Call Me
Brooklyn

Call Me Brooklyn

Eduardo Lago

Translated by
Ernesto Mestre-Reed

DALKEY ARCHIVE PRESS
CHAMPAIGN / LONDON / DUBLIN

Originally published as *Llámame Brooklyn* by Ediciones Destino, Barcelona, 2006

Library of Congress Cataloging-in-Publication Data

Lago, Eduardo.
[Lámame Brooklyn. English]
Call me Brooklyn / Eduardo Lago ; Translated by Ernesto Mestre-Reed. -- First Edition.
pages cm. -- (Spanish Literature series)
"Originally published as Llamame Brooklyn by Ediciones Destino, Barcelona, in 2006."
ISBN 978-1-56478-860-3 (pbk. : alk. paper)
1. Journalist--Fiction. 2. Friendship gsafd I. Mestre-Reed, Ernesto. II. Title.
PQ6712.A45L5313 2013
863'.7--dc23
2013022257

Partially funded by a grant from the Illinois Arts Council, a state agency

This work has been published with a subsidy from the Directorate General of Books,
Archives and Libraries of the Spanish Ministry of Culture

www.dalkeyarchive.com

Cover: design and composition by Tim Peters
Cover photo: George Bradford Brainerd. *Street Scene Near Brooklyn Bridge*, ca. 1872-
1887. Brooklyn Museum, Brooklyn Museum/Brooklyn Public Library,
Brooklyn Collection, 1996.164.2-1778

Printed on permanent/durable acid-free paper

One
FENNERS POINT

"The dead exist only in us."
MARCEL PROUST

On reaching Fenners Point, the county road makes a sharp turn to the west, inching away from the coast toward Deauville. At the height of the curve, on the seaside, is a metal plaque that reads:

DANISH CEMETERY

Underneath it, a green arrow points to the beginning of a path that leads into a pine grove. Some two hundred yards in, the woods open to a clearing overlooking an endless swath of the Atlantic. The coastline rises to vertiginous heights at Fenners Point. There, two strips of land jut out into the water, forming an ominously shaped enclosure. Within its walls, the surf ceaselessly pounds against an archipelago of black reefs. This strange feature of the shore has come to be known as the Devil's Pitchfork.

The best place from which to appreciate Fenners Point and its surroundings is the northern end of a tunnel carved through solid stone on the edge of the shore: Along the coastline, a series of gigantic vaults recede into the distance. At intervals, the ceilings seem on the verge of collapsing into the void. Below, amid the jagged rocks that the joint labor of time and the waves have ripped away from the shore, there's a narrow beach of white sand, inaccessible by land or sea. When night falls, a web of lights alerts ships to the dangers off Fenners Point. It was only after these lights were put up that the fateful history of shipwrecks that haunted the memory of the residents near the Devil's Pitchfork came to a stop.

When I began to put Gal Ackerman's papers in order, I came across an article published in the *Deauville Gazette* on June 7, 1965. It says:

> ### BEACONS INSTALLED OFF
> ### DEAUVILLE COAST
>
> *Last Friday, a system of light signals was installed at the so-called Devil's Pitchfork. Given the perennially dangerous conditions of the sea at Fenners Point, the work had to be delayed repeatedly, until the weather allowed. Shortly before noon on June 4, two helicopters from Linden Grove Naval Base made a visual inspection. Hovering in the air, not far from the reach of the waves, ropes were let out from the aircrafts. Two men carrying precision instruments climbed down.*

I smiled. It was just as well the article didn't have a byline. To me, the identity of the author was self-evident.

> *With remarkable speed, the men anchored some twenty steel bars to the surface of the tallest rocks. Each of the beacons is topped with a light that can be activated by a radio signal. Maintenance workers from the county's engineering services observed the installation from official vehicles parked along the road. After a little more than half an hour, during which the sound of the helicopter blades echoing off the stone walls mixed with the roar of the waves, the ropes were lifted, and taking in their human cargo, the aircrafts*

rattled away along the coastline. Ever since then, when darkness falls, the reefs take on an eerie appearance. With this often-delayed task accomplished, the authorities hope to provide the county coastline with a more adequate level of safety . . .

I have returned many times to Fenners Point, driving alone up the road that leads to the cliffs. And I have to say that the eeriest view is not the lights that twinkle on the reefs at night. In the clearing between the pine woods and the shore there is a small cemetery surrounded by a stone wall. To go in, all you have to do is push open the wrought-iron gate. Inside is an abandoned chapel with a handful of gravestones scattered in front of it. All save one are anonymous, adorned with nothing but crosses carved on the surface of the marble. Next to the door of the chapel, there is a plaque that reads:

IN MEMORIAM
On May 19, 1919, the freighter Bornholm of the Royal Danish Navy crashed into the reefs at Fenners Point. Only thirteen bodies, which could not be identified, were recovered. The others rest forever at the bottom of the sea. Say a prayer for their souls.
Consulate General of Denmark
New York City,
September 21, 1919

MARINE CEMETERY

"To gaze and gaze upon the gods' repose!"

PAUL VALÉRY

Brooklyn Heights, April 17, 1992

Yesterday morning we buried Gal. It had to be that way, like in one of his favorite poems, in a cemetery by the sea swept at all hours by the wind, where the cawing of the seagulls mingles with the incessant murmur of the water. His grave overlooks the magnificent and often roiling Atlantic, although just yesterday it was calm, with the flat blue of the ocean stretching out to the horizon. Everything makes sense; Gal had found the place he was destined to rest forever, alone. "Danish Cemetery" said the sign that he had seen countless times as he passed through Fenners Point by bus on the way to Deauville to see Louise Lamarque. One day, driving by with her, he told her to pull over when he saw the sign. They went together down the dirt road that crosses through the pine grove until they reached an esplanade at the very edge of the cliff. The cemetery was there, a tiny place hidden from human sight. Louise explained to me much later that it had begun as a resting place for the remains of a group of shipwrecked Danish seamen, the crew of a merchant ship carrying a cargo of wheat. Gal never told her that he liked the idea of ending up buried there, but when Frank called Louise with the news of Gal's death, the first thing that came into her head was that they needed to bury him in Fenners Point. Frank loved the idea. Gal had spoken to him about the Danish Cemetery more than once. Thanks to his connections, in less than forty-eight hours the *gallego* had managed to secure a permit for the burial. Only Gal's closest friends attended, although later in the afternoon many others stopped by the Oakland. Gal Ackerman didn't have any family. His father Ben died in '66, his mother Lucia Hollander in '79. Nadia Orlov didn't show up, of course. They'd lost track of her years before, and no one knew if she was dead or alive, although those of us who knew Gal felt something akin to her presence throughout the whole ceremony. As Frank said, if she was still out there, sooner or later she'd hear the news. The burial was very simple, as Gal would have wanted it. No one prayed for him, unless the racket of the seagulls flying above our heads was some sort of prayer. Louise read a few lines from a Valéry poem, and that was it. After the workers hired by Víctor had covered the coffin with earth and set up the gravestone, the motorcade returned to Brooklyn Heights. Frank posted a note on the door of the Oakland announcing to its patrons that there would be an open bar in memory of Gal Ackerman that night. People kept arriving into the wee hours of the morning. Gal would have loved it, just as I'm sure he'll appreciate resting forever at Fenners Point, by the edge of a cliff, in the company of a few Danish seamen, all good drinkers no doubt, as if he had never truly left the Oakland.

THE DELIVERY

Gal, do you recognize the date of your death? April 14. The anniversary of the proclamation of the Spanish Republic. Knowing you, I doubt it was a coincidence. It was exactly the type of joke you always liked to play, convinced that nobody else would get it. But you can't fool me. It's been two years now. Just in case, I've chosen exactly the same day to bring you *Brooklyn*, that way I can laugh along with you. You were one of a kind; when you died, a whole species disappeared with you. The truth is that it's difficult for me to accept that you're no longer among the living. Every time I set foot in the Oakland, my heart sinks realizing I'm not going to see you there sitting at one of the tables. You talked about death so much, wrote about it so much, and now you're there on the other side as well. I had never lost anyone close to me, and didn't know how to deal with it. You used to say that the dead don't depart completely, that in some fashion they remain among us. But the hard truth of the matter, for me, is that you're not here. You've left forever, Gal, anything else is meaningless. Yes, yes. I know you too well, you don't even have to say it. I didn't spend all that time putting your writing together not to pick a few things up. Just now, I hear your voice crisp and clear, mocking me: If that's what you believe, what the hell are you doing here standing on my grave, talking to me as if you were convinced that your words could somehow reach me? All right, you win, but that doesn't change the fact that today, on the 14th of April, it's been two years since your death, and the anniversary of the Second Republic in Spain seems like a perfect date to bring you your book. Yes, yes, I've finished it. Here's your novel, Gal, *Brooklyn*. I'll leave it here in the niche that Louise asked Frank to carve in the gravestone. Like they say the Egyptians did, so it keeps you company in death. Forgive the cliché, but when I saw it from far away as I came in, alone and facing all the others, your gravestone made me think of a blank page. It is the only one without a cross. I like that very much—no epitaph, only your initials and two years, as if the inscription were just a watermark on a sheet of paper:

GA

1937–1992

It was a foregone conclusion, you had to come to the same end as the characters in your novel. Now that I've finished it, I don't have a clue what I'm going to do with my life. I've realized that the time has come for a change of scenery. I've become a little bit like you, not comfortable anywhere. I don't know why, but every now and then I'm overcome by such a sense of panic that the only way to stop it is to run away. For the moment, I'm still in Brooklyn (in your studio), but that can't last long. Although who knows. For people like us, there comes a time when it's no longer possible to continue fleeing. It happened to Louise Lamarque with her brownstone in Chelsea. She's been there for more than twenty years, talking to her dead, like you used to do. Although painting keeps her together, which is what should have happened to you with *Brooklyn*. You know, aside from Frank, she's the only other person who's seen a copy. Three readers. Not bad. You never said it in so many words, but I know you didn't much care about being read, so long as the right people read you.

Louise. I owe my friendship with her to you. It was your absence that brought us closer. We met the day you were buried. You'd spoken to me about her so much that having her right there in front of me made me shudder. She was exactly as I had imagined her: an older woman, tall, elegant, mysterious. That day she wore a very simple black dress, her face hidden behind a veil. So you're Néstor, she said when Frank introduced us, holding her hand out to me and lifting her veil. Her face was slashed with wrinkles, her eyes steely. There wasn't time to say much more. She'd arrived extremely late to the funeral parlor, and Frank had been impatient because the limousines were supposed to have headed out to Fenners Point by then. You'll have time later, he said, and accompanied her into the chapel so she could have a moment alone with you before they closed the coffin.

It was a perfect day, sunny and warm with a light breeze. After the ceremony ended and we were leaving the cemetery, she asked me to sit next to her on the ride back. The two of us were alone in the enormous interior of the limousine. In front, separated from us by a pane of tinted glass, were Frank Otero and Víctor Báez. At first, we went a long time without saying anything. The cliffs were to the left of the road, and our eyes involuntary drifted toward the sea. Every once in a while, the trees obstructed the view of the ocean. When the road finally pulled away from the coast, Louise looked forward and without lifting her veil said in a very soft voice:

It's not that it took me by surprise. We all knew that it was going to happen at any moment, but I just don't have the strength for this anymore. I'm too old to withstand such blows. How many dead do you have?

I wasn't sure what she meant, so I didn't respond.

Three for me, she continued. That's not a lot, but it's not really a matter of numbers. It's how hard it is to put up with their absence as time passes. Three, not counting my mother. She died when I was only a few months old, and I have no memories of her. The first death that really affected me was my father's, when I was fourteen. I almost lost my mind. Are your parents still alive?

I answered yes, and she nodded.

At first, I didn't understand what had happened. I denied the evidence. I couldn't accept that my father had abandoned me. When after a long time I was finally able to come to terms with it, something changed in me. How do I explain it? I had been suffering for over a year and, suddenly, without my noticing it, the pain had transformed into something else. Rage, fury, I'm not quite sure what . . . if it wasn't hatred, it sure felt a lot like it. I wanted to make him pay for having left my side.

Then she lifted her veil, and for the second time I was able to look at her face. Her eyes were a clear blue, strangely cold. She took out a pack of Camels from her purse and held it out to me.

Do you smoke?

I said no, but she didn't budge. It took me a few seconds to react. I grabbed the pack and found a plastic lighter inside. I pulled out a cigarette, handed it to her, and lit it. Louise lowered the window a crack and, letting out a mouthful of smoke, she asked me in an almost inaudible voice:

Am I talking too much?

I shook my head.

The next death was even worse. I don't know if Gal ever told you about Marguerite. She was my companion for more than ten years . . .

Even though it was practically impossible to smoke the cigarette down any further, Louise took one last drag before she tossed it through the slit in the window. The butt seemed to strike some invisible wall, leaving behind a trail of sparks in the air. She put the pack of cigarettes back in her purse and lowered the veil. Her fingertips were yellow from nicotine.

Gal was my best friend, if not the only one. My one true friend,

I mean. We had known each other for almost thirty years . . . She clicked her tongue, making a face that I didn't quite know how to interpret. His death is a sign, I'm sure of it. I feel as if the scales have been thrown out of balance forever.

A long silence ensued, broken by Frank as he lowered the glass partition. He announced that we were almost arriving and asked Louise if she wanted to have a drink with us at the Oakland. She replied that she wanted to be alone, so Otero told Víctor to drive her to Manhattan. As we were saying good-bye, she held my hand tightly:

Come by my studio at dusk some day, she said. I think we have a lot to talk about. Although you wouldn't know it by today, I assure you that I'm a good listener.

She emphasized her words with a burst of dry laughter. It was the first time I had heard her laugh. There was something strangely familiar about it.

Ever since, I've visited her Chelsea brownstone regularly. She almost always has guests over: art collectors, critics, musicians, poets, and, above all, young artists who have a deep admiration for her work. Eventually, her assistant Jacques finds a way to get everyone out of the house and leave us alone. I usually talk about the work I've finished during the day, just as I used to do with you. She is so talented that it's hard to believe it took the world so long to recognize it. But what's most astonishing is her indifference to all of it. She couldn't care less what anybody thinks about her. Jacques says that she's always been like that. The first time I went to see her, one of her guests, a very young sculptor, said something in French that I didn't quite get, although I understood enough to realize that it was about her fame. Louise let out a burst of laughter identical to the one that had escaped from her when we had said good-bye after returning from Fenners Point. Louise's laugh is solemn, deep, just like her voice—the laugh of a smoker.

She pressed her cigarette butt on the ashtray and repeated the young man's words, as he watched for her reaction anxiously. Right then, I suddenly understood what attracted you to each other, Gal. Louise mocks the things that most people worry about, just like you used to. She doesn't give a damn that at the end of her life she's mobbed by this attention that she never once sought out in the first place. Both of you despised the ways of the world equally. That's why she said that your death had thrown off the scales. You left her all alone, Gal.

When she doesn't feel like talking, she suggests that we take tea in her library. Watching her wrinkled face, seeing her light one unfiltered Camel with the butt of another, I've learned to recognize in her the same inner strength that you had. I don't know what to call it. It's not disdain or indifference, but rather a kind of dignity that she uses to defend herself from I don't know what. I had seen this same strength in you many times, strange but positive, charged with an almost violent vitality. Both of you needed to be near danger, although she's much less vulnerable than you were. When Louise feels cornered, she turns in on herself; you, on the other hand, drove yourself crazy, and you wouldn't settle down until you had managed to hurt yourself, the worse the better.

In the library there's a portrait of you in which she was able to capture one of those rare moments in which your spirit was at peace. This will seem like a ridiculous association to you, but that portrait reminds me of one of the most beautiful things you ever wrote: I'm talking about your piece on Lermontov. One afternoon at the Oakland, you spoke to me about him, and when I confessed that I didn't know who he was you were shocked. How can you not know Lermontov? you asked me, astonished. It seemed impossible to you. The Russian poet, you said, lowering your voice and then falling into deep thought. It was one of those silences of yours where I could almost see the shape of your thoughts. Right afterward, you added: He died at twenty-seven, in a duel. The czar had exiled him, and all the locals for miles around attended his burial. When I saw you the following day, you had written a beautiful sketch of his life. You gave it to me, without saving a copy for yourself. Louise has it now. I gave it to her after all the other guests had left the second time I attended her Sunday salon. She led me to the library, sat down in a red leather armchair, and lit a cigarette. When she finished reading it, she said: It's a beautiful piece, but it's not about Lermontov. I shot her a look of surprise and asked: Well, who is it about then? Him, Gal, who else? she asked, amused. I'm sure that he didn't even realize it, though. We shared a laugh. She was right, of course, it was about you. When she handed me back the Lermontov profile, I told her to keep it. I didn't need it for *Brooklyn*.

The more time goes by, the more I'm convinced that you always knew things would turn out this way. I never paid too much attention when you told me that you wouldn't be able to finish the *Brooklyn Notebook* (the title you gave to your novel at first). But you reminded me of it so often, in your own way, without ever saying a word, that before I knew it we had sealed a sort of pact. True: at first, the suddenness of your death made me feel as if I'd fallen into a trap. With you gone, I couldn't back out, and the weight of it was unbearable. *Me, finish your book?* I felt incapable of it, but I didn't have a choice. I was bound to our pact. It was difficult to get started, but when I finally did, I realized that there was a lot already done. At almost every step along the way, I found some clue that allowed me to get a clear picture of where to go next. It was almost like having you there with me, showing me the way. And it wasn't just your notes. Often I'd remember snippets of our conversations at just the right moment. Do you know the first thing that came to mind, before I had even touched a single page, after taking possession of the Archive? (That's what Frank and I called your studio, in honor of Ben).

Surrounded by your papers, I remembered the day that you told me about Kafka's dying wish. He had given his life to his work, but when he felt death closing in, he asked his closest friend, Max Brod, to destroy all his writing.

A trite anecdote, you added, but it's still worth recalling. Virgil did the same thing. Of course, we only know about the cases in which the friends disobeyed. I wondered how many more cases there might have been in which the writer's last wish was respected? How many Kafkas and Virgils have disappeared without leaving a trace?

Which reminded me of another anecdote—one of your favorites. I was hoping you had written it down so I could use it in the *Notebook*, but I never found it among your papers. I'm talking about the story of the English poet who wrote on rolling paper. Do you remember the first time you told it to me? It was one morning shortly after we'd met. I had just flown in from Chicago and went directly from the airport to the Oakland. I was in the middle of breaking up with Diana, and I didn't feel like stopping by our place. Even though we barely knew each other, you had already spoken to me about *Brooklyn*, the book that had been bouncing around in your head for so long.

I don't know what in the hell made you bring up that story about the English aristocrat who wrote poems on rice paper; he'd finish one, then roll a cigarette, and before lighting it would say: The interesting thing is creating them.

I read it in an interview with Lezama Lima, the Cuban novelist, you said. The story, like the ones about the deaths of Kafka and Virgil, came up more than once in our conversations, and it always made me ask myself the same question: *Why does he write?* One day, on our way to Jimmy Castellano's gym to see one of Víctor's matches, I asked you point-blank: *Why do you write, Gal?* You shrugged and picked up your pace. We were half a block away from the Luna Bowl. Cletus, the doorman, was waving at you. Determined to get an answer, I blocked your path and repeated: You heard me, Gal. Why do you write? You winced and waited for me to get out of the way. I muttered an apology and never brought it up again. It was you who never forgot about it. Let me show you something. You must have written this a couple of days later. It's this kind of thing that made me think you had it all planned out:

April 3, 1992

Néstor's question made me think of one of Ben's Spanish friends, Antonio Ramos. They met in January of 1938, when Ben was stationed in a field hospital. One morning, during his rounds, he treated one of the prisoners from the rebel faction. I remember how emphatically Ben stressed that the prisoner was not a fascist. That's the way things were: many people were sent to the front lines before they even had time to choose a side. His name was Antonio Ramos. He must have been eighteen or nineteen and said he was a painter. Aside from the severity of his wounds, he had a weak constitution and for many days wavered between life and death. After he was out of danger, he and Ben became friends. He had a unique sensibility, and my father quickly became fond of him. Often, after making his rounds, he'd return to Ramos's bedside and stay there for some time chatting. There was something special about the boy. Among his things, Ramos had an anthology of the poems of Antonio Machado from which he liked to read aloud—he thought that poetry needed to be *heard* in order to be properly appreciated. On one of the occasions Lucia came to visit him in Madrid, Ben insisted on taking her to the hospital to meet Antonio. When he was discharged from the hospital, he was taken to a military prison. As a parting gift, Antonio Ramos gave Ben the Machado anthology and asked for his mailing address. When the militiamen put him up on the truck with the other prisoners, my father thought that he'd never see him again. He was wrong. Years after the war had ended, a card arrived in Brooklyn. It was postmarked Paris, where Antonio Ramos was living. He had completed a degree in the fine arts in Madrid and had been given a fellowship in Paris—a modest one, but enough to live on. My father wrote back, and in the years that followed, they corresponded sporadically. Finally, on one of his trips to Europe, Ben decided to pay him a visit. It must have been in the early sixties. When he rang the doorbell, a bone-thin, haggard figure opened the door. For a moment, Ben thought that he had the wrong floor. It was only after the apparition gave Ben a hug that he realized that it had to be him. Ramos explained that they had taken out one of his lungs, and that the other one didn't work very well. He lived in a modest apartment, on the Boulevard Montparnasse, and the cold so infiltrated his body that, even though he had a heater running, he had to wrap himself in a blanket in order to paint. He had married a Frenchwoman named Nicole who was a translator for Gallimard. She wasn't there at the moment. Ben asked him how he was doing, and Ramos said that the doctor had forbidden him to paint, had said that if he kept painting, given the condition of his only lung, the toxic fumes would kill him in no time. Ben noticed a number of large, half-finished oil canvases and realized that his friend was paying little heed to his doctor's orders, but he didn't say anything. I know what you're thinking, but you're wrong, Ramos said. I've told the doctor the same thing. It's just the other way around: I'll die if I don't paint. They both smiled. Neither of them wanted to dispel the magic of their reunion. For years, Ramos had been saving a rare bottle of burgundy for a special occasion. When Nicole returned from Gallimard, they threw together some dinner, and the three of them put the burgundy to good use.

So that's why you wrote. I had to wait until you died to find out. As for the trap you made me fall into, the crucial day was April 8. We were chatting in the Oakland and you asked me up to your studio without warning. I had been there before, and this time I had the feeling that things seemed a bit more organized than usual. Pointing to your towers of notebooks, you said:

In the end, everything you see there doesn't matter at all. I keep it because it's my only consolation. Sometimes I open a notebook at random and what I read takes me to another dimension and that's enough. I would be happy to get just one thing out of all this, that's all I need, don't ask me why. Like Alston used to say, one book is enough. I've told you about my friend Alston Hughes, the poet, right? He drank himself to death, like I will. Once, the night before a reading I'd arranged for him, he came home so I could help him choose which poems to read. He took a sheaf of no more than a hundred pages out of his bag. Everything he had written in his sixty-three years was there. He leafed through the sheets very slowly and when he finished he said: How embarrassing to have written so much. He could give a rat's ass about publishing. He read with two other poets, a Chilean who had been Neruda's secretary and a sweet woman with a demure look, a Peruvian, I think. I don't remember their names, but both of them had published many books. Alston was the only one who was unknown. No one had the slightest idea who he was, and if he had been asked to read, it was only because I'd insisted to the organizers that he be included on the panel. It took me forever to convince them, but in the end they trusted my judgment. His reading was astonishing, although the audience didn't know quite what to make of it—they had nothing to compare it with. They wavered between bewilderment and scorn. But the young people reacted very differently. As soon as the reading was over, they surrounded him, asking him where they could find his books. Nowhere, he told them with delight. I have never published anything, and I never will. Now I think that someone in Paris is putting together a collection of his work, but of course he's dead. If I learned one thing from Alston, it was precisely that: *You don't write for fame or notoriety.* Then, raising your right hand, you pointed into the air and added:

There you have every sort of manuscript, things that writers have insisted on sending me all these years. Some are from friends, some from people I barely knew. Flawed stuff mostly, although once in a while I've come across something interesting. I store them up there, you said, and I saw you meant the pair of doors above the armoire. You know what I call that spot? You let out a long cackle before continuing:

The tomb. You want to see inside the crypt, Ness?

I didn't get it, but before I could react you had grabbed a stepladder and told me in a peremptory tone:

Get up there.

You insisted I open the doors, and sure enough, as I was doing it, they seemed like the mouth of a crypt.

Go ahead, look inside. See what's in there? A few months ago, I went to get a manuscript and I felt like a gravedigger exhuming some remains to move them to another hole in the ground. It was then that I christened it. Look in, look in and you'll see.

I did as I was told. It was a rather deep, wide hole with cement walls. Inside, as little particles of light refracted amid a cloud of dust, the whitish reflection of the manuscripts made me think of a pile of bones scattered in an open pit. There was a damp smell. Truthfully, it made me a bit anxious, so I immediately got down. I didn't touch anything, although you had told me to rummage around. As soon as I came down, you climbed to the top of the stepladder yourself and with a theatrical gesture exclaimed:

A manuscript cemetery! You burst out laughing, unable to stop. There's everything here, Ness: novels, poems, insufferable texts without any literary worth . . . Incredible, right? And their common fate is that they will never be read, never be published. So many dreams of fame and money, everything that most people who want to be published dream about. So much time and effort, for what? So much vanity and bitterness and frustration. So many dashed hopes. Here, let me show you.

You began to read titles aloud from the top of the stepladder. You were laughing riotously, but the whole thing made me shudder. How could you do such a thing? It hurt me to see you this way. This was your dark side, and at that moment I found it unbearable. Thank God, the whole thing didn't last long. Abruptly, you stopped laughing, you closed the crypt (you did it very gently, don't think I missed that). You climbed down, folded the stepladder, and took it to the kitchen.

As you know, I never keep anything to drink in here, you said. I'm going to the liquor store for a second. I'll be right back.

When you returned you found me browsing through the books in your shelves. You had brought back a flask of vodka, one of those small bottles that sold for a few dollars, as well as two glasses. You filled the glasses up and said:

You can have anything you want from my shelves. All those names that meant so much to me once, but no longer speak to me. Books have bored me for a while now. Until recently, I used to reread them from time to time, but now I don't even do that. I feel very close to the end, and I'm tired. I think Alston Hughes had the right idea. Leaving *behind* just one book. Posthumous publication. I wrote mine in the absurd hope that Nadia would read it, someday. Or do you think I wrote it for my health? Damn it, Ness, I've invested my whole life in it and I'm not quite sure why.

You approached the towers of paper, saying:

Here it is, Ness, *Brooklyn* . . . bits of my novel scattered throughout the pages of all these notebooks. Well, technically, it's not finished, but it's close. At this point, you could say it's a race against time. If I live a little longer, perhaps I'll finish it. But if not . . . Do you know that it was Nadia who made me realize that this was a race? I talked to her so much about the book that I was going to write. I told her what it was about, filled her in on the details of its structure. I listed for her all of the titles that I had come up with to see which ones she liked best. I told her about the sections I was thinking about adding, many of which I never got to write. One of those times she asked me when I thought I was going to finish it. Never, I replied, completely serious. Nadia was used to my retorts, but this one left her completely rattled.

> I don't understand.
> There's nothing to understand, it's just a fact.
> But why?
> I don't know, it's like a curse.
> That can't be.
> Why?
> Because it's not up to you, Gal. The book exists already, scattered in all your notebooks.
> But I'm not sure I can retrieve it.
> If that's the case, then someone else will do it for you.
> Right?

That's from one of your notebooks. Do you remember it? You wrote it yourself. That was the pact, wasn't it? A great way to start, don't you think? Going back to that day, the vodka sat untouched in our two glasses. You opened the curtains, and the morning light erupted into the room, making you say:

Look at this light, Néstor. It's the light that Louise talks about in her poem. The Brooklyn light.

You closed the curtains again, as if you found it impossible to continue chatting enveloped by such brightness.

What I told Nadia is true. There's something in me that

prevents me from giving a final shape to anything I write. But she was right too, the book already existed, scattered in my notebooks.

Later, I found the page that told the full story. That day you failed to mention that Nadia had been clairvoyant enough to realize that *someone would finish it for you*. But you didn't need to bother. The deal had already been made, though I didn't know about it yet. Then you gave me the key to your studio and got up. You didn't say anything else and neither did I, because again we didn't need to. Our fates had been decided long before you asked me up that day. You didn't even let me drink with you. That shadow that I had grown to know so well crossed over your face. You were far away, alone, lost in your thoughts, barely conscious of your surroundings. Without waiting for me, you took your glass and emptied it in one gulp. You glanced toward the curtains, as if you were afraid that the light might break in. With a slight tremble in your hand, you took my glass and drank it as well. Then you headed for the door without saying anything, as if I wasn't even there. I didn't follow you out. I stuck my hand in my pocket, unconsciously playing with the key you had given me. It was the last time I saw you alive.

On April 9, I left for a trip to New Mexico on assignment. On the night of the 14, when I returned to the hotel in Taos, there was a message from Frank Otero asking me to call the Oakland immediately.

Bad news, Ness. Gal died yesterday at Lennox Hill. He was in a coma for three days. I called the newsroom. Dylan Taylor told me how to get a hold of you. He said you're coming back tonight, so you'll be back on time. The burial is the day after tomorrow at Fenners Point. I'm waiting for the permit, but I have my connections and I'm sure we'll get it in time.

I had never heard of Fenners Point, but I didn't ask because it wasn't the time for explanations. When everything was over, I told Frank that you had given me the key to your studio and asked him to come up with me. Everything was just as we had left it the last time I was there with you. Then I told him about our last conversation in detail.

I don't have any plans to rent it, was all he said. Do what you need to do with what's in here.

It has been two years, two years of organizing the enormous amount of material that you left behind, destroying anything that wasn't destined to become a part of *Brooklyn*. In the studio, surrounded by your pictures, your letters and memories, it was as if you were there with me. When the work began to take shape, I often stayed overnight, and after a few months, I moved in so that nothing could take me away from the work.

Reading your words, I could hear your voice perfectly clear. More than once when a piece of furniture or the wood floor creaked, I turned, thinking you were in the room and were about to say something.

One afternoon, a little after I had moved in, I emptied the tomb, not daring to peruse the manuscripts. I asked Frank to help me. Together, we took several boxes down and one by one burned the manuscripts in the chimney of the Oakland. Watching them catch fire, I couldn't stop thinking about what you liked to say about manuscripts that are born condemned to oblivion. We're like the priest and the barber in *Don Quixote*, Frank said, except that we won't grant clemency to a single title. It made me laugh.

That was only the beginning. Honoring your wishes, I began to fill in the gaps you had left. I went over everything meticulously, the letters, the reams of papers, the notebooks, the files, your diary, and Nadia's. At the end of every day, I went to the bar to burn the material that was no longer needed. You have made me into an extension of your shadow. That's right. Two years of obedience to a voice that never went quiet, a voice that had been preparing me to do what I was doing from just about the first time we met, although I didn't realize that until after you were gone. But it's finished, we're done, Gal, you and I. Here's your damn novel: *Brooklyn*. Nadia was right: the book already existed. You were its maker as well as its only obstacle. We had to get you out of the way. To save it, it just needed someone capable of really listening to your voice, and that couldn't be you because your own voice consumed you. It wasn't easy. Hundreds and hundreds of hours of silence and solitude, lost: hours in which I put my writing at the service of yours. When I finally finished, I realized that if anyone still had doubts, it was me. Many times, on rereading what we'd done, it's difficult to distinguish your voice from mine. Although, in truth, there's only one voice in control, yours: each time that I had to intervene, I did it imagining how you would have done it. It has been a long apprenticeship, but I am grateful. Thanks to you I can say that I am a writer. Before this I always felt as if I couldn't live up to that word.

I have nothing else to add. Everything is in the book. But one last thing, we have to celebrate. I bought a small bottle of vodka like the one you brought back that day, a pint, identical to the ones you liked to put in the altars of the Navy Yard. I'll leave it here with the book to keep you company. But first, I have to account for the drink you didn't let me have the day we sealed the pact. You didn't think I would forget that, did you?

Two

DEAUVILLE

"It is not down in any map;
true places never are."
HERMAN MELVILLE

Deauville, October 13, 1973

I awoke before dawn, anxious. I couldn't remember the dream at all, but I knew it had something to do with Sam Evans. I got up, went to the kitchen, lit a cigarette, and, while I brewed coffee, read Louise's postcard again. It was dated Friday and was about nothing particularly substantial, but when I finished reading it, I had the strange feeling that somehow it was connected to the nightmare I'd just had. I felt the urge to go to Deauville. It was so sudden, I didn't even have the patience to have a second cup of coffee. I threw a few things in a duffel bag and raced to Port Authority. The terminal was half-deserted when I got there. I bought a roundtrip ticket and went down to the 40th Street stop. A bus had just arrived and the passengers were getting off. After the last one exited and the doors shut, the driver remained at the steering wheel jotting something down for a few minutes, and then he too left. Alone at the stop, I glanced at my watch and realized the next departure was not for almost half an hour. I leaned back against the brick wall and, catching sight of my reflection, I watched how the light changed as it hit the surface of the glass door. It was a gray day, but past my figure I was able to discern the shadows of several buildings and a large swath of sky. The wind dragged groups of black clouds toward the Hudson.

I lit a cigarette and opened my journal. There were only a few blank pages left; I would have to buy a new one before returning to New York. I leafed through it and stumbling upon an entry that bore today's date, I realized I was returning to Deauville exactly one year after my last visit. I wasn't sure why, but I associated the coincidence with the unease I had felt about Louise's postcard and the nightmare that had awakened me. I tried to recall the dream, but the images had grown even more fragmented and elusive than before; the only thing I could remember were snippets of my last conversation with Sam Evans. As if the key to the dream were to be found there, I reread what I had written about him a year before.

Deauville, October 13, 1972

As always, I asked the driver to drop me off in front of Stewart Foster's ranch, half a mile before the Deauville town limits. I have always found the sight of thoroughbreds on the loose fascinating, even awe-inspiring. Their odd mixture of vulnerability and power, the almost-human helplessness in their eyes, the grace and elegance of their movements. Stewart is seventy-six and has spent his whole life breeding horses. When the bus stops at the edge of his property, the old man comes out to the porch to see who's getting off. He enjoys when people admire his animals. He recognized me right away, waved, then went back into the house. A mare that had recently given birth was grazing next to her foal. As I approached, she raised her muzzle from the grass to look at me without changing the position of her body, then trotted away followed by her colt. I can spend hours watching the horses, but this morning there was a storm brewing, so I went back to the road and headed toward the gas station. I wanted to say hello to Sam before it started pouring. I love chatting with Sam; my visits to Deauville will be very different when he's gone. There's very little known about his past. He's a very old, blind, black man. He came here almost fifty years ago from Bogalusa, a town in Louisiana, to work as a migrant during harvest time, but he felt so at home that when the season ended he decided to stay. He immediately became known for his honesty and responsibility, and the townspeople began to hire him to do all sorts of jobs. He was never out of work; then, one day, some fifteen years ago, he lost his sight in an accident. I don't know what happened. He's never told me the details. But, ever since, he spends his days in a rocking chair at the station with Lux, his Belgian Shepherd, lying at his feet. I still haven't figured out how he does it, but as soon as I set foot on the gravel path leading to the gas station Sam knows it's me. Could it be he knows my tread by heart? Sam practically doesn't move from the entrance of the general store the whole day. That's his work station; and for him it's sacred. He's not one to beg, so after the accident left him incapacitated, he had to come up with a decent way to make a living. In the end, he devised a rather original business for himself, and like he says, to do it right you gotta have the soul of an artist. The way he sees it, the fact that he was born sixty miles away from such a cradle of creativity as New Orleans just made things easier. And he's right; a wandering artist at heart, the idea for his trade was inspired by the street musicians and tap dancers he saw perform so many times in the French Quarter. People appreciate his talent; and he makes a living from what they give him.

Unless the weather is bad, he sits at his work station by the door of the general store: a small, three-legged table covered with a flower-print cloth. On top of the table, he sets a beat-up, black leather Bible and a small basket. In the center of the table, on a piece of white cardboard, carefully scripted in thick black letters, reads:

SAM EVANS
MEMORIZER OF THE WORD
OF GOD

He leads a very simple life. He sleeps in a shed next to the back of the garage, for which Rick, the superintendent of the gas station, charges him a negligible rent. Kim, a black woman from Atlanta who works as a cook in a nearby diner, prepares his meals and does his laundry, for very little money. He washes in the bathroom of the gas station. His hours vary with the seasons, following a simple pattern he has adhered to his entire life: working from sunrise to sunset. His method is both simple and infallible. Rick has advanced arthritis, so he can't pump the gas himself. When customers arrive to refill, the first thing they see is a sign that says that gas has to be paid for in advance. The moment they're about to cross the threshold, Sam stands up, sticks out his arm, and puts the Bible right under their noses. No one has time to react. By the time they realize what's going on, they have the book in their hands, with Sam urging them to open it at any page. The situation is so unlikely and absurd, no one is capable of ignoring the old man's instructions. Don't mess with fate, he says when he hears the ruffle of the pages. It's best not to think about it and let the book decide on its own.

He always knows the exact moment when the search has come to an end, and without letting his unwitting clients catch their breath, he orders them to recite the book, chapter, and verse their eyes have fallen upon. I don't remember having opened a Bible in all the days of my life till the day I arrived in Deauville and Sam put me through his freakish test. When

I thought about it later, it seemed like an absurd proposition, but the truth is that once you fall into his trap, you have no choice but to do as he says. The funny thing is that nobody protests or offers the least resistance. Although I've tried many times to figure it out, I still don't know why I followed his instructions. The fact is that when he asked me what passage I had stumbled upon, I responded Ezekiel 34. He didn't allow me to say anything more, but recited in a grave and pompous voice:

> *And the word of the LORD came unto me, saying, Son of man, prophesy against the shepherds of Israel, prophesy, and say unto them, Thus saith the Lord GOD unto the shepherds; Woe be to the shepherds of Israel that do feed themselves! should not the shepherds feed the flocks? Ye eat the fat, and ye clothe you with the wool, ye kill them that are fed: but ye feed not the flock.*

Astonished, I waited for him to finish reciting the entire passage. What he did with the Bible made me think of the I Ching, and I thought it might be best for me to keep a record of this message. Before leaving, I copied down the appropriate passage in my journal and left a ten-dollar bill in Sam's basket. My aim was to memorize it, imitating Sam on a small scale.

I've seen Sam in action many times, and he never fails. Most people react as I did, making sure that what they hear corresponds with the text. So far, no one's ever caught Sam out. Rarely does anyone suspect Sam of some sort of imposture; but whenever one of his "clients" does ask him how he does it, Sam lets out a guffaw and responds that there is no trick to it, he's simply memorized the entire Bible. And, as they return the book to him, few are stingy enough not to leave a tip in his basket. When the weather's bad, Sam sets up shop behind the counter with Rick's blessing.

Damn it, Gal, he said when I showed up today. He always greets me the same way. So what's cooking in Hell's Kitchen? Did they finally can you or was your brain just getting scorched from that city air? Come here and give me five!

Perhaps because he's lived so long, Sam's existence tends to be a series of repetitions. He has a specific greeting for each of his friends. No matter how long in between visits, this is the one he uses with me, and he always repeats it in the same tone without adding or subtracting a word.

I looked at his dog, Lux, surprised that it didn't stir when I came in.

I'm afraid he doesn't have a lot of time, Gal, said Sam. (Another one of his abilities is that he always knows which way you're looking.) Before next summer, I'm going to have to take him to the vet, have her put him to sleep. I'm procrastinating, but I don't think I can do it too much longer.

Lux turned his head toward his master.

I'm sorry, you know I don't want to, the blind man told the dog, patting him on the head. Lux got up, his tongue hanging out, and came up to sniff me. These things have to be done at precisely the right time, Sam went on. You have to watch out for the signs. When there's too much suffering, it means that we've lived beyond our span. And that's not right, Gal. Life is never wrong. I don't know why people can't accept that.

I offered him a cigarette and he put it to his lips with a shaky hand. Maybe Sam was right about the dog, but it was he who seemed to have deteriorated most. He had aged remarkably in a matter of months, and the Parkinson's symptoms had grown alarmingly worse. He took a deep drag, spit to the side, and sat up attentively, craning his neck forward, as if he were trying to make something out. Lux pricked up his ears, attending to that same inaudible thing just as intently as his master. Moments later, a prolonged clap of thunder sounded, and it began to rain violently.

I closed the journal and looked around. The Deauville bus was docked in a narrow alleyway boxed in between two brick walls off 40th Street. The front faced 9th Avenue. To my left, toward 8th Avenue, a line of about twenty people had formed. A sliver of light flashed on the surface of the glass of the door and I was startled by my reflection once again. Above my head rose the brick wall and the towering silhouettes of the skyscrapers underneath an overcast sky. The same driver I had seen before came back, unlocked the door on his side, and, a few minutes later, the door on the passenger side opened noiselessly, splitting my reflection in two. As I was about to board, a young woman carrying a heavy travel bag appeared above me at the door. The bus had been parked for more than fifteen minutes so it was shocking to discover the presence of a passenger on board so long after the arrival time. The only explanation is that she had fallen asleep and somehow the driver hadn't noticed. He didn't seem to be too concerned, anyway.

Please make room, he said, poking his head from behind her, and went back to his seat. Her bag must have been as heavy as it looked, because she had to switch it from one hand to the other to make it down. As she did this, the fold of her skirt slid to the side exposing her bare thighs. With a brusque gesture, she smoothed down the skirt with her free hand, which made her lose her balance. In order not to fall, she tossed the bag away and grabbed the steel handlebar.

I caught the bag in mid flight and stumbled backward, feeling the bite of a metal buckle on my cheek. When I regained my balance, she was on the sidewalk barely a step away from me. Her face was hidden by her hair, which she shook vigorously, revealing a very white complexion. She couldn't have been much older than twenty. Her large, green eyes met mine for a moment. Before I could react, she grabbed her bag and rushed away down the sidewalk. I felt the pressure of the other passengers behind me, forcing me to board the bus. I strode along the aisle, found my seat, and fell into it, bewildered.

I was out of breath, my pulse racing. My right cheek throbbed. I touched it with the tip of a finger and when I withdrew it, I saw it was stained with blood. Loosening the collar of my shirt to get some air, I looked toward the station through the tinted glass and I saw her slim, erect figure going up the escalator, the bag at her side. Upon reaching the main lobby, she bent down to pick it up, and then, before heading for the exit and vanishing, she looked back for just a moment. I felt helpless. The sight of her naked thighs suddenly came back to me. Details that I hadn't even known I'd perceived appeared before me with stunning clarity: the color and texture of her skin, the shape of her thighs, her pubis, barely glimpsed. When the image dissolved, I felt a sudden stab of desire.

I jumped up as if obeying an order, and pressing past the bodies moving down the aisle, I headed for the exit. I ran toward the escalator, climbed it three steps at a time, and without stopping raced through the door that led into the terminal. Only then did I pause. The atmosphere in the main lobby was completely different from a half hour before. Rivers of people were flowing in and out incessantly. There were long lines at the ticket windows and groups of passengers gathered under the departure board. I began to wander aimlessly, not knowing where to start looking for her, bumping against others trying to make their way through the crowd. When they announced the departure of the bus to Deauville over the loudspeaker, the whole situation felt unreal, as if the woman from my vision hadn't really existed.

I turned around, resigned to returning to the bus, and then I saw her. She had her back to me, buying a pack of cigarettes at a counter. She lit one and began to walk away with an absent air. She moved toward a wooden bench, put down her bag, and sat down. For the first time I had a chance to look at her in detail. She wore black mid-heel pumps, a denim skirt, and a gray T-shirt. She opened a magazine, and began to leaf through it. I had to speak to her at any cost.

Before I took the first step, a figure emerged from behind a column, heading toward the stranger. She recognized him and stood up with a smile. He was a thin man, a bit taller than her, about the same age, and with long, straight, black hair. She ran to him and they embraced. When they pulled apart, the girl noticed my presence but immediately looked away. Her friend picked up the bag and waited while she retouched her makeup looking into a folding mirror; when she finished, they left the terminal arm-in-arm, laughing. I followed them until I lost them among the crowd. After a moment, I saw the double silhouette of their heads floating against the light. The morning sun struck the large windows of Port Authority with full force; the panels of the revolving doors engulfed her first and then him and they disappeared into the bustle of 42nd Street.

Everything had happened too quickly. The terminal clock read three minutes to eight. Unconsciously, my eyes wandered to the place that her body had occupied on the wooden bench. The magazine she had been reading was still there. I grabbed it and returned to the bus. When I arrived, the engine was running and the door open, waiting for me. As soon as I sat down, the bus lurched. We moved down a curved ramp and came out into the avenue. The Manhattan streets were bustling with life. When we got to Lincoln Tunnel, I surrendered to the chaos of my sensations. First, I saw Sam Evans's expression just before the storm erupted; right after that, flashes of memories began to mix in with fragments of dreams. I saw the pasture where Foster's thoroughbreds grazed, the wooden houses on the shore of the river, and the deserted bus stop where I had been reading my journal. Then, in slow motion, the moment the girl's skirt split open, until I was blinded by the sunlight as we emerged out of the tunnel.

We were in New Jersey, in a labyrinth of highways surrounded by industrial yards and parking lots crammed with hundreds of identical vehicles as far as the eye could see. As we were passing the cargo terminals of Newark Airport, I stopped looking out the window and began to leaf through the magazine without paying much attention to its contents. A small, rag-paper envelope slipped out from between the pages. Intrigued, I grabbed it and saw a name written in ink, followed by a number:

Zadie (212) 719-1859

My first instinct was to tear open the envelope, but I stopped myself. If I did things correctly, this number could possibly lead me to her. The area code indicated she lived in Manhattan. I placed the envelope in between the pages of my diary and put away the magazine in the net pocket in front of my seat. Only then did I pay attention to the cover, a Native American with a scar on his face, wearing sunglasses, meticulously dressed up, standing by the door of a casino and holding a leather portfolio in his right hand. The masthead was in white letters—*New York Times Magazine*—followed by today's date: October 13, 1973.

I began to make conjectures about the girl. What was her name? Had she taken the bus from Deauville or boarded at one of the other stops on the way? I pictured myself calling this Zadie, whoever she was, talking to her, or with some other stranger, or leaving an anonymous message on an answering machine, offering incoherent explanations to some faceless other.

I don't know when the rolling of the bus lulled me to sleep. The last sight I remember before drawing the curtain to shield me from the sunlight was of a wooden house, half-hidden by some maples. When I awoke, we'd already arrived at our destination and most of the passengers had already exited the bus. I rushed to grab my bag from the overhead bin and, when I got off, I couldn't help but laugh, thinking I had been on the verge of doing exactly the same thing as the girl in Port Authority: staying asleep on the bus. I managed to wake up at the last minute, but even so, it bothered me, because I had broken my routine: get off before arriving in Deauville, watch Stewart Foster's horses grazing in the pasture, pay my ritual visit to Sam. The thoroughbreds could wait, but something told me that I should go to Rick's gas station right away. I had a feeling that once there the mystery whose shadow had been haunting me since that nightmare woke me up in the middle of the night would be solved. I left the bus station and stood on the side of the road. Farther off in the distance I could clearly see the Texaco sign next to the gas station. But it wasn't lit. It couldn't be more than half a mile to the gas station, which was at the intersection of the old highway with the county road. I threw my bag over my shoulder and with an uncanny feeling of unease began to walk, my eyes fixed on the neon sign.

On the way, there wasn't the least indication of life. No cars passed me by. No one came out to welcome me or waved at me from afar. When I arrived, there wasn't a soul in the old service station; the place felt ghostly without Sam and his loyal Lux by the entrance of the store. Someone had ripped off the sign telling clients to pay for their gas inside before pumping; in its place, hanging on a rusty chain blocking the entrance, was a wooden board that said STATION CLOSED. That was it. No other explanations. The door and the windows of the general store were sealed with boards of plywood. My premonitions began to become a fearful reality. I walked on the gravel path leading to my friend's shed, listening closely to the sounds of my steps, trying to understand how in the hell he always knew it was me. The place was empty: not a single piece of furniture, or utensil, or any other trace of his presence. Mechanically, I walked toward the small vegetable garden by the stream that ran behind the gas station. It didn't take long to confirm my suspicions. On the other side of the wire fence, I saw a small gray headstone and a succinct inscription.

1958–1973

Et Lux Perpetua

I went up to the tiny grave and touched the epitaph with my fingers, finding it strange that someone like Sam would have used such words. The name, I supposed, was down to the Bible, and how it colored his idea of the world. Lux. That's why he had taken up the animal after he lost his sight. The dog became the light that was missing from his eyes. If Sam too had died, as I was beginning to worry must be the case, they would have buried him in the small graveyard by the Anabaptist church in Deauville. I tried to imagine Sam's epitaph, thinking that no one could improve on what he had written about himself on the day he began to practice his last profession: "Sam Evans, Memorizer of the Word of God." May he rest in peace, I said aloud, looking at the rectangle of white pebbles that marked the contours of the place where Lux had been buried.

As I returned to the front of the station, I saw an approaching pickup truck slow down until it had come to a full stop. The driver opened the door and, sitting up, waved his hat at me, signaling me to approach. He was around fifty years old and was wearing a very dirty pair of denim overalls. When I reached him, he explained:

The gas station is closed.

I see that. What happened? Has something happened to Rick or Sam? You must know them. Are you from around here?

Yeah, of course. Rick is fine, but old Evans passed away a

couple of weeks ago. I stopped because I saw you didn't have a car. What brings you to Deauville? You need me to drop you off somewhere?

I told him I was a friend of Louise Lamarque. Everyone knew the Manhattan painter who spent long seasons alone in the windmill house.

If you want, I can take you there. It's on my way.

I accepted his offer, thanking him, and put my bag between us in the front seat. I told the man in the overalls that I had seen Lux's grave.

The poor thing could have probably held on for a bit longer, but before letting himself die, Sam took him to the veterinarian.

The memory of the old man's grave voice echoed within me:

And the word of the LORD came unto me, saying, Son of Man, prophesy against the shepherds of Israel.

He was a good man—Sam, I said. I don't come here a lot, but it's hard to imagine Deauville without his stall.

What finished him was the new gas station they opened in town. Just like that, people stopped coming here. Rick was offered a good retirement, but he asked for permission to continue to manage the old gas station, and they let him do it, out of pity. What they couldn't do is give him a job in the new station and much less let Sam put up his stall, as you call it. People are too busy, gas prices have gone up too much, and you can't bother customers with that sort of thing. Everyone knew that the only reason Rick went on working was that if he left he would have deprived his old friend of the only way he could make a living. But the situation was absurd. Now and then some old acquaintance stopped by to say hello, people like me, but for the most part, Rick and Sam were two solitary shadows stranded in that deserted service station. A couple of weeks after all this, Sam decided to put Lux to sleep, saying he was way too old. Sam wanted to go on living in the shed just the same, and there was no way to make him change his mind. Finally, Rick stopped working, although he kept on coming to the station every day. He brought Sam the meals Kim prepared him, and they did his laundry. He always stayed for a while, keeping Sam company, but that couldn't last. Rick offered to pay for a room in town, but Sam was too proud to accept anything like that.

One Sunday morning, when Rick came to pick Sam up to take him to church, Sam wasn't by the entrance to the store. Rick found him dead on his straw mattress. The doctor couldn't find any good reason he should've died. Natural causes was what he said in the end. I say, if that's what happened, if he died of old age, without suffering, he didn't have it so bad. Hopefully we'll all go that way when our time comes.

We had arrived at the intersection with the windmill. The man in the blue overalls stopped his truck and shook my hand. We had forgotten to introduce ourselves.

Walker Martin, if you ever need anything, he said.

Gal Ackerman, I replied and thanked him.

No need to thank me. And before taking off, he added: If you want to see Rick, he's at his sister Sarah's house on Red Creek, right next to the hardware store. Have a good day, my friend. Sorry to have been the bearer of bad news.

No problem. I'm not as surprised as you might think. In fact, I was at the gas station because I had a premonition . . .

After he drove off, I threw the bag over my shoulder and followed the path toward the windmill. The door to the house was locked, but there was a light on in the studio. I stamped off, each footfall reminding me that never again would anyone recognize me simply by hearing the sound of my steps.

Three
ABE LEWIS

March 9, 1964
I felt the impact of the landing in my stomach and looked out the window. It was still nighttime, and in the darkness, Barajas looked like a ghost town. Two rows of bright specks stretched back to the end of the runway. Near the ground, strips of fog wrapped themselves around the beacons. When the aircraft changed directions, I made out the shapes of other planes. Against the outline of the hangars, they seemed like sleeping monsters. Finally, the plane came to a stop. I stood up, dazed, and headed for the door with the rest of the passengers. Outside, a gust of wind slapped my cheeks. I noticed a neon sign that read AEROPUERTO DE MADRID-BARAJAS, the letters blurred by the fog. A dim glow floated over the open field on the other side of the wire fence. It had snowed. Sleepily, the passengers climbed down the steps and boarded a bus that had been waiting for us with its engine running. I sat by the driver and adjusted my watch to Madrid time. It was a few minutes before seven.

In the terminal, everyone was smoking. A border guard stamped my passport and handed it back to me. In the baggage-claim area, there was a group of civil guards whose three-cornered patent-leather hats I had seen in the photographs that Ben kept in the Archive. Outside, there was a line of black cars waiting. I noticed that in Madrid, taxis had a red stripe painted on the side.

I went to the front of the line, where a cab driver took my bag and put it in the trunk. Where to? he asked when we were both inside. Atocha Station, I replied. The driver, a man with a wispy mustache, sallow skin, and a surly disposition, nodded silently, wiped the windshield with the sleeve of his shirt, and pulled down the meter lever. Imitating him, I wiped my window and saw that daylight had begun to break over the snowy landscape. We passed by factories, old brick buildings, chalets, houses, and groves separated by large tracts of wasteland and empty lots. We had made it to the outskirts of the city when the soapy smudge of the sun rose above a row of low houses.

A few minutes later, we entered an elegant residential neighborhood. Everything caught my attention: the stately mansions, the blocks of apartment buildings no higher than five or six stories, the balconies and terraces on the houses. The shops weren't open yet, but the streets were already bustling with life. It was evident that the people of Madrid were not used to the snow. For them, it was a rare occurrence that disrupted their daily routine. Because I had seen them countless times in the photographs and documents that Ben kept in the Archive, many places seemed familiar, but no particular names came to mind until the taxi stopped at a red light, a few meters away from the Cibeles Fountain. The sight of the statue called up a vivid memory. I was fifteen. Ben and I were in the Archive in Brooklyn. My father was showing me pictures of Madrid during the time of the Republic. In one of them, there was a group of militiamen smiling and posing in front of the bags of sand they had placed around Cibeles to protect the goddess from Fascist bombs. The traffic light changed to green and the image vanished from my memory like a movie fading to black. The taxi went around the fountain, and as we entered the Paseo del Prado the lampposts lining the street were all suddenly turned off, plunging the city into a murky pool. We jolted down the cobblestoned boulevard until we reached a second plaza with a fountain presided over by Neptune. I recognized the statue, as well as buildings of the Museo del Prado behind it. The avenue flowed into a huge esplanade occupied by a sort of giant roller coaster whose slopes consisted of the maze of ramps connecting all the arteries flowing in and out of the esplanade. The metallic structure of the roller coaster was so big that you couldn't see the buildings on the opposite side no matter where you were positioned. The taxi drove onto a steep ramp that went all the way up then wound down to the side entrance of Atocha Station. Here we are, the mustachioed driver said, lifting the meter lever. He called out the amount of the fare and got out to collect my bag from the trunk. I told him to keep the change and he thanked me without deigning to smile. I got lost in the crowd milling about the station. It was an unpleasant morning with a cold breeze stirring the dirty snow. I climbed a stairway that led to the esplanade. From there, the traffic junction seemed stranger and even more gigantic than from the taxi. The tentacles of the giant metal octopus took over the whole surface of the plaza and reached out into all the surrounding streets, clogged with smoking cars.

Taking a detour, I crossed to the other side and got lost in the labyrinth of the hilly side streets, not worried about where I was or where my steps were taking me. Distractedly, I read the signs of the pensions and hostels along the sidewalk without going into any of them. I wasn't in a hurry, and it felt good to wander around the old quarter, despite the weather. After walking for a good while, as I turned a corner, I came upon a plaque that read Pensión Moratín, 3rd and 4th Floors, and for no good reason, I decided to try my luck there. The pension looked out on a tiny triangular plaza. I pushed the front door open, came to a dark lobby with a wide wooden stairway, and walked up to the third floor, where I saw a door with a sign that said, *Enter without Knocking*. I pushed it open, and found myself in a reception area where a woman in her forties was reading a newspaper with a striking name, *Ya*. When she saw me, she stopped reading, folded the newspaper, put it down on the counter, and greeted me with a stern smile. After jotting down my information in the registry book, she accompanied me to my room, one flight up. It was spacious and had a balcony that looked out on the triangular plaza. When I saw the room, it occurred to me that it may not have been all that much different from the room Ben found for my mother almost thirty years before; he had taken her to a pension in Cuatro Caminos, where she stayed for a few weeks right before giving birth. There was a chipped white metal chamber pot under the bed, and in a corner, by a rolled-up rug tied with a string, a gadget that upon closer inspection turned out to be an electric heater. I plugged it in with a certain apprehension, making sure that it was far enough from the bed. I took off my shoes and fell fully clothed on the frayed, white bedcover with its faded green embroidery. I closed my eyes, allowing myself to be flooded with images of the journey punctuated by the faltering echo of Ben's voice telling me which places in Madrid I could not fail to visit, no matter what. When I succumbed to fatigue, I dreamed I was at the Archive in Brooklyn. The afternoon light streamed in from the garden surrounding the figure of my father. Standing with his back to the light, Ben was telling me about a bar called Aurora Roja.

It was near the Cuatro Caminos Plaza. The owner named it after the novel by Pío Baroja, the Basque novelist that Hemingway had admired so much. I say *it was* because I suppose it no longer exists, and even if it does, it's surely changed its name by now.

Ben walked up to me and showed me a very old picture.

That's where I met your mother.

I took the photo with utmost care, but when I went to look at it closely, the image had vanished. The rectangle of paper had become the window of an airplane. The sun slid far away over a carpet of resplendent clouds. I scrutinized the horizon, but it was impossible to make out anything in that vista cut through by a never-ending light.

When I awoke, it took me a few moments to realize where I was. I got up, opened the shutters of the balcony, and looked out at the plaza. All around me was a panorama of snow-covered roofs. The bells of a nearby church began to peal, and I was overcome by a sense of unreality. I just couldn't come to terms with the fact that I had been born in this place. I went back into the room, took a change of clothes and my toiletry bag from my suitcase, and went to shower in the bathroom down the corridor. When I got back to the room, it was still too early to call the man with whom I had made an appointment. Trying to make some sense of the situation I found myself in, I sat in an armchair with faded upholstery and read Abraham Lewis's letter for the umpteenth time. Nominally, it was addressed to Ben and Lucia Ackerman, but the true recipient was me.

Sarzana, October 6, 1963

Dear comrades,

My name is Abraham Lewis, Abe to friends. I am from Florence, Alabama. Like you, I once enlisted in the Lincoln Brigade and arrived in Albacete in October of 1937. After a training period, I was deployed as an ambulance driver, first in the rearguard near the Ebro and then in a hospital near Gerona. I was repatriated against my will at the end of 1938, as were most of the other members of the International Brigades. After some time passed, I re-enlisted as a volunteer in 1940. I was sent to Italy this time, which had very important consequences, as you will soon learn. Since the end of the war, we spend half the year or so in Sarzana, because my wife is from here, and the rest of the time in the States. I wish things had taken another course, but cruel, cursed fate, or whatever you want to call it, chose me. So be it. Enough with the prologues. When someone gives his word to do something, the best thing is to do it as quickly as possible, that's the best thing for everyone involved. So I'll get to the point: the reason I'm writing is that three months ago someone crossed my path, or I crossed his—Umberto Pietri.

I lifted my eyes from the paper. It didn't matter that I had read the letter countless times. It still hurt me to see that name. Every time Lewis got to a part of his story in which Pietri figured, it felt as if someone was twisting a knife into my guts. I skipped ahead as if these lines were laced with poison, and in the following paragraph I read:

Last month, my wife and I were traveling in Tuscany. One night after dinner, in a small town called Certaldo, Patrizia (my wife) said she wanted to go back to the hotel. I walked her there, but then decided to go out for a stroll by myself. There were a lot of people sitting outside, at the main square. As I passed by a table, I heard something that made me stop cold. It lasted just a moment, no more than a few seconds, but it was unmistakable. Someone was whistling a ballad from the Brigade days. Impossible, I thought. I felt like someone was walking over my grave. I looked at the man and he immediately stopped whistling. He was more or less my age, wearing a long-sleeved shirt. He was alone. We recognized each other at once. I mean, he knew exactly what had made me stop and stare. It wasn't the first time that I'd stumbled across an old comrade. I'm sure you've had the same experience, at some point. The guy probably hadn't even realized what he'd been whistling. Reaching out my hand, I introduced myself and told him the name of my unit: Abraham Lewis, Lincoln Brigade. Without standing up, which surprised me a bit, he told me his name:

Umberto Pietri.

So now you know why I'm writing you.

He didn't mention the name of his unit, which would have been the normal thing to do, so I was forced to ask him. But even then he hesitated. Finally, out it came: the "Squadron of Death," also known as the Malatesta Battalion; he kept his eyes on me, waiting for a reaction. Realizing I wasn't going to say anything, he made clear that, strictly speaking, it couldn't really be considered one of the International Brigades.

I don't know what you know about Pietri's unit. Maybe you don't want to know. But I did a little research after that encounter. It was a very dark business. The Squadron of Death was the brainchild of Diego Abad de Santillán, the anarchist union leader, who proposed to the Generalitat the founding of a unit made up of Italian anarchists. I've seen photographs. Apparently, their uniforms were very flashy and when they marched through the streets of Barcelona it looked more like a circus than a military parade. They were quite ostentatious and became famous before going into combat. The funny bit is that after such macho displays they were crushed by the Falangists in their first battle. I apologize for going into excessive detail, but I think it's pretty likely you haven't kept up with things— and you need to know the details if you want to understand what happened.

As for himself, to make a long story short, Pietri explained to me that he was from Certaldo, and that after returning home from his time in the Brigades, he never left his village again—except during World War II, at which time, he said, without going into too much detail, he was in hiding. His voice was tense. It was clear he was in a hurry to tell me something in particular. He pulled out his wallet, opened it, took out a photograph, and set it on top of the table. When he did this, he winced as if in great pain. His eyes closed and his head fell forward. I stood up, worried that he was going to faint. But he immediately reopened his eyes and kept them on me, although he himself didn't seem quite there. He made a gesture with his hand as if to assure me that he would recover momentarily; when he did, he explained to me that he was very ill, but he didn't seem to think this worth dwelling on. As if what was happening to him was unimportant, he insisted I have a good look at the photograph, and so I did.

It was a very young militia woman, barely out of adolescence, with large eyes. Teresa Quintana, mi compañera, he said. His tone stuck with me; it was biting and sharp, not the least bit somber. He hadn't told me what he wanted, yet, but he had my attention.

At twelve noon, a multitude of bells began to peal loudly (the Angelus, the woman at the reception desk told me when I asked her later what it meant), and I thought it would be a good time to call Lewis. I put the letter back in its envelope and went down to the third floor. The receptionist told me that the phone worked with tokens and handed me one. It was about the size and color of a peseta, but it was missing the image of the dictator and its surface was crossed by a pair of deep striations. The woman looked up the number of the Hotel Florida in a phone book that had no covers. I went up to the phone, put the token in the slot, and watched it slide down a thin, glass-covered chute till it hit bottom. When I said that I wanted to speak to Abraham Lewis, the operator didn't understand my pronunciation, so I had to spell the name for him.

After a few seconds, I heard a deep voice with a strong Southern accent on the other end of the line.

That and the laugh that punctuated his words made me feel less removed from the world I had left behind fewer than twenty-four hours before. Lewis asked me to meet him at a bar that was right next to the Cibeles.

It's called Cervecería de Correos, and it's on the left hand side at the beginning of a street that rises uphill toward the Puerta de Alcalá. You won't have any trouble finding it, Ackerman. From your hostel it's a very pleasant walk if you don't mind the cold. Is one thirty okay?

Yes, but how will we recognize each other?

I am fifty-four years old, with a buzz cut—I'm six-foot-three, have wide shoulders, and if there's any doubt left, I'm black.

He let out a long laugh. Once more, his voice, the way he spoke and laughed, had a deep calming effect on me. Fifteen minutes later, I came out of the hostel and leaving behind the labyrinth of side streets that surrounded it arrived at the Paseo del Prado. On the other side of the boulevard there was a tall wrought-iron gate and beyond it a garden. I crossed toward it. The wind was freezing, but at least it wasn't snowing. I walked very slowly, rather distracted, registering what I saw without realizing it, mixing the sensations of the present with very distant memories. Early that morning—it seemed now like all that had been the day before— I'd looked at the city without being contaminated by its reality, as if the taxi had been a sterile bubble that protected me from direct contact with things. Now, walking along with other people, putting one foot in front of the other on the pavement, breathing in the mixture of smells that floated in the air, everything was different. *Madrid.* The city was getting into me through my pores, my eyes, my nostrils. The photographs, the movies, and the documentaries that I had seen so many times in Ben's Archive, the things my father had told me, it all seemed to belong to some other dimension. It was as if I had awakened from a very strange dream to discover that reality was stranger still.

If someone had pinched me and shown me that I was in fact strolling across the surface of the moon, and even told me that I'd been born there, it wouldn't have been too much more disconcerting. A few hours before, as she handed back my passport after writing down my details in the registry book, the woman at the pension had exclaimed, But you're from here! Who would have guessed with a name like that? Remembering those words, alone in my room, I'd opened the passport and read:

Place of Birth: Madrid, Spain.

Madrid. Spain. Each of those two words contained an entire world locked within it. The *M*, with its mountain-shape, was the sierra where Ben had fought; and then the *S*, the sibilant *S* that Spaniards find impossible to pronounce without putting an *e* before it, and whose sinuous contours refer to the labyrinth of the conflict itself. The shape of the two letters put together gave rise to echoes of countless stories. It took Ben fourteen years before he'd confessed it to me, but I was a Spaniard. Another fourteen years had passed, and for the first time since Ben had taken me to America, back when I was only a few weeks old, I was physically here, in the city where I was born.

My childhood was one long parade of ex-Brigade men marching through our house in Brooklyn. They always showed a special affection for me, because they knew I was actually *from there*—the only one, really, among all those people whose memories were so vividly stamped with the months or years that they had spent in *my* country. For them, Spain was a painful memory because of how the war had ended—but no amount of pain was enough to efface all the marvelous moments they'd lived through there despite all. Ben and Lucia never tired of repeating that it had been the most extraordinary experience of their lives. And I, with my dark skin and Mediterranean features, so different from the Ackermans, both of them unequivocally Anglos, I was the living proof that such tragedy (to employ the same word Lewis used in his letter) had not been a dream.

I took one last look behind the gate of the Botanical Gardens (I didn't know what it was, at that point—all I saw was a mysterious park, overgrown and wild, but somehow outside of time, like so many corners of the Paseo). Snow covered the flower beds and pathways not yet trod upon, it stuck to the trees reproducing the contours of their trunks, the silhouettes of the bare bushes. I continued toward the Museo del Prado, imagining that on the other side of the walls marked with niches occupied by unknown goddesses, the halls would be empty, its usual visitors kept away by the cold. I knew many of the works there very well. Ben had a catalog published during the Republic days that he held in great esteem. When I was a child, he liked to show me the reproductions, accompanied by anecdotes and explanations that my childhood mind turned into fairy tales of sorts. Later, when I was a teenager, the explanations became more technical. Art history was one of my father's frustrated passions. He had insisted so strongly that, if or when I ever went to Madrid, I had to go to that *extraordinary place*, now that I was just a few steps away from all those masterpieces in there, I felt a strange tension. I'll go see them soon, I said aloud, as if Ben could hear me.

When I reached the corner by the Ritz Hotel, I paused to observe the plaza of Neptune, and a title came to mind. *Piedra y cielo*. Whose was it? One of the poets that Ben liked to read, probably. I decided to write a story using the same title. How many times I've started to write something without the slightest idea where my imagination would take me, guided exclusively by the particular resonance of a few little words . . .

A tug on my coat shook me from my reverie. In front of me, a child of about ten with a very serious expression offered me a newspaper without saying a word. I saw some enormous headlines and, to one side, in red ink, the name of the publication, *Diario Pueblo*. I gave the kid the first coin I found in my pocket, but I didn't take the paper. The diminutive vendor shrugged and ran off.

A few steps beyond, I stopped to look upon a flame burning in front of a stone tomb at the foot of a monolith surrounded by an iron fence. I read the inscription, which referred to the heroes of the 2nd of May, and I remembered one of my favorite pages in Ben's catalog, Goya's firing-squad executions. A somewhat disquieting association. It made me feel like a participant in a history with which I refused to integrate. At the same time, I was impatient to finally hear what Abe Lewis had to tell me. I asked myself again why, after so many doubts, I had decided to meet with some stranger on the other side of the Atlantic, and, as always, the answer escaped me. You have to do it—not so much for us, for Lucia and me, but for you, Ben had repeated to me to the point of exhaustion. That wasn't how I felt about it. I had lived twenty-eight years without knowing anything about the man they said was my father, and had felt no need, was not even curious, to know his story.

Ben again:

As much as you refuse to accept it, there's an unresolved issue in your past. Only by going to Madrid will you be able to settle it. The only way you can say that your life belongs to you completely is if you do this. And the place is also important. Of course, you could always wait until Lewis comes back to the States, but it wouldn't be the same. You have to return, set foot on the earth of Madrid, hear the language that Lucia and I made sure remained alive in you. But, most of all, be among your people, for in the end it's as one of them that you came into this world.

After months of hesitation I made plans to travel to Spain, and the expression of relief on Ben's face made it all worthwhile. But now that I was there, alone, there were many moments when the grand gesture I'd made seemed to me completely absurd.

When I reached the end of the boulevard I scrutinized the statue of Cibeles. Riding on a carriage pulled by lions, the goddess of Earth, mother of Neptune (suddenly I realized the connection between the two statues), looked off into the distance. In her wake, two granite children were at play turning over a pitcher from which poured a stream of water. Surrounding the fountain, palaces and gardens formed a circle that seemed designed to protect the stone image, magnificent in her solitude. I continued toward the Palacio de Comunicaciones and arrived at a wide street on a hill. Above, to my right, I saw the arches of the Puerta de Alcalá and, in front of me, on the other side of a crosswalk, the Cervecería de Correos.

The place was packed and smelled of sawdust. A crowd, three-rows deep, made it impossible to approach the bar. A waiter called out to me from afar, asking what I wanted, and in an instant I had before me a tin mug atop a thick cork coaster in a tiny space the waiter had miraculously found for me. I saw the man I'd come to meet before I had taken the first sip of my beer. He was seated at a marble table in the front room to the left. Although I hadn't described myself to him on the phone, he too had recognized me. His head raised, he followed my every movement. Without taking his eyes off me, he stood up and made a sign for me to come to him. When I got to the table, he shook my hand firmly.

Finally, we meet in person, he said, scrutinizing my face with a strange urgency. How was your trip?

The truth is that I don't know what the hell I'm doing here, I replied brusquely. I'm doing it for Ben. But I've spent all morning thinking that coming here was a huge mistake. I feel like I'm floating in space, not knowing where to plant in my feet.

That's normal. Give it some time.

Time for what? It was hard for me to talk about it. What do I care about this guy Pietri? I managed to ask. I had never even heard about him until the day Ben gave me your letter to read. Once more, just like when I was fourteen, I have to change all the coordinates of my life? And you, throwing all of this in my face all of a sudden, who the fuck are you? Was it really necessary for you to write that letter? I had brought my hand out of the pocket of my jacket and was brandishing it. Why are you all so certain about what needs to be done, as you say?

Who are you referring to?

You Brigade people and your infallible sense of "what's right" . . .

Lewis endured my diatribe as if he had known beforehand that this was the way things were going to be. When I'd finished insulting him and had put his letter back in my pocket, he looked me in the eyes and pressed a firm hand into my shoulder.

Have you had anything to eat?

Eat? I asked, as if I didn't know the meaning of the word.

I'll get us something, he said, signaling for the waiter.

Although you may not like to hear it, he noted after the waiter had taken our order, Ben's right. That's why I took the liberty of pressing this point. He's a very special person—you're very fortunate.

What do you mean?

It's just my impression. I only know him through a pair of letters. I'd like to know more about him.

Like what?

His story.

The waiter dropped off tapas at our table and left. Abe Lewis was laughing.

What? I asked him.

You cross the ocean because you think that I've got something life-or-death to tell you, and the first thing I do when I see you is ask *you* to tell *me* stories . . .

It's fine. You're right about Ben. He is very special. And I apologize about what I just said about the Brigades. I was out of place.

Lewis went on laughing.

Well, let's eat something, see if we can cheer up.

At that moment, the front door of the bar opened and group of people came in cackling and yelling. Their coats and scarves were sprinkled with snow. A burst of frozen air snuck in with them and reached our table. The newcomers blended in with the other patrons around the bar, leaving the door open. We looked outside. It was snowing harder now—for a few seconds the white filled the frame of the door. We saw whirls of snow glowing under the streetlights, sucked down by the storm, till a burly man came in from the street and closed the door after him.

It's too loud here, Lewis said. Why don't we go next door? It's a perfect place to chat.

I shrugged, which in the code that we had begun to develop meant, it's fine.

The snow drove itself into the reddish marble façade. I raised my eyes, barely able to make out the gold letters that read Lion D'or. A double set of glass doors created a buffer space that prevented the warm air of the cafeteria from escaping. Inside, a thick cloud of acrid smoke lingered, making it difficult to breathe; it stuck to the walls and clouded the mirrors. The curtains and upholstery on the seats were red velvet, the tables marble topped with wrought-iron legs. The light from the lamps floated ghost-like in the haze.

We sat in a corner next to a window and remained silent for a long while, getting used to each other. A waiter with a reddish complexion, an enormous mustache, and slick hair, asked us in a smug tone if we wanted anything.

Watching it snow. Trapped in a strange web of geometric intersections. The lights of the cars going both ways on Alcalá projected cones of light that beveled the curtain of snow. Same with the edge of the table; or the plane of the sidewalk that met the floor of the café at an acute angle. The windowsill almost touched the ground.

What's the origin of your last name Ackerman? Is it Jewish? People always ask me that. Same thing with my first name, Gal. Neither of them are necessarily Jewish. Ackerman is a German surname. My great-grandfather's family was from Alsace, although he was born in Brooklyn, in 1858. He ran a bakery in Bensonhurst. My grandfather, David Ackerman, worked all his life for the *Brooklyn Eagle,* a great newspaper, the best one ever published in Brooklyn. Walt Whitman was one of its most renowned contributors, but there were others. It shut down in 1955, after one hundred and twenty-three years. The death of a newspaper is a very sad thing, don't you think? My grandfather started as an apprentice when he was seventeen and he ended as a head typesetter. He never went beyond that, but now and then they allowed him to write a few things, and finally, right before he was about to retire, he got his own column, which was published weekly.

What did he write?

Political commentary, anecdotes, op-ed columns, random notes, but above all, stories about the different neighborhoods of Brooklyn. He knew Brooklyn like the back of his hand.

Do you still have the articles?

Of course, as well as hundreds and hundreds of index cards about the history of Brooklyn. He had vague plans to write a book about the borough.

Was he a communist?

Anarchist, although he didn't like to talk about it. He was viscerally repulsed by any type of proselytizing, on top of the fact that he was a very reserved and solitary person.

What about your grandmother?

Her maiden name was Gallagher. May Gallagher. She and my grandfather couldn't have been more different. Her family was from Pennsylvania. They moved to Brooklyn at the turn of the century when she was sixteen or seventeen. Everyone called her Sister May, because she had the look of a nun about her. She was a very devoted and generous person, but with a strong personality. She met David at a street dance not long after arriving in Bensonhurst, and a few months later, they married. They had two children, a daughter who died a few days after she was born and Ben.

When was all this?

Let's see, Ben was born in 1907, and May, I'm not sure. Around 1883, I figure—she and David were about the same age.

Did you get along with him?

With my grandfather David? Very well. I loved him. My grandfather and I had a very special relationship. He would pick me up on Sundays and take me out to explore Brooklyn. He liked taking me to places where we not only had a good time but learned something as well. He was a Brooklyn history fanatic. I have very vivid memories of our visits to the Navy Yard, the Red Hook Harbor, the Botanical Gardens, Prospect Park, the Brooklyn Museum, the Public Library, and many, many other places. One of my favorite outings was when he took me on a stroll around Brooklyn Heights. He knew the history of each building, down to the last brick. He was a member of the Brooklyn Historical Society. That's where he got the material that he later used in his columns for the *Eagle*. But the greatest was when he took me to Coney Island. He called me his "research assistant" and we spent two summers going there several times a week. It's a shame he never got to write that book. Have you ever been to Brooklyn, Abe?

He shook his head, smiling:

No, but after today, I have no excuse.

The truth is, it's like a world without end.

And you said he never talked about politics?

Not ever. I knew he was an anarchist, because I heard everyone else call him that, although I wasn't exactly sure what the word meant. He was obsessed with culture and progress. He liked to take me to all kinds of cultural events: concerts, lectures, and once in a while to the movies or the theater. Only once did he take me to a meeting.

How old were you then?

Fifteen, but I remember it vividly. My grandfather and I spoke about a lot of things, but what brought us together most were the long periods of silence that we shared. We understood each other perfectly well without having to talk. Many times, on the subway or the trolley, when the noise was too much, instead of raising his voice to make himself heard, my grandfather would interrupt whatever he had been telling me and just sit there quietly. I soon grew accustomed to his silences. That's what happened the day he took me to the meeting; when we came out of the subway station, instead of going toward the Fulton Street Market he took me to Boerum Hill without offering any explanation. Halfway down one block, we saw a throng of people by the front doors of a theater. If I'm not mistaken, the place is still there. We got in line. I remember that in the lobby there were three very tall doors, but my grandfather took me by the hand to a stairway on one side, and on reaching the upper level we went into a box in which there were five or six other people already seated, waiting for the function to start. I looked down. In the orchestra, there was an immense sea of heads, but there were also people in the aisles and just about everywhere else in the theater. Soon the house lights were lowered and a murmur passed through the audience. Spotlights shone on the stage, where I saw a long table, a podium, and a few chairs. Some people filed up onto the stage and sat on the chairs as the crowd burst into thunderous applause. A woman of around fifty approached the podium and addressed the audience. I hardly paid attention to what she said. Other things caught my attention. There were little red and black flags all over the theater, and on the stage there was a banner. I didn't make out what it said because I couldn't take my eyes off what I saw on the wings of the stage. They were portraits of two men twice the height of a normal person, painted with broad brushstrokes and in strident colors. They looked like cartoon characters. They wore no vests and their shirts were unbuttoned. One had brown pants and the other navy-blue ones. Their heads were disproportionate to their bodies. But what frightened me most were their eyes, which in spite of the shrill colors, seemed to me very real and unsettling. I had the feeling that they were looking at me, only at me, as if they knew who I was and were accusing me of something. Only after I grew accustomed to those eyes was I able to discern the words on the banner. Now of course it's impossible not to know those names, but when I read them that day, they lacked all meaning:

Sacco and Vanzetti (1927–1952)

The speakers came and went from the podium at regular intervals. Their words were all clearly enunciated, exalted, booming. Every once in a while, the crowd interrupted the speeches, cheering and applauding. Although I was right beside him, my grandfather seemed unaware of my presence. Not once during the entire business did he look at me or say a word. What most surprised me about his behavior was that of all the people who were in the box, or probably the entire theater, he was the only one who didn't raise his voice or clap. Even so, I was perfectly aware of the changes in his mood, because I saw how he frowned or how his hands clenched into fists. The function was rather long and was pretty boring for long stretches, though you couldn't help but get wrapped up in everyone's enthusiasm—after a while, although I wasn't sure why, every time the crowd clapped or screamed out this or that slogan, I felt a strange mixture of excitement and fear.

When we got out, my grandfather quickly said good-bye to

his friends and we left hurriedly, finally heading to the Fulton Street Market. Not once did he mention the meeting. After a few minutes he picked up the story he had left half-finished when the noise of the subway had drowned out his words, as if only a few minutes had passed. At the Fulton Street Market, he took me directly to the shoe stalls and helped me pick out a new pair. Well, in truth, he chose them for me—I couldn't make up my mind. When we got home, he wanted me to put them on so that everyone could see how well they fit me. Then he went into the kitchen to have some coffee with the other grown-ups. Later that afternoon, he came to give me a kiss and said good-bye. Ben and I accompanied him to the porch. Before reaching the corner, my grandfather turned around and waved. The sun was low and hit the front of the house head-on.

Who were Sacco and Vanzetti? I asked Ben.

And, just then, I realized how tight my shoes were and I knelt down to loosen the laces.

Take them off before you get blisters, I remember Ben saying.

I went into the house carrying the shoes in one hand and dashed to my room, followed by my father. We sat on the edge of my bed.

Where did you hear about Sacco and Vanzetti? he asked me, and I told him about the meeting in Boreum Hill.

It's his way of telling you that he considers you a man, Ben said after I had finished. He did something similar with me when I was your age.

Four
BROOKLYN HEIGHTS

June 19, 1990
11:29 on the gas station clock. The metal shutter of the Oakland closed. My suitcase in the middle of the sidewalk where the Sikh left it. The shadow of the Chrysler fades in the distance, a yellow haze heading around a corner. Time seems to have shrunk since I last set foot in Queens. The distance between O'Hare and LaGuardia felt considerably shorter than the trip from New York to Chicago. My internal, subjective time. The feeling that things are happening faster than usual. The world's unassailable external time. I try to make sure that these two do not unravel. 9:43. My suitcase appears on the baggage belt, the first one out, and for a minute or so, the only one. Arrivals area. 9:45 according to the Marlboro ad. At the taxi stand, a man wearing a saffron turban practically rips the suitcase from my hands and forces me to get into his cab. 10:07 according to the red digits on the dashboard clock. The Sikh smiles, waiting for my directions. Hicks and Atlantic, Brooklyn Heights, I tell him and the cab lunges forward, tires screeching as they grind on the asphalt. We swerve past trucks, delivery vans, and school buses, the regular morning traffic on the BQE. I like the taxi driver. For some reason, his aggressive driving doesn't make me anxious. I settle into the back seat. I read on the yellow-card license that his name is Manjit Singh. As if he's somehow picked up on the direction I'm looking, the Sikh

raises his right hand to his turban and smiles at me in the rearview mirror. He's in his early twenties, has a black beard and his teeth and gums are red from chewing betel. He slows down, apparently in the mood to chat. He slides open the partition and points to the stone mansions and stately buildings. We pass by streets named after fruits. Do I live in Brooklyn Heights? he wants to know. I'm going to visit a friend, I explain. Good neighborhood, very elegant, he says. On Atlantic Avenue, Manjit Singh lifts his foot from the gas pedal and lets the Chrysler glide to a spot right in front of the Oakland, perfectly lined up with the curb. He gets out solicitously, and with a succession of quick movements, deftly opens and closes the trunk, leaving my suitcase in the middle of the sidewalk. He presses his hands together in front of his chest as if in prayer, bows his head, and says good-bye before getting back into the taxi. He takes off with a lurch, as he had at the airport, leaving behind a trail of smoke that smells like gasoline and burned rubber.

There's a light on in the back of the Oakland.

I push my hand through the grate and knock on the glass door. I hear the tinkling of the keys that hang from the lock inside, and a few moments later I glimpse a figure approaching unsteadily. I try to figure out who it is. Not Ernie, not Frank . . . till I realize it's Gal Ackerman; it hadn't occurred to me he would be here. He presses his face to the glass, sees me, turns the key, and pulls the door open.

No one's here. Everyone took off for Teaneck to see Raúl's new house. Ernie won't open up till this afternoon.

He takes a drag of his cigarette then tosses it to the ground and steps on it, even though it's almost whole. Something is clearly wrong. He shrugs and turns around without saying good-bye, which gives me time to put my hands through the bars and grab him by the sleeve of his vest.

Gal, please, let me in. I just got here from the airport.

He shrugs again, pulls the key ring out of the lock, and passes it to me through the grate.

They locked me in without realizing it, he explains with the hint of a smile. I can unlock the inside door, but not the gate. You have to do it. Here, it's one of the small keys.

How was Chicago? he asks once we're both inside.

I'm surprised that he keeps up with my affairs.

All right, I respond . . . I'm really sorry to bother you, it's just that . . . I almost tell him why I've come straight to the Oakland from the airport instead of going back to my place, but I hold off. It's too early to go into the newsroom, I say absurdly.

Gal gestures to a pot of coffee steaming on top of the counter.

It's fresh, he says.

I leave my suitcase on the floor, pour myself a cup, and sit with him. On top of the table there's a section of the *New York Times* folded in half.

Look at this, he says, pointing to the headlines. He flips the paper around so I get a better look. The news is from February 21.

MAN ACQUITTED OF KILLING
AND BOILING ROOMMATE

He lets out a nervous laugh.

What's so funny? I ask.

He puts an index finger to his lips, leans on the wooden edge of the marble table with his elbows, flips the newspaper back, and continues to read silently. After a while, he says:

Daniel Rakowitz. The thing is, I knew this guy. I was always seeing him around Tompkins Square Park when Louise lived on 12th Street. Shit, now that I think about it, Louise bought some grass from him once. Remember the May Day concerts in the park?

Sure.

He goes on reading. When he's done, he says:

I remember him perfectly. You must have seen him yourself. Doesn't he sound familiar? You were in New York last February, right?

Gal . . .

Do you remember the guy who used to traipse around Alphabet City with a chicken on a leash as if it were a Chihuahua? The poor critter ran around behind him while its owner sold bags of marijuana around the park for five dollars.

Sounds familiar.

He was from Texas. Came to live in New York in 1985. One of the witnesses, Bart Mills, a homeless man who lived in Tompkins Square Park, testified that Daniel Rakowitz used to show up in the park with a pot and a ladle and offer the beggars loitering there a bowl of stew, beef and potato or something. But the thing is that according to Mills's testimony, one day when he and a few of the other beggars were feasting on Rakowitz's stew, one of them found a human finger in the bowl, with the nail and everything. That's what it says here.

I spit out a mouthful of coffee.

Look, I just added his index card to my files for the *Death Notebook*, with his picture and everything. Name: Daniel Rakowitz. Age: Thirty. Accused of first-degree murder. The case number follows, and then in this clipping, the jury's verdict. How about that? But the truth is the guy has a sense of humor. When he appeared before the judge, after a group of psychiatrists had examined him, he said that he would prefer jail to the psych ward, because he had learned how dangerous drugs were, and in jail they wouldn't stupefy him with pills. Read it yourself if you don't believe me.

Gal holds the *New York Times* aloft for a few moments and then brings it back down slowly to the table, smoothes it over, reading the news story to the end. When he finishes it, he gives me a brief summary.

He lived at 614 East 9th Street, right in the middle of Alphabet City, and once in a while, he worked at Sahak, an Armenian restaurant in the East Village, when he needed the money . . . hey, Ness, is it noon yet?

I point to the clock on the wall. The minute hand is about to reach the highest point in the circle. By the time Gal glances over, the two hands become one.

Perfect. It's time. My internal chronometer never fails.

Time for what?

To give the demons a drink! Someone has to take care of them.

He takes a bottle of vodka out of a brown paper bag that he has hidden under the table and pours a long shot into his coffee.

He murdered a Swiss girl who was studying contemporary dance at the Martha Graham Academy, name's Monika Beerle, I think.

Sounds Dutch.

Could be. According to the reporters, Rakowitz had proclaimed himself to be the "God of Marijuana."

He sits in thought a while.

Go on, Gal.

Some detectives from the narcotics division who were watching the area began to hear rumors about how this Rakowitz had boiled a body. Don't tell me that doesn't make your balls shrink! You're a journalist, explain to me what the hell that means: *Rumors that he had boiled a body*? Can you imagine a junkie telling someone else in the park: Hey, that Swiss girl hasn't been around for a while, I think the dude with the chicken killed her and boiled her body?

Yeah, right.

He laughs, but on seeing that I won't join in, stops.

Gal . . .

All right, all right, don't get upset. It's just one hell of a fucking story. So, anyway, a pair of plainclothes detectives headed over to Rakowitz's place with a warrant. They took him down to the precinct to question him, but he roundly denied having anything to do with killing anyone. He'd found the body, that's all—found it and soaked it in bleach before boiling it! He he he he! Unbelievable! He said he wanted to disinfect the bones. They really grilled him, and half the things he said contradicted the other half. That's when he told them that the head was at Port Authority. When they took him there, he led them to a bucket of kitty litter in the baggage room, in which—to make a long story short—there was the skull of a female wrapped in newspaper and in an advanced state of decomposition. Seems the bleach didn't work very well.

He laughs and laughs, unable to stop.

Wait, he manages to say when he recovers, that's not all. It gets better. You want to know what Rakowitz said to the members of the jury after they had delivered their verdict? Let me read it to you, otherwise you're gonna think I'm making it up:

After jurors returned their verdict yesterday in State Supreme Court in Manhattan, Mr. Rakowitz thanked them and said, "I hope someday we can smoke a joint together."

"I won't fault you for your verdict," said Mr. Rakowitz, who had frequently interrupted the six-week trial with bizarre outbursts. "The prosecution had an overwhelming case against me. But I'll be getting out soon and I'll sell a lot of marijuana so I can bring to justice the people who actually committed this crime."

He he he he. But you haven't heard the best part.

During the trial, after both sides had rested, the judge delivered a peremptory speech to the jury about its responsibilities, then ordered it to go deliberate. When the court gathered again nine days later, the jury declared Rakowitz not guilty by reason of insanity. What do you think of that?

I don't know, Gal.

What the fuck do you mean you don't know? I've told you the whole story from beginning to end, don't you have an opinion?

If they didn't think he was sane, then they couldn't hold him criminally responsible. That's the law.

That's bullshit: then who was responsible for the girl's murder?

Gal, you shouldn't start drinking so early.

I didn't know you cared so much about my health. He punctuates these words by drinking directly from the bottle before adding:

To me, the little pebble that keeps rolling around inside my shoe is the fate of that girl, Monika Beerle. It's disturbing that the article barely has anything to say about her. No details about her family history, not even her age. It's almost as if she were a footnote to the case.

I apologize, Gal, what time you drink or don't drink is none of my business. Anyway, I have to get to the newspaper. Thanks for letting me in, and for the coffee. If you don't mind, I'm going to leave my suitcase in Frank's office. If you see him, tell him I'll come pick it up this afternoon.

Gal responds by taking out a pen from his shirt pocket and burying himself in his papers.

Later. A sticky wind blows down the avenue. Frank still hasn't returned. I know because his Plymouth isn't parked in front of the Oakland. Ernie is reading the *New York Post* at the bar, clenching a pipe between his teeth. Gal isn't around. Perhaps I'd offended him that morning?

Ernie, have you seen Gal?

He puts his paper down and takes his pipe out of his mouth:

Damned if I know. When I got here at three, there wasn't a soul in the place. Haven't seen you for a few days, now. Where have you been?

Chicago. So you don't know where Gal is?

Fuck no, I just told you. This morning he was here, we left a set of keys for him, but when I got back to open the bar, he'd taken off. As you know, I don't keep tabs on the clientele. I've got enough problems of my own.

How has Gal seemed to you these days?

I haven't noticed anything. Truth is, I don't understand all this concern about him.

What if something's happened to him?

Something like what?

Don't be cynical. You know exactly what I'm talking about.

Forget about Gal. He can take care of himself.

Has he been talking a lot about Nadia recently?

Ernie snorts.

Oh, here we go. I don't know and I don't care. But, speaking of women, some gorgeous little number just moved in upstairs. She can't be older than twenty.

The remark surprises me. The motel is a taboo topic in the Oakland, and if anyone ought to know it, it's Ernie Johnson. If Frank had been sitting there, Ernie wouldn't have had the guts to make a comment like that.

Watch your mouth, Ernie.

He asks me if I want something to drink, chuckling. I ask for a Heineken. He puts an ice-cold bottle in front of me, mutters something incomprehensible, and disappears behind his copy of the *Post*. I go to the table where I had been seated with Gal that morning, the Captain's Table. As I put the bottle down on the marble surface, the image of him reading the Rakowitz story comes to mind, but then it is superimposed by a much more distant memory.

(I'm doing okay, right, Gal? Dialogue without quotation marks interlaced with action, just as you like it. And now I am going to do something that I also learned from you: insert fragments of my diary. I never had a chance to tell you how I first found out about you.)

Dylan Taylor told me that they were putting on Norman Mailer's *The Deer Park* at the old St. Anne's church.

You want to cover it? Maybe Mailer will show up. He lives right there. Why don't you go by?

Mailer lives in Brooklyn Heights?

Yeah, right on the promenade. The last of a long line of famous names. It's inexcusable that you still don't know the neighborhood. Wait a second.

He goes out of my cubicle and about thirty seconds later comes back from his with a book. He tosses it on top of my desk. It's Truman Capote's *The Dogs Bark*.

What's this for?

Take a look at the piece called "A House on the Heights." Going back to the Mailer piece, it doesn't have to be long. Three hundred words or so is good. We can publish it Saturday.

You can read the Capote thing in twenty minutes. Dylan is right: Thomas Wolfe, W. H. Auden, Hart Crane, Marianne Moore, Richard Wright, the Bowleses, and Truman Capote himself—among others I can't remember now—all have lived in the Heights.

I told Dylan that I'd take a stroll around the neighborhood after the performance.

Some images that have stayed with me: the gaslights on Hicks Street; a window through which could be seen the peaceful image of a girl playing a violin, like a still from a silent movie; the Grace Court alleyway, which reminds me of a Vermeer canvas, with its uneven cobblestone road, the enormous gates of the old carriage stables, and the hook from where the hay was once hung to feed the horses; the engravings on the medallions from the enormous dining room doors of the sunken cruise liner *Normandie*, now adorning the giant metal doors of the Maronite church Our Lady of Lebanon.

I turned the corner on Hicks and Atlantic and saw a sign, *Oakland, Bar & Grill*, in red and white neon letters above a window made of thick cubes of frosted glass. I pushed open the black iron door with some effort. On the other side there was a narrow space with tall ceilings and red velvet curtains. On parting the curtains, I had the sensation that I was leaving the waking world behind and walking straight into a dream. I had come to a space packed with people in costumes. It seemed like a masquerade ball was taking place in an old cabaret, or in the dance hall of a cruise ship. The wall to the right was covered with a fishing net, a hatch half hidden underneath its folds.

The bar was to the left. A wooden panel hung from the ceiling, following the contours of the counter. There were all sorts of tools and gadgets related to marine life on it: rigging, buoys, lifesavers, lamp globes, a ship's wheel . . . In the middle of the bar there was a mirror on which the flags of Denmark, the United States, and Spain had been painted in the shape of a cross. Against the wall, rows of bottles flanked by more maritime objects: a miniature lighthouse, the busts of a mermaid and a ship's captain, and strings of lights wound around several masts. In the back of the bar, to the right, there were two wooden phone booths next to a jukebox. The ceiling and support columns were adorned with paper garlands in vibrant colors. Two of the columns formed an archway that led to the dance floor. On the walls were photographs and posters (I remember one of them was an announcement for a bullfight at the Plaza de Toros in Sada, dated 1910), as well as shelves placed at various heights displaying model ships, some quite huge, inside glass bottles.

Then I saw him. He was a man of about fifty or fifty-five, the only one in the whole place (aside from me) who wasn't wearing a mask. He was seated in a corner, implausibly oblivious to everything happening around him, scribbling in a notebook. Around him there was a cloud of smoke that seemed thicker than the one that floated through the rest of the place, as if he were in a bell jar. Now and then he paused to take a drag from a cigarette or to have a sip of his drink.

Someone wearing a feathered cape and an owl mask grabbed me without warning and dragged me to the bar. Dipping a plastic glass into a bowl of reddish liquid, he filled it and told me to drink it in one gulp. I did as I was told. It was a potent brew that made my eyes tear and I broke into a coughing fit. The man let out a laugh, gave me a mask as monstrous as the one he was wearing, and wouldn't leave me alone until I put it on.

When I got rid of him, I went back to the spot from where I had seen the solitary man writing, but he had disappeared. On his table was a cigarette butt still burning in the ashtray next to an empty glass. I searched every corner of the place, at each step having to throw off people who insisted that I dance, but I couldn't find him. Maybe they had forced him to put on a mask, as they had done with me. I was dazed because of the concoction I'd been made to drink, and then this whirlwind of new experiences, and I was finding it difficult to make my way out of there. Finally, I located the exit, and after going through the red curtains and out the iron door, the silence of the night seemed like a miracle.

I started to walk, a bit unsteady, and on passing by a shop window, I mistook my masked reflection in the glass for a stranger, and jumped, startled. Taking off my mask, I walked on toward the piers, as had been my intention from the start. I was feeling strangely anxious, though I couldn't understand why.

It was months before I went back to the Oakland, although on several occasions a passing memory of it mingled with other things I had seen on my first trip to Brooklyn Heights. Everything had made a profound impression on me, starting with Mailer's play, and then all the singular spots I'd discovered in the neighborhood. But of all these powerful impressions, none surpassed the one left by the masquerade ball in that strange sailors' bar. Every time I thought back to it, the image of that one man writing in a notebook, seemingly oblivious to the strangers packed into the place around him, came to mind.

I'm about to order another beer when Frank and Víctor arrive.

Look at this, our friend the reporter is here, Frank says, taking off his golf cap and sitting down at the Captain's Table. Víctor smiles a hello and goes to the bar to chat with Ernie.

Ernie, a cold beer here, please! Frank shouts out. What do you want, Ness? I thought you were in Chicago.

I got back this morning, and I don't know why it got into my head to come directly here from the airport.

Ernie puts two Heinekens pearled with frozen sweat on the table.

Ah, and today they handed Raúl the keys to his new house.

Gal told me. Good thing he was here. Oh, and I left my suitcase in your office. Hope you don't mind.

The Oakland is your home, man, you know that.

Thanks, Frank. Gal was in a weird mood this morning. Did you see him?

He was around, but we were in such a hurry, I didn't pay him much mind. Why? Something wrong?

He started drinking too early, at noon, something he hasn't done in a while. And it's also strange that he's not around now. Because lately this is his favorite time to write. Unless things changed while I was in Chicago.

You're right. It's the first time in a good while that he hasn't been here around now. Who knows, maybe there's an interesting fight at the Luna Bowl, although I doubt it. Víctor would have asked for permission to go. Víctor! he yells out. Do me a favor, call Jimmy and ask him if he's seen Gal.

It was at the Luna Bowl, Jimmy Castellano's boxing gym, where Gal had discovered Víctor, Frank's aide-de-camp (as he calls him sometimes), a little while after the Puerto Rican, recently arrived in Brooklyn, had begun to work out there. One afternoon, the trainer of one Ricky Murcia, a mastodon from the professional circuit who weighed over 260 pounds and had come to New York to take part in an exhibition match in Madison Square Garden, offered Víctor fifty dollars to spar for eight rounds with his fighter. Murcia pounded the young man mercilessly until he lost consciousness at the end of the fifth round. It seemed strange to Gal that Víctor would have let himself be put in a position where he would take such a beating, because he was at least two weight classes below Murcia. Cletus explained to Gal that Víctor needed the money, and besides he didn't have a manager. Intrigued, Gal decided to approach the young man. Their conversation convinced him that the Puerto Rican was no good for boxing. It wasn't about his physical aptitude, but his personality. The boy was a dreamer. He was too sensitive for such a profession. Gal told him that a friend of his was looking for an assistant and gave him the Oakland's business card.

His last name was Báez. He was tall and thin, twenty-five years old, a mulatto with curly hair and greenish eyes. Although he'd been boxing for some time, his face was untouched, except for a light scar on his right cheek. He's quick, throws a good punch, his legwork couldn't be more agile; he's a good fighter, Gal told me. Technically, there's not a thing wrong with him, but he's just not very competitive. He is completely devoid of malice. When Gal introduced him to Frank, Frank understood him completely. He has the soul of an artist, Frank told Gal, only he was born poor and black. Don't worry, I'll take care of him. In about week, Víctor had become irreplaceable. It took some doing, but eventually, between Gal and Frank Otero, they were able to get the idea of becoming a professional boxer out of his head. What they couldn't quite put an end to was that now and then he would sign up for amateur fights.

Gal isn't at the Luna Bowl, boss. Old man Cletus claims he hasn't heard a peep out of him for weeks.

Do you think he's at the Shipyard? it occurs to me to ask.

Frank and Víctor exchange an alarmed look. Gal only goes to what he calls the Shipyard during his darkest moments. The last time he disappeared, they found him unconscious in some debris at an empty lot.

Let's hope not, Frank says.

I'm going to go check, just in case, I say. If I don't see him, I'll probably just head on to Manhattan. Do you mind if I leave the suitcase in your office till tomorrow?

Frank is so lost in thought he doesn't hear the question.

On the way to the Shipyard, I think back to the first time Gal took me to the Luna Bowl. I remember exactly how his eyes lit up when the boxers climbed into the ring. Disconcerted, I asked myself what he was looking for in such a place. It was evident that the thrill of the sport fascinated him. But why? What sense did it make for him to watch such violence? We'd come for one of Víctor's fights. By the time the bell rang for the first round, however, I was no longer there for Gal. When it was all over, what most surprised me was the number of people who came to say hello to him after the fight. The aspiring boxers, punch-drunk old men, the employees, everyone liked him. When we first got there, I also noted that Cletus Wilson, the black doorman who was almost eighty, refused to charge us admission. Maybe it's my imagination, but I think there's something in Gal that makes people feel he's living in the shadow of some unspecified threat. That's what I'd felt the first time I saw him: a vulnerable creature weirdly separated from his environment by a bell jar. Perhaps what people pick up on when they approach Gal is his own sensitivity to the suffering of others. I've never met anyone else so careful not to hurt other people. Gal is only capable of hurting himself. I've never heard him say anything mean-spirited or offensive about anyone, not even when he's drunk. He never loses his dignity. He has an amazing ability to hold on to it even at the most extreme stages of drunkenness. Even physically. To me it's a sort of miracle how he manages to coordinate his movements even as he's about to lose consciousness.

Night has begun to fall. Venus glitters all alone above the cranes of the port. The sky darkens so slowly that I notice the luminous points of the stars appear one by one. I go over the events of the day: the taxi race from LaGuardia to the Oakland; Gal telling me the Rakowitz story; six hours at the newspaper; the conversation with Frank. It's not just that I'm worried about Gal. I'm also on my way to the Shipyard because I need to see him. Something he said this morning has been haunting me. *Someone has to take care of the demons.* He was talking about his own, but if I find him, I'll ask him to take over mine as well.

Cletus Wilson comes out of the ticket booth to say hello. Before I open my mouth, he tells me it's been weeks since he's heard from Gal. I tell him that I know, that I was with Frank when

Víctor called from the Oakland. Then what the hell are you doing here? he asks. I tell him that I'm going to have a look around the Shipyard. Cletus's eyes open wide when he hears this. Just to be sure, I clarify. Before I go down, I chat with him for a while under the green awning at the front.

It's just turned dark. Next to the water tank is a roofless telephone booth. A few steps away, I see a jumble of iron with the sign for the phone intact, as if someone had ripped it out taking care not to damage it. Surprised, I confirm that the phone is working. I decide to call the house, as much as I know there's no sense in doing it. I know Diana won't be there. I'm certain that she left the same day I flew to Chicago. I have nothing to reproach her for. I know she did it to make things easier. I'll look for a note but I won't find one, because no note is needed, just as my phone call now is unnecessary. Everything has been settled. And still, in Chicago, the first thing I did after I checked into the hotel was to call her. As expected, the machine picked up. I would repeat that same futile gesture every night after work. The only thing different today is that I am back in New York. I'm half an hour away from our apartment, a few stations on the subway after crossing under the river that separates Brooklyn from Manhattan.

I'm about to punch in my number when a strange melody rips the night air. It's a woman's voice. It takes me a few seconds to realize that it isn't live. Someone must have put on a record, but where? There's nothing around the Shipyard but abandoned lots and ruins. The sweet voice sings a sad lament with an Eastern air. Trying to locate its source, I reach the conclusion that it must be coming from an alley whose entrance I can barely see from where I'm standing. There's a bar frequented by Albanian immigrants there. I decide to go, enthralled by the melody. I watch my shadow ahead of me on the brick-paved alleyway. Almost at the end, there's a narrow opening that casts a square of yellowish light onto the sidewalk. When I get there, I part the colored plastic straps that cover the entrance. Inside is an old man with a red wool cap seated in a rocking chair. I remember him from the times I've come here with Gal—I also remember the woman tending bar. She's around sixty, wears a headscarf, and has a vertical blue stripe tattooed on her chin. At a table, some men around my age playing cards turn for a moment to look at me. The old man signals for me to come in. I say hello and approach the jukebox, still hypnotized by the song. When it's finished, I leave a couple of dollars on the bar and return to the phone booth.

I pick up the receiver, seeing the stars tremble through the rectangle cut above my head; it feels strange to be within four glass walls looking at the sky. A swath of misty, pulverized light blurs the outline of the constellations. I feel the cold of the receiver in my ear, the querulous buzz of the line. I dial, imagining the acoustic signal travelling under the bed of the East River, through the length of a tube of bundled cables, carrying all my anguish along with it. The signal gets to Manhattan in a matter of seconds; after two rings, I hear a long beep and then my own distorted voice, suggesting I leave a message, and then nothing. As I hang up, I see the tail of a comet glitter fleetingly.

I'm not sure exactly when the abandoned grounds begin to fill up with shapes. Leaning in a corner, a thin man with a black leather jacket watches the movements on the block closely. Every once in a while someone approaches him and there's a quick exchange. Heroin, I imagine. The shadows of a prostitute and her client cross a vacant lot. I follow them with my eyes until they disappear behind an abandoned boat. I still can't decide if I should move away from the phone booth. Some time passes—I don't know how much—when I hear a very high-pitched whistle that reminds me of the cawing of wild birds, and the street again empties out. A few moments later, I see the red-and-blue glare, and moments after that the beams of light sweeping the asphalt. The patrol car advances down the street toward me. The glass of the booth reflects the multicolored lights. I hear static crackling, the clamor of voices coming from a radio. I feel eyes on me. The car slows down even more as it passes my booth, but it doesn't quite stop. At the dry dock, it turns right and vanishes as eerily as it had appeared.

Gal is nowhere to be seen. There's no sense in my hanging around any longer. I cross various lots, leaving behind the Shipyard. I go up a slope sparsely covered with shrubs and arrive at a deserted street that winds along the river. I walk on, and as I turn a corner, the violent blaze of the skyscrapers on the southern tip of Manhattan surge up before me, a black mountain range whose peaks of varying heights are pierced by quadrilaterals of light. A street-sweeper rumbling by shakes me from my reverie. I follow behind, walking in the middle of the street, stepping on the glittering puddles of water it leaves in its wake until I see the distant glow of an empty cab and hail it. I climb in unsteadily and give him directions to my place. We take a side ramp onto the Brooklyn Bridge. 1:06 A.M. on the Watch Tower clock.

Five
ZADIE

Hell's Kitchen, October 23, 1973
When I woke up, the insistent noise that had infiltrated my dream, something like the howling of a siren or the squawking of a seagull, had faded into the drone of an engine that was coming from the courtyard. The alarm clock glowed in the darkness. Six-thirty. What day of the week was it? I walked up to the hallway still half-asleep, opened the door, and retrieved the *New York Times* from the doormat. It was Sunday. Back inside, I lit a cigarette. The flame illuminated the hallway revealing my face in the mirror, haggard and unshaven from the night at the Chamberpot hanging out with Marc and Claudia. In the kitchen, with the lights off, I heated coffee from the day before and tossed the newspaper on the table. A photograph of Nixon, under some headlines that I couldn't make out, shimmered under my eyes. The first sip of coffee helped me piece together last night's events. After the Chamberpot I had gone to Claudia's place. I had a vision of her naked body, her lips descending toward my cock, fucking. The first brightness of the morning—a pale, second-hand light came in through the window looking out on the courtyard. I drew the curtain to block the view of the brick wall across the way, turned on a lamp and placed the Underwood on the kitchen table, the best place in the house to write. I slid a sheet of carbon paper between two pages and rolled it in, then stared at the blank page.

I needed to break the spell. But my mind was as blank as the page. The Underwood was at the mercy of a whirlwind of possibilities, storm clouds gathering over the slanted horizon of rounded keys, each with a letter or punctuation mark protected by a sharp-edged metal border. One idea, one word, one phrase, is enough to destroy the latent magic. Or to set it off. Marc says that he writes much better when he's hungover, with his antennae clean and his sensibility raw, but I couldn't get going. I caressed the cold steel frame of the Underwood, and then I glimpsed the corner of the letter protruding from the side of a pile of papers. I had slid it in between the pages of a notebook I bought in Deauville when I went to see Louise. Now, a tiny paper triangle peeked out of its pages, laying claim to my attention. I still hadn't used the notebook, so its binding was stiff. I pulled at the corner of the envelope. It had been a week since I had opened it the morning after finding it in between the pages of the *New York Times Magazine* at Port Authority, and I hadn't resealed it. I had looked at the contents of the envelope endless times. The image on the surface of the Polaroid was in danger of being worn down from having been looked at so often. I examined it one last time before putting glue on the edges of the flap and sealing the envelope. I liked the feel of the thick, double-weight paper, rough and soft at once. I passed my fingertip over the traces of ink, going over the name and phone number, letter by letter, digit by digit—large handwriting, rounded, somewhat childlike. I read the text aloud, as if doing so could provide more information.

Zadie (212) 719-1859

It'd be better to call tomorrow, Monday. For some reason, I've concluded that it's a work number, although I have no real basis for my guess. It's irrational, as was the reaction I had when the envelope slipped out of the pages of the magazine and I tried to cover it up, instinctively, as if I had just stolen it and was afraid someone would notice. In Deauville, news of Sam Evans's death made me forget about the letter for a few hours, but that night, alone in my room, when I was about to start writing in my notebook, I came upon the envelope again, which brought to mind everything that had happened at Port Authority. I thought that the best thing would be to open it very carefully and then, depending on what was in it, reseal it. I decided to wait until the next day and then steam it open in the kitchen while Louise painted upstairs in her studio. Another irrational urge. Why did I need to hide it from Louise? The entire operation of opening the envelope with steam was also a touch absurd. I had seen a character do something similar in an old black-and-white spy movie. I set myself to it. Mesmerized, I watched the flap of the envelope ripple and unseal like a wound with the stitches coming loose. But I hadn't counted on the sense of unease I would feel when I emptied the envelope. First, out came some sheets of rag paper, identical in texture to the envelope. As I was unfolding them, a Polaroid glided out and fell face down on the table. I flipped it over. It was a blurry picture, of very poor quality, but it was her, the girl from Port Authority. When I recognized her, my stomach knotted up just as when I had seen her in person. She was different in the Polaroid, dressed more formally, with her hair short. Her face and eyes, so alive when I had seen them up close, were devoid of expression.

The man who was with her in the picture was the same one who had picked her up at the terminal. They were in a seaport, in wintertime, it seemed. He had his arm on her shoulder and they both smiled. There were scattered dots of light all over the surface of the Polaroid; that's why the image was so fuzzy The note said:

> Dear Sasha,
>   I am so glad about your new job, although now it will be even

longer before you come to see your Nadia. Or am I wrong? I hope I am and that you come to visit New York soon. I am very happy with my violin classes. I am killing myself rehearsing for three concerts. I have also found a job. Well, three days a week, in the archives at the public library in Lincoln Center. Since she took up with her boyfriend, Zadie almost never comes to Brooklyn. I have the apartment practically to myself. The subway ride is too long, especially at night, but I like the neighborhood a lot. In Brighton Beach, almost everyone is Russian, and you almost don't need to speak English, which is funny to me. My building is huge and I don't like it except for one thing: I live on the thirtieth floor. The view of the coastline is amazing, you can see all of Coney Island and beyond. In the morning, the light in the dining room swallows you up. I'm not going to ask you to write, but you could call once in a while at least. Please don't let so much time pass before we speak, and don't make me be the one who has to call all the time. Tell me how things are going for you. Call, even if just to say that everything is okay. Has Boston changed a lot? I don't know why I ask you all these questions that you will only ignore. I'm sick and tired of it, actually, but you should know that your sister misses you and loves you.

Nadj

October 24, 10 A.M.

Leichliter and Associates, good morning.
  Good morning.
  How can I help you?
  May I speak with Zadie?
  Zadie Stewart? (Professional tone. I note the last name.)
  Yes, please.
  What is this in reference to?
  It's a professional matter.

(A long silence.)

Who's calling?

Gal Ackerman.

One moment, please.

(Two short beeps, then a click, then another voice.)

Hello?

Ms. Stewart?

Speaking. What can I do for you, Mr. Ackerman?

Well, actually, it's not a professional matter at all. Although I wouldn't say it's personal either, exactly.

I'm afraid I don't follow you. (A soft, patient tone.)

I'm sorry. I'll get right to the point. I'm calling because I need to return something that belongs to you or to someone you know. Around ten days ago . . . eleven to be exact, on the thirteenth, I picked up a magazine that someone had left on a bench at Port Authority. When my bus left New York, I started to look through it and inside found an envelope on which was written only a name, Zadie, and this number.

And?

I came back to the city on Saturday and thought I'd better wait till today to call. I don't have the slightest idea what's inside the envelope, but I thought it might be something important. That's it.

I'm sorry, I'm not sure I understand. An envelope with my name and phone number?

Right. It was inside a *New York Times Magazine* I found on a bench.

Got it. I appreciate this, you're very kind. Did I hear you say that you weren't at all curious about what's inside the envelope?

Of course I've been curious. Very curious.

But you haven't opened it?

(I hesitate before answering.)

No.

(Silence. Ms. Stewart has realized that I am lying.)

I see. In that case, I suppose, you can't tell me any more than you've already said.

(Obstacle cleared. Relief on my part.)

Indeed. If it's all right with you, Ms. Stewart . . . Zadie. May I call you that? I can bring the envelope to you in person. (Silence.) I live in Midtown. I freelance, so my schedule is very flexible . . . (Terrible excuse, made worse by my nervous giggle.)

You're very kind, Mr. . . . . Ackerman, but you really don't have to put yourself to more trouble. I would appreciate it very much if you mail the envelope to Leichliter and Associates, care of me. The address is 252 East 61st, 10028.

Are you sure you don't want me to just bring it over?

Very sure. It really isn't necessary. Thank you again, Mr. Ackerman. Have a good day.

(She hangs up. The hum of the line.)

1 P.M.

Strange and intense these last ten days, like a long tunnel between two nightmares, literally: one before leaving for Deauville and the other on my first night back in Hell's Kitchen. I have to think, go over what's happened, I've barely had time to take it all in. It was good that I went to Deauville, as always, despite the unexpected blow of the news of Sam's death. I hardly wrote anything, not even in my diary; I spent the time strolling around, reading, thinking, and chatting with Louise. She's doing well. She understands me like no one else, and leaves me alone most of the time. She works all day. She's up to her neck with the preparations for an upcoming exhibition. At the end of the day—she always stops working the moment the last light fades—she likes me to go up to her studio. She pours herself a whiskey—a vodka for me—and she shows me what she's done, smoking, not saying anything. We go back down to the kitchen and then we talk and talk. She asked me about my stories. I told her about the one that was getting published in the *Atlantic Monthly*, and gave her the last story I had written. I finished it the day before leaving for Deauville. It's called "The Lights of the Synagogue," and it's about a Sephardi from Granada who one day decides to return to a Jewish neighborhood in Brooklyn in search of his American ex-wife. It's not exactly true that I didn't write anything during my stay in Deauville. I wrote a biographical sketch of Sam, a memory, a good-bye piece, not even a tribute. It was hard to write. While I was on his turf, his absence was something very real. One morning, I went to see Rick, and by chance while I was there, Kim showed up—the woman who used to wash Sam's clothes and cook his meals. Afterward, I walked to Stewart Foster's ranch. He took me to the stables, filling me in on his new acquisitions and the most recent births. He insisted I stay for lunch, and, naturally, Sam came up during our conversation. That afternoon, while Louise painted, I wrote about Sam. But ever since returning to Hell's Kitchen, my memories of him have become insubstantial. Everything has been tainted by that run-in at Port Authority—the letter, the picture. I don't know why all of it is affecting me so much. Absurd, given it's someone I don't even know. But the fact is that I can't get that woman Nadia out of my head.

2:30 P.M.

When I arrived on Saturday, there was a message from Marc on the answering machine telling me to stop by the Chamberpot around eight. He was with his buddies, drinking and playing pool. It felt good to see him again. He asked me to go walk with him to his place and when we got to his door, he asked if I wanted to come up for a drink. I told him I was tired but he insisted. Hours later, I woke up in the middle of the night, disoriented, thinking that I was still in Deauville. I was awake for a long time, smoking and looking through his books, and when I realized I wouldn't fall back asleep, I left him a note and came here.

9:30 P.M.

Marc, you're there. I've called you a few times.

I was in Long Island, just got back. What mess have you gotten yourself into now? You better be careful, you saw what happened in Midtown yesterday.

What happened?

Haven't you seen the papers? The Westies executed somebody right in the middle of the street. When I saw the picture, I recognized the guy. You know him too. He used to go by McCourt's a lot. He's the third one to go down this week. They're not kidding around.

I didn't know. It's been days since I've read a newspaper.

You're missing out. This Westies thing is better than a novel.

Not to change the subject, but we have to talk.

About the girl in the photograph?

How did you know?

Because it's the only thing in your head, apparently. Nothing else interests you—and you just proved it. Yesterday it was all you talked about all night.

There's been a development, that's why I'm calling you.

Oh, yeah? Go on then.

I finally called the number on the envelope this morning, and spoke to that Zadie woman. She works for a company called Leichliter. I didn't ask what kind of company it was, but it sounds like a real-estate agency or something. I have the address. It's not far from my place, but as much as I insisted, she didn't want me to deliver the envelope in person. So I need your help.

Me? What do you want me to do?

To come with me to her office. Sending that envelope by mail is out of the question. I think you should give it to her in person, pretending you're me. I'll wait for you in a coffee shop nearby. This way I can follow her around without her suspecting anything . . . until I can meet up with my friend again.

You mean the girl from the bus?

Who else? Her name is Nadia.

Yeah, yeah, I remember. You've told me like twenty times. So when do you want to do this?

As soon as possible. Not now, of course. Can you get away tomorrow? Please. It's important to me.

I've noticed. But you're in luck. I can go sometime before lunch, around eleven thirty. Is that good?

October 25

Things turned out pretty much as I expected. Almost right across the street from Leichliter there was a bar called the Next Door Lounge. I sat at a table by the window and somewhat anxiously followed Marc's movements. Midtown is full of people at that time of day. Walking with an exaggerated seriousness, Marc crossed the street and lifted the envelope over his head to signal at me. A couple of passersby turned to look at him. Then, becoming even more solemn, he walked up to a mailbox and made as if to put the envelope in. He put his right hand over his eyes, squinted, and pretended to scan the horizon. Finally, he showed me the envelope again, and making a slashing gesture across his throat as if I were putting his life at risk, headed for the front of Leichliter and Associates. Now I was the one who was squinting, trying to see what was happening on the other side of the street. I could see that he had spoken to a receptionist and was waiting. After a few moments, an assistant came up to him and he disappeared into one of the offices. Less than five minutes later, he was on his way back to the Next Door Lounge with a confused look.

How was she?

Who? Zadie? A beauty. We're having dinner tonight. Too bad I don't like girls.

I'm taking this seriously, Marc, whether or not you think it's worth it.

Okay . . . the receptionist said that I could leave the letter with her, but I told her that I had instructions to deliver the letter to Zadie by hand, so she called her assistant who led me into Ms. Stewart's office on the third floor. That one up there if I'm not mistaken.

He pointed to a window on which the name of the firm was printed in an arch. From our spot, all you could see inside the office were some tubes of fluorescent lighting.

And?

Ms. Zadie Stewart is a normal, run-of-the-mill executive, although if you picture her dressed in some other outfit, you can make out that she's not half bad . . . and that's it, Gal, whatever else you want to make of it, there's nothing more. She seemed very busy and, in spite of her apprehensions, wasn't too bothered by the fact that Mr. Ackerman showed up in person to hand her the envelope despite her protests that it wasn't necessary.

What did you tell her?

That I lived less than fifteen minutes away, that I had spent all morning writing and needed to stretch my legs and after hearing her voice I couldn't resist the temptation of meeting her in person. Don't laugh, that's exactly what I said.

And what did she say?

She thanked me, called her assistant, and asked her to please show Mr. Ackerman out. Before I left, I shook her hand and she smiled. Slightly.

What's she like?

She seems intelligent.

Physically. If I were to follow her.

Black hair, dark skin, maybe Italian or something. Tall, with black-rimmed glasses, gray blouse and skirt.

What time does she leave?

Well imagine that, I forgot to ask her. If you want, I'll go back in and find out. I think you're going to have to wait a while. If you're lucky, she'll go out for lunch, and since this place is so nearby the office, she may even show up here. I should probably leave, so she doesn't see me with you. Seriously, Gal, I'm outta here. I don't have all day to be playing detective.

Thanks very much, Marc. Are you going by the Chamberpot tonight?

No. I have a date with Zadie at La Côte Basque. The dream of a lifetime fulfilled, having dinner at Truman Capote's favorite restaurant. I can afford these luxuries now, they gave me a raise, I forgot to tell you. So, good luck with your Nadia. Au revoire.

Thank you, Marc. I really appreciate it.

For you, baby, anything.

But Zadie Stewart didn't go out for lunch. Around twelve thirty, a heavy thunderstorm started up and the café stayed fairly deserted. I ordered something to eat, and then one coffee after another, to pass the time. After I ordered my fourth cup, the waitress took pity on me and started coming over to chat during her free moments. Around three, I almost left. I asked for the check, explaining to the waitress I was supposed to have met someone but that the other person seemed to have forgotten. It happens, she said, smiling. I gave her a good tip and said good-bye. When I got to the door, though, I changed my mind. Seeing me back at the same table, the waitress smiled and brought me a cappuccino. On the house, she said. At five, when all the offices spewed out all their employees at the same time, I decided to wait outside. I found a spot directly across from Leichliter and Associates. At five twenty, I set a limit on the amount of time I would wait, and then another and another. It took a concentrated effort to convince myself that it was absurd to throw in the towel after so much time invested, especially since I knew that Zadie Stewart still had to be inside the building. A little after six, I saw her come out with a man who was wearing an elegant suit. Just as Marc had said, she was slim with a dark complexion. She too was wearing a suit jacket, and she did in fact have black-rimmed glasses. Zadie Stewart and the man chatted for a few minutes by the front door of the building. I crossed the street and, knowing that they wouldn't suspect me, I pretended to look at a window display, dangerously close to them. It wasn't long before they parted.

I was relieved when I saw Zadie Stewart walk off. If she had gotten in a taxi, I would have lost her in traffic, not even taking into account the fact that I didn't have enough money on me to give chase. Where was she headed? Brighton Beach? And if she wasn't going there, how would I ever find Nadia? Wouldn't it be better just to ask her directly? I thought about it, but decided to see how things went first.

On the corner of 60th Street, she took off her high heels and put on a pair of sneakers. When she got to Lexington, she went down into the subway. There were a lot of people in the station so I hardly stood out. I followed her, hidden in the crowd. She changed trains twice, once on 51st Street and then again at Rockefeller Center. Yes, she was going to Brooklyn. I settled down at the other end of the car, a newspaper in front of me. I read the story of the murder committed by the Westies that Marc had told me about. One more change of trains. Finally, around seven thirty, we arrived at Brighton Beach. Before going to her place, she stopped at a supermarket and then picked up a suit from the cleaners. Her final destination was an enormous hulk of an apartment building without a doorman on Neptune Avenue. She opened the front door with a key and disappeared into a hallway. I memorized the number of the building and looked at the time. Almost seven thirty. I felt as if I were losing the spirit of the thing. Was this the way the chase ended? I crossed to the opposite sidewalk and looked at the huge building, not knowing which one of the cells in that beehive was hers. Night had fallen. Nadia would be in the apartment with her. And if that was the case, perhaps they would go out for dinner. After some five or ten minutes, a pair of old folk appeared at the end of the hallway and I went up to the door, timing my arrival to coincide exactly with the moment that they opened the door. The woman rebuked me in Russian; I thanked her and smiled. Ignoring the protests of the couple, I shrugged and went into the building. I headed toward the hallway to the right as I had seen Zadie Stewart do and at the end saw a wall covered from floor to ceiling with metal mailboxes. Not all of them were labeled with a name, but I read every one of those that were. I began to lose hope when finally I found what I was looking for: on a yellowing card I read Zadie Stewart, in typescript, and written below by hand, Nadia Orlov. The apartment number was 30-N.

I left the mailboxes behind and came upon an open rectangular space. There were three elevator doors but only one call button. The center door opened, and I got into the box and hit the button for floor 30. After an interminable wait that probably was only about a minute long, I exited on a landing that led to a narrow hall flanked by doors of an indefinite color somewhere between gray and blue, eight on each side. At the very beginning of the hallway, to the right, there was a large window that offered an expansive view. I stopped and looked out, following the line of the beach with my eyes ending in the burst of lights from Coney Island. I walked slowly down the hallway until I found myself in front of apartment N. At my feet, a strip of light. I listened closely. After a few moments, I could make out the muffled sound of a television; that was all

I lingered for a moment in the hallway and decided that the best thing to do was to go back out on the street. I stationed myself in the front of the building again, unsure of how to continue my investigation. I tried 411. Information, how can I help you? said a woman's voice. I gave her Zadie Stewart's name and address and crossed my fingers. I'm sorry, sir, but there's no one by that name listed at that address, the operator said. I thanked her and hung up. It would have been too easy. Or worse: I could have wound up having to risk ending my quest with a single phone call. I headed for Brighton Avenue, which is lined with Russian restaurants and bars. I picked one at random and went in. On a stage was a fat singer with a sequined suit and a tie, being accompanied by an electric organ; a few middle-aged couples were dancing out in front. There was no bar, only a handful of communal tables that gave the place the air of a Soviet mess hall. A waiter appeared. His name was Metodi, wasn't Russian but Polish, and didn't speak a word of English. I asked for an order of blini and a measure of vodka. That's how you order it, by volume, Metodi made me understand, and I liked the concept. The alcohol helped me put things in perspective. After I finished eating, I went out for a stroll on the boardwalk. I got a bit emotional, remembering the walks on Coney Island with my grandfather David when I was a kid. There were a lot of people out, groups of old folk and children. Lights from the ships out at sea, far away. And, all in all, as Nadia had said in her note, almost no one was speaking English. I passed by the amusement park and arrived at a subway station. Out of the back window of the last subway car I looked out upon Coney Island, taking it all in, the giant Ferris wheel, the Cyclone—the roller coaster of my youth—the Parachute Jump, opening like an atomic mushroom into the sky. I arrived in Manhattan at eleven. There were two messages on the answering machine, one from Louise and another from Claudia.

Nadia Orlov, I said aloud. I sat at the kitchen table. There were two blank pieces of paper with a carbon sheet in between rolled into the typewriter; I had forgotten to take them out. I typed out the name and looked at the letters. I could write Nadia Orlov a letter, and make up some excuse to meet her . . . or I could hire a private detective. I let out a laugh remembering my brief foray into that profession. Can you afford all this, Gal Ackerman, or is this another of your fantasies? I asked myself. The answer was in my pocket. I reached in and felt the check for five hundred dollars. It was the first story I'd ever sold. And it hadn't even been my idea to send it out. Marc was the one who sent it, pretending he was me, because he knew that I would never do it myself. The important thing was that, thanks to him I would be able to make the first payments.

The best thing would be to look in the Yellow Pages. The only copy I had was three years old, but it would have to do. I leafed through various letters until I got to the one I wanted. It was a couple of pages long. I skipped through various professions and activities and began to narrow the field: Dentists, Design, Diamonds. But no Detectives. I flipped to the index in the back of the book. There I found Detectives . . . *see* . . . and then, amid various references, finally, Investigators.

It was like consulting an encyclopedic dictionary. There was so much information just between Hotels and Jewelers. I stopped at a few names for no real reason. On coming across Meyerson and Associates, Inc., I thought about Leichliter, and it occurred to me to look it up in case it might itself be a detective agency. Which would be amusing, but of course there was no Leichliter listed. The closest name was Lincoln . . . Lincoln Controls, Inc. Not having any criteria for choosing one agency over another, I allowed my eyes to drift over the page at random, letting the entries present themselves to me as they will. Some of my finds were quite funny. For example, this one, in big bold letters:

PINKERTON CONSULTING & INVESTIGATION SERVICES.

An agency with historic pedigree and literary prestige. I dragged my index finger across the page for the address: 30 Wall Street. Possible . . . not a bad location. In another column, more discreetly announced, I read:

HOLMES DETECTIVE BUREAU, INC
ESTABLISHED IN 1928

Speaking of literary prestige. But I decided to keep on looking. In a box in the right-hand corner at the top of the page, I read CLARK. The name didn't bring up any immediate associations, but then I saw their ad, which made me decide to go with them after all. There was a magnifying glass, and under the glass, as if trapped in flagrante delicto, the letter *C*. But what made me laugh is what apparently had been caught by the magnifying glass. In the middle of the circle there was a dark spot that could suggest anything. I looked at it closely, trying to decide what it was supposed to be. It could be a fly, but what it most resembled was a clump of pubic hair. I read on: twenty years of proven experience. Specialists in surveillance. Armed and unarmed agents. Discrete and professional. Reasonable fees. A phone number, but no address. I went back to the alphabetic listing and got it from the appropriate column. I liked the cartoon so much that I ripped it out and put it in between the pages of my diary, after taking down all the information I needed:

Clark Investigations and Security Services, Ltd.
31-10, 56 Woodride, Manhattan, (212) 514-8741
See our ad on the following page.

October 26
It was a ramshackle place that made me think of the office of a neighborhood dentist or a shady immigration lawyer. There were

a few clients in the waiting room, two women who looked like a mother and daughter and a white man around forty-five years old, in a suit. He was wearing a polka-dotted bow tie and had a violin case with him. In the magazine rack were various old issues of *National Geographic* and *Sports Illustrated.* The receptionist made me fill out a four-page questionnaire. Some questions were so peculiar as to be funny, but I completed it in all humility and handed it to the girl at the desk.

That will be fifty dollars for the consultation, she said. Will you be needing an armed operative?

I laughed. I don't think that'll be necessary.

Detective William H. Queensberry will be right with you. Have a seat, please.

I looked around the waiting room. The guy with the violin had left; the mother and daughter (if that's what they were) were about to go into an office at just that moment. Some ten minutes later, I saw a blonde woman come out of another room. The receptionist got up, led her to the door, and then, coming over, asked me to follow her to the same office from which the woman had left. She followed behind and handed the detective the questionnaire that I had filled out.

Mr. Ackerman, Detective Queensberry will assist you, she said and left the office, closing the door without making a sound.

Queensberry stood, shook my hand, and gestured for me to take a seat.

With an exaggerated concentration, moving his lips in a way that made it all seem rather grotesque, Queensberry began to read my answers in a low voice. As he did so, he followed the lines with his chubby index finger, emitting perfectly unintelligible sounds, as though he were singing under his breath, although maybe it was a way of commenting to himself. Eventually I understood that it was a technique to help him think. Every once in a while he stopped reading, seemed distracted for a few moments, then looked me over. I too looked at him closely as he read. Given the profession he had chosen, Detective Queensberry's physical appearance was hardly the most discrete. He had the face of a bullfrog, and his body reminded me of a comic book character I couldn't quite call to mind. He was fat and some five foot nine in height, with pink skin splattered with freckles. He had an enormous double chin and swollen cheeks, his hair buzzed almost down to the skull. He wore a short-sleeved white shirt, with a flower-print tie, the knot to one side. It was clearly too tight around his neck. He was around thirty-eight and two hundred and twenty pounds. Behind his reading glasses glimmered a pair of tiny porcine bluish eyes. As if all that weren't enough, Queensberry was a squinter. He stood up to get a paper cone of water from a cooler in a corner near the window. He moved gracefully in spite of his corpulence.

It took him ten full minutes to finish reading the questionnaire. When he did, he leaned forward, planted his elbows on the desk, and said:

What do you say we get down to business, Mr. Ackerman?

His voice was deep and each word ran together with the next. I took out a pack of cigarettes and offered him one, but he declined, taking a visibly tooth-marked plastic cigarette out of his shirt pocket, which he immediately brought to his mouth.

Thanks. I'm trying to quit.

I laid out my case. Queensberry's plump fingers stuck like suction cups to a small notebook in which he took notes at great speed. I asked him if he wanted me to speak slower.

Actually faster, Mr. Ackerman, he responded. That way we both win. Time and money.

When I finished, he put down the notebook and asked:

So you're a writer? What do you write, Ackerman?

A bit of everything.

I figured out his game by the way he looked at me. He was just more comfortable passing himself off as a fool. A moment later he was back to his old self.

Nadia Orlov, he said, savoring the syllables. He bit down hard on the plastic menthol cigarette. It's a ludicrously easy case. I don't want to talk you out of it, per se—after all, this is how I make my living—but are you sure you want to spend your money on such a trifle? I guess you do, if you're here. I'm just saying, maybe you want to reconsider—from what I hear, writers are always starving. No offense intended, after all, appearances can be deceiving. Let's see. I can give you a definitive report this coming Monday morning. I want to watch her over the weekend as well, that way you'll get more for your money.

And how much will I owe you?

Five hundred dollars. Including the consultation fee. You can pay the rest when I give you the report.

I put my hand into the pocket, to make sure that the *Atlantic Monthly* check was still there.

Six
BEN'S ARCHIVE

Character is fate, Ben said. He thought for a moment and added: You're old enough to enter the Archive. That's what he called his office. It was a secret room that was always locked, a sacred place, a sanctuary to which I had been denied access while I was too young to understand what it meant. For a moment, I thought I must've misheard. That's where my father kept papers and books he treasured. Inside were the filing cabinets full of letters and pictures and all sorts of other documents and materials. And there too is where he held secret meetings with his old comrades. Over the years, I had caught a glimpse of the Archive on many occasions; I'd even been allowed to go inside once or twice, but always only for a brief moment, and never by myself. This time was something different; the Archive was being opened expressly for me. I remember the excitement I felt when my father pushed open the door and stepped to one side so I could go in. The room was dark and it smelled musty. Ben turned on a lightbulb that hung from a beam. The walls were covered with bookcases from the baseboard to the ceiling, and the shelves were all packed. There was a single window that looked out on the garden. Ben drew the curtains, raised the blinds, and lifted the window wide open. Air and sunlight rushed into the cloistered space; I was blinded for a moment. When I opened my eyes again, hundreds of specks glimmered on the clouds of dust. Ben sat on the windowsill, surrounded by the gradually diminishing day, and said, repeating what he had told me a few minutes before in my room, while I was changing my shoes:

It means he considers you an adult. When I was allowed to go in, there was a lot of violence in the air. It was the time of the Sacco and Vanzetti trial. One day, your grandfather got home very agitated and announced: We're going to Manhattan, son, get ready. Manhattan? For what? To a demonstration. Hurry up, we don't have much time. I'll explain it to you on the way. Put on some light clothes, we're going to have to run.

That was his way of trying to explain things. In that sense you could say I was luckier than you. Your grandfather never says anything; he lets people come to their own conclusions. But, that day, he was more loquacious than usual. He explained to me who Sacco and Vanzetti were, the case that had been mounted against them, the intricacies of the judicial system. Finally, he told me they'd been condemned to death a few days before. A wave of indignation has surged through the world, he said. Protests have been organized in countless cities trying to stop this travesty. I want you to come with me—you're almost a man.

We got out of the subway at Rector Street. Many of the side streets off Broadway were crowded with police troops, both on foot and mounted. The demonstrators had gathered at Bowling Green, near Wall Street. It was a cloudy day, and there was great tension in the air.

We meandered through groups of policemen and eagerly joined the crowd. It was difficult to move amid so many people. Your grandfather told me to hold on tightly to his vest and not to let go under any circumstances.

Suddenly, the crowd began to push toward Broadway. At first I heard some isolated screams, but after a few seconds your grandfather and I found ourselves engulfed by the deafening roar of the multitude. I could feel my temples pounding. The cops egged on their horses. They didn't charge head-on right away, just passed us quickly, barely missing us, trying to disperse us. It was so terrifying that I can barely remember isolated scenes. At one point I saw clouds of rocks flying through the air and the horses stampeding from panic. At an officer's command, the police charged, and the crowd scattered in all directions. I heard screams, loud thuds, horseshoes striking the cobblestones. There were people fallen on the ground, windows being shattered, cars turned over. Somewhere, flames rose up, further frightening the horses, which began to kick and rear, getting rid of their riders. People with bloodied faces, many of them women, kicked and punched the fallen policemen. After I'm not sure how long, we were running through the graves of the small cemetery at St. Paul's. Your grandfather lifted me up and threw me over a hedge as if I were a bale of hay. We kept on running alongside other demonstrators, and didn't stop till we left behind all signs of violence, well past the outskirts of Chinatown. It's a miracle that nothing happened to us.

There were demonstrations all over the world, not only in New York and other major cities in the United States, but that didn't affect the course of things. We held out hope till the very last moment, but when the day arrived, May 17, 1927, the two anarchists were executed in spite of the fact that there had been no conclusive proof against them. A few days later, your grandfather David published an incendiary article in the *Brooklyn Eagle*. Many times over the years, I heard him say that it was the best thing he ever wrote. Maybe so; the fact is that the article made quite an impact, and some passages were quoted in other papers, including the *New York Times*. Numerous letters of support arrived at the *Eagle*'s offices. The execution was followed by more violence. And around that time, the police showed up at our house with an arrest warrant for David Ackerman, accusing him of inciting violence in his article—which, as you can imagine, was full of invective against the judicial system of this country. They put him through all types of interrogation and coercions, but after the seventy-two hours of the habeas corpus, not having enough proof to charge him and realizing they weren't going to get anything out of him, they just let him go. He remained an anarchist until the end of his life, but, never losing sight of his own sense of repugnance at any sort of proselytizing, he never tried to inculcate anyone with his ideas.

Maybe that was the reason, I went on, why Ben didn't inherit his father's ideology. He was a well-intentioned intellectual, a liberal, to be sure, but free of specific political affiliations. At most, you could say he was a sympathizer of the Communist Party, or, more accurately, a latter-day adherent of utopian socialism. As for me, despite my heritage, I've never cared for politics one bit.

Lewis nodded:

My kids neither. Each generation responds to the world according to unforeseen patterns.

The protest at the southern tip of Manhattan and the meeting in Boerum Hill are connected in one important way: each event represented the moment at which David Ackerman felt that his son and his grandson had, respectively, become men. And, of course, the meeting I attended with my grandfather was in honor of the two anarchists who had been legally murdered twenty-five years before.

Thinking about it, I realized that the event that David had made me attend in Boerum Hill had two consequences at a symbolic level: first, my grandfather had welcomed me into the world of adults, something that he'd managed to do before my father had even thought of it; second, and for me this was the most important one, because of David's gesture, I was at last allowed into the Archive. It was a decisive moment for me: I was giving up one haven for another. I was leaving behind the paradise of my childhood, which I had not yet completely abandoned, to enter into one filled with books, which I would never leave again.

Ben gave me free access to the Archive a couple of years later, in 1954. By then, however, I had begun to accumulate my own papers, dating them and documenting all my writing. The difference being that Ben never wrote anything, only collected it, while I felt the need to record everything I saw. On the other hand, I began to fathom the most profound side of my father's character. The fifties, as I don't have to remind someone like you, were a very difficult time for people like him. McCarthy was in his heyday, doing his thing, and ex-Brigade men had it tough. The worst part was that they had to hide their past. The noble ideal of which they felt legitimately proud and for which they had risked their lives had become something criminal and embarrassing. They had no other choice but to hide.

The events of 1927—the demonstration in Bowling Green, the executions of Sacco and Vanzetti, the agony caused by the detention of my grandfather—were a revelation that left a seed planted in Ben's conscience. For the moment, the floodwaters ebbed and he could lead a normal life like the rest of the kids his age. When he finished high school, he spent a summer working as a forest ranger in Vermont, and in the fall, he enrolled in the school of engineering at the University of Pittsburgh. He was always a good student. By the time the Spanish Civil War broke out, he had finished his sophomore year with excellent grades. The news of the fascist uprising surprised him in the middle of the summer, while he was working at the Brooklyn Navy Yard. What had happened in Spain—and this I don't have to tell you either—caused quite a stir in liberal circles in the United States. There was an overwhelming show of support for the republican cause, both from conscientious workers and from the intellectual class. Ben didn't have to think about it twice. He was twenty-three years old and had led a rather uneventful life. Up to that point, his studies had taken up most of his time and energy.

Ben's told me many times that what was going on in Spain was the catalyst that awoke his political conscience, which had been dormant for so long. During the first few months, he followed news of the war in the papers with great restlessness and anxiety. One year after the hostilities had erupted, things began to look bad for the Republicans. In October 1937, reading the *Brooklyn Eagle*, he saw the announcement for a meeting that was going to take place at a hotel in Manhattan, and he decided to attend. He had good reason to go: he had made his mind up to enlist in the International Brigades, and was going to do it without telling his family. The keynote speaker was the British novelist Ralph Bates—you know who he is, of course.

Lewis slapped his thigh and let out a loud laugh:

Do I know who Bates is? Who hasn't heard of *El Fantástico*? A brilliant man.

Then you'll remember that the republican government had asked him to make a tour of North American cities to recruit volunteers and raise funds to fight the rebels. That was the meeting Ben went to. As far as my father was concerned, however, Bates was preaching to the converted. The idea of enlisting in the Brigades had been bouncing around in his head for a while, and he had already made up his mind before hearing one word of the Englishman's harangue.

Funny the way people's paths cross, Abe said. I met Ralph long after the end of the war, in 1951, during the yearly reunion of the International Brigades in their New York quarters, on Broadway. In the United States, Bates had been pretty well-known as a fiction writer before '36. He had published a couple of novels and collections of stories dealing with Spain, although literature was only one of his many interests. Have you read him?

I haven't, but Ben likes his work very much. Some people say that his stuff about Spain is better than Malraux's or Hemingway's. There are a few of his books in the Archive: *Sierra, Lean Men,*

The Olive Field . . . and some others I forget now. Have you read him?

I don't read fiction. I said the same thing to Bates when I was introduced to him, to justify my not really knowing his work. A few days later, I got a copy of *The Dolphin in the Wood* in the mail, signed and dedicated. It's not fiction, the dedication said—and it wasn't, as such. It was his autobiography. A beautiful gesture, and I have to say, I was impressed by the book. He's had a fascinating life.

What ever happened to him?

He's been forgotten. I think he spends half of the year in the island of Naxos with his wife and the rest of the time in Manhattan. Sort of like I do. As far as I know, he teaches at NYU, these days.

Has he stopped writing?

When I last saw him, he had long since decided not to publish ever again. He gave me a rather peculiar explanation: the more politically disenchanted he had become, the less he cared about literature. Before the war, he had been very prolific. After Franco's victory, he went to Mexico as so many others had. He didn't know that he was in for yet another terrible blow: the news of Stalin's pact with Hitler. When he found out, he almost completely lost faith in his fellow man. He tore up his party card after having been a member for twenty-four years. But, in spite of everything, he had just enough faith left in him to finish *The Fields of Paradise*. That was in 1940, after that there was a ten-year silence. When we met at that reunion on Broadway, he told me that *The Dolphin in the Wood* was his farewell to writing. And the nail in the coffin was still to come: the McCarthy era. That's where Ralph Bates's public life comes to an end. There's not a trace of him after the early fifties.

It can't be.

It is. End of story. He became disenchanted with the world,

with politics, with human beings, with literature, and disappeared from the face of the Earth. That's how it turned out. That's the simple truth. We'd know by now if he had any more to say for himself.

It had stopped snowing and was getting dark. The Lion D'Or was still packed, a few of the groups who had been there when we arrived still chatting away. Before starting on another subject, let's go somewhere else, Lewis said. I propose that we continue this conversation in a rather peculiar place—you'll see what I mean when we get there. You probably don't know who Chicote is, do you.

No.

You haven't missed anything. A questionable character, a Francoist. But political differences aside, everyone knows that his bar serves the best cocktails in Madrid. It's on the Gran Vía, a few steps from the Hotel Florida, where I want to go afterward. Of course, if you have a problem with that, we'll go somewhere else.

Anything's fine with me.

In that case, the best thing to do is knock back a *carajillo*. I can't believe I didn't think of it before. Do you know what that is?

There was practically no one on Alcalá Street. It was no longer snowing, the air was crisp, and a sharp wind cut at the skin. Just as we reached Recoletos Avenue, the facade lights of the buildings around Cibeles went on. That morning, crossing the plaza by cab, I had seen the opposite: the streetlights had all turned off. With them on, the city looked different, more beautiful in a way. We were in front of a building crowned with a winged god; Ben told me the name, once, but I'd forgotten it. Alcalá Street meets the Gran Vía there, two bright avenues disappearing into the distance. Patches of clouds sped across the sky. The glow of some straggling lightning shimmered far away. We walked slowly, not saying a word, soaking in the mystery saturating the air of the city.

At Chicote, the waiter brought two steaming cups and put them on the table, warning us not to touch them.

Unless for some reason you feel like getting burned, he said, dead serious.

Ben was in one of the first contingent of brigades that set sail from New York in '37, I went on. From Albacete, they sent him to the Guadalajara front and he was wounded in one of his first confrontations. He was treated in a hospital in Madrid where he became friends with an American doctor named Bernard Maxwell. During his convalescence, he also met a fellow countrywoman spending a few days in Madrid: Lucia Hollander. Lucia spoke Catalan as well as Spanish, which is why they'd stationed her in Barcelona, where she worked for intelligence. She met my father at a party in the house of Mirko Stauer, a Montenegrin aristocrat who was active in the party. Ben and Lucia fell in love at first sight and got married then and there, in the middle of the war.

In the same manner that I can only associate the word father with Ben Ackerman, for me there has been no maternal figure other than Lucia Hollander. And yet, from the first time my father told me about Teresa Quintana and showed me her picture when I was fourteen years old, there hasn't been a day I haven't thought about my biological mother. At first, when all my imagination had to go on was the young militiawoman in the picture, a thousand questions hammered the inside of my head. What was she like? How did her voice sound? Was anyone in her family still alive? What had her life been like in that little town in Valladolid, whose name Ben couldn't even remember? And what was the young man standing beside her in that photo like? At night, before falling asleep, I repeated her name aloud, as if I could summon her ghost that way, or stir up some memory

I didn't have. Somehow, my sadness made its way to Lucia, who appeared in my room and sat at the edge of my bed, trying to console me. But it was only Ben who had met her in real life, and when we were alone in his studio, it was him that I implored to tell me again and again the tale of how they'd met. A thousand times I asked him to repeat it, and he always complied, although there wasn't much to add to what he had told me the first time. When it comes down to it, Abe, I know very little about her, and I can sum it up in very few words.

Ben and Teresa met each other in Madrid. Lucia, like I said, was stationed in Barcelona. She and Ben still hadn't gotten married and communication between them was limited to the phone calls Ben was able to make from work, once a week if they were lucky. In spite of the war, daily life in the capital of Spain went on with tenacious vitality. Ben was always saying that Madrid is the most fun-loving city in the world. He was staying in a *pensión* near Cuatro Caminos. One morning, while he was having his coffee at the Aurora Roja, he saw a girl walk in. She caught his attention because of her pale skin and because of the mixture of sadness and determination that he saw in her face. The girl sat a few tables away and ordered a glass of milk and some cupcakes. Ben's like that, sometimes he doesn't notice the glaringly obvious, other times he zeroes in on the most trivial detail imaginable. That was it. After a while, the girl left, but for some reason, her image stayed with him. We always tend to think that we'll never see people like that again, when we run into them by chance—I mean people we find attractive, not necessarily sexually, but who capture our attention. Ben must have assumed the same thing, which is why he was shocked when that same day, a few hours later, he saw her at the headquarters of the International Brigades. The girl was speaking to someone who had a British accent. She seemed very nervous and the Brigade man was trying to calm her down. The girl's black eyes rested for a moment on Ben, not quite seeing him. Although he was at some distance, he caught bits of the conversation. The Englishman was telling the militiawoman that the unit her *compañero* was in had been wiped out near the hermitage of Santa Quiteria, and that there wasn't news of any survivors. You know about that better than I do.

The snippets of conversation Ben heard had intrigued him and when he called Lucia a few nights later, Ben told her about the militiawoman with the black eyes. He asked her if she'd heard about the Squadron of Death, and Lucia told him that it was a unit of Italian anarchists. She promised that she would make inquiries among her comrades in the intelligence services, and that she would have some answers the next time he called. When she did, she confirmed everything he had half-heard: the expedition had been a catastrophe, the members of the squadron had fallen like flies, exterminated near a hermitage in the mountains of Huesca and there was no word of survivors.

For some reason, Ben was certain he'd see the girl again, and it wasn't long before he was proved right. Some days later, she showed up again at the Aurora Roja. This time, as soon as she walked in, Ben realized she was pregnant. Her state was so evident that he didn't understand how he hadn't noticed it before. Teresa asked for a coffee with milk and sat down. Every so often, she glanced impatiently at the clock on the wall, as if she were waiting for someone who was late. After a bit, a man arrived and sat with her. This time, Ben didn't have to make an effort to hear their conversation. The man was quite effeminate. The girl called him by his name several times: Alberto. Grabbing her by the hand, he told her that he was very sorry, but that he still had no news for her. The catastrophe of the Malatesta Battalion had given rise to anger and controversy in Republican circles. According to his sources, two things seemed clear: one, what had happened could only be explained by some type of betrayal; and two, there was now talk that some of them *had* survived. A name came up repeatedly: Umberto. That must have been the militiawoman's companion, although the Italian never mentioned a last name. Alberto told her that there was no news, and insisted that the best thing was to try not to think about it until they had some reliable news. As for him, they had just told him he was being transferred to the Luigi Longo unit. When she heard this, the girl began to cry. The Italian tried to calm her down as best he could, and soon enough he succeeded. After about half an hour, he excused himself. They agreed to meet the following day. When he saw that she'd been left alone, Ben approached her table and asked for permission to join her. She gave him a desolate look but did not refuse his company, probably because—aside from the fact that she felt helpless—Ben was wearing his Brigade uniform and had a foreign accent.

Every time that he gets to this part of the story, Ben laughs.

The first thing she asked him was if he was Italian.

American, Ben said, taking a sip of the coffee he had brought with him. What's your name?

Teresa.

How old are you?

Nineteen.

Are you from Madrid?

No, I'm from a town in Valladolid.

On his right ring finger, Ben wore a thick gold ring.

Are you married? she asked.

Engaged, he answered, following the direction of her eyes.

Is your fiancée Spanish?

No, an American, like me.

What's her name?

Lucia.

And you?

Ben. Benjamín in Spanish. Are you married?

No, Teresa said smiling. But I'm going to have a child. Its

father's name is Umberto. He's Italian.

From the Squadron of Death?

The girl gave a start. Ben detected a flash of panic in her eyes.

How do you know that? Are you a spy or something?

No, no, he said, amused, but yesterday I was at the headquarters when you were asking for information from that English officer. I also heard you talking with your Italian friend just a moment ago. I know what you are going through, that's why I asked if I could sit with you. I'd like to help you.

Why? You don't even know me. How do you think you could help me, anyway?

Lucia, my fiancée, really is a spy. But on our side. It sounds like a joke, I know, but it's true. She works for intelligence in Barcelona. They should have more information there.

Teresa lowered her eyes. She was about to cry but immediately composed herself.

But no one knows anything. My friend, Alberto Fermi, the Italian who just left, says the squadron was wiped out. According to him, people are saying the whole thing might have happened because of a traitor in the unit. That's what he told me.

I've heard something like that too, but the news is vague and it would be unwise to come to any hasty conclusions. At least they're saying there might be survivors now. Not all of them are prisoners, according to my sources, which makes it possible that your Umberto may have escaped with his life. I'm not telling you this just to make you feel better, believe me.

I won't take any convincing. I already know he's alive, Teresa said.

Ben looked at her, surprised:

It's possible.

It's not only possible. I know.

How can you be so sure?

I can't explain it. I just know.

Then you have reason to be happy.

There's something else, Benjamín. Something strange.

Such as?

I don't even know. A premonition, I guess you'd call it.

She had grown very pale.

Are you all right?

I'm dizzy. I feel very weak.

Where do you live?

In a hostel on Luchana Street.

Do you want me to take you there?

No, the last place I want to be is there. I go back at night when I don't have any other choice. Don't worry. This'll pass. I'd rather be out.

But why? In your state you should be resting.

You don't understand. Things there aren't good. I feel like a pariah. They can't stand me because I'm broke. I don't even know how many days I owe anymore. They only put up with me because the owner is a party member and I'm pregnant, but his wife is bent on making my life impossible. She made me move into a room without windows, and you can't fit anything in except the bed—and for that favor I have to help cook and clean. Even when there's nothing to do, she makes things up just to put me in my place. She can't stand to see me around there.

Ben offered to get her a room at the boardinghouse where he was staying. She absolutely refused. But my father is as stubborn as they come; nobody refuses him. It took some convincing, but he finally got her to relent. He went with her to pick up her few belongings and set her up in a room adjacent to his. Seeing that she was so weak and her pregnancy so advanced, after a few days he took her in to be examined by a doctor friend. She was diagnosed with a severe case of gestational anemia and prescribed bed rest and a proper diet.

In the days that followed, Ben attended to Teresa, taking care of her as if she were his younger sister. They chatted, read, and went out for walks and to see movies. The worrisome thing was that the closer it got to the delivery date, the worse my mother looked. On one of their first days together, he asked Teresa what she was thinking of calling her child, and she responded without hesitation: Gal.

And what if it's a girl?

It's a boy, she replied, without a shade of hesitation.

How can you be so sure?

There are things that can't be explained. I just know. That's it.

It didn't take long for the rumors to be confirmed. The Squadron of Death had been wiped out and no one knew if there were prisoners or survivors, although more and more people were saying there were both. As a military action, it had been so disastrous that it had set off an investigation to determine if anyone should be held responsible. Despite all her efforts, Lucia had found it impossible to get any reliable information about Umberto Pietri.

Then Ben asked her where she had come up with a name like Gal.

You might think it's silly, but it means a lot to me, Teresa replied happily. A short time after having arrived in Madrid, I attended the funeral of a high-ranking Brigade man. The ceremony was presided over by the chief of his unit, the Polish General Joseph Galicz, alias Gal. He might have been a great warrior, but that day, at the funeral of his comrade, I saw him cry.

Someone had put a bouquet of red carnations on the grave. General Galicz was silent for a long time, pensive, his back to everyone. Finally, he knelt down on the ground, picked up one of the carnations, and turned. I was directly behind him. Our eyes met for an instant and it was then I realized why he had taken so long to show his face. He had been crying. His eyes were still teary, but he didn't bother to wipe them. He held my look for a few moments and then, handing me the carnation, moved on with his head held high. I noticed that on his army jacket there was a strip of cloth with the letters GAL stitched in black thread.

Stories about that Polish general's cruelty came to Ben's mind. It took him a while before he asked:

But how do you know what he's really like?

Teresa said that she didn't know, and Ben told her that General Galicz was renowned for being rather bloodthirsty.

Although it could be just talk. You know how these things are.

I don't know, and I don't care. I had never seen him beforehand and I have never seen him since. What counts for me is what I saw that day.

When her water broke, she was only eight months pregnant. They took her to the Hospital de Maudes in Cuatro Caminos. Her labor was long and complicated. Ben was asleep on a sofa in the waiting room when a midwife woke him up with a very stern look on her face. The doctor who had attended to Teresa was beside her. It was clear from the way he spoke that he thought Ben was Teresa's husband

Sometimes, the doctor told him, we are faced with the necessity of choosing between the life of the mother and the life of a newborn. That was not the case today.

Nervous, Ben asked him to explain exactly what was going on.

The child is fine, but the mother has died, the doctor said, declining to beat around the bush a moment longer. I'm very sorry.

In those days of constant carnage, the loss of a single life didn't have much weight. Ben made a quick assessment of the situation. He knew that no one would claim the body. Teresa had gone off on her own to join the militia; whenever Ben had asked about her family, she'd been evasive. He thought about contacting her best friend, Alberto Fermi, the Italian from the Aurora Roja who had been transferred to the Longo Brigade. He sent him a letter, but never did find out whether it had ever arrived. What could he expect from Fermi anyway? The only thing that mattered now was the fact that the fate of the newborn was in his hands. He didn't have to check with Lucia; he did what she would have expected of him. Given the circumstances, there was only one thing to do. He claimed that Teresa was his lover and that the boy was his.

They made him go into a room where there was a representative from the General Union of Workers. Ben handed him his papers and then Teresa's. When he told the man that they hadn't been married, the official gave him a look of complicity and said with a baleful smile:

Because there was no bond of matrimony, you're not obligated to recognize the child, comrade . . . your choice.

I'm not simply declaring a birth. The mother has died. What do you want me to do, leave the child here and go?

The man took a step back and preened his mustache.

You must be a foreigner, with an accent that strong. Where are you from? Are you a son of the British Empire or something?

I'm the son of your whore of a mother, you sorry motherfucker, Ben replied. How do you like my Spanish?

The official apologized, made him sign a few registry books, and gave him copies of both the birth and death certificates. Teresa Quintana's remains were transferred to the Fuencarral Cemetery the following day. Her suitcase was at the boardinghouse. Ben went through the contents and kept a pair of mementoes, nothing much.

For Benjamin Ackerman, truth was a religion, and it had always been clear to him that he had no right to keep it from Teresa Quintana's son. What he never explained is what prompted him to tell me the story of my origins precisely on the day I turned fourteen. We were in the Archive, and Lucia was with us. As you can imagine, Abe, I wasn't at all prepared for what was to come. Perhaps there's no way to prepare someone for such a revelation. I don't remember his exact words, only the effect they had on me. It was an indescribable shock. My world teetered and became incomprehensible. I felt as if someone had severed the mooring lines to my reality and I was floating in space.

My bond to them took on even greater significance when I found out the reason why they'd never had any other children: Lucia was sterile. She had told my father when he proposed, and although Ben loved children, he didn't want to give her up. Naturally, the limits of my life went beyond what happened in the house. My world was Brooklyn and its streets. At times, when filling out papers for school, I was often surprised when I had to write down that I'd been born in Spain. Well, perhaps it wasn't so strange after all. I had classmates from everywhere, students from distant states, even from other countries, children of Italian, Irish, and Polish immigrants. Believe me, Abe, I really can't complain— it would be unfair. Ben and Lucia gave me all the love they were capable of giving. They went out of their way to make sure I had a good education. When I finished high school, I went to Brooklyn College. Those were happy years, at least in retrospect. And now that I'm telling you this, who knows why, the figure of my grandfather David cuts a path right through my memory. He wasn't in the library that afternoon, and what I'm saying right now doesn't really have anything to do with him. But for some reason that still escapes me, I connect—not just now but always—that afternoon in the Archive to something which happened much later, on the day I graduated. Perhaps the connection comes from the fact that I understood then that I had to face the world on my own. The truth is that I didn't have the slightest idea what I wanted to do with my life; but the day of my graduation when my grandfather asked me what I wanted to do with the rest of my life, I answered him resolutely that I wanted to be a writer. I don't know what the hell made me come up with that. I spoke without thinking, but on that very night, I found myself dwelling on my reply, and realized that I had spoken the truth. But back to the story—it would be entirely impossible for me to describe how I felt. At some point, I became aware of Ben's voice again, but as if it were very far away. I understood what he was trying to tell me, that he wanted to show me a photograph of my parents. He had held on to it all those years and the time had finally come to give it to me. I hesitated before telling him that I was afraid to look at it. I didn't want that chasm to open beneath me, but Ben was adamant. They're your parents, he said. Lucia took my hand and held it tight. Truth exists independent of whether you want to accept it or not. There is no use in denying it. I finally relented, half-scared, half-curious. I felt like crying, but I was incapable. After what seemed like an eternity, I reached out my hand. It was a picture of a couple. Both very young. She's nineteen, I hear Ben say. He's a bit older, maybe twenty, or twenty-one at most. I contemplate the image as though from an unspeakable distance.

They both, in the photo, seem very attractive, beautiful, and full of life. He is beaming, wearing his militia uniform, and she is holding his arm. He's a slim and dark young man, with sharp features and a straight nose, very good-looking. Maybe it's my imagination, but they seem very much in love—particularly her. She is clearly pregnant. With me. Her eyes are large, black, a bit sorrowful; one hand rests on her belly. His foot is on the ledge of a stone fountain inscribed with the words: República Española, 1934.

These are not my parents. That's what I said, looking at Ben and Lucia. You are my parents. I felt very calm after having said it; tears would have been unnecessary, now. I'm sure they were feeling worse than I was. Not knowing what to do with it, I handed the photo back to Ben. It was clear that he had given it to me because he wanted me to keep it, but he didn't dare say it. Finally, he affirmed: It's yours. I've waited years for the right moment to give it to you. Please take it.

I simply couldn't. I was afraid to touch it again. I remained as I was, still, without saying a word.

All right, as you wish, Ben said. To him it was like being forced to drink from the same bitter cup as I. I'll keep it here in the Archive, as before. His sense of duty made him add: With or without the picture, your mother is Teresa Quintana; no one can change that. He put his fingertip on the surface of matte print. Above the crescent shape of his fingernail was the childlike face of the militia girl. Ben slid his finger to the right a little, and for a moment I was expecting him to add: And your father, Umberto Pietri. But he said nothing. Now the tears burned my eyes a second time, but were no more willing to emerge. My throat was very dry and gritty, as though clogged with sand.

At the bottom of the cup was the remainder of the *carajillo*, a coffee and brandy concoction. Abe Lewis picked up his pack of cigarettes from the table, took one for himself, and offered me a Lucky Strike. After lighting both of them with a certain slowness, he took such a deep drag that his head disappeared for a moment, enveloped in smoke.

I had made Ben and Lucia repeat the story of Teresa Quintana many times but about your Umberto Pietri, Abe, I never knew a thing. I don't think I even heard his name once. All I knew is that Teresa's *compañero* had vanished with the rest of the Squadron of Death. That's it; there was no other trace of him, in Santa Quiteria or elsewhere. Not that I cared very much. I simply thought that he was dead.

Seven
THE DEATH NOTEBOOK

"If you are Death, why do you weep?"
ANNA AKHMATOVA

January 1993

I sat where I had seen you writing so many times, at the Captain's Table (the command bridge of the Oakland, as Frank used to say). I swept the place with my eyes. You were right. From that spot, every angle of the room was perfectly visible. Nélida, the Puerto Rican waitress, was on the phone seated on a stool at the far end of the bar. The long spiral cord made a straight line from where she was to the opposite end. The dance floor was completely dark but for the weak glare of the building's lobby on the other side of the revolving doors. At the far end of the bar, the poolroom looked like a giant aquarium. Boy and Orlando were playing a game. Their figures silently circled the table, submerged in a fog of neon that took on a greenish cast from the paint on the wall. Crouched behind the cash register was Raúl, Frank and Carolyn's adopted son. (His parents, you told me one day, had died in a car accident when he was a child. He is thirty-five and four foot seven. Everyone calls him Raúl the Midget, which he doesn't seem to mind. He's an accountant, and every Wednesday he passes by the Oakland to look over his father's books.)

There was only one person I had never seen before, an old albino seated on a stool at the back end of the bar. He was leaning on the wall made of blocks of frosted glass while Manuel *el Cubano* (more on him later) whispered something in his ear. When they noticed me, everyone said hello, even Boy and Orlando who were rather far away. Manolito left the old man alone at the bar, punched in a bolero on the Wurlitzer, and then went to the bathroom. Raúl raised his right hand, a familiar gesture that meant he was buying whatever I wanted. Nélida put her hand over the receiver, blew a kiss, and walked up to the trap door behind the counter. The phone cord followed her as if she were herself plugged into the wall. She pulled on the iron ring, lifting the trap door, and went into the basement. When he saw her disappear, the old man got up and ran to the jukebox. A dreadful thundering suddenly shook the foundations of the bar, as if someone had set off an explosive device. The albino had raised the volume all the way up using a hidden button on the back of the Wurlitzer. Excited by the deafening noise, he was bent over with laughter holding onto his belly as if his intestines were about to spill out. Nélida ran up from the basement and cut off the racket with one stroke. In the sudden silence, the old man began to gesticulate spasmodically, mimicking the arm movements of an orchestra conductor, each time with less force, until he was completely still, like a wind-up toy doll that had run out of battery power. With a resigned look, Manuel *el Cubano* came up to him and helped him back to the same stool he'd recently vacated, keeping an eye on him now. Raúl gave me a sign that he was going into his father's office to work.

At that moment, a light flashed briefly. Somebody came into the Oakland through the revolving doors in the back, cut across the dark dance floor, and on reaching the archway that separated it from the rest of the bar, paused. It was you. You exchanged a silent greeting with Manuel *el Cubano* and walked toward me. You put a notebook on top of the table. Nélida brought a bottle of vodka and a glass without your having to order it.

Do you know him? you asked, signaling to the albino.

No.

Looking at him, no one would suspect, but before he was twenty-five years old, he was the chief mate of a Danish merchant ship, you said. You made a face, poured yourself some vodka, and downed it in one gulp. I owe him a strange debt. His story was the origin of the *Death Notebook*. You passed your hand over the notebook. Claussen first came to the Oakland long before me. But I noticed him from the moment I arrived. He was always in the same spot, that one corner, like another piece of furniture, but we never said a single word to each other over the years—at most a simple nod of the head. One afternoon, unexpectedly, he came up to my table. With a voice that didn't make sense coming out of his desiccated face, he asked for permission to sit down. I was flabbergasted. The official story was that he had lost his mind. For me he had always been some lifeless thing, nothing more. So all this was like watching him being reborn from his own ashes.

You're a writer, right? he asked.

I looked him over, having trouble believing he was actually capable of speech. It was the first time that I had dealt with him as a human being, the first time I had taken note of his features, his eyes, the tone of his voice; the first time I could confirm that he did in fact have a face, eyes, a voice of his own. I imagine I responded that I was a writer, the truth is I don't remember. What I do remember is what he did afterward. He put his hand in the inside pocket of his blue jacket and pulled out a newspaper clipping. I must have spent a long time looking at his dirty fingernails and the wrinkled and greasy piece of paper before I finally grabbed it. He asked for permission to sit down again, but I still couldn't get used to his presence, to the fact that he was able to express himself almost normally. I read what he had given me. That clipping and what he told me during those few minutes he had use of his reason led me to begin this.

You touched the notebook again. It was black, a good size, with a hard cover and yellow edges. A band held it shut vertically. You poured yourself a second shot of vodka and emptied it as vehemently as you had the first. I was frightened by how you were looking at me; it made me feel an indefinable giddiness, as if I were trespassing into what had been a forbidden part of your world.

I can understand someone leaving everything behind for a woman that he's only just met. But I don't understand why you have to pay so dearly for it. Always. There's something in that that I'm not sure I grasp yet, Chapman . . .

(Were you thinking about Nadia?)

You took a deep breath, pushed away the empty glass, and said:

I'll show you what he gave me later; but let me tell you the story first.

Some ten or fifteen years before the Oakland opened, Otero owned a bar by the piers. It was called Frankie's and was in an area where Danish ships used to dock. (By chance, I imagine, since I know of no regulation that says that ships of a certain nationality all need to dock in a particular place.) So when he closed that bar to open the new location on Atlantic Avenue, the Danes all stuck together and followed him there. That was in 1957. One of those Danes was Knut Jansson, the captain of a mid-sized cargo ship. His first officer, Niels Claussen, was that old man who just turned up the volume on the jukebox. Come here, I want to show you something.

He pointed to the word AALVAND, neatly inscribed on the ring of a life preserver hanging on the wall. In the space circled by the floating device, Frank had placed a picture of the ship's crew posing in full uniform. Captain Jansson, you said, pointing to a figure with your index finger, although his rank was perfectly recognizable by his uniform. It wasn't necessary to point out who Niels Claussen was either. His albino head stood out a mile, as though a drop of acid had fallen on the surface of the picture there. You studied the photograph silently for a few moments, then came back to our table.

The *Aalvand* docked in Brooklyn twice a year on average. The photograph was taken around the time the Oakland opened. Jansson and his men arrived at port on the night before Labor Day. The neighborhood was partying. The Caribbeans were putting on a music festival. Parade floats crowded with bands playing reggae and calypso rolled down Eastern Parkway. The partying spilled over to the adjoining neighborhoods and the sailors celebrated as sailors do. Don't ask me where they took Claussen. In theory, he went to see the parade with a few other sailors; but when they got together at the Oakland before curfew time, someone reported that the first officer had met a green-eyed brunette who had relieved him of his senses.

Must have relieved him of something else too, we heard Frank say. We had been so engaged in our conversation that we hadn't even noticed when he arrived. Good afternoon, gentlemen. You poured yourself another vodka. Nélida approached the table to tell her boss that his son Raúl was in the office going over the numbers. I'm sorry, Frank said, conscious of how brusquely he had interrupted us.

So, the story about the albino and the mulatta, he said, uncomfortably. He stole a glance at the old albino who at that moment was heading to the poolroom with Manuel *el Cubano*. How come?

From the bar, Nélida tried to get Frank's attention, letting him know that his son was asking for him.

Excuse me one second, I'll be right back.

It gets Frankie's goat whenever Niels's story comes up. He

never said a word about it until the day the Dane approached me. After that, he saw it fit to provide me with further details. I understand his initial reservations. Anyone would have trouble taking in the story of that poor sailor.

I don't know, Frank said when he returned, scratching his ear without making a move to sit down. I see you guys are so deep into it, I'm not sure if I should get involved.

His words gave you pause, apparently. You pulled out a chair, offered it to him, and said:

You're at your table, captain.

Frank sat down.

So why are you talking about Niels?

Because it's the first time Néstor's seen him.

Ah, that's right. Well, he's been sick. And Manolito took him to spend a couple of months with him and his mother in Florida when he was recovering. Takes care of him as if he were an only son, even though the Dane is more than twenty years his senior. You know Manuel *el Cubano*, right?

Yeah, in passing.

(Another one of the regulars. Gay, a real chatterbox, always dressed to the nines, with his *guayaberas*, his linen pants, his white shoes, and sunglasses, which he never takes off, so no one notices his glass eye.)

It was difficult for you to pick up the thread of the story again. In spite of his apologies, Frank was in a good mood, but the story took on much darker overtones after you nodded and got it back in hand:

Her name was Jaclyn Fox and she was Jamaican. I've never seen a picture of her, so I can't describe her physically.

I saw her in person, Ness—nothing to write home about, Frank interrupted. I'm not talking about her face, body—that's a taste thing. I just didn't like the way she looked at people, didn't like the way she presented herself, so accommodating, submissive.

I didn't trust her, and she realized it right away. Since she knew she wasn't going to get one over on me, she did her best to treat me like dirt. I felt bad for Niels. He didn't have much experience with women and went bounding into her jaws like a lamb.

The important thing, you pointed out, as far as our story goes, is that after being with her, Niels couldn't get her out of his head. It was as if he'd come down with a contagious disease, as if she had poisoned him and he'd become dependent on the poison that only she could administer. He was obsessed. The very thought of being apart from her tormented him. And his mates from the *Aalvand* needled him about it. They laughed in his face, telling him that all women had what the Jamaican had. Claussen didn't care. For him, the only thing that mattered was knowing that, once the *Aalvand* departed, it would be six months before he saw her again, and six months is simply too long to ask a woman like that to wait—especially since he knew that, even if it worked, he'd just have to shove off again sooner or later and wind up in the same predicament.

I'm sorry, Gal—this was Frank—but aren't you romanticizing it just a bit? These stories of sailors with doomed loves, aside from being boring and repetitious, are just not true. The truth is that they get married like everyone else, and their wives are faithful or they aren't, it's all down to chance. As for the men, the vast majority of them head right for a brothel the minute they set foot on land. And that's no secret; all you have to do is make the rounds of the joints near the port. Or around the Oakland. And that's what happened to Claussen—he got hitched to a whore.

She wasn't a whore, you protested. She had a decent job and . . .

If she wasn't one by trade, she behaved like one. Anyway, go ahead.

The *Aalvand* docked in Brooklyn again in March . . .

February—sorry. I know because it was cold as hell. There was a few weeks' worth of snow accumulated on the streets. Mountains of dirty ice.

So February. Five months, then, not six. Five months is a long time, but in this case not enough to erase memory of the toxic desire inspired by Jaclyn Fox. The *Aalvand* returned and with it Claussen. They'd be here a week, same as always, and every night the Danish seamen came to the Oakland to see Frank. The day before their departure, Niels came to the bar with his captain. Their ship would sail first thing in the morning.

It was a while before you said anything else. You needed some time to recapture the sense of intimacy that we'd shared at the beginning of our conversation, before Frank showed up. When you were ready, you again brought your glass to your lips.

And that's why, Frank said, abruptly jumping in, I almost lost it when the following day in the middle of the afternoon I see Niels Claussen walk into my bar.

He went silent, expecting you to go on.

He was carrying a knapsack and dressed like a civilian, you said, eventually; his ship had sailed some hours before. You didn't have to be a brain surgeon to figure out what had happened. The first officer of the *Aalvand* had deserted. The first thing that Frank asked him was where he had left the Jamaican woman. Claussen replied that she was waiting outside. He put the canvas bag with all his belongings on a chair and asked Frank if any of the rooms that he rented on the floor above were available.

The question annoyed the shit out of me, more than you can imagine. I told him I didn't know what the hell he was talking about; and who had told him that I had anything to do with any fucking motel? He looked so shocked by my outburst that I reined myself in and told him that it had nothing to do with him, he was always welcome at the Oakland. But he didn't come back, and we never did find out how they managed to live, the two of them—except for the fact that they hardly had time to enjoy their little love nest. The only thing that was known for sure was that they had gotten married and lived in Fort Greene.

On the other hand, you continued, Captain Jansson remained faithful to his custom of coming to see his friend Frankie Otero every time the ship docked in the port, and when the *Aalvand* returned to Brooklyn a few months later, it wasn't long before her skipper showed up at the Oakland. He wasn't coming to ask questions. It wasn't necessary for Frank or anyone else to tell him what had happened—he knew that Claussen had left it all behind for a woman.

The combination of rage, hurt, and disdain with which he spoke to me about the man who had been his best friend surprised me, Frank said. Of course, such vehemence made clear how much that betrayal had hurt him. According to him, the Jamaican woman had dragged Jansson through the sexual mud, so to speak—as if *he* were a bitch in heat. For his own good, he said, referring to Niels, I hope not to see him here.

Some months went by, about six or seven—no, Frankie? The next thing we knew about Niels, he was no longer living with the Jamaican.

She'd gotten bored to death with the albino and had taken off with another man. That's what my regulars told me. According to the rumors, she was living with an Irishman. Obviously she had a thing for white men, although this one wasn't as white as the Dane, of course. Poor fuck. He was already losing her the very day he stripped himself of his uniform.

What did he do then? I asked.

Jaclyn and her Irishman, Frank responded, lived near Prospect Park. Trying to put some distance between them, Niels went to live in Bedford-Stuyvesant. As Manolito says, he must have been the only white man in the neighborhood.

Then, one day, completely out of the blue, Niels gave signs of life, you began to say, but Frank interrupted you.

I was in the office when my wife Carolyn came in with a very serious look on her face and told me some strange man was asking for me. She couldn't tell me exactly who it was. I went to see and found the albino. He was skinnier and more haggard than ever. He wanted to know if Janssen still came by the bar when the ship docked in Brooklyn. Yes. Why? What do you want with him? I asked. His desertion must have been weighing on his conscience. He had betrayed not only his captain, but his best friend. But my attitude toward the albino changed completely after what happened.

We haven't gotten there yet, Frank.

What the hell are you two talking about? I asked.

About the newspaper clipping that Niels Claussen showed me on the day of his resurrection. Now that you know the background of the story, you replied, I can show you.

Pulling off the rubber band that sealed your black notebook, you opened it to the first page, slowly enough that I could read:

DEATH NOTEBOOK

You leafed through a few pages, pulled out a very worn clipping, and gave it to me.

BODY OF WOMAN BRUTALLY MURDERED FOUND IN PROSPECT PARK

The Brooklyn Eagle, September 23, 1958.
At 5:27 A.M. on Friday, a 911 call alerted the authorities to a body in Prospect Park. In the reported place, the police found the remains of woman around 20 years old. The body showed . . .

You grabbed it from my hand without letting me finish.

This is what Claussen gave me the day he came up to my table to talk. As you can imagine, I read it with the same confusion you're probably feeling right now. I thought my head was going to pop when he told me in that otherworldly voice:

The victim was my wife.

I looked at Frank and then back at you.

Are you saying that . . . ?

Just that his wife was found brutally murdered in the park, Frank interrupted. The woman was Jaclyn Fox, obviously.

But . . . who did it?

The Irishman. See, she tried to pull the same stunt on him that she had on Niels, but this time she'd picked the wrong guy. You couldn't fuck with the Irishman. The news spread like wildfire through all the bars near the port and the joints frequented by seamen. The ships sailing from here carried the news to other places. When Jansson returned to Brooklyn, he already knew what had happened to the woman for whom Claussen had turned his life upside down.

You needed another shot of vodka before you could go on. You asked Frank and me if we wanted to join you, and turned to Nélida to ask her for two more glasses, but we both said no.

You emptied your glass in one gulp and said: Stunned by the old man's revelation, I stared at him like an idiot.

His complexion looked like cracked quicklime. His white hair stuck to his forehead and cheekbones. His eyes were translucent, vacant, the pupils almost invisible. I tried to give the newspaper clipping back to him, but he raised his hand, and asked again:

You're a writer, right?

This time, I'm sure I didn't give him an answer. The question didn't require one.

I saw how darkness had descended upon his reason. And before leaving me to take up his usual spot in the corner, he'd once again become the living corpse that he'd been since Frank rescued him and brought him here. He had only been a real person during the fifteen or twenty minutes that we'd talked. I kept the clipping and put it in a folder, not knowing what to do with it.

You were on edge. Pausing to pick up the vodka, you filled your glass to the brim and emptied it again. When you next tried to speak, you were having trouble articulating, as though you couldn't breathe.

You turned to Frank and asked him to take over.

So there was that poor bastard, the *gallego* said, right in front of me, in my territory, helpless, not telling me what was going on. I invited him to sit down, asked him if he wanted anything, if he needed help. In response, he produced the newspaper clipping. He carried it with him everywhere, showing it to everyone, like someone who likes to flash around pictures of his kids—until he gave it to Gal, that is. No doubt, it was the first sign of madness.

Have you seen this, Frankie? he asked me.

Making sure I didn't hurt his feelings, I told him that he shouldn't carry the clipping around like a trophy. With a contrite air, he put it away and told me that this was how he had found out about it himself, from the newspaper. That was the beginning of the most ludicrous part of the story. It was then that he told me that he had written Jansson a letter and that he wanted me to give it to him when the *Aalvand* docked in Brooklyn again— something that, according to his calculations, should happen soon. I told him that it wouldn't be a problem at all, that I would give him the letter the moment he came in. Niels handed it over, thanked me profusely, and left. And I have to leave you as well, Frank added, apropos of nothing, as though looking for an excuse to get out of our way. My son Raúl needs me.

It was a while before you said anything else. When you were ready, you again brought your glass to your lips.

What Claussen expected to achieve with the letter we'll never know. He didn't speak to me about that. One thing is certain: it only cemented his humiliation. An outsider might have concluded that Jansson's response was needlessly cruel, but the truth is that—putting myself in his place—I understand. You strapped the band around your notebook again.

Keeping his word, when the moment came, Frank told Jansson that Niels Claussen had left a letter for him. The captain of the *Aalvand* shook his head. Of course, he didn't want anything to do with his former chief mate. To which Otero could only nod.

He didn't ask any questions. And never brought the subject up again. It wasn't long before Claussen called Frank to ask him if he had given the letter to Jansson. The *gallego* told him that the captain had refused to take it.

At this point in the story, you began to drink more slowly. Inexplicably, you had attained an almost unbearable lucidity, despite the vodka. Hoping to retain it, instead of emptying another glass in one gulp, you took small sips to fortify your words.

Jansson had been in Brooklyn for three nights when Claussen showed up at the Oakland. He shouldn't have done it. Jansson's decision didn't really leave room for misunderstanding. But human stupidity knows no limits, and Claussen did the worst thing he could have done. He appeared at the Oakland in full navy uniform. It was a surreal scene that Frank tells me still haunts him. It was nighttime and the bar was packed. Frank's place is a closed world. Everybody knew the albino and his story perfectly well, so the sight of the former chief mate in full regalia caused an appalling silence to fall over the room. Niels looked around for his old captain, headed toward his table, and when he was a few feet away, he paused, not knowing what to do next. Jansson frowned, stood up, and asked Otero to go get him the letter. When it was brought to him, he approached his former subordinate and made to return the envelope. But instead of taking it, Claussen stood at attention and saluted.

Frank says what happened next was like a dream. Jansson's right hand trembled, and after an endless moment, he let the letter drop to the floor. Who knows what was going on in his head? He was likely offended that Claussen had had the temerity to show up dressed in the very uniform that he had desecrated. His hand began to shake more violently. For a moment, Frank thought that he was about to return the salute, but instead Jansson reached back and delivered a slap that sounded like the lash of a whip in the silence of the bar. Niels stumbled back, but managed to quickly recover and hold his stance, still saluting. He was a sorry sight, surrounded by people who couldn't take their eyes off him. He looked like a marionette abandoned by its puppeteer. His face was tense. A drop of blood appeared in the corner of his mouth. Jansson turned around and continued chatting with Frank as if nothing had happened. Niels remained still for a long while, trying to contain his tears, until—having had his fill—he let his arm drop, and amid the intolerable silence, crouched down to pick up the letter, turned on his heels, and went back to wherever he'd come from. At Frank's signal, Ernie Johnson hurried to play some music. The noise from the Wurlitzer was like a sudden storm, overshadowing what had happened.

You passed your finger over the edge of your glass, delaying the moment before you took another sip, as if you knew that you were now at a point equidistant between lucidity and drunkenness. The line of vodka in your glass seemed to mark the frontier between the two states.

Did Jansson ever explain himself to Frank?

There was no opportunity. He stopped coming around. He disappeared. He asked to be relieved from the North Atlantic route and they never saw him again. There was some news about him from the Danish seamen who never stopped coming regularly to the bar, over the next few years, but that's all. Jansson retired in 1964. In the late '70s, after many years of having heard nothing about him, a telegram arrived at the Oakland with news that the old captain of the *Aalvand* had passed away. It was an official telegram, signed by someone or other ...

What about Niels?

At first, everyone thought that he had gone back home—but no. Last thing anyone knew, he was still living in Bedford-Stuyvesant, but that had been before the murder. One day, a friend of Frank's told him he had seen Niels in Red Hook, begging for change and completely out of it. Later news confirmed that he was in effect living in a bit of parkland next to a garbage dump with a bunch of other homeless guys. Frank went to look for Niels and recognized him right away. He saw a foul-smelling wreck collecting cans, glass bottles, and plastic containers that he would later exchange for a negligible amount of cash at a supermarket. But his height, his hair, and the color of his skin were unmistakable. It was the albino, all right.

Did Niels recognize Frank?

By then he had completely lost his mind. He had already become the man you see sitting there. The only difference is that now Manuel *el Cubano* takes care of him. The albino doesn't remember a thing. You can tell him anything you want about his past, he won't react. Once we put him in front of the photograph with all of them on the deck of the *Aalvand*, and he laughed like an idiot—we might as well have shown him a picture of monkeys fucking, shall we say. That's why, when I told him that Niels had come to my table to talk, Frank didn't buy it, and only believed me after I showed him the clipping.

Speaking of clippings, you said, tapping your notebook with your index finger, Jaclyn Fox's was the first. From then on, every time I come across news of that sort in the *New York Times*, I cut the article out. I'd been doing it for years, not knowing why, until one day I decided to turn one of the news articles into a story. I thought that if I did that, perhaps I would be able to make some sense of it all. So I began to take notes in a journal—different from all the others I keep. I didn't have to think much to come up with a name for it. It was clear that the common denominator of all those stories was death. But I still didn't know what shape I wanted to give my material. Little by little, I've been writing stories based on the articles I've been collecting . . . but not Niels's, that remains to be done.

We looked hard at each other, probably to avoid looking at Niels, although he was far away by now, watching Boy and Orlando play in the poolroom. You pushed the notebook toward me and invited me to open it. I was impressed by how carefully organized it was. It was a veritable catalog of the horrors of which human beings are capable—of the terrible things that we live with but don't pay attention to, since they appear routinely in the newspaper as part of our day-to-day lives. The monstrosities recorded in the *Death Notebook* repeated themselves with a mesmerizing monotony. It was strange, very strange, going through it. There was so much pain in those clippings. I flipped through the pages without daring to read any in detail, barely even looking at the headlines. They seemed like windows opening onto evil itself. Which is your phrase, not mine.

You filled your cup, pouring interminably. Soon the fire of the alcohol began to burn in your eyes. Your voice shook. Your words were more spat out than spoken.

To understand, simply to understand how anyone can commit such atrocities, you said, slurring a bit. That's all I want.

I noted something inside you, then, that I would only see again when I was with you at the Shipyard; I didn't know what to call it, but whenever I saw it, I made sure to keep my distance. Raúl had come out of the office, but he didn't come over, and I'm sure that Frank was staying away to avoid seeing you in that condition. Raúl went to sit with Niels, who was dozing off peacefully in the poolroom. He looked like a gargoyle perched on the arm of the sofa. Manuel *el Cubano* was sitting beside him, one hand on his back.

Anyway, you shouldn't pay too much attention to me, Ness.

It was the last thing you said, and it was said with a great deal of effort. You managed to get to your feet, but when you tried to take the *Death Notebook*, you couldn't quite grasp it, and I had to hand it to you. You went to pour yourself another vodka, but all you could manage was to pour the little liquid left in the bottle right out onto the surface of the table. Everyone in the place was watching you, now. With a surprisingly steady step, you walked toward the dance floor, but after making it into the middle of the darkness, you stopped. I came up from behind you to turn on the light and waited until you crossed the empty floor. You made it to the revolving doors and disappeared into the lobby of the building.

The glass panes continued to revolve for a few seconds; when they finally stopped, I saw a figure reflected there. It took me a moment to realize that the shadow lost among the ghostly lights of the dance floor was me. Had I not heard Nélida calling my name at that very moment, I would have been lost, I think— adrift in time and space.

Eight
DO YOU KNOW WHO
YOU'RE DATING?

Clark Investigations & Security Services, Ltd.
341 West 56th Street
New York, NY

CASE # 233-NH (CLASSIFICATION ID 08-1)
DATE OF CONTRACT: October 25, 1973
NAME OF CLIENT: Gal Ackerman
Report prepared by William S. Queensberry, Jr.
SUBJECT OBSERVED: Nadia Orlov. Age: 23. Born in Laryat,
Siberia, May 17, 1950. Daughter of Mikhail and Olga, nuclear
physicists. The Orlovs sought and obtained political asylum in the
United States in 1957. Associate professors at the Massachusetts
Institute of Technology. Mikhail died of pancreatic cancer in 1965;
his widow continues to teach and lives in the family home in Boston.
After graduating from Smith College, Nadia Orlov was accepted at
the Juilliard School of Music in Manhattan, where she is in her third
year. Current address: 16-62 Ocean Avenue, # 30-N, Brighton Beach,
Brooklyn. She shares the place with Zadie Stewart, vice-president and
director of publicity at Leichlter and Associates.
ADDITIONAL FACTS: The subject works three days a week
(Monday, Tuesday, and Thursday) at the New York Public Library
for the Performing Arts in Lincoln Center from 3 to 6 in the afternoon

(5 to 8 on Tuesday). Saturdays and Sundays she works as a waitress at the Paris Bistro at 764 Avenue N in Brooklyn. No criminal record. She does not seem to be currently involved in a romantic relationship. Activities during the weekend: she arrived at the restaurant at 5 P.M. and left after midnight. Returned to Brighton Beach by taxi. Her routines offer no new revelations: shopping; a visit to the post office; a concert at Carnegie Hall on Saturday afternoon; a stroll in Coney Island on Sunday morning by herself. Her roommate, Zadie Stewart, didn't show up at the apartment all weekend . . .

Good morning, Ackerman. Queensberry walks into his office and shuts the door. I'm sorry I made you wait. Well, at least you got a chance to look at the report.

I make as if to stand, but Queensberry asks me not to bother and shakes my hand. He has a plastic cigarette is in his mouth, making his enunciation less clear.

Don't take this the wrong way, he says, leaning on his elbows, but this is probably the blandest case we have had so far this year. I warned you. But, hey, it's your money. The only thing even slightly atypical about the case is the age of the subject. This sort of job is most common with people who've been married a certain number of years. One or the other party starts developing irrational jealousies out of sheer boredom. It's just another way of throwing away money, like I said, although, actually, we tend to get better results than psychiatrists—when our clients read their reports, they tend to calm down right away. As you can see, this girl isn't hiding a thing.

I slip the brief report prepared by Queensberry into a gray envelope.

I also took a few pictures, he goes on, having stopped chewing on his so-called cigarette. Mostly to entertain myself. From a professional perspective, they're perfectly irrelevant, although if you may permit a frivolous remark, there's no doubt that the subject is quite attractive.

He hands me another envelope, the same color as the first. The intercom buzzes as he does so. Queensberry pushes a button. A female voice is heard, somewhat distorted.

Thank you, Tracy. Put him on hold on line two, please. Excuse me, but I have to take this call. Your case is closed. I wish you the best, Ackerman. I'm glad I was able to be of some help. It's been a pleasure.

William S. Queensberry, Jr. stands up and shakes my hand.

Same here, I make sure to say. But as soon as the detective picks up his phone, I've ceased to exist for him. Before turning the doorknob, I read on the glass in the door:

.ЯႱ ,YЯЯƎႱƧИƎƎUϘ .Ƨ MAIᒐᒐIW

When I close the door behind me, the letters, written in gold letters, appear rearranged in their natural order. The receptionist who attended me on the first day stops her typing and comes up to the counter, smiling. On her blouse is a plastic name card: Tracy Morris. I give her a check, duly filled out and signed. She studies it for a few moments before giving me a receipt and then leads me to the outer door.

Thank you, Mr. Ackerman. Have a good day.

There's no one else on the landing. As I wait for the elevator, I examine the envelopes. One has the CLARK logo, next to the magnifying glass with the stain that could be an insect or a clump of pubic hair. The other one, firmer to the touch and without any markings, contains the photographs. On each of the envelopes is a white label with the name William S. Queensberry, Jr. typed in. When I described him in one of the notebooks, I nicknamed him *Bullfrog*. Just like that, no frills, with a capital *B*, as if he were a boxer, the Bullfrog. So sorry, Queensberry, I think as I pull the photos out of the envelope, I tried to come up with another nickname, but I'm afraid that one is in your genes.

The morning sun falls gently on southern Manhattan. The streets are full of life; people are wearing light clothes enjoying the outdoors. I would like to return to my place on foot but I have to finish a job for McGraw-Hill, so I decide to take the bus. I think about Marc. I really need to speak with him, give him all the minute details in the report, show him the pictures so he can see what Nadia looks like. Nadia. I go over the set of pictures again, studying them one by one. They are good-sized enlargements that bend a bit when I take them out. As photographs, they leave a lot to be desired, but they're better than Polaroid snapshots. In truth, there's only one that's any good. I go back to it when I finish with the rest. Queensberry caught Nadia right at the moment that she was coming out of the library at Lincoln Center. Her left arm is blurry and in her hand is something I can't quite identify at first, but after looking closer decide are sunglasses. She brandishes them as if they were a gun. It happens sometimes, even in bad-quality pictures, that the camera fortuitously captures a moment of everyday mystery and freezes it in time. Nadia looks at the camera with a fixedness that betrays some anxiety. I think of a deer that has suddenly sensed the presence of a hunter amid the silence. Muscles tense but perfectly still, an animal captured in a fragment of time a mere tenth of a second before fleeing. Nadia too has detected a vague danger. I linger on the shape of her lips, on the eyes whose depth fills me with unease. I can sense her restlessness, trapped in the moment when fear turns to anger. My instinctive reaction is to protect her, but she doesn't need protection, there's an aura of strength about her. Her expression is in fact familiar. It's the same one I saw just before she threw her bag at my face in Port Authority. I'm so absorbed studying the details of the photograph that I don't notice the bus arrive. When it stops in front of me, the screeching of the brakes makes me jump. Although I'm at the head of the line, I step aside for everyone else waiting to get on. I put away the pictures and climb in, restless because I'm not sure what the next step should be, now that I'm acquainted with the details of Nadia Orlov's routine. I throw a handful of coins into the slot as I hear the muffled sound of the door closing, leaving the world behind.

After the radiant sun in the street, my place feels like a black hole, but I don't turn on the lights. I'd rather wait until my eyes get accustomed to the darkness. I leave the envelopes on the table and call Marc at work. He answers on the first ring. It's good to hear his voice and I begin telling him everything hurriedly, overwhelming him with the details of Queensberry's report, my words tripping over each other.

Gal!

But I keep going.

Gal! What's gotten into you?

And I realize that I didn't even bother to say hello.

Sorry, Marc, I'm a little shaken up.

At first there's a silence on the other end of the line, then the murmur of a distant voice. Someone must have come into his office.

I need to talk to you.

I can't now, I'm sorry. I have a business lunch. Marc's voice sounds different, mechanical, professional. I won't be back to the office for the remainder of the day. Why don't you drop by the Chamberpot tonight?

What time?

After eight. Sorry, Gal, I have to go.

A beam of light sneaks in through the window. The midday sun appears from behind the skyscrapers that keep my building in the shadows all day. Except for now. Fifteen minutes. That's it. At this time of the year, there are only fifteen minutes of natural light a day. Fifteen minutes during which, if the sky's clear, the sun shines particularly bright as it runs the course between the two skyscrapers that box in the courtyard of my building. A patch of light appears on the kitchen floor. I go to the window, close my eyes, and wait for the sun to hit me square in the face before it vanishes for the day. When I feel the shadow again through my eyelids, I let the curtain fall and sit at the table.

I know the search isn't over. After so much expectation, everything's happened too fast. I found the girl in the photograph. I know where she lives, where she works, what she does every day. I know the external details of her routines, and if I want, I can burst into her life; but something tells me I shouldn't do that yet. It's as if I've reached the border of some new land, shrouded with fog. I've cheated fate till now—to take the next step will mean danger. But wait. I push away my doubts and make a quick mental calculation. I have time to finish correcting these galleys and turn them in to McGraw-Hill before she finishes her shift in the library.

It's a hot afternoon. Since mid-September, the weather has been consistent: an anomalous, cancerous extension of summer. After dropping by McGraw-Hill, I walk up Sixth Avenue, and on reaching the southern edge of Central Park turn left toward Columbus Circle. I like this route because on the side that borders Central Park there's a long line of carriages hitched to horses. I love passing near them, feeling the uncanniness of their presence, not even bothered by the acrid smell of their feces. I turn up Broadway, approaching Lincoln Center. It's been a long time since I've been there. Right after it opened, I used to go frequently. When it appears at 62nd Street, the sheer audacity of its concrete and glass architecture surprises me as if I were seeing it for the first time. I go up the steps facing the stone pedestal with the fountain in the central plaza. The noise of the city doesn't seem to reach in here, as though it's been absorbed along the way. I stop to watch the play of the clouds in the sky, a procession of elongated patches that travel slowly westward. The light has acquired an intense metallic blue that adheres tightly to the edges of the buildings. In the lobby of the Met, up front, hanging on the walls, I see the Chagalls, two gigantic canvases in which strange beings float weightlessly in an impossible space. A uniformed doorman comes out from between the columns of Philharmonic Hall. He must have seen me smoking and asks for a light. A Hispanic with a trimmed beard, he speaks to me in English and I respond in Spanish. On hearing his language, he smiles and leans forward, stretching his neck. He puts his cigarette to mine and inhales deeply, stealing the fire.

Gracias. It's a beautiful day, no? he says after taking a drag, and bringing a hand to the visor of his cap, he disappears in between the columns of the building.

I go in toward the northern square to the right. The two rectangular spaces might as well be separated by an imaginary wall. When I walk from one side to the other, I feel as if I'm crossing an invisible barrier and that everything on the other side, even the air, is different. In the area by a pool is a patch of trees. Marble pots rest on the cement grid floor, a young tree planted in each. Their leaves are changing color but all are still hanging on. The treetops are brilliant with the colors of fall, a blaze that runs the gamut of ochre, red, and yellow. The entrance to the public library is in the back of the square, boxed in between the side of the Met and the entrance to the Vivian Beaumont Theater. To the north, on a higher level, is the Juilliard School of Music. I imagine an invisible thread connecting these two places where Nadia Orlov spends so much of her time. I walk along one side of the pool at a measured pace. The surface is a perfectly smooth gray sheet that takes in the reflection of the trees, the buildings, and the clouds whose inverted shapes seem to plunge into the depths of the water. The two pieces that make up Henry Moore's reclined figure, partly submerged, sit in the middle of the pool, at once peaceful and restless. I go up the stone steps that lead to the conservatory and the first thing I see when I reach the landing is the library. Groups of students mill near Juilliard. I lose myself among them, watching with special interest those who are Nadia's age, trying to imagine what their lives are like, what secrets I would uncover if I decided to hire an army of Queensberrys to investigate their everyday comings and goings.

At ten to six, I decide to go down again. At the top of the stairs, a girl hugging a violin case smiles at me as I pass by her. The sun has started to set and the north square is beginning to fill with shadows. When I reach the edge of the pool, I lift my eyes and see the last embers of the day's light floating in the air. I sit on a bench by one of the trees. From there, I can see the entrance to the library, but as soon as I sit, I see her appear. Instinctively, I get up and step behind one of the potted trees, as if the trunk, hardly thicker than my arm, could hide me. She walks off quickly. I follow her. As we approach the main square, I lose her for a few moments. When I get there, I realize they have turned on the lights of the fountain. On the other side of the plumes of water, I make out her figure. I wait until she disappears and decide it's enough for the day.

I return to the library to familiarize myself with the place where she works. The entrance hall is very spacious. Toward the back is a group of people waiting for the elevator. I go up with them. I slowly explore the three floors of the building, going down the stairs from one landing to the next. In the mezzanine, I look for the music archives where, according to Queensberry's report, Nadia works. There's a counter, a few empty chairs, and a door with a sign that says: *Employees Only*. I cross between the stacks and reach a reading room. There are a few people reading at the desks. I sit in one of them, at random, deciding I will return the following day. That was all I needed, just enough time to catch sight of her. Now that I've managed to see her again,

I realize that the unexplainable restlessness that came over me when our paths first crossed at Port Authority hasn't settled in the least. Tomorrow I will come out the other end of the spiral down which I've been plummeting. There is no sense in leaving the wound open any longer.

That night, at the Chamberpot, I show Marc the pictures. He looks through the stack, studying them with interest.

Nadia! Nadia! Nadia! Always her! he exclaims. And what about my friend Zadie Stewart? She's not in a single one of these.

He looks at me, smiling, and continues to flip through the pictures. When he's done, he pulls out the same one that had initially caught my attention and looks at it more closely.

What do you think? I ask.

He puts out his cigarette in a metallic, triangular ashtray.

The truth?

The truth.

He turns the picture toward me and says:

It's like she was designed for you.

We spend a couple of hours drinking and chatting. I don't like playing pool, but Marc loves it. Every once in a while, if someone's up for it, he challenges them to a game, but today he doesn't find any takers. Neither one of us notices when Claudia comes in. She has a whiskey in her hand and is writing her name on the board, which is completely unnecessary, because no one else is waiting to play. We say hello from afar. She winks and comes toward the bar. There's almost no one left in the place, just the two of us and a pair of shady characters near the door. Marc suggests that we go to Keyboard, a new place they just opened on 46th Street.

I finish my drink and say:

Not me. I have a lot of work to do tomorrow.

Like all of us, Marc says. Claudia laughs.

It's an urgent job for McGraw-Hill. They need it by noon, I can't be late. It pays really well.

Whatever you want, Marc says, shrugging. And then: So? Are you going to play me? he asks Claudia.

Yes, but only one game and then we go to Keyboard and check it out.

Marc looks me in the eyes, makes an exaggerated bow, doffing an imaginary hat, and heads for the pool table. Claudia remains at the bar with me for a moment.

Everything all right? she asks, reaching out and caressing my cheek.

I smile. She goes to the pool table and blows me a kiss. I watch the beginning of the game. Marc pulls the lever. I hear the rolling of the balls inside the pool table. When Marc finishes rounding them up with the rack, he gestures to Claudia who leans over the table and strikes the cue ball hard. The colorful triangle shatters with a dry crack that reverberates across the room.

Outside, the streetlights are reflected on the road as if it's just rained. At a distance, I see the rear lights of a garbage truck. There is no one on the streets. On the corner of Ninth Avenue, there's an old man covered by a blanket inside a cardboard box. He's awake, talking to himself in a low voice. When I pass by, I take in the nauseating stench and move on, not even looking at him. There's quite a bit of traffic heading toward Lincoln Tunnel. It's a moonless clear night, a cold wind blowing in from the Hudson.

I spend Tuesday morning finishing my urgent assignment. At noon, I go to McGraw-Hill, turn in my work, and from there head for Lincoln Center, taking the same route as the day before. I cross the streets at the same spots, turn at the same corners, as though following my own tracks. I like the ritual of retracing my steps, although today everything happens faster, because I know that I'll see her when I get there. After I make the twists and turns through Lincoln Center and before going into the library, I sit on the same bench as yesterday by the edge of the pool and try to imagine what will happen. But I can't imagine anything. I shake my head and move toward the library with a determined step. I go directly to the archives. The same employee as yesterday is at the counter facing the readers. My desk, however, is taken. I look for another spot, near the back of the room, next to the large windows facing Tenth Avenue. More than half an hour goes by without a single sign of her. Perhaps she decided not to come to work today, I think, but the thought has barely crossed my mind when I see her appear between two rows of bookshelves carrying a folder full of papers. She sets it on top of a table near the counter, sits down, and begins to separate the files, arranging them in different stacks. For a long time, no one approaches her with a request. From the moment I saw her at the end of the hall, I haven't taken my eyes off her.

I watch her movements so closely that I don't even realize how tense my body has become, twisted into an absurd posture, neither sitting nor standing. I am watching her so intensely that it's a wonder no one has noticed how weird I'm acting. Nadia herself hasn't noticed a thing. She's so absorbed in what she's doing that she has no clue that in the back of the reading room someone is scrutinizing her as if his life depended on remembering every detail. One of the other people here, a man of around fifty wearing a denim jacket, approaches the counter then and blocks my view of her. It's only now that I feel the tension in my body and fall back down on my chair, trying to relax. Above the exit door, the clock says five twenty. Today the library closes two hours earlier than usual, at six, exactly when her shift is over. I decide to kill some time browsing through a book I pulled out arbitrarily from one of the shelves. I didn't even notice the title till this moment. *Silence* by John Cage. I browse through it distractedly and, when I finish, I close it, put it aside, and take out the book and notebook I always carry in my bag. It's a futile gesture—I know it'll be impossible to write or read anything. The man in the denim jacket returns to his desk and Nadia stands up. I fix my eyes on her again. She goes to the back wall and climbs a stepladder to get a book from one of the top shelves. I see now that she's wearing the same skirt as that day at Port Authority, and there's a flash of naked thigh. After a few moments, she returns with a bundle of documents bound with a red ribbon and sits back down at her desk.

The sound of a high-pitched bell warns readers that it's closing time. I haven't been able to read much. As if in a dream, I look up to the counter and I realize that she's looking at me. I feel out of place, ridiculous, like a child caught doing something wrong. The hands of the clock make a perfect, straight line. The second closing bell rings. A security guard walks between the desks ringing another little bell, hurrying the readers lagging behind. Nadia and I are the only ones left. We look at each other across the room. Then, she turns abruptly, picks up her things, and rushes out the door. I throw my book and notebook back in my bag and jump up. At the door, the security guard asks me to open my bag. I wait for him to give me the okay, and hurry outside, afraid to lose her. I cross the length of the northern square but don't see her. I continue, almost running, but just as I turn the corner of the Met, I come to a dead stop. She's there, at the foot of the fountain, with her legs slightly apart, waiting for me.

Brooklyn, October 24, 1973

I felt ridiculous. My behavior was absurd, considering my age. She was the only person in that section of the square. Behind her, on the other side of the curtain of water, tiny figures moved about. I advanced toward her. She was standing, her head tilted to one side, in a mildly defiant pose.

Are you following me?

No. Yes.

Since when? I mean, aside from the library.

She grimaced slightly.

It's not what you think, I said.

What do I think?

You must think . . .

I remember you, she broke into a brief laugh.

What?

From Port Authority, a couple of weeks ago. I fell asleep on the bus.

My hand drifted up to the spot on my cheek that had been cut by the buckle.

Are you the guy who went to see Zadie?

Zadie Stewart, your roommate? Yes . . . I mean, no.

Are you Gal Ackerman?

Did your friend tell you?

Of course she did. But the person she described was different.

Listen, I . . . I can explain.

Just tell me what you want from me.

I don't know. Why don't we go somewhere?

Fine, where would you like to go? she replied.

I suggested we go to Café Bordeaux, a place I'd passed by so many times without ever going in. As we started walking together, my thoughts and feelings began to settle down, clarify.

What do you know about me? she asked.

A lot.

Like what?

Well, you may not like this . . .

What is it that you know? I have every right to ask, she said

You were born in Laryat, Siberia. Your parents came here when you were very young, you study violin at Juilliard . . .

She raised her hands in shock. Thinking that she was going to run, I grabbed her wrists.

I'm sorry . . . Please, if you don't yell, I'll confess everything to you. Only then did I realize she'd had no intention of running. Promise me you won't get angry, I said.

She snapped her hands away. She was strong. I took out the envelope with the pictures. I asked her if we could keep walking. There was something going on between us that I'm having trouble putting into words. A sudden drunkenness of the senses. It felt as though I'd been waiting for ages for just this scene, just these words, just these gestures. She should have been mad at me, afraid of me, of what I might do, but instead of running or yelling for help, she just stood there, somehow as confused as I was.

Now you're going to have to tell me something about you, she said. She spoke without an accent, but her pronunciation was somewhat peculiar, sharp, as if having to enunciate the end of phrases made her impatient.

I freelance, editorial work, proofreading, translations. I also write.

What do you write?

Everything, articles, some essays, stories, personal stuff.

Have you published anything?

I remembered the story that Marc had sent to the *Atlantic Monthly* without telling me.

Not yet.

We never made it to Café Bordeaux. I'm not sure that either of us knew what we actually wanted to do. When we passed in front of Coliseum Books, I couldn't help but stop and look at the titles in the window. It was something I did mechanically. We were silent for a while, then we went down Broadway until we reached the cascade of lights at Times Square right at the moment when the sun had begun to set. We were at the edge of my territory, near the border of Hell's Kitchen.

I'm thirsty, she told me.

I suggested we go to Eighth Avenue, where the dives that Marc likes to haunt are. Almost all of them we discovered together on nights when we went down looking for trouble into the caverns of Manhattan, as he used to say. I didn't take her to any of those places, but to a Greek café I'd never been to before. It didn't matter what we spoke about, words were unable to take us anywhere, but they were the only thing we had. She talked to me about music, about the piece she was rehearsing, the essays she was writing, about Bach's violin sonatas. About her parents and her brother Sasha who lived in Boston. From the time they were very young, they had been inseparable. When they arrived in the United States, the world became unintelligible. He had been her only support, especially in school. It was impossible for her to put into words how much she missed him, she said. I asked her if she remembered Siberia. She said she did, but the memories were very distant, as if, instead of having lived them herself, someone else had told her about them or she had read about them in a book.

Tell me about yourself, she said. But I couldn't.

We sat there in silence for a while. Her hands were very white, her fingers thin and delicate, the nails small, covered in transparent polish that reflected the lights of the café. When she spoke again, she told me that she lived by music and for music, to play it, to study it. That it was the only thing that had given her the wherewithal to separate herself from her mother and brother. Listening to this, I thought that I would have loved to hear her play, but I didn't say anything.

What were you reading in the library? she asked.

Oh, that. It's not the type of book I usually read.

Let me see it.

I gave it to her. She opened it, pulling back the green silk bookmark from the page and reading for a few moments, in silence, to herself; then she recited the lines I had underlined aloud.

The sweetheart sings one song; another, woe!
The hidden, guilty River-god of Blood

She closed the book, looked at the cover, and handed it back to me without a word. She kept her hand on top of the table, with the fingers slightly apart. I reached out with mine, the skin much darker, a trembling animal slowly approaching another. Once again, I asked the question that I had asked when we were standing in front of the fountain.

What do we do now?

Whatever you say, she replied again as quickly as she had before, smiling with her eyes.

We went up the wooden staircase, very slowly, led along as though in some hypnotist's act by our own desires. We hardly spoke, as though we'd entered some sacred place where words would only sound shrill and vulgar.

The railing was painted blue, like the doors. When we reached the third floor, there was a lonesome bark. It was Theo, the dog of an old Armenian woman who I often helped to carry up her groceries. The animal quieted down when it recognized my smell and went up to the door, whimpering.

We went into my place. I saw my shadow behind hers in the blurry surface of the mirror. The living room window was open to the brick wall of the building across the way. She went up to it.

I love the view, she said, smiling.

I drew the curtains. The light in the entrance hall was the only one on. I asked her if she wanted anything to drink. She said no. Before kissing her, standing there facing her, I told her that since the day I had seen her in the bus station I hadn't been able to rid myself of her. She began to undress.

The bedroom was dark and moonlight seeped in from the window, an icy moonlight that outlined the contours of her body with extraordinary precision. She leaned back, very slowly, still holding me by the hand. Her eyes shone in the shadows. She dragged me toward her, gently. Later, she would graze my sex with her tongue, contour the living flesh of her mouth to it, but it's not this tactile memory that has remained with me, nor the moment when I penetrated her. It was before. She had finally pulled her hand away from mine. Holding the shaft of my penis firmly, she maneuvered it so that it entered her smoothly. When that happened, I lost control, and not just bodily. It was then, I came to realize later, that I became attached to her forever, despite myself.

Nine
UMBERTO PIETRI

But Umberto Pietri hadn't died, he had returned to his place of origin. And I had to be the one who bumped into him. I wouldn't have chosen to meet him, but there are some choices we don't get to make for ourselves. He had been waiting decades for the chance to tell someone the terrible truth he had been hiding, and he'd long since lost all hope that it would ever present itself . . . till I ran into him. He told me things that he'd never told anyone. There was so much to tell that he needed two full days to do it. When I talked to Patrizia, my wife, about it, she saw as clearly as I had that it was imperative for us to get in touch with Ben Ackerman, tell him that Pietri was alive and suggest that we meet in Madrid. You and I, because at the end of the day, his story was meant for you. It makes the most sense this way, because here is where your parents met (Umberto and Teresa; Ben and Lucia), because you were born here, because here is where so many people's dreams of freedom were lost forever. And because here is where . . .

I raised my hand to prevent him from finishing this thought. I knew what he was going to say and I didn't want to hear it.

. . . where your mother died.

The nausea began in the pit of my stomach, rose to my chest, and burst into my head. I couldn't get it under control.

[There's a large blank space here. In retelling his conversation
with Abraham Lewis, Gal seems to rely on the letter Abe
wrote to Ben Ackerman as a guide. I haven't found the original
in the Archive. I only know it by the fragments Gal transcribed
in his notebooks.]

It was rather late by the time we left Chicote. It felt good to
walk down that elegant avenue lined with colorful shop windows.
After a few minutes, we arrived at Red de San Luis Square. That's
another thing that I love about Madrid: the charm of place-
names. At the Florida Hotel, a uniformed doorman opened the
door for us. Letting me go in first, Lewis told me that the hotel
had been a meeting place for foreign journalists during the war.

General Hemingway had his headquarters here, he said. I
picture him at the bar at all hours of the day. And speaking of
bars, there's no better city in the world for them. Don't you agree,
Gal? Think about all of the places we've been to today. We've
never had to think twice about where to go next.

We took the elevator to the top floor. On the other side of
a pair of glass doors was a wide, carpeted room with a dimly-lit
bar and dozens of tables widely spaced from each other. Large
windows that looked out onto the Gran Vía lined the far wall.
On seeing Lewis, a waiter who seemed to be expecting him led
us to a corner where there were two leather armchairs in front of
a fireplace. Without further ado, Abe picked up the conversation
at the exact point he had left it at Chicote.

Every time I remember that night, Lewis said, the first thing I
see is the huge round moon over the main square of Certaldo.
Umberto Pietri put away the picture of the *miliciana* in between
the pages of a book he carried in his pocket. When he was
assigned to the Squadron of Death, Teresa Quintana was six
months pregnant. A mutual friend, Alberto Fermi, promised to

take care of her, although he too was going to be sent to his unit any day. Pietri didn't tell Fermi, but he was certain that this was it: once he was separated from his girlfriend, it would be the last he'd ever hear of her, and that's how it turned out.

On top of the table was a bottle of mineral water. Pietri brought it to his lips and drank with great effort, his Adam's apple bobbing frenetically. Avoiding my eyes, he told me that they had detected a tumor in his liver and he had only a couple of months to live. He remained silent for a few moments before saying that when they told him the news he thought that he had to find a way to get in touch with his son.

[A thick notation in blue pencil, crossed out but perfectly legible: Get in touch with me]

At the very least, he should know what happened, he said in a thin voice, although by this time it may not matter. It's not just for him. I need to tell everything before I burst, even if it's the first and last time.

[...]

After the war ended, Pietri continued, I didn't hear a thing about Teresa, Alberto, or anyone else, of which I was glad, as you'll understand soon enough. That is, I didn't know anything until the day that Alberto Fermi showed up here in Certaldo, quite unexpectedly.

When was that?

October of forty-six. I don't remember the exact day.

[There's a gap in the text here.]

When the order came to join the Luigi Longo Brigade, Alberto Fermi, Ben Ackerman, and Teresa Quintana got together at the Aurora Roja. When the time came to part, Ben and Alberto exchanged addresses. Such gestures are almost always futile in times of war, but as soon as he set foot in Brooklyn, Ackerman wrote Fermi telling him everything that had happened since they had last seen each other. He wanted Fermi to know that Teresa had died giving birth but that the child had survived. At the hospital, everyone had thought that he was the father, and he didn't say otherwise. In fact, that's how it appears in the civil registry. The child was legally his. Shortly afterward, he married Lucia Hollander, and when the Brigades were repatriated, they took the baby to the United States and raised him as their child.

Pietri was drawing on his last reserves, giving out fact after fact, each more surprising than the last. He told me that he was glad that the son he'd had with Teresa had found a family. Over the years, he never gave the child a thought. Later, as he got older, he would occasionally remember that he had a son, and wonder what he might be like, but it was all idle speculation—he had no real interest in meeting the boy. Only now that he was so close, he felt that . . . It wasn't just about his son, he insisted. He needed to relieve himself from the hell he had lived through, telling the story of the Squadron at least this once. Which is why he thought that our encounter was some kind of sign.

I'm not sure I'm reproducing Abraham Lewis's words faithfully. If there's some confusion here, it's my fault, because he told the story with perfect order and clarity. It's possible that I got too emotional, occasionally losing the thread of his narrative. To be sure now and then I lost track of his voice while listening to him in the bar of that hotel. At times, I could hardly see him, let alone hear what he said, and now that I'm trying to transcribe his words in the *Notebook*, it's even worse. But I must leave a written record of everything, regardless of my feelings.

Why did Pietri seem so upset whenever he mentioned the Squadron of Death? Abe wondered—and I wondered too, intrigued. When it became obvious that he wasn't going to get to the topic on his own steam, I decided to ask Pietri point-blank: Whatever had happened at Santa Quiteria? Pietri flapped his right hand around as if he were tearing away a spider's web, and fixing me with a stare that might as well have been from Death itself, he rasped:

I betrayed them, Lewis. The whole unit was lost. Everyone died . . . I saved my skin at the cost of having them all slaughtered like rabbits. That's why I am still alive. I'm a coward and a traitor.

When Abe made that vicarious confession, something teetered in me. I had been lying to myself. My feelings were far stronger than I was willing to admit. My vision grew blurry. I looked around, peering into the darkness of the bar. Again that sensation that I'd been feeling intermittently ever since I set foot in Madrid. I didn't want to be there. I felt utterly exhausted.

What . . . what time is it, Abe?

He leaned toward me.

I haven't finished, Ackerman, he hissed. But if you want, I'll stop.

No, there was no point. Why bother trying to save myself.

It's too late for that, I said. Go on till the end.

Pietri broke into a copious sweat. It seemed he was fighting a terrible battle against himself. Finally, he shook his head and begged my pardon, telling me that perhaps it was best to leave things as they were. There was such helplessness in his eyes, it was easier for me to let him know that it was all right, that he could tell me anything he wanted, that I was perfectly willing to listen to him.

Pietri stood up and left some money on the table, murmuring

to himself:

I should get the hell out of here. Anyway, I'm glad that you crossed my path, Sergeant Lewis.

But he didn't leave. He remained there, standing with an absent look, infecting me with his own nervousness.

I've never told anyone what I just told you, he finally said, and I don't regret it. I've just begun to uncover something that has been very deeply hidden. And now that I've started, there's no other way but to confess the whole truth. I need you to hear me out. Of course, I'm perfectly aware that I have no right to ask such a thing. The fact that both of us were in the Brigades doesn't give me any privileges, I know . . .

Pietri leaned on the table and asked me if, when my wife and I stopped at Castelfiorentino, we had visited the monastery of San Vivaldo. I shook my head, and he explained to me that it was southwest of the town, past the old village of Montaione in a densely wooded area.

Taking for granted that we would meet again the following day, he gave me driving directions and specified that he would be there at eight, before the heat became unbearable. There was a lot weighing on his conscience, he said, but he stressed that if I decided not to show up, he would understand. He didn't shake my hand before leaving. He simply walked to the opposite end of the square with a stumbling, uncertain step.

Back in the hotel, I couldn't sleep. What Pietri had begun to tell me had left me feeling disgusted, but I was sure I would go to the meeting. I read what the guidebook said about the villages of Certaldo, Montaione, and Castelfiorentino. You're a writer, so you'll appreciate the fact that Boccaccio spent the last thirteen years of his life in Certaldo, in a place known as Castello, which is said to be the setting for the *Decameron*. The history of Castelfiorentino also has its interesting points, but what most caught my attention was the description of the labyrinth of chapels erected in the vicinity of the monastery of San Vivaldo.

Early in the morning, I told Patrizia—in broad strokes—of my encounter the night before, and likewise that I had decided to get to the bottom of Pietri's story. I promised I would be back at the hotel for lunch. The trip was very short. I arrived at the grove of century-old cypresses where Pietri had said he would wait for me. I found him seated on a stone bench, next to the ruins of a wall whose arched window had a view of the entire valley. He was wearing a white shirt with the sleeves rolled up, black pants, and sandals.

Thank you for coming, Lewis, he said, when I came up to him—thank you very much. I wasn't sure you would show up.

That was all he managed to say, at first. After a moment or two, his face contracted violently, a wince of pain accompanied by a wave of nausea. Leaning on the ledge of the window, he retched violently, trying to vomit, but all he could get out was a thin string of reddish saliva. I tried to help him but he stopped me with a determined gesture. After a few minutes, he wiped his mouth with a handkerchief and, leaning on the column that divided the window in two, pointed to a spot in the valley.

I live in Certaldo, he said, but my work is in Castelfiorentino. You see that compound with a red-tiled roof near the bridge? The one with all the cars parked in front? That's my workshop.

When he felt he had the strength, he suggested we take a tour of the chapels. He pointed them out to me, telling me stories about each, but not going into any of them. Finally, we reached a wall covered in ivy, and he pulled apart some bushes, revealing an opening.

The whole area is full of hidden nooks like this. When we were kids, we came to play here a lot. Imagine—what could be more fascinating and mysterious for a child. I suppose I have some memory of each corner of this forest. It's a place charged with hidden meanings. Back then, of course, all the chapels were intact. When I came back to the woods of San Vivaldo after the war, half of them were in ruins. In a way, I was glad. The wounds of the stones reminded me of my own. Come, follow me.

The darkness inside was only pierced by whatever rays of light filtered through the many cracks. Umberto Pietri took out a flashlight and turned it on. He advanced cautiously, shining the light on the walls. Amid large bald spaces where the paint was flaking off were the vestiges of what seemed to be an old fresco. We were in front of the wall farthest from the entrance at the back of the chapel. Pietri swept the light of the flashlight over the painting.

The Tabernacle of the Condemned, he said. Can you see it, Lewis?

Large patches of faded colors dissolved in the space, becoming one with the darkness.

Whose is it?

It's a copy of a Benozzo Gozzoli. There are paintings by the master everywhere in the area. The original is in the Church of Santo Tomasso e Prospero in Certaldo. If you can, go see it with your wife—it's quite deteriorated, but it's still impressive.

He brought the light closer.

I painted it, he said. It took me years. It has no artistic merit whatsoever but I've always felt good about it. At home, I have many copies of masterpieces, but the *Tabernacle* is different. Normally I try to restore the perfection of the work as it was when it was first created, but in this case, my intention was to remain faithful to the decrepitude of the original.

Pietri went carefully over different parts of the fresco.

The faces of the condemned, almost intact, suggested their terrible torment. At mid torso, some of the figures in the *Tabernacle* began to lose their color. The lower parts in gray and rosy tones were reminiscent of tissue devoured by cancer. Pietri was right, the strange allure of the painting was the result of its decomposition.

When we returned to the garden, he summed up the story of the place.

Vivaldo was a hermitage founded by St. Gimignano. According to legend, he lived in the trunk of a hollow chestnut. One day they found him dead, still kneeling to pray. The Franciscans erected a monastery in his honor. Some two hundred years after his death, a friar decided to build a New Jerusalem in these hills. Thirty-four chapels representing passages in the Way of the Cross. So that the symbolic journey would be more real to the pilgrims, the insides of the chapels were decorated with frescoes of polychrome terracotta and other materials. Today, only half of the chapels are standing.

A long silence followed. Staring out into the valley, Pietri said:

I know it's just my imagination, but the view from here makes me think of Santa Quiteria. Often, when I can't sleep, I drive here in my pickup and it's as if I'm reliving that night.

[. . .]

We had been in the hermitage three or four days when we detected troop movements in the surrounding area. We organized a raid at dawn and took five fascist prisoners. Before we executed them, they confessed belonging to a contingent that was headed for Huesca. That night, I had guard duty with a comrade named Salerno, a Neapolitan who confessed to me he had forged his birth date to be able to enlist. He was seventeen, two years younger than me. We were alone on a bush-covered hill from which we could monitor several hundred meters of the surrounding terrain. Salerno was very nervous. He saw the enemy everywhere; any noise, the murmur of the river, the rustling of leaves, a gust of wind, made him think that fascists were bearing down on us. In the end, he made me nervous too. When the moon came out and a silvery glow spread over the trees, Salerno became even more anxious. It seemed to him that the bushes were alive. Then, after a couple of hours, we finally did hear a real sound. Crouched behind a boulder, we saw a column of rebels advancing through the bushes.

We had to alert the garrison, communicating with the nearest squad some two hundred meters below so they would in turn alert the following squad until the news reached the heart of the unit. This would prevent anyone from being taken by surprise and, if it was a large force approaching, reinforcements could still be called by radio. Salerno signaled to me that I should go to the post below while he tried to slow the enemy down from the rearguard. But there was only one thought in my mind, then: to save my own skin. I came up behind Salerno's back, covered his mouth, and slit his throat with a single slice of my bayonet. He struggled a bit, but I held him firmly until I was sure that it was over, then let him fall. I was bathed in blood. All those soft, barely perceptible night sounds we'd been hearing now became a roar a thousand times greater than any of Salerno's imagined threats. Still, I managed to control myself. The fleeting flashes that we'd glimpsed a few minutes before were still there, glinting among the bushes, getting closer: a buckle, a helmet, a belt. The fascist column advanced stealthily up a path that would allow it to reach the back of the hermitage without being detected. It was evident that they knew the territory. Perhaps a patrol such as the one we had surprised that morning had managed to explore the region around Santa Quiteria and return without being caught. Everything must have happened in a matter of minutes. I waited until they had passed, and when they were far enough away, I took a shortcut that led directly to the river. It wasn't long before I heard the explosion of grenades and the rattle of machine guns. They must have dropped like rabbits, but I was on the move away from there, safe and sound . . .

Pietri spoke to me from the other side of death, Lewis said.

He told me the memory of his actions had rotted inside him, had become a pus seeping into his soul for more than thirty years, more powerful and repugnant than the claws of the cancer now devouring his insides, he said. It's not that I have a good memory, Ackerman, it's that these words are difficult to forget. It all came down to a monstrous sort of paradox. Now that he had no way to avoid death, Umberto Pietri had at last been able to gather the courage he had always lacked in life.

I could barely make out Abraham Lewis's features, only the brilliance of his eyes, a feverish, diseased glow that compelled him to keep talking. That was the most unsettling thing—although, for me, Umberto Pietri had no face, his voice was there inside Lewis's, hidden in his monotone, repetitive diction, listing these atrocities dispassionately, an agonizing and endless litany. The words I was hearing hurt me, but I still clung to them. I was afraid, I guess, that Abe would stop talking. Let the world end, but in the meantime, let his deadpan voice go on tearing me to pieces. But only this once, so that afterward I could transcribe it all, as I'm doing now. I know that I will never go back over what I'm writing at this moment. Pietri's words will remain here, trapped in this notebook. After that, my memory will be clean. What I heard at the bar of the Hotel Florida must have been a hallucination, just a malignant dream that I need to set down exactly as it was, while it's still fresh. Trying to anchor myself in reality, I looked out those large windows with a view of the Madrid night. The gaslights of the Gran Vía floated outside, tempting me to flee, but I pulled my eyes away from them and looked at Abe, who was saying:

You can imagine the hell I've been living in, Lewis, the Italian told me. There's been no room in my life for anything else. It's a debt that cannot be repaid. When someone commits such an atrocity, no punishment is sufficient. But this is not the time for rhetoric. You're an intelligent man and you know that I don't expect your compassion or anyone else's. It's enough that you've listened to me. And he repeated that I was the only one he'd ever told, Lewis continued. He thanked me again for having come to see him. Now I really have nothing more to add, he said. You'd better go. And that was it—Pietri stopped talking. Another wave of nausea came over him but this time he was able to vomit.

He didn't last as long as he thought he would. Only three weeks later, the telegram he had said would come arrived in Sarzana. The text in faded blue ink, with capital letters printed on a narrow strip of white paper, said succinctly, in Italian: UMBERTO PIETRI DIED AUGUST 3 RIP. The signature was the initials C.P., which I imagined belonged to his wife. That very night I began to write to Ben Ackerman the letter you are now carrying in your pocket.

[The text continues on several folded pages that seem to have been ripped out of another notebook. Blots of ink make a good part of the first page illegible as well as a number of phrases throughout the remainder of the text. I've reconstructed the first paragraph as best I can.]

Abe Lewis insisted on calling me a cab, but I told him that I wanted to walk back to the boarding house. It was late and it was very cold but I was yearning to breathe the chilly air, to feel the coolness of a night after snowfall. I'd already fallen for this city to which, I was sure now, I would never return.

[After this the text is perfectly legible.]

We stood up at the same time. Lewis was much taller and stronger than I was. He opened his arms as wide as he could and hugged me tightly. He gave off a powerful smell, but I was glad of the affection he was offering. Putting his hands on my shoulder, he said in his low baritone voice:

There. Mission accomplished.

I told him that I needed to be alone for a moment and went out to one of the balconies overlooking the Gran Vía. I needed silence, no voices, no more stories; I needed to lose myself in my own head, to forget for a while who I was and why I was there. At eye level, I noted the idiosyncratic architecture, the fanciful cornices on which stood the statues of goddesses and warriors riding chariots drawn by mythological creatures. The veil of clouds had begun to tear, giving way to numerous clear patches. I looked up at the sky that had been continuously overcast since I arrived and witnessed a beautiful atmospheric effect: a gigantic halo behind the Telefónica Tower. A few minutes later, the only remaining traces of the storm were the dry cold air and the gusts of wind hissing through the Madrid fog, grazing an incomparable landscape of terraces and tiled roofs. The globe of the moon, clean and round, rose over an oriental-looking dome on the other side of the Gran Vía, spreading its rays over the skylights, the tiles, the spires and statues crowning the buildings of this strangely beautiful city. I closed my eyes, to see farther out, and I imagined the sierra under the canopy of night and, more distant still, the fields of Castile. I remembered what Ben's books said about that city founded by the Arabs: Magerit. I saw stories of palace intrigue and revolution. I don't think I can explain myself. Everything, not just this landscape of ghostly and aristocratic garrets, began to seem unreal.

I waited to calm down before I went back inside. Lewis was standing next to the dead chimney.

You all right? he asked when I returned to him.

I nodded.

Now that we've gotten all that behind us, I heard him say,

we can concentrate on lighter things. Tomorrow we'll go to the Prado. It's Ben's idea. You said you're staying near Atocha? Give me the exact address and I'll drop by to pick you up at eleven. Is that okay?

We took the elevator down to the lobby. Abe Lewis walked me to the entrance of the hotel and shook my hand without saying anything. I crossed to the other side of Montera Street and turned around. The black Brigade man was silhouetted against the canopy of the hotel. I swallowed him up with my eyes, trying to record his image forever.

[On the plane, right after taking off.]

I'd felt out of place, then, on the balcony of the Hotel Florida— banished from the coordinates of my own history, as if nothing of what I'd heard that night had anything to do with me. Madrid might as well have been the Baghdad of the *Arabian Nights*. I had arrived thanks to TWA, but I might as well have come in on a magic carpet. Who the hell was Umberto Pietri? What did he have to do with me? The people and places in Abraham Lewis's story paraded before me, no less unreal than the nocturnal view of the city, than the reflection of the lights on either side of that cosmopolitan and elegant avenue in southern Europe. No, I didn't feel bound to the history of that man who needed to get lost in a labyrinth of chapels beginning to atone for his disgrace. As for Abraham Lewis, I wasn't sure what to think of him. Ben had said that he was "a good man, his only real loyalty is to doing the right thing." But there was something strange, almost suspicious about him. Why had it been so necessary for him to tell me everything that Pietri had told him? But the question was moot; there was no turning the pages back. What he'd told me would always be with me.

[After a dozen crossed out lines, the following is legible

in thick and firm strokes.]

I woke up very early because of the time difference. I had an appointment with Abraham Lewis, but from the moment he'd suggested it, I knew I wouldn't be there. I picked up my luggage, paid the bill, and went out on the street. Near Atocha Station, I hailed a cab and told the driver to take me to Barajas Airport without even knowing when the next flight to New York was scheduled.

[...]

What to tell Ben?

The same thing I would tell Teresa, if she were alive—that is, anything but the truth. I will invent a heroic past for Umberto Pietri.

Or perhaps there's no point pretending, and I will tell him the truth.

Ten
DIALOGUE OF THE DEAD

June 1, 1992

I first confronted the raw pages of what would end up becoming *Brooklyn* on June 1st, a date with the greatest symbolic weight in Gal's secret calendar. I was browsing through used books at a street market on Court Street when I felt a tap on my shoulder.

I greeted him cheerfully, but his gloomy disposition made me change my attitude instantly.

Is something wrong, Gal?

I wanted to talk to you, and since it's Wednesday, I thought that maybe you'd come by Fuad's.

Sure enough, the days the street market sets up there, I like to drop by. Fuad is from Beirut, around sixty. He spent years in Panama, so he can find his way around in Spanish. In his stall, among the most disparate objects imaginable, there's always a box full of used books, and if you take the time to look through them, it's not uncommon to find some real surprises, beginning with the fact that a lot of the books are in Spanish. Gal had told me about Fuad's books soon after we met, and it wasn't unusual that we would run into each other at the Lebanese's stall. That day, I had just come across a Mexican edition of Valle-Inclán's *The Lamp of Marvels*, so old that the yellowish pages seemed as if they would crack simply by being turned. I was going to show my find to Gal when he grabbed my sleeve and asked with unusual seriousness:

You know what today is?

I had to think about it for a second.

June first, why?

Don't you get it?

Get what?

It's Nadia's birthday.

Nadia's birthday?

Well, I guess there's no reason you should have known that. The thing is, I've decided to surprise her by calling her to wish her happy birthday.

I didn't reply. It'd been four years since anyone had heard from Nadia. She had disappeared without a trace.

I'm serious. I'm going to call her.

Call her where?

Vegas.

Vegas, I repeated.

Not knowing what else to say, I handed him the book and pretended to continue to explore the contents of the box.

After her disappearance, Nadia had been silent for a few months, after which a letter arrived at the Oakland. Gal had thought it was a one-time thing, but a few weeks later a second letter arrived and others soon followed. At the beginning, she wrote sporadically, but after a year, she began to do it more regularly, once and even twice a month. There was never a return address, so Gal couldn't respond to or send the letters back. But thanks to them at least he knew that Nadia was still alive and thinking of him, that she needed him, as he told me once. Toward the end of the second year, the time between letters began to grow longer, until they stopped coming altogether. The last time she had written was early in 1987, a letter accompanied by a postcard from Vegas. After that, there had been no news of her.

How do you know she's still in Vegas? I asked, my back still to Gal. I turned to face him when it became clear he wasn't going to answer me.

He was leafing through the Valle-Inclán. I saw that he didn't want to talk, so I didn't push it. Nadia's silence had become an enigma that infected every inch of the Oakland, Frank had told me. He said that he had even gone so far as to hire a detective, not only because he'd never seen Gal so down, but also because he was rather intrigued by the situation himself. It was a futile gesture for which he was shaken down to the tune of three thousand dollars. I thought of Queensberry's report when Gal had hired him. If he were to hire him now, Queensberry would just need four words to complete his report: *erased from the map*. But it wasn't that it seemed out of the question to me that Nadia might have finally given Gal some sign of life after so many years. On the contrary, such sudden, crazy reverses suited her character. If I was certain that Gal hadn't heard from her, it was because I knew that if he had, his reaction would have been markedly different from what I was seeing. So I didn't know where all this was coming from. Obviously, it was all in his head.

Carefully, he closed the copy of *The Lamp of Marvels* and studied the cover.

Not bad.

You like it? I'll buy it for you.

You don't believe me, do you? You think I'm delirious or something. He put the book back in the box. Well, you're wrong. You're absolutely wrong. All of you are wrong. You think it's been ages since I last heard from her, but you're mistaken. I have an infallible way of communicating with her, not that I expect for you or anyone else to know it. That's right . . . an infallible means of communication . . . with Nadia and with . . . the others, with all the rest of them. You don't know a thing about it, none of you.

I noticed a hardness in the depths of his eyes; it was new to me, and I didn't know what to make of it.

Gal, I wish I could stay and chat, but Dylan called a staff meeting today and I can't be late. I can meet you later at the Oakland, if you're planning to be there.

That's what I wanted to talk to you about. I can't be there this afternoon, but if you're going, I want to ask you a favor.

Of course, what?

He pulled out a green folder.

Will you give this to Frank, or to whoever is working there today? I'll pick it up when I get back.

Fine.

Ness . . .

Yeah?

If you want . . . Well, that's some of my writing there . . . You understand, being a writer yourself.

Don't you worry, it's in good hands.

He just stood there. He wasn't done yet.

It's not that. I just wanted to tell you that . . . Well, only if you want to, of course, but perhaps you could take a look at it? If you want to understand—to understand me, anyway—that's probably the best way.

I stared him down, trying to catch sight of any ulterior motive, but if it was there, I missed it.

When I had the folder in my hands, he thanked me and headed toward Montague Street.

I was dazed. What did it mean? What was Gal Ackerman after, trusting his writing to me? Was this a test? Or maybe . . . I had the feeling that he'd given me something more than just a bunch of papers. I pushed those thoughts away, reached into the box of books, and rescued the catch of the day. When I went up to Fuad, he put his hand on his heart and greeted me warmly in Spanish.

So good, *habibi*, he said, casting a fleeting glance at the book. What happen to our good old Gal? Where he go in such a hurry?

I shrugged and asked him how much he wanted for *The Lamp of Marvels.*

Good stuff, very ancient, he said caressing the cover. For you, only a dollar, *habibi.*

I didn't think about Gal's papers again for a few hours. The meeting Dylan Taylor had called was rather short. I went back to my cubicle and began to type out a rather long article I had written in longhand. When I do this kind of work, I'm on automatic pilot, and I let my imagination go wherever it wants. I was just about finished when the midday light flooded through the skylight above my desk. I reread the closing paragraphs quickly and turned in the article. As if he'd somehow been spying on me from his office, the minute I finished, Dylan opened the glass door and peeked in.

What now? How about some lunch?

I glanced at the green folder on my desk.

I'll stay in today. I need to have a look at something. Would you mind bringing me a sandwich, any type?

I gave him a five-dollar bill.

Okay, doc, Dylan said, taking the money and heading out.

The light that had been coming in from above began to move away. I pulled off the rubber bands, opened the folder, and exclaimed:

All right, Gal, let's see if I can understand you!

Inside were three thin plastic folders of different colors. I smiled. Although most likely there was no logic whatsoever behind it, it seemed to me that Gal was using some secret, personal code, a system of color variations, using pencils and different kinds of ink to make corrections, just as there seemed to be some sort of meaning behind the colors of the notebooks and folders. I spread out the three folders. One was blue, the other yellow, and the third transparent. On the first one, there was a label that read:

DEATH NOTEBOOK

I began to read.

April 29, 1991
Grand Army Plaza
So many things happen in New York on a single day that it's impossible to register even an infinitesimal part of it in these notebooks. Should I play Todd Andrews and transform the floating opera of life into a sheaf of pages, adrift? There's no need to force the imagination, it's enough to flip through a newspaper. I've spent the morning at the public library in Grand Army Plaza, looking through the day's papers. I found the piece of news first in the *Post*, then I read it in the others. They all stick to relating the events with the same rigor. The only thing that changes is the style. After careful consideration, I chose the *Times*.

Right after that, a note says "based on an article by G.J." followed by a version in ballpoint pen of a newspaper article:

IN TRASH, A BRIEF LIFE
AND A NOTE OF LOVE

At 1:30 P.M. on Monday, April 29, a phone call came into the 83rd precinct in Brooklyn reporting the body of a newborn found in a garbage dump in Bushwick. The call came in from a phone booth in front of 12 Cornelia Street, a three-story building. Lt. Nicholas J. Deluise, the chief detective in the precinct, immediately sent

Officers Kenneth Payumo and Maureen Smith to the scene. The officers reported finding a yellow plastic bag containing the remains of a newborn baby girl wearing flower-print pajamas and a diaper, and wrapped in white cloth, to which a note was pinned. "The baby was neatly wrapped, very neatly wrapped," Officer Payumo said. "It was immaculate as a matter of fact."

"Unfortunately, we get a lot of calls like this," Lt. Deluise commented.

What Gal labeled "version" was his own transcription of the story he had read in the *Times*, which he had edited slightly. The original clipping wasn't in the folder, although he'd cut out and preserved a picture of the note that had been pinned to the blanket used to wrap the child. Gal had taped the picture right below his version of the article:

> Please Take Care of my Daughter.
> She was Born on April 26, 1991 at
> 12:42 pm. Her Name is April Olivia
> I Love Her very much
> Thank You

> She Died at 10:30 am
> On April 29, 1991
> I'm sorry.

In the second folder there was a sort of sketch of the area Gal called the Shipyard at the Brooklyn piers. Looking at it brought back memories of the time I'd been there with him. In the margins of the paper, outside the perimeter of the Shipyard there were some names I recognized: Atlantic Avenue, Luna Bowl, the Oakland. An arrow originating from the first name pointed directly to the middle of the avenue and next to each of the other two names, there was a cross, penciled in blue, from which there emerged a second and third arrow pointing to two buildings on the map. I noted too that there were places Gal had singled out within the boundaries of what he called the Shipyard: the names sounded familiar from Gal's conversation, although I wasn't quite sure what they meant to him. I read the words many times over, as if they held some hidden meaning: Dry Dock, Round Tower, Water Tank. Elsewhere on the page, Gal had written the words "temple" and "altar." There were five or six spots labeled in this way, scattered around the Shipyard. There was also a series of dotted lines, the meaning of which I was unable to decipher: some of these joined together different places marked on the map, while others seemed to float in space, where nothing had been written. Lower down on the page was a date: June 1, 1989. So the map of the Shipyard was two years old. Before putting it away, I studied the sketch at length, and as I did, I began to remember more and more clearly details from the one time I had gone to the piers with Gal. His imaginary geography wasn't entirely foreign to me. The temples, the altars . . . I had been there with Gal. He had shown me those places, explaining what they meant. I had stood before those mounds he had decorated so strangely, and I had climbed the steps of the decrepit, yellowish brick building that he had named the Temple of Time . . .

In the third folder was a carbon copy of a letter from Nadia that Gal had typed up with great care. As is the case with the letter that Abe Lewis wrote to Ben Ackerman, letting him know about his encounter with Pietri, I have not been able to find the original manuscript or typescript.

January 20, 1980

Dear Gal,

I'm writing from Coney Island to tell you that there's something wrong with me, and I don't know what it is. I feel like crying but I can't. Remember when I told you that sometimes when I'm in this kind of mood, I see images of the sea that seem to be coming to my rescue? You used to laugh, but that's exactly how I feel now. A little while ago, I heard a tiny, weak voice—it was hard to make it out. No, it's not one of my episodes; let me tell you. It was me, my own voice when I was a little girl in Laryat. You have to believe me. I made a test. I closed my eyes and I could see everything as it was back then: an opaline sky and a lake. No, it's not in Laryat and it's not a lake. It's the sea and I am four years old, because that was my age when we came to America. On the beach road there's Dad's blue Mustang, and it's Nantucket, because that's where we spent our first summer. Sasha is not with us. I don't know why. My parents are very young, younger than I am now. The very idea of that makes me uneasy, but let me go on with my memory. I see father's masculine, athletic body; he's wearing a black, tight-fitting bathing suit with a white stripe on each side. He comes up to me smiling, lifts me in the air, and gives me a kiss. My mother is sitting on a towel. She's wearing sunglasses and is smearing a white lotion on her legs. Gal, do you think it's possible for me to remember things from when I was four years old in such detail?

My father puts me back on my towel. He darts off toward the shore, runs into the water, and when it reaches his hips he dives in without a splash and my mother returns to her book. The crests of the waves move in an orderly fashion, forming hollows in which the figure of my father surfaces and submerges. I can't take my eyes off the tiny dot of his bobbing head, which looks smaller each time till it disappears. I panic at the thought that he may not come back, that the sea has swallowed him. I look at my mother, but she doesn't seem the least bit alarmed. Although she must have noticed something, because she takes off her sunglasses and smiles at me, as if to say I shouldn't worry. I have a picture of her on that same beach. She's looking at the camera holding her sunglasses in one hand, wearing the same bathing suit, a floral print with anemones that contrasts against her tan skin. Her toenails are painted a very bright red, a red I can see now in all its vividness even though the picture is in black and white.

Papa hasn't drowned, his head resurfaces; I see his arms flashing rhythmically as they go in and out of the water—a wake of foam trailing behind him. When I see him swim back, getting closer and closer to the shore, I scream with joy. Unable to control myself, I run up to meet him, and he takes me in his arms. The water is freezing and I get the chills, but I love it. He walks up to my mother, who puts her book in the straw bag next to her and gets up. From this moment on, she's the only living thing in the entire universe to me. She puts on her swim cap, gathers her hair and tucks it in, leaving only the soft hairs at the back of her neck visible, and fastens the rubber strap under her chin.

She does things differently from my father. She doesn't plunge; she walks into the sea and when the water covers her knees, she crouches, splatters her shoulders and chest carefully, then goes on until she can't touch bottom. She's an elegant, delicate swimmer. And she doesn't stray from the shore but glides parallel to it. And I'm never, ever afraid that she will drown, not only because she's always careful enough to stay within sight, for my sake, but especially because, knowing that I'm watching her, every now and then she stops to wave at me.

Papa isn't much of a reader, so he always comes up with something else to do with me. He takes me by the hand and tells me stories about everything around us. I loved hearing his explanations, always so detailed, and the way he pronounced certain words, whose meaning only he knew. He made me repeat them till I'd learned them by heart. There were a lot of them. Remember I used to recite them to you? The rocks on the breakwater were *tetrapods*. One word that I couldn't pronounce without cracking up was *coelenterate*. I can't tell you how much I loved those walks, which my father called "verbal hunting expeditions." Our games ended when my mother began to swim toward the shore and we went to wait for her.

Once, shortly after one of our games, while the three of us were sitting on the sand, we saw a disturbance way out in the water. My father explained to me that it was a school of dolphins. A few days later, on the ferry, the waters by the side of the boat began to swirl. We leaned over the railing and I asked my mother whether it was sharks, and she laughed and said no. No, Nadj, my love, they are dolphins, just like the ones we saw on the beach. Don't you remember? She said it in a way that made it obvious she cared very much about them. You really like them, don't you, Mama? She said she did. And when I asked her why, she said, Because they are just like you, Nadj: they're little kids. Dolphins have the souls of children. And Papa explained to us that the reason why humans were always cheered up by the sight of them was the fact that they laughed, even though we couldn't hear it. The dolphins remained with us for a good while, on that trip, as if they were interested in what we were saying.

One day, taking a stroll at the Boston seaport, I saw one up close. It was dead, with its mouth open—very small. It made me feel so sad because it was just a baby. I asked my mother what made men kill such innocent creatures. She explained to me that they didn't do it on purpose—the dolphins became tangled in fishing nets. It wasn't enough, though, that explanation—I went on thinking that the fishermen must have been killing them on purpose.

It's so strange being in the Brighton Beach apartment without you. When I came in, many memories came rushing back, most of them of you. It's been years since I was here. The place is mostly empty. Zadie got married and is going to sell it. You don't know how much that saddens me. I want to see you so badly, have you here, next to me, but not quite yet. I need to be alone for a while, get used to the pain of the loss. I know exactly what's wrong with me. The irony of it is that it's you of all people that I need to tell. It's not fair, but I can't help it: Gal, I've had another miscarriage. Not again, please, I said, and went to the gynecologist, who explained to me that the likelihood of my carrying a child to term was getting smaller every time. I thought I'd die from the grief, at first. I've heard people say that drowning is an especially agonizing way to die, but I find that hard to believe; on the contrary, I imagine it must be a very sweet death compared to this, going numb bit by bit until you're gone. Forgive me, Gal, I'm talking nonsense but I don't know what else to do to relieve my suffering. And I have a good reason to suffer. I most likely will never be able to bear children.

There are chance occurrences that I don't know how to interpret. I guess they mean nothing. Coincidences, that's all. The day I went to the clinic was my twenty-ninth birthday. It seems impossible. Where has the time gone? You turn a corner and you're old. Look at my mother, sixty-one years old already; it seems inconceivable to me that she's lost that stunning beauty that once turned heads. In the mornings, when I get out of the shower, I look at my body, check up on the damage, the ravages of time on my face, the wrinkles around my eyes, my lips; nobody else can see them, they're too subtle, but I know they are there. I'm not complaining—it's not that. The truth is

I don't mind getting old. It's inevitable, so it makes no sense to try to pretend it's not happening. But above all, Gal, I don't mind getting old because I am not afraid of what's in store for me. I've lost all hope. I'm trying not to deceive myself. I'm approaching the future as if it were the edge of a cliff. There's nothing out there waiting for me, in the void. Sometimes I find beauty in moments, places, or people. But I'm not capable of holding on to anything, of risking it all for someone, Gal. You know that better than anyone. No one knows me like you do. Something in me keeps me searching, even though I couldn't tell you for what. Is that why I wanted to have a son, I mean, a daughter? Or was it just a whim, something irrational, inexplicable? Maybe it was just Nature, although of course I know women who would shudder at the idea of having kids. A child, Gal, a daughter. I guess I'll have to resign myself to the fact it won't happen. That's why I'm satisfied with the smallness of certain moments. Beauty is just about the only thing that comforts me, although often it's tinted by sadness. You know, the world is full of people who know what they want. They'll do anything to get it. But me, I just don't know, I've never known what I really want. I don't try to impose my will on the world: I accept things as I find them. And if I can ever manage for a moment to peek behind the veils that hide their true nature, sometimes a little miracle happens, an instant of real peace or beauty. We should be happy with that. In the end, that may be what it means to get old. It's like autumn, a prelude to the death of things. Like snow, like fire. Things that are simply beautiful. But for me they are also sorrowful—I can't help it. I write all this thinking that one day you will read it. As I write it, I feel that my ideas become clearer and I understand things better. When I was with you, I could never talk to you this way: it's not possible when someone is so close to you. When there's so little space between us, all we can do is to understand each other through our bodies. You told me that. If I had you here, I would like to touch you, to bite you, sweetly or in anger. That's what happens when desire takes over. As it is, so far away, while night falls, I'm writing words that, when we were together, didn't know how to be born on their own. They rush toward me now, here, and here I leave them for your eyes only.

Let me make a confession, Gal. All of a sudden, I stopped writing, just for a moment. I needed to speak to you, hear your voice, so I went to the phone, and without lifting it off the hook, I dialed the number of the Oakland . . . several times. Each time I did it, I said to myself: what if I call him for real? Only to remind myself that it can't be. I let the dial rotate back one last time and when it came to rest, I went back to this letter. I mean, let's suppose that it's a real one, even though I'll probably never send it. You know, in the clinic, when I came to, I spoke Russian for a while with the nurse who was attending me. She was Ukrainian, from Kiev, and her name was Inna. I asked her about the gender of my unborn child. She gave me a reproachful look for asking something that we both already knew. I was seven weeks pregnant. But when she saw me cry, she said it was a girl. I asked, What do they do with it? She turned around indignantly and walked out. But, really, Gal, what do they do? What is it that they do with these unborn children? Something horrible I once heard came into my head: they use them to make cosmetics. Their tissues are so delicate that they're perfect to make products to help people look young. It was a girl. When they told me, I remembered how you said once that one day we would have a baby girl and we would call her Brooklyn. Brooklyn, imagine that. Sorry, sorry. How strange it is to need to talk to you so badly when I know that you can't hear me. How strange that this is the only way I can talk to you. Now I'm positive that the best thing would be not to send you this letter in which I'm just jotting down my wandering thoughts. I probably won't. I know it wouldn't mean the same thing to you. It would make a big difference to you, yes, but most likely I won't. At any rate, whether I send it or not, it's already done me good. It's enough for me to know that you are there. I feel that if I put my thoughts down on paper, they'll somehow get to you no matter what. I can even hear your voice, soothing me, telling me that everything is fine, saying I should go to sleep. You always told me I was very fragile, but that's where you were wrong. I'm actually very strong. As a matter of fact, you've always been the weak one. Weaker than me. I'll leave you now because I'm very tired. I've taken a pill and I don't know what I'm writing anymore.

A kiss from your

Nadj

After reading Nadia's letter, there was a riot of conflicting memories in my head. I put the folder away, feeling almost feverish, as if this action could shut it all away—the story of April Olivia, the scenes evoked by the map of the Shipyard, today's date, and now Nadia's words, which brought her to life for me for the first time as someone real, not just some ghostly projection of Gal's imagination. All of it filled me with dread. I had a premonition that, though vague, didn't presage anything good.

Dylan stuck his head inside my cubicle, making me return to reality.

I brought you the special of the day. Here's your change.

Thanks, Dylan. Listen, something's come up. I have to go.

What about the sandwich?

I'm not hungry anymore.

And the article?

Typed up. I edited the ending a bit, though.

Non ti preocupare de niente . . . I'll take care of it. But hey, you seem upset. Did something happen? Are you all right?

Yeah, I'm fine. It's Gal.

Something happen to him?

I don't think so, I don't know. Enough questions, Dylan. I'll explain everything tomorrow.

You got it, boss. My apologies . . . He was going to add something, but I rushed past him down to the lobby.

Outside, I practically threw myself in front of a cab. When it stopped, I barked at the driver to take me to Brooklyn Heights.

Frank was at the bar, chatting with Víctor Báez.

I blurted out everything about my run-in with Gal that morning at Fuad's place. Frank listened attentively and, when I was finished, raised his right hand urging me to calm down, and told his assistant to call the Luna Bowl. Infected by my nervousness, Víctor rushed to the phone booth by the jukebox.

Spoke to Jimmy, he said as soon as he hung up. He's got his eyes peeled too. It seems that old man Cletus told him he had seen Gal wandering around near the gym in the afternoon, although he never went near the door. According to Cletus, he seemed very upset. He went up to him to make sure he was all right, but Gal ignored him and went off toward the piers. He was making weird gestures. Cletus says he saw him trip a couple of times and almost fall.

Frank took off his cap and scratched his head.

What's today's date, Ness?

June first.

Damn, of course. How could I forget?

This is the folder he asked me to give to you, I said. He insisted I look inside. Everything has to do with Nadia, today's date, and the piers.

I gave him the folder. Frank handed it to Víctor with a thoughtful expression.

Put it in my office, please.

[Copied from my diary, August 6, 1989. Notes toward a pastiche of Gal's style.]

"On How Néstor Oliver-Chapman Heard about the Shipyard for the First Time."
(A Very Brief Account)

One morning the police showed up unexpectedly at the Oakland. Apparently, some teenagers who had been messing around shooting at rats with pellet guns around the garbage dumps near the Dry Dock had found a man passed out near one of the piers. The closest thing to an ID that they had found on him was the Oakland's business card, with Frank's name. That's why they had come.

Frank's voice:

They were two tall guys, one dark-skinned, Italian-looking, and the other one was this big kid, with a very wide handlebar mustache, blond hair, and blue eyes—Irish, apparently, from the nametag: MacCarthy. The Irish cop's belt was more than a little lopsided, so he reached down to hoist it up and told me they had just come from the piers. An ambulance had taken the unidentified man to Long Island College Hospital. The business card they had found on him . . .

Frank interrupted to tell him he knew exactly who the man was and gave the copy all the pertinent information: his name, that he lived in a studio Frank had rented him since '85, that he spent long periods of time away from said studio . . . (the Irishman jotted everything down in a notebook) . . . A writer, proofreader, translator, all that shit. Of course, I told him that I would take charge of him, and Officer MacCarthy offered to take me to the hospital in his patrol car.

I went, of course.

Acute alcohol poisoning.

No, Ness, it wasn't the first time that they'd found him unconscious like that, although it was the first time that it happened in the Shipyard.

Maybe I should just go look around the piers. He has to be there, don't you think, Frank?

No doubt—the question is, in what state? I don't know if you should go alone. He took a drag from his cigar and put it back in the ashtray.

If he's back at it, you're going to need help. But let's not get ahead of ourselves, there's no reason to think anything bad's happened. Let's do this: since it's still early, you head over first. I'll give you till it starts to get dark. If we haven't heard from you by then, I'll send the guys in.

Who?

Boy and Orlando. You know them. The boxers who come to play pool almost every afternoon.

Right. Okay, perfect, Frankie.

Ten minutes later, I was in front of Jimmy Castellano's gym. Cletus wasn't at the ticket booth, but I didn't need him. What Jimmy had told Víctor was all I needed to know. Before going down, I looked toward the Shipyard for a few moments. There was a good view of it from the front door of the Luna Bowl. In truth, it's just a succession of vacant lots scattered with filth, transfigured by Gal's imagination. By the position of the sun, I estimated there were around two hours of daylight left. I wasn't exactly sure where to begin my search. The day he took me to visit his domain, we had also started at the door of the gym. I tried to retrace our steps, but it was difficult because there are no landmarks by the piers, the empty lots just repeat with no paths except for the ones that Gal said he saw. The only changes in the landscape were due to the evolution of its various junk piles—

what had been left behind and what had been taken. From our previous foray, the place that stuck most distinctly in my memory was a yellow brick house atop a concrete platform surrounded by an iron fence. It looked like a small, abandoned warehouse. There was a porch out front that extended over the concrete platform. The façade looked out onto the water and had a frontispiece that gave the building a vaguely Greek air. Gal always called it the Temple of Time.

I looked for the places that Gal had named on the map. Leading off the piers, there are cement ramps that sink down into the dirty water. It's been years since any of them have been used. On Gal's Dry Dock, there are no ship hulls to repair, only the sparse weeds that grow in between the remains of a metal fence. What Gal calls the Water Tank is a huge cylinder of cracked wood on which seagulls perch. The Round Tower is a gray structure whose windows are sealed with rotted planks.

The outer limit of the Shipyard is marked by a toppled barbed wire fence lying on the ground. The only things left standing were the cement posts that had once held it up. I crossed the street and went in, pushing aside some bushes that had grown on the edge of the sidewalk, then began to walk down the side of a hill. Something was in the air, I couldn't say exactly what; it felt as though I really had entered a parallel world. As I approached the middle of a hollow in which there were a bunch of rusty barrels, I remembered the afternoon when I had been there with Gal. I felt something crunch under my feet and saw that it was the skull of a seagull. Two other very large ones with dirty white feathers flew past me, perched on one of the barrels, then took off letting out strident caws. When the birds were gone, it seemed to me that I could hear Gal's voice in the distance. I thought I could make out his drunken screams, echoing and distorted, disembodied, coming from nowhere in particular, and I thought about what he said, that the rules are different in this place, that strange things can happen here, things that aren't necessarily possible in the familiar world.

Everything is here, Ness, everything, he had told me then. All the shit and some things that aren't shit. The good and the bad, and above all, my people. We're surrounded by presences. Don't you sense them? Here, sometimes—not always, it's not wholly dependent on me—I have been able to speak with Teresa, but it's not easy you know, sometimes it's not very clear. But it doesn't matter. I know it's her and that she's speaking to me and that's all that matters. Same with Nadia. I can hear her much better because she's still here, so to speak, while Teresa, Teresa died giving birth to me, you know? We always take a little bit away with us—from things, from places, from others. There are fragments, shreds of other beings that remain stuck in us like splinters. And it hurts, it hurts a lot, like right now. But that's not what's most important, what's important is that they're here now. I can hear their voices, I hear them all the time, how they talk, what they say, or shriek, if they shriek. Don't you hear anything? It's important to listen—that way you know what's happening to them, what they're feeling, whether they regret things, resent the way their lives went. Did you know that they sing, sometimes? Crows, seagulls, mermaids. Here they are, I have their screams here. Look at them, take a good look at them. Do you see them or not? All of them are here, men and women, no one's missing. There are also people I don't know. I see faces, shadows. But I can't tell you their names, because they're listening to us and they might not like it. Sometimes they gather behind that wall. They need the support of something material to hold on to. Don't turn around now, just keep on talking as if nothing's going on. Nadia is right across there. She's staring at me and apologizing. She's changed a lot, but that's normal after such a long time. It's even hard for me to recognize her voice—it's not the same voice that I remember. Then there are the spiders and the iguanas scurrying around me and laughing and calling my name: Gal, they say, hey, look at that! Hey, Gal! These last words he screamed. Then he went quiet. He was shaking, and his forehead was covered in sweat.

Seeing him so delirious, I said: Let's go, Gal—trying not to hurt his feelings. Don't you see there's nothing here? Just old tires, used condoms, empty crack vials, weeds, and seagull bones. Or don't you see that? Please, Gal, let's get out of here.

Don't you ever say anything like that again. You hear me, you fucker? If you don't understand it, fine. No one has to understand it. But don't you dare say there's nothing here. The thing is, you don't see it, you can't see it because you have no faith. I shouldn't have invited you. You shouldn't be here. You have no right. This has nothing to do with you. We're approaching the Temple of Time, there! Do you believe me now? A temple facing the sea, that dirty, oily sea, all we have left of the wine-dark Hellespont. They know and that's why they come. How is it possible that you can't feel that they're here? And you know why they come? To talk to me. That's why I've erected these mounds and altars, to summon them, and they have heard my call, they know, they all come, Ness. All of them. The dead and those who are not yet dead, like her. This is a good place, I like it. Soon I will die, but before that happens . . . Never mind. The important thing is that I can call up anyone I want, Teresa Quintana, my grandfather David, even Umberto Pietri, whom I never got to meet. You know who they are, right? Do you or don't you? I haven't told you about them yet? I will soon. They're my ghosts for now, but soon they will be yours. Even little Brooklyn, the girl Nadia was never able to have. Did you know that we were going to have a baby girl and call her Brooklyn? How do you like that name for a girl, Ness? Ness . . .

I felt utterly confused and out of place, as if I had been in fact transported to that distant afternoon. I could hear Gal's words, or so I thought, as if he were actually speaking them at that very moment. I had to make an effort not to lose my bearings completely. The echoes of Gal's deranged screams were still floating in my head when I spotted him. Just as I had suspected, he was at the Temple of Time, in front of the main altar, where he had set countless empty bottles of all shapes and sizes. As he put them in place, he counted them, solemnly reciting each number. Every once in a while he made a mistake and started over again, like a child learning his numbers. There was something about that ridiculous ceremony that inspired respect. Somehow, Gal sensed he was being watched and so turned around and said hello. He was calm. When I reached the foot of the steps, he turned to me as if we'd been together all afternoon and I was just returning from some errand he had sent me on. He considered the rows of bottles with an expression of great concentration, as if he were making a very complex calculation or trying to decide if he was satisfied with the décor—he'd stuck sundry weeds into some of the bottles, as if making a floral arrangement. Everything must have been as he wanted, for he sat on the steps and tapped the spot beside him, gesturing for me to sit by him.

One day, he said, Nadia came to the studio in a very good mood and told me she had a gift for me. It was supposed to be a surprise, although you didn't have to be a genius to figure out what it was. The silver wrapping paper had the shape of a bottle. It was held together with a blue ribbon. When I opened it, I saw that it was a small bottle filled with a violet-colored liquid. *Parfait Amour*, said the label. I picked it because of the name, she said, because a perfect love is something that cannot possibly exist, but if it did, it would be reserved for us. All very like her. Wordplay aside, though, I have to say the stuff was pretty disgusting—I almost threw up—but the thought was nice, and we drank it together. Nadia loved the slop. Since she barely drank, she preferred her liquor on the sweet side. We started giggling. I don't know if the name had something to do with it—it never occurred to me that it could be an aphrodisiac, somehow, but the fact is that we started making love like teenagers. Can you imagine drinking almost a liter of *Parfait Amour*, straight up, without ice or anything? No fucking way I'll ever touch it again. But, will wonders never cease, there are people out there who actually enjoy it. The proof is that I found an empty bottle out here. I've put it up on the altar, right in the middle. Do you see it?

He pulled out a pint of the cheap vodka he liked to drink from the pocket of his jacket. It was almost full, but he drank it down in one long slow gulp. When he finished, he stood up, took a deep breath, and exhaled violently. Almost immediately, he was overcome with a spasm. I went to help him, but he pushed me away, brought his hands to his stomach, and puked out the liquid he had just swallowed. When his stomach was empty he went up to the altar, stumbling, gnashing his teeth, and taking in big gulps of air. He went rigid then, lost his balance, and fell on the altar of bottles, as if a sniper had gunned him down.

That's when the sun began to set. I felt an intense panic that couldn't have been mine alone but must have come from him as well; it permeated the atmosphere. I didn't know what to do. I put a hand on the back of my fallen friend as if that could ease his suffering, and in the paralysis of the late afternoon, I couldn't help but contemplate the extraordinary beauty of the twilight casting a curtain of red and yellow fire onto the clouds floating over New Jersey and the Hudson. I looked one last time at the burial-mound made of bottles, half of them now scattered all over the temple, and picked Gal up as best I could, carrying him over my shoulder. He was heavy, so when we made it to the barrels, I stopped to rest.

Voices came from the top of the hill. Two figures descended toward us: Boy and Orlando. They came up to me, grabbed Gal's body and easily carried it away, laughing. To them, Gal might as well have been weightless. I told them they had to take him to the Oakland. That's where we came from, they said. Frank sent us. He said it was urgent and didn't even let us finish a single game of pool.

Víctor was waiting for us at the door. When Frank saw Orlando and Boy come in bearing Gal on their shoulders, he made a face that was difficult to interpret. The boxers asked him what he wanted them to do with the sack, still laughing. Frank told them to take Gal into his office, where they dropped him on the sofa. The boxers asked Nélida for sodas when they came out. Frank served them, also giving each a twenty dollar bill. He looked at me for a moment and then went to the back and returned with a blanket. He was going to put it over Gal, then changed his mind.

Why don't we just take him up to his room? Have you ever been upstairs?

I told him I hadn't.

More sacred ground. But in a different way.

Víctor took Gal upstairs without the slightest difficulty. Nélida opened the door with the master key. Everyone went into the studio, but I didn't dare cross the threshold. I saw a window with the shutters open; on top of a table was a typewriter, paper, and a pile of books. Frank set the green folder there.

Once we were all back below, he insisted I have a drink, but it was impossible for me to stay in the Oakland even a second longer.

I appreciate it, Frank, but I need to get some rest. It's been a very intense day. I'll see you tomorrow. You think Gal will be okay?

The *gallego* took off his cap and scratched his head.

Don't worry about him, Néstor. None of this is new. Tomorrow, when he wakes up, he'll say he doesn't remember anything. Frank tapped me on the shoulder, saying good-bye, and added, No, he won't say that, if I know him. He won't say anything at all.

Eleven
CONEY ISLAND

When I was a boy, our world ended at Coney Island. That beach on the outer reaches of Brooklyn was our *Finis Terrae*. Everything began in the summer of 1947. David sent the publisher of his newspaper a handful of articles and the guy liked them so much that the next day he offered him a weekly column. It wasn't the first time that he'd published something, but this was different. He'd been working at the *Brooklyn Eagle* for more than thirty years, then—had done all kinds of jobs there before being promoted to head typesetter, but his secret dream had always been to write. He told us the news on my birthday, when the whole family was gathered. He said that he wanted to bring the hundreds of stories hidden in the many neighborhoods of Brooklyn to life. What he had sent the publisher was only a sampling—he had a lot more where that came from. Since there was so much to tell, he would write a series of articles about each neighborhood, beginning with Coney Island. After saying this, he put a hand on my shoulder and told my parents: I need a good field assistant. Grandma May went into the kitchen and returned with a raspberry tart adorned with ten flaming candles.

The trips began on the first day of summer vacation. My job basically consisted of keeping him company, listening to him, and occasionally jotting down instructions in a notebook whose only function was, I now realize, to give me something to do. At his house, David had a file cabinet in which he kept the material relating to each neighborhood. He never called them by their real names. Coney Island was the "Haven of Dreams"; Brooklyn Heights, an "elegant and stately enclave of writers." Did you know, Iacchus, he asked me once (I'll explain the origin of my nickname later), it was there that the first edition of *Leaves of Grass* was published? He showed me a copy signed and dedicated by Whitman himself. "For David Ackermann [sic], Cordially, your friend," and, below, the impeccable signature of the poet. When we went to Red Hook ("volatile and phantasmagoric, full of mysterious taverns, riddled with side streets paved with blackened cobblestones"), he loved to stroll through the port. He couldn't mention East New York without adding "sordid and bloody," nor Brownsville without repeating for the umpteenth time that it was the "frightful theater of operations of Murder, Inc." He was fascinated by the stories about that band of criminals, to which gangsters of the caliber of Lucky Luciano, Meyer Lansky, and Frank Costello had belonged. More neighborhoods. Williamsburg was never simply Williamsburg but "motley Williamsburg." Ineluctably, an explanation would follow. Like "the neighborhood's packed with innumerable different peoples and cultures—to give just one example, there are twenty different sects of Hasidic Jew within a few square miles," and so on and so forth. He usually concluded his stories with some solemn aphorism. My favorite was this one: "In one word, each neighborhood is a world unto itself, and Brooklyn the whole universe." We didn't agree on everything, of course. He had his preferences and I had mine, but there was one thing on which we were always in agreement: the best neighborhood in Brooklyn, light years beyond all the rest, was Coney Island.

The trip on the subway took around an hour and a half, in those days. David came to pick me up very early. Right before we left the first day, he took out a map and, putting his index finger on top of an orange strip that was shaped like an upside-down bicycle seat, dragged it slowly over the name, revealing the letters one by one.

C - O - N - E - Y   I - S - L - A - N - D

After passing the Seventh Avenue stop, the train emerged from under the ground. The view of the city from the elevated tracks was amazing. At Brighton Beach, the train made a sharp turn, leaving the sea on our left. The view of the beach was impressive, thousands and thousands of bathers milling around on the sand, a restless mass that pushed into the waves like lava. The most thrilling moment was after we crossed a stone bridge and the visionary architecture of the amusement parks rose before us: domes, needles, minarets, the gigantic Ferris wheels, the silhouette of the roller coasters, and the metallic structure of the Parachute Jump presiding over everything

Normally, my first reaction once we had arrived was one of terror. To get out of the subway we had to cross a long unlit passageway where the diabolic laughter of one of the automatons could be heard. I would squeeze my grandfather's hand. Turning to Greek mythology, as he always did, he would tell me: Have no fear, Iacchus. This is just the Mouth of Hades, there's nothing to worry about. We were at the entrance of an artificial cave that had once been part of a ride called Hell Gate. A gigantic devil spread its wings several yards wide, standing guard and watching over the people waiting in line to get in. No matter how my grandfather contextualized it, to know that we were about to enter hell wasn't especially reassuring, but when we came out of the cave the explosion of life and color changed everything.

Going back to Coney Island after so many years has filled me with an overwhelming sense of nostalgia. I asked Nadia to come with me to get some copies of my grandfather's articles that Ben kept in his Archive. On reading them, I am Iacchus again, the boy who explored a world of fantasy holding his grandfather's hand, and although I still see David as I saw him then, the adult that I have become feels closer to him as a man. Above all, I've discovered the writer in him.

My relationship with Coney Island has changed, and not just because of Nadia. Everything is different, the people, the streets, and—maybe more than anything—the light. In the old days, we would always go there in the summer. Now it's winter. There's very little going on, and besides, the days are very short and silent. In the morning, I walk Nadia to the subway and stroll through the streets of Brighton Beach, then go to a coffee shop and sit down to read and write.

We sleep late when Nadia doesn't have to go to Juilliard, and if the weather is nice enough, I take her to the places I discovered with my grandfather in the old days. I like watching her as she reads David's articles. Very often, once she finishes reading one, I pick it up and read it myself, trying to imagine what she had felt:

Coney Island looks out at the sea from a long, meandering boardwalk made of solid wood planks. The beach is a wide strip of fine white sand—one single beach, even though the signs give the successive stretches different names: to the east, Manhattan Beach; in the middle, Brighton Beach; and to the west, Coney Island Beach. From time immemorial, ships were not considered to have arrived at the New York harbor until they reached Sea Gate. Sitting on one side of the bay, Coney Island kept a restless eye on the ocean like an ancient city-state. It is a relatively small peninsula: half a mile wide by two and half miles long. Two sandbars protect the shores from the pounding of the sea. When the explorer Henry Hudson arrived at what would become New York City aboard the

Half Moon, the ship landed on the shores of Coney Island. There are at least two competing theories about the origin of the name of this place that was once nothing more than sand and marine soil, and each relates to a different animal totem. One of these popular theories attributes the name to a tribe of Indians who lived on the island: a subset of the local tribe that the Europeans incorrectly dubbed the "Canarsie" (after their own word for their home territory, it's said): these early islanders were supposedly known as the *Konoi*, or "Bear Band." The second and more familiar etymology, these days, goes back to a word in the language of the first European inhabitants of the area: *konijnen*, which is Dutch for "rabbits."

David's stories are no less powerful for me printed as when I heard them spoken. Yesterday, I came across an article that took me back to one of our first trips. My grandfather had asked me to write down the name of all the avenues that we crossed on our way. One day, reaching a corner, I spotted a street sign that read:

NAUTILUS AVENUE

Captain Nemo's ship! I shouted, thrilled. My grandfather stopped, smiled, and patted my head. A detail like that was all he needed to set off a new story:

Open Letter to My Grandson, Iacchus

Dear Iacchus,

The nautilus belongs to the family of mollusks, along with clams and oysters; the difference is that they have very elaborate shells and, above all, Iacchus, that they are a very rare species. Their natural habitat is the southern seas, the Indian Ocean especially, and to a lesser extent the Pacific. The nautilus lives inside a spiral-shaped shell divided into chambers, and whose walls are coated with mother-of-pearl. Of special note is a creature known as the "paper nautilus," which belongs to the genus of *Argonauta*. While they aren't nautiluses, properly speaking, there is a great resemblance between the creatures, particularly the females, who secrete a paper-thin shell used to hold its eggs (a nuptial chamber, if you will). I surmise that you don't know where the name "Argonaut" comes from. It goes back, like so many things, to Greek mythology. The myth—though this is not the place to go into detail—concerns the story of the sea voyage of the heroic Jason in search of the coveted Golden Fleece. One day I will tell it to you. But, regardless, the nautiluses and their cousins are travelers—not only above the waves, like Jason's ship the *Argo*, but through the deepest chasms of the ocean. So it's no coincidence that Jules Verne would choose that name—which is, indeed, very beautiful—for the submarine in which your beloved Captain Nemo traveled his twenty thousand leagues under the sea.

One of the places I was most eager to see again was Cooper's Corner. I went there without Nadia. I was afraid that I would find the place completely different or even leveled. My grandfather was always perfectly aware that it was impossible for us to set foot on Coney Island and not stop there. It was and is difficult to imagine its like—the heaps and piles of toys, comic books, marbles, candy, trinkets, and just about any other thing you could conceive of that might take a child's fancy. And nothing had changed. Just as it had been back then, there was a noisy conglomeration of kids in the shop, all of them busy trying to load their arms with as many treasures as possible. I remembered a day at Cooper's Corner when, busy trying to decide on what I wanted David to buy for me (I was only allowed one goodie per visit), he came up to me with a luminous yo-yo in the shape of a mermaid. He said that the mermaid was the symbol of the island, and told me to look around and note all the pictures of mermaids everywhere when we went back out. The yo-yo wouldn't make it out of the store (a comic book won out), but I saw that my grandfather had been right. Coney Island was swarming with mermaids: they were painted, sculpted, drawn, made of plastic, wood, and neon; in bars, store windows, ads, and decorating the amusement parks. The yo-yo had given him the idea for the topic of his next article. During our reconnaissance strolls, if he found a striking detail, he pulled out a journal he carried in his pocket and took note of it. When he thought that he had enough material collected, he took me to Dalton's, the beer garden on Surf Avenue. Seated on the terrace, with a mug of beer in front of him, he asked me:

Do you know where mermaids come from?

I invited Nadia to come with me to Dalton's. I'd never been by there during the off-season. The windows were closed and the terrace and the garden—from which there was a good view of the ocean—were deserted. I imagined the sea crowded with mermaids. I had told David, that day, that I didn't know where mermaids came from, and asked him in what part of the world— if nautiluses lived in the southern seas, as he had said—we could find one. He came out of the web of his thoughts for a moment, gave me an odd look, and said:

Don't be silly, there's no such thing.

Which was a bit confusing, at the time—after all, his stories were full of cyclopes, centaurs, Amazons, chimeras, harpies, gorgons, and other such fantastic beings. The catalog was endless, really. Was he telling me now that I would never be able to see a mermaid or a nautilus or any of those other creatures firsthand?

With a hint of a smile, he told me that it depended. Nautiluses, for example, did exist. To a certain extent you could also say that about Amazons . . . At least they *had* existed, in the distant past, and then the popular imagination had transformed them into fabulous beings. Mermaids were a borderline case. That is, there was a species of aquatic animal, the manatees, which looked a lot—well, more or less: from a distance, anyway—like women with fish tails, and they were the origin of the legend; but as far as actual women with actual fish tails living in the sea . . . well, no. As for centaurs, chimeras, and all the rest, there's nothing to them. Completely imaginary. They've never really existed.

We were seated at one of the garden tables. The waitresses were dressed as Valkyries, sang in German, and did everything they could to keep the customers drinking. That was the afternoon, come to think of it, when my grandfather gave me the nickname Iacchus—which he only used when we were alone. As always, he had ordered what was considered at Dalton's a small mug of beer, although I thought it was huge (later I would find out that the "small" was a full liter). Usually, when I finished my soda, he allowed me to wet my lips with some beer—no more than that— which delighted me. What I'd never seen David do, however, no matter how much they insisted, was allow the Valkyries to serve him a second mug. That day, I'm not sure why, his will weakened. He drank half of his second mug easily enough, but afterward he found it hard to keep going. On that day, he let me take as many sips as I liked. I realized that he was somewhat drunk when, after taking a last, long sip from the mug, he set it in front of me and challenged me to finish it. He was thrilled when I stood, picked up the mug, and drank down the inch or two of beer that remained. Tittering with joy, he patted me on my shoulder, put two fingers on my forehead as if he were anointing me, and in a hesitant voice declaimed:

Son of the god of wine, from this day on you will be known as Iacchus.

Among the hundreds of index cards kept in the Archive, I found one that read:

Iacchus—One of the epithets of Dionysus. It was at once a name and a ritual cry to greet the child-god during the mysteries of Eleusis. Iacchus and Bacchus were avatars of the same deity, although in other versions of the myth Bacchus is considered to be distinct from Dionysus. Iacchus was the son of Persephone: a peculiar child, who laughed ominously in the womb of his mother.

David wrote about so many things—far more than seem to have wound up preserved in the Archive. I wonder what's happened to all that material. For instance, I can't find any written record of all our visits to the public library on Mermaid Avenue (where Cooper's Corner was), nor of our visits to the archives of the *Brooklyn Daily* and the *Coney Island Times*, the two newspapers in the neighborhood. I also can't find any reference to the Miss Brooklyn contests that used to take place every summer at the Atlantis Club, organized by the *Brooklyn Eagle*. And who knows what other things I myself might be forgetting, or only remembering partly. I keep taking Nadia to places that were once important to me, but when we get there, as often as not, instead of the corner treasured by my memory, we find ourselves facing an apartment building, a supermarket, or a bank. Holding her hand, I point at them and tell her about what had stood there before.

It also happens that the past sometimes returns without my searching for it. Last night, walking around with Nadia, I heard a laugh that hadn't changed one jot with the passing of the years. The Tunnel of Laffs, I exclaimed, pointing to the entrance of one of the few attractions that was open all year long, and told her about the first time I had gone in there with my grandfather. The amplified guffaws of the automatons ricocheted off the vault and the walls of the tunnel. A faint light passed through one of the skylights, barely allowing me to make out the silhouettes of the creatures that emitted such sinister laughter. We had been riding on a train for a few minutes when out of the darkness popped a clown wearing a black polka-dotted suit and a cone-shaped hat studded with stars. He was moving toward us on the tracks, taking fitful steps that made his metallic joints screech. When our car reached it, the dummy let out a hair-raising scream. I thought we had run over it, but after a few minutes of silence, its gloomy laughter returned with renewed force, repeating the same never-ending cadence with the same inflections. I grabbed Nadia's arm tightly, getting goose bumps from the mere echo of something that had terrified me so long ago.

That summer I made an important discovery. It was a while before it made sense. A series of isolated episodes gradually revealed to me what it was all about. One day at dusk, watching from a hilltop, we saw a long line of couples on a dock, waiting to board boats bound for a rock in the middle of an artificial lake. After the last one was launched, a tunnel of green canvas unfurled over the row of boats, hiding the lovers from view. The Tunnel of Love, David remarked when the couples disappeared, and he told me that when he was a young man, there had been a replica of the Moulin Rouge at Coney Island—a famous cabaret in Paris, he explained. (Well, his exact words were "It was a Temple of the Flesh.") You're too young to understand these things, he said, and we left our lookout.

He wasn't entirely right. I hadn't told him, but I was already learning the nature of that lingering anxiety which sometimes took hold of me. On the basis of what I had seen, what I had heard grownups talk about, and what I had read in books, one day I realized that I had fallen in love. I wasn't expecting it, and I kept it to myself—not a word to anyone, not even to my grandfather.

I knew enough to be embarrassed by what had happened: I was all of ten years old and had no precise notion of sexual desire, although more than once I had seen what some couples did underneath the boardwalk.

Many an afternoon we passed by a booth with a miniature racetrack. Small crowds gathered to watch and bet on the horses. My grandfather and I usually kept on walking, but one day he asked me if I wanted to play and I said yes. As the barker urged onlookers to lay down their bets, I noticed a very special mannequin nearby. She was life-size, with blonde hair, blue eyes, and very white skin; she wore a short light green skirt and high heels and seemed to have been designed to look about eighteen. It was a mechanical doll. Her movements were very limited: smiling, moving her eyes left and right, and once in a while lowering her arms to adjust her skirt. As soon as a race started, she stood stock-still. Everyone aside from me kept their eyes on the horses, while I stood staring at that blonde mechanical doll. We left as soon as the race was over, but for the rest of the afternoon I couldn't keep the mannequin out of my mind.

Because of me, stopping at the booth became a ritual for us. Although we didn't bet, I always insisted on staying for at least one race, and David always complied. As he watched the horses, I stared at the mannequin with the green skirt, lost in the contemplation of her figure, the outline of her arms and legs, her eyes and lips, all of her features, sketched to be sure, but which I found utterly exquisite. My grandfather never caught on as to why I was so eager to go to that booth, nor did he realize that it wasn't the races I was interested in. I myself didn't quite understand what was happening to me. It was simply enough to watch her, if only for the few minutes of the race. The mannequin didn't have a name, and once we went home, it shifted into the background of my feelings, although lingering traces of her remained despite my best efforts. Some nights, I even had what you'd have to call amorous fantasies about the mechanical doll, innocent and vague, but still full of longing. My love story only lasted a few weeks. When the summer ended and we stopped going to Coney Island, the feeling began to dim until it disappeared completely. Fall and winter passed, and during that time the mechanical doll came to mind infrequently at best, and when it did I thought of it no differently than I did the other summertime attractions. Nevertheless, when we returned to Coney Island the following year, the first thing I did was drag my grandfather to the booth with the miniature racetrack.

Everything was the same. The barker in his derby hat and black suspenders shouted out the bets in the same gravelly voice as the summer before. The horses were the same and the pretty toy jockeys mounted on them hadn't aged. The background scenery had the same motifs, painted in the same colors. The only thing missing was her, the mannequin without a name. On top of the old pedestal (a truncated cone, speckled with stars) they had placed an effigy of Sherlock Holmes.

In the articles that he wrote during that second summer, David explored the world of action, the craziness of the bowling alleys, the shooting arcades, rides like the Whip, barrels, and Ferris wheels. As was only proper, he reserved a very special place for the roller coasters, going over their history. He gave precise details of the ones that had been taken down—a long, sad list. Past or present, no two were alike in origin, height, speed, and length. In one article, he listed their given names with all the gravity of an epic poem. He also made me repeat their names till I knew them by heart: Tornado, Thunderbolt, Cyclone, Jumbo Jet, Wild Mouse, Bobsled . . . His favorite one was the Tornado and mine was the Cyclone. The day Nadia and I rode it, the Cyclone had just reopened in Astroland—the last great amusement park of Coney Island.

The Cyclone and the Parachute Jump were naturally paired off, iconically—the latter the most dangerous of all the attractions on Coney Island. They weren't too far from each other, so photographers were always looking for angles from which they could capture the two great symbols of the island in one shot:

> The first thing you see when you approach Coney Island by land, air, or sea is the Parachute Jump. Its silhouette is reminiscent of the Eiffel Tower, although it also looks something like an oil rig, and then, because of its metallic petals, something like a mushroom cloud as well. From the wide art deco base an iron stem rises, gets narrower as it rises toward the sky, and on reaching its maximum height opens out into twelve curved projections. A carefully folded silk parachute is hooked up to each. Designed in the thirties for the Air Force, it was the last test the recruits were meant to take before parachuting out of an aircraft in flight. Transferred to New York for the World's Fair (1939–1940), it was dismantled thereafter and installed permanently at Coney Island, where it occupies a privileged spot. Here's how it works: riders sit on canvas seats at the base of the tower, each of which is fitted with a large, closed parachute; they are lifted up by six guide cables, and when they reach the top of the tower, a lever is tripped sending the riders into free fall. After a few seconds, a white and orange parachute mushrooms into the air. Descent is further slowed by the tension in the cables. Although there is a whole system of shock absorbers built into the platform below, they say the landing is almost as rough as the real thing. It's a dangerous attraction, and naturally such a system invites all sorts of mishaps. It's not unusual for the cloth of a parachute to become tangled in the metal frame, leaving customers violently lurching in midair until attendants can climb up and free them. The rescuers are in almost as much danger as the parachutists,

and because all this is conducted in plain sight of the public, one can only wonder that so many people are still interested in having a try themselves . . .

Among the boys in my class, it was quite clear—without anyone having to say so aloud—that whoever hadn't ridden the Cyclone before they were eleven years old, and then the Parachute Jump before they were twelve, would never be a man. In the Jump's ticket booth, in fact, there was sign forbidding anyone under the age of ten from riding, but because it was difficult to confirm a kid's age, there was a notch at a certain height on a metal post, and when it came down to it, this was the only valid method to determine who could and couldn't ride. Although I was already of age, the first year my grandfather and I made our rounds, he never gave me a chance to express an interest in the Jump. But toward the end of the second summer, I put my foot down and told David I wanted to try it. There wasn't that much time left, and I didn't want to wait any longer to prove my manhood, even if nobody would know but us. I didn't tell my grandfather *why* I wanted to do it, and although he'd warned me that he considered the Jump unsafe, when I told him I wanted to try it, he said yes, and said that he would even go along. When we got to the ticket booth, an attendant wearing military dungarees approached us, measured me against the post, and gave his approval. He helped me get settled, and once I was in place on the worn-out canvas seat, he adjusted the leather harness with a brass buckle. Three of the four other chairs were occupied. When the attendant confirmed that everything was sufficiently safe, he pulled on a lever and I began to rise in fits and starts. A few seconds later, I saw David rise. I felt a tingling in the pit of my stomach as the cables lifted us into the air. The people grew smaller under our feet as the music coming from the attractions grew fainter until it was silenced completely by the plaintive screeching of the cables. The amusement park shrunk. The people became a mass of black particles covering the beach and the boardwalk. My ecstasy turned into a momentary panic when, at very nearly the highest point of the tower, I saw the shape of one parachutist plummet right beside me, and then another and another. When I reached the top myself, not exactly knowing what I was feeling, I took in the beauty of Coney Island in all its splendor. This new rapture was interrupted when I heard a metallic cracking sound under my seat. It seemed as if everything—my life, the world— had stopped, and the silence grew thick around me. This was followed by a dry pop and the indescribable terror of knowing I was collapsing into the void. I thought about death, and after an immeasurable period, I was enclosed in a pocket of hot air and heard the strident screams of the people watching us fall. I'll never forget it: the ground rose toward me and the blotches that were faces got rushed at me, a sea of featureless masks. I crashed into the springs of the platform, and bounced, once, twice, maybe up to six times. The attendant who had tightened my harness rushed in to rescue me. He passed his hand over my head and said, Are you okay, son? My legs were shaking and I could hardly walk. If the ride had been too much for me because I was a child, it had been just as bad for David because he was an old man—but to admit as much would have violated the manly code of Coney Island. My grandfather was pale. Without saying anything, he put his hand on my shoulder and led me to the boardwalk, where we held on to the railing for a long time, taking in the beauty of the sea.

At the beginning of August, the publisher of the *Brooklyn Eagle* called David to tell him he regretted to inform him that his column would be cancelled come September. Something about restructuring, nothing to do with the quality of his work. He was leaving the door open to the possibility of reinstating him as a staff writer in the future. My grandfather didn't take it too badly, but the suddenness of the news put him in a difficult position, from a technical point of view. Which of his stories should he publish of the many he had yet to tell? His column came out on Saturdays. He only had space to publish three more. I have them with me. I've just now read them through, one after the other, and when I was done with them, I didn't feel nostalgia, as I had anticipated, but joy that I could share something so important to me with Nadia.

The article dated August 16th, "A Stroll on West End," is a meditation on the destiny of the great hotels of yesteryear, of which there were barely any left at the time of writing. On the boardwalk, up on 29th Street, David stops in front of a visibly deteriorated building (the structure is still majestic) that had been converted into a Navy Hospital during World War II. Given its current state of abandonment, its fate, as approved by the municipal commission, was to become an old-age home. Do any passersby know that this building was once the most opulent hotel in Coney Island's history? asks the columnist. Leaving the question unanswered, he proceeds to describing the Half Moon Hotel during its period of splendor, when the cream of society took a trip all the way from Manhattan to attend the fancy balls thrown in its grand rooms. David speaks of the elegance of the women, the opulence of the decorations, and the audacity of the building's architecture, with its Ottoman dome covered in colorful mosaics and topped with a weathervane in the shape of Henry Hudson's ship, from which the hotel took its name.

In "Kid Twist," published on August 23rd, David Ackerman returns to one of his favorite subjects, the golden age of Murder, Inc. when its gangsters, also known as the Brownsville Boys, did as they pleased all throughout Brooklyn. The authorities were powerless to put a stop to the machinations of the bloodiest and most calculating gang in the history of New York (more or less).

The article ends retelling the story of an event that made the Half Moon Hotel headline news in all the papers in the country:

> Although it was as meticulously engineered as any powerful corporation, Murder, Inc. was doomed to collapse due to an act of betrayal. One of its historic capos, the gangster Abe Reles, aka Kid Twist, decided to cooperate with the authorities. He had so much to tell that the New York Police Department filled 75 notepads with the details of hits on all sorts of clients carried out by efficient assassins on the payroll of organized crime. After the interrogations Kid Twist was taken to the infamous "Rat Suite": aside from being heavily guarded to prevent its tenants from giving in to the temptation of suicide, as well as to protect them from any attempts on their lives, all the windows faced the ocean. As it was, in Abe Reles's case, all precautions were in vain. One morning, Kid Twist went out the window. Whether he committed suicide or was murdered has never been determined. The bed sheets with which he allegedly attempted to descend from his golden cage are preserved in the police archives at 32 Chambers Street in Manhattan along with the 75 notepads that cost him his life . . .

The last article, "The Island of Dreams," dated Saturday, August 30, 1947, is in front of me, top of the pile. It's about Dreamland, the amusement park that, according to David, really captured the spirit of Coney Island. How like him not to have chosen the legendary Luna Park, or Steeplechase, the two most emblematic parks in Coney Island's history. No, David preferred to dedicate his final article to a failure. Dreamland had been designed to be the grandest park of them all, but it ended up being the most ephemeral.

The columnist tallied up the facts: Founded in 1904, it was razed by a fire seven years later, in 1911, which didn't leave a trace behind. The fire started at Hell Gate, appropriately enough, the same place David always talked to me about as we came out of the subway, after it had been rebuilt. The article goes on to recount how the fire devastated the incredible Lilliputia, a miniature city inhabited by three hundred midgets and designed as a half-scale replica of fifteenth-century Nuremburg, albeit with all the modern conveniences. For reasons I've never understood, my grandfather doesn't say a word about the fate of the inhabitants of Lilliputia, just as he doesn't mention what happened to the premature babies who were exhibited in the Baby Incubator attraction overseen by the celebrated Dr. Courtney.

As always, in the middle of September, the Haven of Dreams began to empty out. In a matter of days, the majority of the installations had been disassembled and the bathhouses closed; the boardwalk was already half-deserted, and the beach practically empty. The neon signs stopped flashing. The doors and windows of hundreds and hundreds of wooden buildings disappeared from sight, blinded by gray boards nailed up by the owners. By October, only a handful of stores remained open, and the human element was reduced to the yearlong residents, of which there weren't too many. Before I met Nadia, I had only gone there in the off-season a few times. There are wintry images stored in my memory, views of a ghostly Coney Island swept by an icy wind, but never had I witnessed the unusual phenomenon of the beach covered with snow.

Still, even in the middle of the winter, there are people on the sidewalk. Saturday it was sunny and we went out for a stroll. We saw men and women in the solariums, tanning with the aid of tinfoil sheets. A group of middle-aged Russian bathers, male and female, even risked the beach. After doing some warm-up exercises, they plunged into the water and swam, indifferent to the floes of ice bobbing along the crests of the waves. We continued walking west. I wanted Nadia to see the Kensington Hotel (the articles don't mention it), which had survived so many vicissitudes. Its structure was intact under the skeleton of the Thunderbolt. When this roller coaster had been built, the engineers had been very careful to ensure that it would in no way affect the Kensington building. We continued walking, keeping to the edge of the shore until we arrived at the Sea Gate. Near Dead Man's Rock, a spot where many swimmers had drowned over the years, we saw the rusty shell of a shipwrecked ferry. I walked Nadia to the subway (she had a rehearsal at Juilliard), then wandered around until four that afternoon, when it began to get dark.

It's midnight and Nadia is asleep. I watch the ocean from the living room. It's the view that I had never seen as a child: the lighthouses twinkling, the ships glimmering in the distance, the sea shrouded in darkness. To the west, sparkling, the tiny red dot of the Norton's Point lighthouse. Further out, toward the south, I see three more lighthouses whose names I don't know. I would need David here to tell me that sort of thing. It's a clear night and the crisscross of reflections on the water—with some ships near the shore and others far away—makes the ocean look like a map of the firmament. I think about Nadia, sleeping in the adjacent room, and it continues to astonish me that of all the lost corners of the five boroughs of the city, she came precisely to Brighton Beach when she arrived in New York. The last time I was here must have been ten years ago.

Returning to the world of my childhood fantasies has been such an intense experience that I want Nadia to share something similar from her own life with me. I ask her to tell me about her childhood, and she does, but it's hard for her. She had just turned four when she arrived in the United States and it was as though a door had closed between her and the memory of Siberia. She says that at times a handful of unconnected images come to her: a house in Laryat, her parents' bedroom, the community vegetable garden full of frostbitten purple cabbages, snowflakes stuck to the classroom windows in her school. Then after they left, she recalls the deck of a ship, her mother lying on the canvas of a folding chair, reading. After that it's Boston Harbor; the silent hilly streets lined with trees. A tea shop, her brother Sasha playing with her in a small park. As soon as I let her, she goes quiet; she prefers when I tell the stories.

A few days ago, going by Hampton Road, we ran into Chuck Walsh's grocery shop; he was an anarchist buddy of my grandfather's. Every time we went in, in those days, Chuck gave me a handful of ginger candy. When the dark blue wooden storefront appeared ahead of us, I was overcome by the usual wave of emotion. We went in, of course. The man behind the counter was a young man who looked nothing like Chuck. He asked how he could help us and I turned to Nadia. She looked around a bit, then pointed to a box of oranges that were individually wrapped in tissue paper; once the clerk had handed it to her, she put it away in her bag as if it were a very valuable object. Back on the street, she told me that the first time she ever saw an orange was in a market in Boston, not long after arriving in America. She would never forget the delicate taste of the juice in her mouth when her mother gave her a slice to try.

Twelve
NÉSTOR

He lost his head over her . . .

Frank was going to add something when Nélida hung up the phone, rushed toward him from the other end of the bar, and whispered something in his ear. The *gallego* nodded and waved the waitress away before he finished what he was saying.

There's no other way to describe what happened, Ness. He lost his head over her.

He took a sip from his cranberry juice and added:

Maybe we should talk in my office. By the way, I have a surprise for you. Did I tell you that Larsen is here? His ship just came in from Havana.

He turned on a floor lamp once we were in his office. On top of his desk was a box of Cohibas.

Every time Larsen docks in Cuba, he remembers his old friend Frankie Otero. A nice touch. Of course, I don't treat him too bad myself. There was a movement at the door. Víctor! Frank shouted.

Good morning, boss, his assistant said.

Look what we've got. Geez, you must have smelled them! Come on in.

Víctor greeted me with a nod and stepped behind Otero, leaning against the wall like a bodyguard. Frank tore the paper seal and opened the tin latch of the box with his thumbs.

Do me a favor, open the window, will you? he asked, turning toward Víctor. Let in a little air.

The mulatto put up the blinds and pushed the shutters out, exposing a damp brick wall covered in dirty moss and crisscrossed with wires and tubes. The light from the courtyard was so dim that Frank left the floor lamp on. He carefully lifted the wooden lid, rolling back his eyes and taking in the aroma that came out of the box. He stroked the top layer of cigars, and finding the texture to his liking, picked one out and offered it to me.

Thank you, Frankie, I said, but it'd be a waste. I wouldn't appreciate it.

I've never been able to understand how anyone exposed to such a pleasant fragrance can resist succumbing instantaneously to the temptation of smoking. All right, your loss.

I heard the flick of a lighter. Víctor's gold tooth glimmered in the dark. Frank brought his cigar to the flame. Pulled by the force of his lungs, the fire penetrated the rolled leaves of tobacco forming a circle of live embers at the tip. A cloud of blue smoke enveloped Frankie Otero's silhouette and broke up in thin wisps that were dragged out through the open window by the breeze.

Víctor, why don't you drive out to Astoria and have a look at Raúl's Camaro? I don't know what the fuck's wrong with it, but he couldn't get it started this morning. He just called to tell me, and since there's never much to do around here till later in the afternoon, I thought that maybe you could help him out. And don't give me that face, Frankie is not going to forget about you. Here, take one of these for yourself, give the other one to my son.

You didn't have to do that, boss, but I sure appreciate it. Putting both cigars in the top pocket of his jacket, Víctor turned to me. Take it easy, Chapman, he said, before heading out.

Frank took a tentative drag from his Cohiba.

Where do you want me to start? he asked, savoring the

smoke.

There's a gap in the notebooks and I'm having trouble reconstructing the part of the story I'm working on. I'm not sure whether the material was lost or if Gal got rid of it on purpose. I've found a few clues, but that's about it. I'm lost in the fog. But, you know, apart from that, and despite all the loose ends, for the first time since I set up shop in the Archive, I feel like *Brooklyn*, the novel that Gal had in his head, is really beginning to take shape.

Which part of the story are you talking about?

The bit when both of them were living in Brighton Beach. The trail breaks off all of a sudden.

And what can I do for you?

I really don't know. Just talk, I guess. Tell me what you remember. Something will come of it, I'm sure.

Don't be so sure. I barely knew him then. But I'll tell you what I know.

When exactly did he start coming around the Oakland?

Exactly a year after that time you're talking about. It was '74. He usually dropped by in the afternoons. I remember him sitting in a corner, writing while he sipped from a screwdriver that he liked to have continuously refreshed, not talking to anyone. The second or third time I saw him, I went up to his table, introduced myself as the owner of the place, and bought him a drink on the house.

Did he ever come in with Nadia?

Almost never. Those early days I must have seen her three or four times altogether. Many nights, Gal didn't come to his room. I imagined he was staying in Brighton Beach. That was before they went on their first trip.

What trip? There's no mention of a trip in the notebooks. Where did they go?

Oh, here and there—a few places, over their time together.

On that occasion, specifically, they went to Oaxaca. Gal had spent quite a bit of time there before they met. He loved it.

Oaxaca?

Yeah. He had been to other parts of Latin America, but he liked Oaxaca because the weather was nice all year round and it was full of expats and Gal felt at home around them. He always said they were the only people he liked—but his main reason to go was to be in touch with the Spanish language. He never told you about that?

No.

He needed to feel that his Spanish was alive. It was his only connection to the past. He never talked to you about any of that? Really?

No.

Didn't you find it odd that he spoke without an accent?

Well, he was different from the rest of you *Americaniards*, wasn't he? English was his first language, his adoptive parents were American. Whereas the rest of you—sometimes I think you've actually managed to preserve a way of talking that's died out even in Spain. There's you, and Raúl—who was actually born here in Brooklyn, yet after forty years still sounds like he just stepped off the boat from Galicia . . . but Gal only ever heard English when he was a kid, so . . .

No, no, English wasn't all he heard—it might not even have been his first language, really.

What do you mean?

He never told you anything about Leonor?

Gal never knew his flesh-and-blood, milk-and-bone mother, but ended up with two surrogate ones. Frank was hesitant to speak about it. He found it very strange that Gal had never mentioned this other mother to me. I had to remind Frank that Gal and I hadn't actually been very close friends; the truth was, I'd just been getting to know him when he died. Well, Leonor had played a crucial role in Gal's early years, but Frank couldn't tell me much else about her. He didn't even know her last name—only that she was from Salamanca, the daughter of exiles from the Spanish Republic who settled in New York after spending some time in Mexico—professors, I think. They became close friends with Ben and Lucia, and were at their place at all hours. Gal told me that it had been Lucia's idea to hire Leonor. She was fluent in four or five languages, including Catalan, which she had learned before enlisting with the Lincoln Brigade, and insisted that her adoptive son speak Spanish perfectly. Thanks to Lucia's conviction, ever since he was an infant, Gal was always around Leonor.

He adored her, Frank continued. She had been an elementary school teacher in Salamanca during the time of the Republic, teaching was a higher calling for her, it was in her blood. In New York, she ran a small school devoted to giving lessons to the children of immigrants and exiles. She taught all kinds of subjects at an elementary-school level, always in Spanish.

Is that right? If she's still alive, I'd like to speak with her.

I don't know where I got the idea, but I'm pretty sure she passed away. She went back to Mexico. I'm not exactly sure when. I think Gal even went to see her once or twice . . . Ness, I'm sorry, if I knew more I would tell you. I did meet her once, though.

When was that?

It was a very brief encounter.

Where did you see her?

Here in the Oakland. One day she showed up with Lucia. And that was the only time I ever saw Gal's stepmother, by the way. They came to see Gal, who was secluded in his room, going through another bad spell. One of those times when he would lock himself up and refuse to see anybody. Gal came down to meet them, but at one point, he and Lucia stepped aside to talk alone, and that's when I approached Leonor. We had a few minutes to ourselves. She told me about the days when Gal took lessons from her. Lucia was so committed to the idea that he had to master Spanish at any cost, she even held him back from grade school so he started a year late.

Never said a word to me about that.

The idea was to have Gal learn to read and write in Spanish before he could in English. He spoke perfect English, of course, but thanks to Leonor his Spanish kept its "viviparous origins," as Gal liked to put it. After he started school, he continued to take lessons from her, a couple of hours every afternoon, so for him Spanish was always a living thing. And when, at fourteen, Ben and Lucia told him the truth about his past, the issue of keeping his native language alive became crucial to him too. It was the key to his true identity, and he did everything he could to maintain it. Aside from being the only thing that kept him connected to Spain, he often said that it was the most beautiful of languages, and to master it was both a duty and a privilege. That's why he went to Mexico so often—and to other places in Latin America as well, although, as I said, less so. That's why he became a translator and why it was so important for him to write in Spanish. And of course to read it; you've seen his collection of Spanish classics. It's impressive. Everything that counts is in there.

(He wrote in both languages, but it was clear he felt more comfortable in English. And, though I've looked and looked, I haven't been able to find any sort of writing left over from his youth, in English or Spanish. As for published work, he mentions in his notebooks that he used the money from a piece accepted by the *Atlantic Monthly* to pay for detective Queensberry's services, but I've looked everywhere and haven't been able to find the story. When I inquired at the magazine, I was told that most likely it had been published under a pseudonym. I knew that he hadn't submitted it himself—his friend Marc Capaldi had done it—but the trail went cold. As for the notebooks, ninety-nine percent of them are in Spanish. There's a handful of texts in English, no more than fifty pages altogether, but of course there's no way of knowing what he might have gotten rid of. I've found a few additional pieces originally written in English in Ben's Archive, and then there are the texts that Gal entrusted to Louise Lamarque, the most remarkable of them being his portrait of Lermontov, but that's outside the scope of *Brooklyn*. At any rate, I have no way of knowing how much he destroyed before he died. I have a feeling that as soon as he realized that the end was near, he began to accelerate the process of destruction, especially the English texts, although I can't be entirely sure about this either . . .)

Frank's face had again disappeared behind a curtain of smoke. Where were we? I asked.

Gal told me that he had just returned from Oaxaca where he'd spent a couple of months with Nadia, and he wanted to know if any of the rooms upstairs was free.

Had they broken up?

I don't know if you could call it that. Theirs was a unique relationship. What I can tell you is that after their trip to Mexico, Nadia started coming by the Oakland more often than she had done ever before. When I say the Oakland, I mean the studio; she hardly ever set foot in the bar. Until, one day, she stopped coming by altogether, and it wasn't long before Gal left New York again. He didn't say a word to anyone. He simply gathered his things and took off. He was gone for such a long time I was convinced we would never see the man again. But I was wrong. After a couple of years, he showed up and asked me if I remembered him. Well, I laughed in his face. He wanted to rent a room but I didn't have any available. Then it occurred to me to offer him Raúl's studio. I had been saving it for my son forever, but he didn't want to leave our house. There was no way to get him out—until I bought him a place in Jersey and he had no choice but to go off on his own. Gal found the studio perfect for writing. And that was it: he was there for the rest of his life. What caught my attention was how much he had aged since he left, as if ten years had gone by, not two. When he left, he was still a young man, but the person who returned was someone else. Maybe that's why he asked if I still remembered him. He was aware of how much he had changed and imagined others saw it as well. And it wasn't just his physical appearance, his character had also changed; he had become more sullen and withdrawn, keeping much more to himself than he ever did before. It was as if his youth had evaporated. The Gal who returned was an older, defeated man, someone who'd lost his battle with life. Very strange.

Did he talk about Nadia a lot?

It came and went. She was definitely always on his mind. There were times when he was more loquacious about her and other times when he would act as if she didn't exist. When he brought her up, I took it with a grain of salt. Not that I thought he was lying, Gal was incapable of that. He just seemed to be revising the past, just as he revised reality, which is what all you writers do, isn't it?

Yesterday she came along to pick up some books Marc had left for me at the Mad Hatter, a small bookstore he was very fond of. Nearby, right next door to the jail on the corner of Boerum Place and Atlantic Avenue, we saw a crowd gathered in front of a very austere building. By the door, there was a sign that read:

FRIENDS MEETING HOUSE

That's what Quakers call themselves: Friends. Noticing us, a tall guy came over: If you're here for Alice Keaton's funeral, he said with a strong Slavic accent, her brother is receiving mourners in the lobby. Nadia and I exchanged a glance. We must have been thinking the same thing. We went in. Alice Keaton's brother was a redhead, around forty years old. He wore a black suit and no tie. The couple who had been talking to him shook his hand and went up the stairs. Nadia and I followed them. On the first floor beyond the double doors was a very spacious square room with high ceilings. Two of the walls had windows that looked out to an interior garden. The other two walls were white and bare. Wooden benches were set up at an incline toward the far end, as in a theater. In the middle of the room was a lectern with a Bible next to a red velvet stool on which sat an open violin case with the instrument inside. The guests filled the rows, sitting two by two or three by three, or alone, leaving a good deal of space between them. The man in the black suit greeted the last mourners at the entrance. When everyone had arrived, he took a seat in the first row. Outside, the afternoon was bathed in an unpleasant, murky light.

A long silence followed. I was moved by this way of paying homage to the memory of the deceased. When I told Marc about it later, he explained to me that the observance of silence is not mandatory. Whoever feels like it can speak, although, on that day, no one did. I was enthralled by that unfathomable, limitless silence. After a time I began to wonder how much longer I'd be able to endure it. Nadia, on the other hand, was imperturbable, seated on the edge of our bench with her gaze lost someplace beyond the windows. I managed to relax, eventually overcoming my resistance to the power of that silence. I lost all sense of time then; it was as if I were floating in a void. My mind dragged me to different places and moments of my life. Every once in a while, I emerged again and looked at Nadia, who seemed just as lost in thought. After who knows how long, however, I saw her expression change. She knitted her brow as if she had come to some decision, stood up, and walked to the center of the chapel. She approached Alice Keaton's brother and pointed to the violin. Outside, it had started to drizzle, and you could hear the raindrops against the windows. Nadia picked up the violin and played a sad sweet melody that she managed to make sound as though it were an extension of the silence rather than an interruption of it. The mourners didn't seem to notice—as if, indeed, the silence had never been broken. When Nadia passed by Alice's brother on the way back, he stood up and shook her hand. Instead of sitting down next to me again, however, Nadia walked out the door.

The rain had almost cleared, and stopped completely after a few minutes. I felt purified, very close to Nadia, still incapable of speech. When at last I managed to say something, I asked her what piece she had played. A Schubert sonata, she replied, so softly I almost thought I'd imagined it, and then the silence continued between us. Time had come to a halt while we were in the Quaker chapel, and now it was difficult to set it back in motion. The air smelled of damp earth and of that acrid scent that trees give off when the air is charged with electricity after it rains. We took a long walk to Columbia Heights.

On the promenade, we sat on a bench to watch the Manhattan skyline. The view of the harbor was beautiful. We marveled at the incredible variety of vessels we saw in front of us: oil tankers anchored in the distance, tugboats, garbage scows, passenger ferries, cruise ships and ocean liners, police patrol boats, yachts, sloops of various sizes, and even a solitary Chinese junk, God knows how it ended up there. Nadia pointed at the masts of the old schooners docked at the South Street Seaport, and finally let her eyes fall on the merchant ships tied to the piers on the Brooklyn side.

The Danish cargo ships captained by Frank Otero's friends are berthed over there, I told her, and explained that the original Oakland had been there many years before. Frank bought the bar from a Dane. That's how the whole thing started.

The sunlight slipped in between two rows of clouds, painting the sky a bloody orange. We had lapsed back into our silence, watching the colors of the twilight change. Then I asked her to marry me.

Her expression didn't change, and she didn't turn to look at me. The water in the harbor, a metallic blue till then, became tinged with violet reflections. When the ball of the sun fell behind the buildings of New Jersey, she asked:

Should we go?

I asked her to wait a bit, because I wanted to see night fall.

As the sky darkened, lit squares began to pop up on the sides of the skyscrapers as if someone were putting together a luminous puzzle. Rows of multicolored lights traced the shapes of the bridges. When the first stars appeared, we got up and began to walk toward the subway, down Montague Street, holding hands. Riding back, silence still reigned. Back at her apartment, Nadia dragged me to the bedroom, and when we made love, it wasn't like the other times. As for the proposal I had made to her on the promenade—it was as if I'd never opened my mouth.

Why didn't they ever live together?

The truth is that everything happened very quickly. It was like a gunshot in the dark. According to Gal, Nadia was too independent; even the slightest hint of commitment terrified her. What Gal liked most about Nadia was what hurt him most, you know? She was the carnal embodiment of his attraction to the void. I don't know how many times I heard him say that.

A few hours ago, in the Astroland cafeteria, I proposed once again and she replied that she was against marriage. She said she hated the idea of tying herself to anybody. She stated these things so forcefully that I didn't really know how to react. I said things . . . things I didn't realize were as foolish as they must have sounded until I saw them written down in my journal:

[. . .]

I asked her if she loved me. She stared at me and it was a while before she said:

Define "love."

There's nothing to define. Or explain. Just answer me.

Please, Gal, enough with the meaningless questions.

Silence again, only now it was different, because I felt the sliver of an affirmation making its way through her consciousness. It would emerge in a moment. I imagined a string of monosyllables falling down through the air, not knowing where they would land. She held my hand, her big green eyes fixed on mine. I must have repeated the question, because I heard her say:

You know that I do.

Then, the question I had asked her on the promenade escaped my lips once more.

She pulled her hand away, closed her eyes, and with an expression of deep weariness, began to reply . . .

I put my index finger to my lips.

I get it, I said. No more questions, your honor. The interrogation is over.

She got up abruptly, grabbing me by the arm, and rushed me out of the cafeteria to the base of the Astrotower. It was Tuesday, so the line was huge; everyone wanted to see the fireworks from the glass elevator that went up more than a hundred yards. I wanted to say no, but Nadia would have none of it. We had never been to Astroland together. I had never seen her act like this—it was as though she had become somebody else. She was very agitated, behaving like a teenager, avidly pointing at everything, her excitement contagious. As we went up surrounded by strangers, her body pressed to mine, I looked down at the park and remembered when I had gone up on the Parachute Jump with my grandfather. The world of fantasy at our feet grew smaller and smaller; we were entering a place whose laws were different from those down below. I thought about my grandfather David, separated from me forever by the cruelty of time. He never got to know Astroland (he died in '58 and the park didn't open until '63), although he would have found its style foreign. All the attractions had something to do with the space age. The elevator was a glass cage that rotated as it went up hugging the outside of the tower, providing a view of the four cardinal points. Below us, people lined up in front of the Mercury Capsule Skyride to go on a simulated journey through space. A panorama of rockets and satellites suspended by cables hovered in the air above the spectators. Presiding over everything were the capricious peaks of the Cyclone. Somewhat farther away, outside the limits of the park, like a symbol of the past, stood the silhouette of the Parachute Jump. Beyond that, the black surface of the sea, splattered with the reflections of the fireworks.

She had it her way. The elevator remained on at the top of the Astrotower for a long time, so we could watch the fireworks finale. After we came down, Nadia was still very restless. She took me firmly by the hand and told me that she wanted us to ride the Cyclone. I followed her in a daze, not knowing why I was humoring her. It was a violent, absurd ride punctuated by hysterical, piercing shrieks. When we finished the nightmarish course, I was trembling, but Nadia was unbowed. We ran through the amusement park, Nadia leading me by the hand. At the exit on Neptune Avenue, she hailed a cab and told the driver to take us to Brighton Beach. Making love in her apartment, I felt as if I were at her mercy. I could feel her despair intensely. When we finished, she forced me to start again. I don't know how I had it in me. It only ever happened with her. For the second time that day, time had been suspended. I forgot about the world, about my fears. Finally, she fell asleep, inaccessible, gone to a distant place to which I would never be able to follow her.

I went down to the boardwalk and took a long stroll all the way back to Coney Island. Seated on a bench reminiscing about all the things we'd shared—thoughts, feelings, silences—I realized that it was precisely what I would have to call her soul that was out of reach . . . no matter how much she took charge of my body and how often she gave me hers.

Her body,
  but
   no:
    it's too
     difficult
      to put the words
       the concepts
      in the place where they belong
    That's why
     I need to write
      about her / about you.

I need to write about you in the diary, because here and only here can I express what I feel without worrying about your reaction. When I'm with you, I just can't speak freely; I feel the conflict and anxiety inside you and dare not open my mouth. I wait until I'm here, alone, to set down all the things I keep to myself when we're together. And yes, I know these are words that no one can actually define. It could be that they don't mean anything—but I need them just the same. Without them I don't stand a chance of beginning to work out what's happening to me. Because of you. What happens to me when I'm with you, what in the world happens to me when I'm inside you. Not to mention what happens to you, then. What do I give you? What do you give me? It's very strange, I've never been a religious person in the least, but somehow, when we have sex, if feels almost holy to me. But no, you won't let me talk like that. I realize that for you it's entirely different. At any rate, you'd rather remain silent about it. Unlike you, I need to verbalize my feelings, wrap up everything that happens in words, then shape them in writing, caressing them one by one. We're so afraid to use certain words. What I'm writing now, though, is nothing but the truth, and it's meant for your eyes only. Perhaps a day may come when you'll read this. Don't think it isn't difficult to write. Having the courage to use words like these makes me extraordinarily vulnerable, in turn. But, one day, all of this will find a form. I will repay you with my writing for everything you've given me. I never knew why I did it, why I wrote it all down, but now I see that it makes sense—because of you. I've always wanted to write this book, this *Brooklyn*—even if I'm not sure what it will turn out to be, in the end. All I know is that the real book is hiding underneath the thousands and thousands of words I can't refrain from writing. I have to dig it up and give it a shape, so that you'll read it. *Brooklyn*. I'll write the book for you, even if you don't want it. *Brooklyn* will be born thanks to you, in spite of you.

He was crushed, Frank said, when he found out that she had fallen in love with this Eric . . . Gal told me a few things about him, but not a lot. It hurt him too much to talk about it. Let's see, what was his last name? Rosoff, I think. Yeah, Eric Rosoff. That's it. He was Jewish and a classmate of Nadia at Juilliard. He was from Boston, very delicate, rather feminine. A pianist. He wore white gloves all the time to protect his sensitive hands. Everyone said he was a genius with a very bright future ahead of him. He was younger than her, must have been twenty. Gal was thirty-seven then, you know? The story of Nadia and the pianist took a jackhammer to Gal's theories about Nadia and him being meant for each other, or whatever. Till then he had been able to keep the fiction alive. He had written the screenplay, so to speak, for the two of them, and believed in his role—really swallowed it hook, line, and sinker.

Following his own cues, he came to the conclusion that Nadia wasn't about to change on his account. It was hard, but he learned to accept her as she was. She wouldn't ever belong to any man. Neither her head nor her heart worked like that. She was fiercely independent, incapable of any kind of commitment, yeah, he used those exact words—but that's what Gal liked most about her, even though it meant having to give her up. She will never be mine, he admitted, there's no way around it. It's been hard, but I've finally learned to accept it. In a way, I'm glad it's like this. I don't care anymore. He would talk about her as if he understood the inner workings of her character better than she did herself, but the truth was he didn't know up from down. Those were very confusing days in every sense. It was clear that the real Nadia had little to do with the one invented by Gal, but he wasn't able to see anything outside his own scripted scenario. For him, it all came down to one thing: in the end, Nadia would always return to him. She needed him—it was that simple. There was some truth to that: at some point she always did go back to him, only it wasn't for the reasons that he would have wanted. Things just weren't fated to last eternally, as he would put it. Or, going back to the screenplay simile: the script worked fine up to the middle of the movie, but then it followed its own path. And Gal didn't see that the hell of it was that he was right about one thing: She would always come looking for him, sooner or later. He was caught in a loop. She would look for him, would show up here, and if he wasn't around she would wait for him. She slept in his studio, wouldn't leave his side for days, weeks. Then they would go on a trip and the cycle would repeat itself: Nadia stopped needing him, all of a sudden, and disappeared. And when she wasn't around he became sullen, disagreeable, hostile. His drinking got out of control. So, yeah, for a long time, the script played out just like that, without much variation. But it was different with the pianist. Once Eric Rossoff came into the picture, the script changed.

Why?

Let's say that Gal had learned to accept that Nadia would surrender bodily to others, to use his terminology . . . He learned that relatively early. But things got out of hand with the pianist. She fell in love with the guy. That was something Gal hadn't anticipated. See, according to his script, Nadia was incapable of falling in love. She was above the passions that affect us mere mortals. In Gal's eyes, that kind of detachment meant that Nadia was a superior being. In his eyes, she was a goddess, and since he was a mortal, he couldn't aspire to her love. According to this fiction, Nadia would remain a free spirit to her dying day. Well, Eric ruined the story. Nadia had never been the goddess that Gal insisted on worshipping. Gal tried not to see it, but it was hard to sustain the illusion.

When she met this pantywaist, she became unrecognizable: She felt about him exactly the same way Gal felt about her. She even moved in with the guy, something she had always refused to do with Gal, and when he proposed, she married him right away, something else that wasn't in the script. Nadia was supposed to abhor the very idea of marriage, see? That was another one of Gal's little homilies: from the beginning, see, Nadia had proclaimed to the four winds her eternal aversion to the institution of marriage. Gal explained it all to me with such gravity he started to seem a bit unhinged. And then one day, naturally: Bam, she got married, just like that. She let him know herself. Gal never got over it. Everything about his relationship with Nadia was a torment to him, her terrible frustration over being sterile—though he didn't see that it would only have hurt him more if she'd had kids with another man. The only thing about Gal's fantasy that had any speck of truth to it was his central thesis—though he didn't see the irony in it, since it seemed to justify all his loyalty, his hope.

What do you mean?

I mean, she really did find it impossible, for some reason,

to sever ties with him completely. In her own way, she went on needing him. And even though they stopped seeing each other, she continued to write him. She told him everything, all the intimate details and preoccupations . . . In fact, the first thing she did when she divorced the pianist was write Gal.

When was that?

A little more than a year after they were married. This business with the musician was nothing but a mirage, that's what Gal thought. Nadia remained true to herself, that's why the marriage was doomed. You'll see—she'll turn up again any day now, he would tell me. And indeed, one day, Nadia showed up at the Oakland. We were all flabbergasted, except for Gal.

That part is in the notebooks.

She came back. I knew it. I knew she would. She came back just like all the other times: because she needs to be true to herself, living, exploring, seeing what the world has in store for her. She's done what she had to do; she went out into the world, and now has returned to base. She called and asked permission to come to the Oakland to see me. I told her that she didn't need my permission for anything, that she knew perfectly well she could show up here whenever she wanted to. She came up to my studio right away. She was so beautiful I couldn't follow what she was telling me; by the time I was able to properly focus on her words, I realized that she was saying something I had heard from her many times already: that she had come back because she needed me, because she felt safe with me, because the world is filled with traps and snares, and she knew that I wouldn't fail her. I felt slightly dazed. I went back to staring at her, tuning out her words. Then I realized something had changed. The woman who was speaking to me was not the Nadia I had known. I understood that there was a huge gap between what she was saying and what I heard. I asked her not to say such things . . . Now it was me who couldn't accept certain words. The purity and authenticity that she was talking about didn't exist, they were a reflection of her anxiety about finding them, and since she couldn't, she attributed those qualities to me. I told her that what she was saying made no sense. I asked her to tell me about her, and as she did I saw clearly what couldn't be pieced together. She hasn't returned for me. She needs me, but not as I'd like her to. She's come back because she got hurt. I let her talk, waiting for her to calm down, and then I said it . . . I asked her to go, to leave me alone, to get on with her life. She looked at me for a moment, turned around, then said: So long, Gal. And I closed my eyes, grateful.

I was shocked to see her back at the bar, Frank said. She seemed pretty shaken up herself. I asked her about Gal, and she simply said that he was fine. I walked her to the door and when we said good-bye I got up the courage to ask her why she was leaving when she had just arrived. I didn't know her well enough to ask her that sort of thing, but she didn't take it the wrong way. Very calmly, she responded that it wasn't her choice, that Gal had asked her to leave. The funny thing is, he wrote this bit out of the story pretty quickly—it wasn't the way he chose to remember that day. But that's the truth: He asked her to leave forever, to never come back or write to him again. And Nadia complied. She abided by his wishes, except of course, for the letters. He'd begged her to stop, but she continued to write him.

Until when?

Until '86. Haphazardly, I mean. At first, she tried to comply with Gal's wishes, I think. There was a relatively long lapse of silence, several months, but then the letters started showing up again, at first just a few and then more regularly. After a while, the process was reversed. She wrote less and less until the letters stopped coming altogether. Then, after another long break without a single letter, a new one arrived, accompanied by the famous postcard of Las Vegas. I say famous because Gal never seemed to tire of mentioning the damn thing to me. For a while, he carried it around with him everywhere, and showed it to me more times than I care to remember. It has to be in one of the notebooks, I'm sure. If you haven't found it yet, you will. It was the last message he got from her. But we've already gone over that a few times, right?

(In the postcard you can see a casino with crazy lighting atop a mixture of incompatible architectural elements. In the background, above what could be a Byzantine dome, there's a neon arch that says: Coney Island. Behind that is a roller coaster. On the flip side in blue ink, it says: *HAVEN OF DREAMS*. This and the letter accompanying it are the only examples of Nadia's handwriting I've been able to see. Her characters are thick, rounded, somewhat shaky and childlike. The letter is dated January 12, 1986.

> Dear Gal: Yesterday I dreamed about you. We were in your apartment in Hell's Kitchen. The details were all very vivid, the wooden table in the kitchen, the Underwood. Then, all of a sudden, I don't know how, we were in Astroland. You were chasing me, your face distorted. At times I thought it wasn't you at all, but then your face was very close, and yes, it was you. We got on the Parachute Jump, which was open in spite of having been shut down for so many years. You kept telling me to jump, but I was afraid. You tried to convince me, assuring me you had done it many times. Finally, you pushed me . . . That was it, the end of the dream. Who knows what it means. I'm spending a few days in this ridiculous place with a journalist friend . . . she invited me down, just a short jaunt. I wanted to be far away from everything. I'll only be here for a few days. My friend hates this place, and wanted some company while doing her stupid assignment. Silly, no? But there's something about this city, I'm not sure what, that I like. What do you think of the

postcard? It's fitting, right? Las Vegas reminds me a little bit of Coney Island, but without the soul, as you would put it. I remember what you used to say when we came out of the subway, that we were at the Gate of Hell, and I liked that, I liked being near hell, and I think you do too. I miss you a lot, Gal. I would like to be with you, listening to your stories until I fall asleep. I'm too tired now, but I promise that I will write a long letter very soon. I have something very important to tell you. Until then.

N.(G.)

There's a coffee stain in the middle of this letter. And around the *G.* in the signature, Gal had drawn a red circle. I passed the tip of my finger over it. It was usually Nadia O., or Nadia R.— her maiden name, her married name. So where did this *G.* come from? I can imagine Gal speculating about it too, not that it's much of a mystery.

She was married again.

Thirteen
THE AVENGING ANGEL
(FRAGMENTS OF *BROOKLYN*)

MIHRAB

[March 1969]

Monday. Louise on the phone: It's a done deal. Sylvie has already moved into an apartment at the Chelsea Hotel. There's going to be a housewarming party on Wednesday, just a small group of friends. I'm finally going to meet her *petite amie* but before that I need to do her a favor. Could I go with her and Mussifiki to an oriental bazaar in Brooklyn Heights? You know who Mussifiki Mwanassali is, she says. You've never met, she hastens to add, but I've told you about him—art critic, historian, professor at NYU. He wrote a book on the rugs of Kurdistan. I tell her I don't remember. Of course you do, you were browsing through his book the last time you came to Deauville. It rings a bell, I say. Louise pauses. I hear the flick of a lighter on the other side of the line. Well, she continues, it turns out that Mussifiki has made one of his usual discoveries. Poking around the Arab stores he knows in Brooklyn Heights, he stumbled upon a very special Kurdish rug and has gotten it into his head that *I* have to buy it. He says that the minute I see it, I'll understand. So we're meeting tomorrow at three o'clock, and I would really appreciate if you came with me. So I agree to go. By the way, she says, it's gonna be great when we all meet on Wednesday. I told you Moreau is coming, didn't I?

233

You know who he is. Robert Moreau, the poet. He has just arrived from Paris. As for Mussifiki, well, he has a screw loose, that's for sure, but I have no doubt that this rug must be something special. It's actually very nice of him to keep an eye out for me. But he's terrified that the rug will fall in the hands of some philistine who won't appreciate it. He claims he'd like to buy it for himself, but there's not an inch of space at his home or office, he says, and that includes the walls and the ceilings. I'm going to buy it for Sylvie, as a good luck talisman for her Chelsea place.

Tuesday. I arrive at the Izmir Bazaar at exactly three o'clock. Louise is talking to a tall, skinny young man with a dark complexion and a thin mustache. He's wearing a deep-red fez with a gold tassel fringe that is clearly part of his business attire. Hi, Gal, says Louise. On time as always, if only everyone were like you. She seems annoyed. This is Jair. We shake hands. He's from Alexandria. He's been in New York for six months and speaks English much better than me. Of course, there's no hope for my English. Waving aside the compliment, the man clarifies that he has a degree from the American University in Cairo. Louise tells me why she's annoyed. Mussifiki just called the store saying he'd be late. He does it to me all the time, she complains. The rug is worth the wait, Jair adds, and he offers us tea and pastries. Louise tells him not to bother. It's no bother, the salesclerk responds. Five minutes later, we're seated on Moroccan leather poufs in front of a Damascene table on which Jair has set a tea service accompanied by some pistachio pastries. The place looks like an illustration out of *The Arabian Nights*. There are mirrors, musical instruments, antiques made of silver, wood, or bronze everywhere. Stained-glass lamps hang from the ceiling, and the walls are lined with tapestries, brocades, silk shawls, and all sorts of handcrafted objects. Louise offers me a Camel, takes one for herself, lights them, and proceeds to tell me the story of Sylvie Constantine, her lover.

She was sixteen when she arrived in New York. Her mother had died a few months before in a car accident near Lausanne. Daughter and husband were out of their heads with grief. Bernard Constantine had been working as an engineer for a Swiss company; when the tragedy occurred, his boss, who was also his best friend, suggested that he take charge of the New York office, whose director had just retired. Constantine would have to work sixty hours a week, which would leave him little time to think. Bernard and his daughter moved into a duplex on the Upper West Side. Sylvie attended the United Nations International School, and when she graduated, she was admitted to Vassar. During her senior year, she studied photography with Demetria Martin, the famous Harlem photographer. Sylvie fell madly in love with her, but Demetria deftly channeled that passion toward the only thing that she thought should matter: photography. She hired her as an assistant on a project about life in Harlem. Sylvie took thousands of photographs at basketball games, street fairs, concerts, book readings, exhibits, protests, trials. She attended weddings, religious ceremonies, graduations, reunions, birthday parties. She captured murder scenes, robberies, fires, accidents. She shot tenements, churches, stores, restaurants, clubs, and coffee shops. Sifting through the enormous amount of material she had amassed, Demetria helped her select some three dozen photographs that Sylvie exhibited at the Tribes Gallery on the Lower East Side. After she graduated, Demetria asked her to work on a second project involving the black population of New York, this time photographing corpses in the funeral homes of Brooklyn; the dead were of all ages, dressed in their finest outfits, scrupulously made up, with serene, vacant expressions, their bodies stuffed into padded coffins with colored linings; nurses, mailmen, basketball players, musicians, bank employees, subway conductors; bodies stricken with cancer, murder victims, girls dressed in white chiffon dresses, teenage boys with colored ties:

inscrutable faces with sealed eyelids and rigid lips. Under each snapshot, they printed the name of the deceased, age, profession if any, and cause of death. They published a coffee-table book that was very successful. After that, Sylvie started getting calls from everywhere. When Bernard Constantine felt strong enough to return to Switzerland, his daughter decided to stay in New York. The thought of living in Europe appalled her. In Manhattan, she had everything she needed in life. Moving anywhere else was unthinkable.

Jair sticks his head in from behind the muslin cloth that divides the showroom from the back office and announces that Mussifiki has arrived. We exit the *haima* to meet him. A man of about fifty is leaning on the counter. He has blue-black skin, almond-shaped green eyes, and fleshy, purple lips. He must be used to getting stared at, because he tells me out of nowhere: My mother is Chinese, from Macao, and my father is Zulu. He shakes my hand and, without any further ado, goes to a stack of carpets and deftly pulls out one from nearly the very bottom. I don't get anything from these deals, he says, holding up a corner of the carpet while the rest of it cascades onto the floor. I do it because it gives me pleasure to know that an acquaintance of mine is going to make something as special as this a part of their household. In a way, it's as if the new owner is sharing the spirit of the carpet with me. He gives it a close look, satisfied. Stunning, no? We all agree that it is. I'm going to tell you about its history, he says, taking a deep breath. Louise interrupts him: Mussifiki, save it for tomorrow, when we bring it to Sylvie. A great choice, Jair says, as he rolls up the rug. There's a hint of sadness in his voice, as if he were reproaching himself for not having detected just how interested his clients were in this piece of merchandise. The price had already been settled the day Mwanassali discovered the rug, and it's too late now to raise it. You're lucky no one else took a liking to it, he says, resigned. I'm going to take it home to touch it up, Mussifiki says, picking up the package. What time are we meeting at the Chelsea, Louise?

Wednesday. I've passed by the Chelsea Hotel so many times, but this is the first time I've ever been inside. Suite 1006 is on the top floor. When you leave the elevator you turn left, then go past a pair of swinging doors and walk almost to the end of a long dark hallway. To reach the top suites you have to go up a creaking wooden stairwell. Sylvie's apartment is almost devoid of furniture. On the far wall, next to a large window, there's a flight of stairs that lead to the rooftop. Take a look, you're going to love it, Louise suggests. I climb up to find myself lost in a maze of dormer windows, glass cabinets, twisted chimneys, gardens, and soil beds in which all kinds of plants, bushes, and even fruit trees grow. You have to come see the terrace at night, Sylvie says when I go back down. I love this woman. She's petite, fragile, very pretty, with blonde hair and large blue eyes, and a very feminine air that perfectly complements Louise's masculine look. She doesn't look you in the eye when she speaks to you. I also like Robert Moreau, Louise's poet friend. He looks like Picasso, but is tired of people telling him that. He has a unique sense of humor that he uses as a shield to protect himself from other people's curiosity. He is in town for Louise's opening at Westway. There's an essay by him in the catalog. Mwanassali pulls the same stunt as the day before at Izmir Bazaar. Just a few minutes away from when everyone was told to arrive, he calls to say he's going to be a bit late. Exactly half an hour later, he bursts into the suite without knocking. Louise makes some quick introductions because Mwanassali is eager to show everyone the rug, which he carries tucked under one arm, wrapped in brown paper and tied with a fine string. He deftly undoes the bundle, spreading the rug open on the wooden floor. He kneels and smiles with satisfaction before he speaks:

The rug is originally from the Gaziantep region in southwest Turkey, on the Syrian border, and, near as I can estimate, it must be around a century old, perhaps a little less. The colors, design, and weaving technique point to a type of carpet common among nomadic tribes. He turns it around. This symmetrical weaving pattern is known as Turkish knot. There are between sixty to seventy knots per square inch. His long, black-blue fingers gently caress the lower fringe of the rug. Mwanassali points at the pattern in the center. That's the mihrab, which means niche, he explains. It's the equivalent of the niches in the walls of mosques at the points nearest to Mecca. Mwanassali caresses the rug as if it were a living thing. Why does it look new, despite its age? Because it has been used exclusively for praying—the rest of the time it was carefully stored. This type of rug is relatively rare because they aren't meant to be sold. Mwanassali stands up. He seems saddened by the necessity of separating himself from the Kurdish rug. All of us admire its beauty in silence. In the days when this rug was first woven, the contemplation of its complexities would be enough to send the mind into an altered state. As though the mihrab were a door that at any moment could open into another dimension. Madame Sylvie, this is a very beautiful gift that will keep you company for the rest of your life. Who knows how many places this rug has been before winding up at the Brooklyn bazaar where I found it, how many owners it must have had, what kind of lives were being lived by those who stepped or kneeled upon it? One thing is certain, the craftsmen who wove it are dead, as are its first owners, and most likely the owners after that. Mwanassali looks around, smiling. When all of us in this room have passed away, its beauty will only have deepened, and who knows where it will be then, and what kind of new owner it will have.

THE PERISCOPE

*[Undated fragment. Probable
date of writing: April 1969]*

The war cry of the Order of the Knights Incoherent was *¡Viva
Don Quijote!* (the same password used by Hughes, Anzaldúa, and
Moreau at the meetings of the Paris chapter, of which I will speak
below). They held their sessions at the Periscope, a bar on the
Lower East Side. The members of the New York chapter were
David Ackerman (my grandfather), Felipe Alfau, Jesús Colón,
Aquilino Guerra (alias One-Eye), and Henry Martínez, aka Lord
Gin. Although some sessions were for members only, the Knights
Incoherent usually brought one or more guests to the meetings.
Sometimes they would invite lecturers, or give talks themselves.
The Order also offered small seminars on a bafflingly wide range
of topics. One way or another, the Knights Incoherent were all
literary types. Although he made a living working as a translator
for a bank, Alfau was a poet, novelist, and short story writer. A
journalist of remarkable talent, Colón nonetheless had no choice
but to take on a wide variety of jobs to make ends meet. As for
my grandfather, he was the head typesetter for the *Brooklyn
Eagle*. The literary ambitions of Aquilino Guerra and Henry
Martínez were much more modest. Guerra was the owner of a
grocery store on 14th Street in which he sold Spanish delicacies.
He bragged that his imported items were highly appreciated by
the locals. He had to ship orders of his signature spicy chorizo
all over the States. Lord Gin, an inventor (he had obtained

various patents for a bunch of rather absurd contraptions), he wrote plays in verse. He taught history at a community college in Long Island. One of his inventions was a literary genre he called "vicarious travel literature." He recast and revised travel articles and books, substituting himself and his friends for the protagonists of the originals. He had made up a list of forty to fifty potential readers—made up of friends and acquaintances—to whom he would send his vicarious travelogues unsolicited. No one took offense, although few of the recipients bothered to read his ridiculous tales to the end. According to the Annals of the Order, on one of the occasions Martínez handed a piece of writing to a fellow member, the annoyed recipient blurted out: We can't read as fast as you write! Martínez took it well, though. Anyway: As stated earlier, there was a chapter of the Order based in Paris. It had only four members: Alston Hughes, Robert Moreau, Jesús (Chus) Anzaldúa, and an honorary member, one "Gilgamesh," of whom I have learned very little, save that he was a compulsory plagiarist. Hughes and Moreau were poets, the former from Panama, the latter French. They were both translators, as was Jesús, who was a native of Navarre and now living in Barcelona, though he traveled often to Paris. Anzaldúa was the opposite of Martínez; he had traveled widely, but never wrote. He said that he lived in a state of poetic vigilance, waiting for the Muse to call upon him. It's up to her, he would respond when asked if he was going to write something for a forthcoming meeting. If she's not interested, I'm not either—I have enough going on already. As for the Knights Incoherent of New York, three of the five founding members were *Americaniards* (Alfau, Guerra, and Martínez). Alfau had come to Manhattan on an ocean liner with his family when he was fourteen years old. He was a Catalan from Barcelona, but considered himself Basque. Colón arrived in this country on a merchant ship as a stowaway; he was Puerto Rican. Guerra was born in a small town near

Murcia, and Martínez came from the village of Dos Hermanas, Seville. The only native-born American was my grandfather, who was a third-generation Brooklynite. By then, David was already writing his column for the *Brooklyn Eagle*. The members of the group covered the political spectrum from one extreme to the other. The Puerto Rican was a card-carrying communist; my grandfather belonged to an anarchist labor union; Martínez and Guerra were left wing, although they didn't know quite how to classify themselves. When Alfau pushed him during one of their meetings, Martínez declared himself a utopian socialist; Guerra wasn't sure what that meant, so for the time being he said nothing, but when the meeting was over he asked Colón what Henry had meant. When he came to understand the concept, he decided to declare himself a *scientific* socialist, to mark out his territory more than anything, although he had to wait for the next gathering to inform Alfau. Alfau himself was right wing, which made his relationship with the rest of the Knights Incoherent rather difficult at times, although generally Jesús Colón was able to put out any fires when things got ugly. I've come to know about the Order of the Knights Incoherent through Ben and David, though somewhat less through my grandfather (he wasn't wont to talk about the brotherhood). In the Archive is a photograph of the eight members of the Society (as they sometimes referred to themselves), the five from Manhattan and the three from Paris (the elusive Gilgamesh is missing). Alfau is white, tall, skinny, gangly, with a thin mustache that makes him look like a Mexican movie star. Colón is black and completely bald, with intelligent eyes and a sincere smile. Henry Martínez has a thick head of silver hair combed back. He has small, porcine eyes and a sharp nose, and is wearing a black cape and a white scarf. Guerra is short, chubby, balding; in the picture he's wearing overalls of some sort. Hughes is a mulatto, tiny, and is giving the camera an arrogant stare. For some reason that Ben couldn't explain, Hughes is dressed as an Arawak, but a woman, not a man, with braids and a skirt. Anzaldúa is tall, self-assured, with a Basque sort of face. Moreau has Caucasian features, an aristocratic bearing, and a shiny bald dome. In the picture, he's wearing a gray suit with black pinstripes and has his thumbs stuck in the pockets of his vest. The idea to name the group the Knights Incoherent seems to have been Alfau's, although there were always lively arguments about who had first come up with it.

In the Archive are numerous texts by the Knights Incoherent, as well as various documents chronicling the activities of the Order. Most literary works are by Felipe Alfau and Jesús Colón. The documents by my grandfather David are kept apart, in a file that includes his journalistic pieces. Colón was a writer of infinite grace. His articles were published in local newspapers, forgotten today, a shame no one has bothered to collect them in a book, because they're masterly. Alfau's manuscripts include carbon copies of the two novels he published in life, and a handwritten letter from Mary McCarthy. Ben told me that one day he turned up at the Periscope and showed the letter to the members of the Order. In it, Mary McCarthy goes overboard praising the manuscript Alfau had sent her. It was titled *Locos* and published in June 1936, three weeks before the outbreak of the Spanish Civil War. Alfau spoke flawless, somewhat archaic Spanish, but he wrote in English and cultivated an avant-garde sort of aesthetic. His only subject matter was Spain. The Knights Incoherent very much liked his first novel (if that's what it was—it's not clear if you can call it that). They would sit in a circle at the Periscope, taking turns reading it aloud. It's set in the Café de los Locos, an imaginary venue in Toledo. Colón was a very different but no less talented writer. He was a kind of Caribbean Figaro—the penname of the great Larra, one of Spain's most incisive literary journalists ever, and a great writer too. Colón was critical, intelligent, funloving, and as opposed to his Spanish model, his work always contained a note of optimism. I've taken the time to confirm the things that Ben told me about Jesús Colón's work, and everything is as Ben said, with frightening precision, even the pseudonyms and the dates on which the articles were published. Ben went to a few of the Order's gatherings and he had total recall of the first time that his father took him to the Periscope. In fact, after David's death, he inherited my grandfather's membership card.

The anecdote I'm about to set down here takes place in the middle of winter. At that time, Moreau and Hugues had shown up at the Periscope with some young women, French artists, one of whom was no other than Louise Lamarque. Frequently, the Order presented avant-garde spectacles at the Periscope, and that afternoon they had put together a performance whose purpose was to poke fun at Vicente Blasco Ibánez. The Valencian novelist was doing very well in Hollywood, but in the opinion of the Knights Incoherent, he had sold out—for them, having a book made into a commercial film was a mortal sin. On the wall, in the back of the room, they hung a caricature of the novelist. Above it, they had written in large letters "BLASCO'S–EYE." The French artists had painted a target in the colors of the Republican flag right on his nose.

The Civil War changed everything. Alfau stopped coming by, and it would be many years before he returned. The news from Spain was unsettling. The Republicans were beginning to lose. Ben went to a public lecture given by Ralph Bates at a hotel in Manhattan. After hearing the Englishman speak, he felt even more strongly about his already firm decision to enlist with the Abraham Lincoln Brigade.

MR. TUTTLE, ALIAS THE SHADOW

*[Exact date of composition unknown.
Originally written in the mid-seventies,
revised in January 1992.]*

Felipe Alfau met Mr. Tuttle by chance. He was seated by the window of a coffee shop at the corner of Chrystie and Hester, about to take the first sip from his mint tea, when he noticed an iron door on the sidewalk rising slowly. With his cup halfway to his lips, Alfau saw emerge from the bowels of the earth a black midget woman wearing rubber boots and a yellow patent leather raincoat. She took a precautionary look around, leaned back into the hole, and signaled to someone who was still underground to come out. A few seconds later, an individual dressed in a frock coat and top hat stood on the sidewalk. The woman went back into the netherworld, and the trap door closed as slowly as it had opened. The newcomer smoothed his coat, adjusted his hat, checked the time on his pocket watch, and walked off merrily. Alfau had heard tell that this was one of the entrances to an underground city in which thousands of people led a perfectly civilized life. But confirming what had never seemed anything more than a legend made a profound impression on him. Leaving his mint tea untouched, he left the coffee shop determined to follow this apparition who seemed more a character from one of his stories than flesh and bone.

Before long, the man in the frock coat figured out he was being followed and began looking back. When he got to

Houston Street, he finally stopped to confront Alfau, and asked him if he didn't have anything better to do than stalk him. The *Americaniard,* who all that time had been looking for an excuse to start a conversation, blurted out: How about a coffee? My treat— you're not going to get a better offer than that today, are you? The man took off his hat, scratched his head—his hair curly and frizzy—and accepted the invitation on the condition that they walk eleven blocks up to Veniero's, because he loved the cannoli there and it was his birthday. Happy birthday! exclaimed Alfau, shaking the man's hand effusively. Better than cannoli, why not a cake and candles and everything? A birthday setup. The stranger seemed to like the idea, and they walked off talking about God knows what. Once they arrived, Mr. Tuttle called a waitress over and ordered a fruit tart, asking her to put three candles on it. Alfau made some calculations and thought that perhaps each candle represented twelve or thirteen years, maybe fifteen, and when the tart arrived he asked the guest of honor why specifically that number of candles. It's because, the honoree explained, I am in the habit of celebrating my birthdays backward. Alfau gave him a puzzled look, and the man felt compelled to explain:

We're all aware of the inevitability of death, but no one really knows—barring some notable exceptions—when exactly it will strike. I am, he announced, one of those exceptions. I know for a fact that I will die the day I turn fifty. Mr. Tuttle looked at Alfau expectantly, in case he wanted to object, but Alfau was hanging on his every word, so the peculiar man resumed his speech. For this reason, he said, after I turned thirty-five, I began to mark my birthdays backward. Ever since, instead of celebrating the years I've lived, I celebrate the years I have left. Consequently, instead of adding candles to the top of the cake, I subtract them. When I turned thirty-six, I blew out fourteen candles, the following year thirteen, then twelve, and so on till today. Mr. Tuttle clarified that on that day, March 16, 1964, he turned forty-seven, so he had to blow out three candles. As a matter of fact, he had already ordered a cake for that afternoon, he added, although two are certainly better than one—yes, sir.

Alfau nodded and asked him if the tart was okay. Very good, thank you very much, Mr. Tuttle replied. You're welcome, said Alfau, and cleared his throat before he pointed out that they hadn't properly introduced themselves. That's easily remedied, Mr. Tuttle said. What's your name? Felipe Alfau, Felipe Alfau said, and you? Mr. Tuttle responded that in the underground city he was known as Mr. Tuttle, but the few acquaintances he had made in the superficial world above tended to refer to him as the Shadow, which was all right by him. You may call me either. My pleasure, Mr. Tuttle, Alfau said. The pleasure is mine, Mr. Alfau, the Shadow replied. Do you live in the tunnels of the Lower East Side on a permanent basis? Alfau asked. Mr. Tuttle responded that he did, but that on the night of his birthday he always booked a room at the Chelsea Hotel. One night a year, that's all? Alfau asked, thinking perhaps he'd misheard. Yes, that's all, the Shadow confirmed.

Alfau asked him whether he had plans to go anywhere after Veniero's, and Mr. Tuttle said, To the Chelsea Hotel, naturally, since his room was already paid for, and having been a regular for so many years gave him the right to check in at noon, two hours ahead of the scheduled time. Having said this, he consulted his pocket watch and got to his feet. Alfau followed suit and asked if he could come along. Mr. Tuttle said he didn't mind. On the way over, covering the distance on foot, the Shadow briefly explained what kind of life he led in the bowels of Manhattan, and Alfau told him, also concisely, about the Knights Incoherent and their activities. Very interesting, Mr. Tuttle observed as they arrived at the entrance of the hotel. It just so happens, Alfau pointed out, that this very afternoon we are having a gathering. We get together in the Persicope, maybe you know it. It's very close to the entrance to the underground city you used today. It would be an honor for the Knights to welcome you as their guest. Unless you have other plans, he added, remembering that the Shadow had told him he had ordered a cake of his own accord. Do you plan on celebrating your birthday with anyone? I'm not sure, Mr. Tuttle said, with women you never can tell. I'm with you, Alfau said, tapping him on the shoulder, and pulling a piece of paper from his pocket he wrote down the address of the Periscope and gave it to him. When you find out whether you're going to be alone or not, and if you feel up to it, you know where we are. We get together on the floor above the bar—it's a gray door. The password, Alfau added before leaving, is *¡Viva Don Quijote!* Mr. Tuttle read the address and walked off across the lobby with a melancholy air.

When Alfau arrived at the Periscope, he told the knights present at the time that a very special guest might show up at the club later that evening, and went on to recount his peculiar encounter of a few hours before. That day's meeting began on schedule: a debate over the advantages and disadvantages of Soviet communism. In the heat of the argument, the Knights Incoherent (particularly Alfau, who was a rabid anti-communist, and thus in the minority) forgot that there was any likelihood of that dapper gentleman who got along so well with the current president of the Order (it was a rotating shift) making an appearance. Soon enough, they were about to come to blows, and the echo of the primary combatants' crescendo of cursing still hung in the air (You, sir, are a fucking fascist! Aquilino Guerra had shouted at Felipe Alfau—And you're a goddamned Stalinist murderer! was his response, as Jesús Colón held this august personage back by his arms) when they heard a knock at the door. Shut up for one fucking second, damn it! Henry Martínez ordered. The echo was allowed to die. Regaining his composure, Alfau worked loose from Colón, took three wide steps, and slid open the cover of the peephole at the door (they did things right). *¡Viva Don Quijote!* someone said from the other side in a voice that managed to be both gruff and timid. Alfau let him in, of course. The newcomer wore a frock coat, top hat, and a green polka-dot bow tie (therefore different from the black one he had been wearing that morning). He walked in very slowly because he was carrying a cake bearing three unlit candles. It's not much, he said, looking contrite. I only ordered a cake for two, but my date didn't show up. Alfau adopted a serious expression and tapped Tuttle on the shoulder for the second time that day. Come in, please, he said. Make yourself at home. The Shadow put his cake on a table and removed his hat. Aquilino took the frock coat and hung it on a bronze hanger. Alfau dashed to the bar and returned with a bottle of González Byass sherry and glasses for everyone. Rogelio Santana, who was Jesús Colón's guest, lit the three candles. Before blowing them out, Mr. Tuttle begged for silence: no ridiculous songs. Sulking, the Knights Incoherent and their guests shook their heads as if reproaching him for thinking they would ever do such a thing. When they finished the cake, Alfau proposed a special vote to decide if the newcomer could be awarded the title of Honorary member of the Order. The five founding members left Mr. Tuttle for a moment with the other guests and deliberated for a few minutes in a corner. Returning to the table, Martínez, the permanent secretary of the Brotherhood, informed the guests that the motion had passed unanimously. At Colón's request, it was resolved not to continue with their interrupted political discussion and from then on the conversation flowed through calmer channels. When Mr. Tuttle excused himself, it was formally agreed to invite him to celebrate his remaining birthdays at the Periscope. Two more, said Mr. Tuttle, signaling with white-gloved fingers, and poured himself another sherry with that taciturn air that never abandoned him. None of them, neither Alfau nor any of the other Knights

Incoherent, would ever see him save on one of his birthdays.

On March 16, 1965, Mr. Tuttle showed up at the headquarters of the Order with a cake and two candles. The following year, there was only one candle on the cake. He had always been a man of few words, and hated toasts, but on that occasion, before blowing out the lonely candle burning atop his cake, Mr. Tuttle said: Thank you, my friends, it has been a great honor getting to know you and being a member of the Brotherhood. He took a deep breath before adding: This will be the last time we will see each other. On March 16, 1966, there was an open house at the Periscope and the place was packed. The Knights Incoherent argued about politics as vehemently as always, but as the debate dragged on, it became increasingly apparent that an undercurrent of anxiety was slowly undermining the discussion, until at last it waned. Near seven, everyone was staring at the clock, a Festina with black numbers neatly sculpted on a faded yellowish background. A few inches above the slot for the winding key, there was a small blue rectangle in the shape of a double door. When the second hand grazed the lowest part of the circle, one of the guests exclaimed: Half a minute till seven! The Knights Incoherent, all seated at a long table on top of a stage, presiding over the large room, held their breaths to a man, eyes glued on the Festina. The little hand swept the left side of the clock with a desperate languor. All anyone could hear in the Periscope was the clanging of the heating pipes mixed with the intestinal noises of Aquilino Guerra, who had eaten clams and beans. When the second hand and the minute hand came together, the little blue doors burst open and out sprang a cuckoo so small it could have been a hummingbird. The tiny bird chirped seven times and went back inside. The Knights Incoherent shifted their eyes from the Festina to the front door, but no one rang or knocked. The first one to break the silence was Martínez, who made his way to the back of the room cracking his knuckles; Guerra lit a cigarillo and threw the pack into the center of the table for whomever wanted to join him; Colón started looking through a copy of the *New York Times*, although he had read it from beginning to end that morning; the rest of them busied themselves with various delaying tactics, including Rogelio, Guerra's cousin, who began to clip his fingernails over a wastebasket. The guests watched the movements of their hosts as if they were witnessing a Grand Guignol performance. At seven fifteen, Alfau opened a bottle of González Byass and poured a round, even setting up a glass for their absent member, conspicuously placed at the head of the table. Martínez proposed a toast, but Alfau reminded him that Mr. Tuttle hated them. Guerra suggested observing a minute of silence, but Colón called him a jinx. My grandfather advocated trying to figure out what had happened, and Martínez asked how. Alfau insisted that the only thing that could be done was to go on with their gathering as if nothing had happened—nothing *had* happened, after all—but this proved impossible. There was an oppressive sadness in the air that prevented the Knights Incoherent from concentrating on anything. Around nine, they realized that they had to act. Someone suggested that a few of them grab a taxi and go to the Chelsea Hotel. After much give and take, it was decided that Alfau would lead the mission, and select his troops accordingly. He picked Colón and my grandfather. When they got to the hotel, they went right to the front desk—the clerk wasn't sure what to make of them. Alfau showed him a picture of the group, taken one year ago, and pointed at Mister Tuttle. The clerk frowned and told them to have a seat in the lobby, and—photograph in hand—went in search of the manager. The manager came out, stood before them, and ceremoniously preened the long, pointed ends of his mustache, which were oiled with Brilliantine. Looking the picture over, he asked them if they were related to the guest. My grandfather said no, they were not. Friends, acquaintances, colleagues? Jesús Colón said they were all members of a club, to whom Tuttle had been admitted three years ago, although he only ever attended on March 16th, to celebrate his birthday.

Same here, the manager of the Chelsea Hotel said. Although I didn't know anything about his birthday. He always makes his reservation far in advance—I mean, he has a permanent reservation and always calls two months in advance to confirm it. He always books room 305, one of the more inexpensive ones. This year he did the same as always.

He asked the clerk to bring him the reservation book.

Aha, here it is. He confirmed on January 16.

An uncomfortable silence ensued.

Well, don't just stand there like a log. Go tell him his friends from the Periscope are here to see him, urged Alfau.

Let's remain calm, my friend. Calm and cordial. When the clerk came to see me with the photo I asked him to call your friend's room, but he's not answering the phone, which means that he is not there.

What kind of reasoning is that? Alfau chided him. If something's happened to him, he wouldn't be able to answer no matter how many times you called.

I asked our friend here, interjected my grandfather, pointing to the clerk, and he confirmed he saw him go in but not come out; on top of which, if you look behind the desk you can see that his key isn't in its slot.

Guests often take their keys with them when they go out, the manager said, now concentrating his preening on the right point of his mustache exclusively.

You know perfectly well that Mr. Tuttle is in his room. But you don't want to cooperate—which, if you don't mind my saying so, strikes me as rather risky.

Risky?

Perhaps he's had some sort of accident. If we delay much

longer, it may be too late.

What the hell are you talking about, sir? asked the manager. Mr. Tuttle most likely just wants a little privacy. He's up in his room, doing who knows what, and isn't answering the phone because he doesn't feel like it.

In point of fact, we have reason to believe something very serious has happened. His life might be in danger—that's why we're here. Actually, it may already be too late. Why can't we just go up and knock on the door? Alfau asked. He seemed to be getting more upset with every new exhortation.

We take our guests' privacy very seriously, sir. It's a sacred trust—especially at a place like the Chelsea. I take it you're familiar with our reputation? We can't just go up and open a door, especially if we suspect the guest is inside. Who knows what we could find in there? I'm very sorry, gentlemen, I just can't. I'm sure you'll see my point if you'd just calm down.

Colón stood right behind Alfau, ready to hold him back in case he lost control. As of yet, the Catalan contented himself with raising his voice. His rage was such that the manager's resolution began to crack.

How many times do I have to tell you that each minute that passes is crucial? Do you give a damn about your guests' lives or not?

Hedging his bets, Colón took this opportunity to grab Alfau by the arms, just in case—which was providential, as it was this gesture that made the manager relent.

José, get me the duplicate key to room 305, he said to the clerk, and up they all went. The manager banged on the door for a full five minutes, putting more and more strength into it until he was forced to give up. Now as unsettled as the others, he put the key in the lock.

David said—as Ben reported—that it was a sight he'd carry with him to the grave. It was a small room, with a checkered marble floor and a small window that looked out into an inner courtyard. It was sparsely furnished: a single-door armoire, a narrow desk, a chair—where Mr. Tuttle had left his frock coat, top hat, and watch—and, incongruously, a bed with a canopy whose green curtains were drawn. A stool had been knocked over and lay on its side in the middle of the room. Mr. Tuttle was hanging from a polka-dot bow tie that he had tied to a hook he had nailed into one of the ceiling beams himself—as the presence of a hammer on the table proved. His tongue was lolling out and his face was swollen and purplish. Around his crotch was a wet mark that ran down the seams to the hem of his pants, which was still dripping into a yellow puddle on the marble tile.

For some reason, before taking his life, Mr. Tuttle had removed his undergarments, which were black, and put his clothes back on. On top of the small wooden table by the armoire, the hotel staff and the delegation of Knights Incoherent could see a pair of socks and a union suit.

OPIUM

[*From a notebook dated 1972.*
Text revised in January 1991.]

Moreau explained to me how access to the smoke rooms in the opium den worked. To preserve secrecy, clients were given cards with directions to different entrances whose locations changed every few hours. These points of entry could be found in all sorts of locales, from the shabbiest to the most luxurious. My guess is that there's a whole maze of passages that connect a web of hidden rooms in homes and shops. The police had been bought off, while they in turn have placed double agents inside the Chinese mafia, so that the relationship between the two has become a hall of mirrors. For security reasons, new "entry" cards are being issued all the time.

I looked at the back of the card Moreau had just given me. You see that gray band? Scrape it off for the address of your entrance. But as soon as the inscription comes into contact with the air, it begins to fade, and in a matter of minutes it's gone. Also, the Frenchman went on, if you don't show up at the place within two hours, the address is no longer good.

What happens then?

Nothing, but when you get there, it could be a flower shop or a children's clothing store, in which case all you can do is buy a bouquet of flowers or a jumper. Or a pound of shrimp if you end up at a fishmonger's, he added, laughing and faking a punch to my stomach. In any case, all the addresses are in Chinatown.

He didn't tell me how much he had paid for the card, but I knew from Louise that they were expensive.

A few friends of mine are going there today as well, he said, I don't know if you've met them. Louise and Mussifiki will be there too. So have fun.

Do I scratch for the address now?

Whenever you want, as long as you're there in the next couple of hours. I bought your ticket at noon. All right, see you later.

I scratched the surface of the card with a quarter.

The address was 120 Mott Street. Below it was a phrase that seemed to be pulled from the *I Ching*: The cranes have built their nests in the snowy garden. I watched the letters fade and put the card back in my pocket. I took the subway to Canal Street and walked north up Mott. I left behind a throng of restaurants, shops, street stalls, specialty stores, teahouses, and a temple with an enormous golden Buddha. I crossed Canal and passed the last fish stores, fruit stands, and warehouses. 120 Mott is half a block north of Grand Street. I stood in front of a wooden door painted brown. I pressed the bell and heard a frayed voice over the intercom. I didn't understand a single word, but when it stopped, I spoke the password as clearly as I could: The cranes have built their nests in the snowy garden, I said. A young woman holding a baby in her arms turned the corner and didn't take her eyes off me until she had gone past. I heard the buzzing of the door and went into a space that looked like a store that had been recently ransacked. The metal shelves on the walls were empty. On the paper covering the wall nearest the street there was the outline of a piece of furniture that seemed to have just been removed after years in the same spot. In the back, behind a wooden counter, there was a sickly man, with a gruff face, looking like a Sicilian from central casting. He had a three-day beard, a black vest and beret, a white collarless shirt, and his fists clenched with knuckles pressing into the counter. Behind him was a red door.

The card, he demanded when he got tired of looking at me.

I took it out of my pocket and placed it face up on the counter. The front of the card was violet, colored with the silhouette of a crane above a row of Chinese characters. The man glanced at it and lifted a part of the counter, letting me by. I reached to grab the card, thinking I could keep it, but the Sicilian (supposing that's what he was) held it down with a finger and signaled toward the red door with his chin. After I went in, the door clicked shut behind me, leaving me in complete darkness. All I could see was a crack of light at the end of the hallway. I groped my way forward slowly, my hand on a damp wall, until I came to a light switch and flipped it on. Farther away, a bulb barely casting any light came on. There were puddles on the floor. A few yards ahead the water swarmed with life. I moved forward, my feet splashing. A multitude of reddish eyes turned toward me, and the hallway filled with high-pitched squeals. I had interrupted a congregation of rats engaged in something or other I probably didn't want to know about. For a moment, I thought they were going to attack me, but soon their shadows shot off in all directions and they disappeared. Some darted through my legs. I stepped around a bundle that gave off an unbearable stench and did my best not to figure out what it might be.

My only guide was the very weak lightbulb at the end of the hallway. When my eyes adjusted a bit to the darkness, I saw brownish stains all over the walls that reminded me of the bat droppings that smeared the Mayan crypts of Palenque. I came to the door at the end of the hallway and turned the knob, afraid it would be locked. It gave way easily, and I found myself at the bottom of a narrow, steep staircase, from which a stream of putrid water ran. Above, I made out a slit of light seeping out from under yet another door. Holding onto the iron railing, I struggled up the stairs, opened the door at the top, and came to a room somewhat better lit than the hallway and staircase I had left behind.

Although it didn't quite match the description of the place that Moreau told me he'd gone through before reaching the opium den, I was relieved to recognize some of the objects he said I would find when I got there. In the middle of the anteroom was an ewer and basin with a towel and a bar of soap. A mirrored armoire took up the far wall entirely. I wiped the soles of my shoes on a straw mat and went to the washbasin. The soap had a delicate aroma of vanilla and jasmine. As I washed my hands, the surface of the looking glass took on a sheen, as if someone had turned on a light on the other side of the armoire. I looked carefully and noticed what appeared to be two human shadows behind my reflection. I turned around. There was no one else in the room, but when I looked into the mirror again, the shadows were still there. I pressed the doors of the armoire with my fingertips and they moved toward me with a slow creak. I opened them wide and saw that instead of a sheet of wood there was a curtain, through which the light of the space behind filtered in.

I drew the curtain and saw a vast room whose elegance was a stark contrast to the spaces I had just passed through. In the middle stood two women. One was blind and old, the other a disturbingly beautiful young lady who looked at me intently. The old woman took a step toward me. She was tall and very thin, with brittle skin and large, bony hands. After carefully feeling my face with her hands, she hummed a tune in a soft voice, then went into the armoire and disappeared. The one who remained in the room with me couldn't have been more than twenty. She was taller than me, was wearing a very agreeable perfume, and had a slightly androgynous air. She offered me her hand, which was white and delicate, and said in flawless English: Come, your friends have been waiting for you for a while now.

The scene that followed was almost comforting, since I'd seen it countless times in old photographs, in books, and at the movies. Men and women were lying on divans and mats, attended by servants who moved about, refilling their opium pipes. The customers had an electrifying air of sensuality and abandon about them. The women weren't bothering to cover their thighs or their breasts. Some were Asian, a few were black or mulatto. The majority were white, European types. They were all luxuriantly dressed—in fact, the ostentation of their clothing might have been more exciting than the sight of their bodies.

My guide led me to a private room where I found Louise and Mussifiki with others I had met on previous occasions, although I couldn't remember where. Louise's eyes met mine for a moment before shutting me out.

She hasn't seen you, she's dreaming, my young guide said, not having let go of my hand. It's your turn now, get comfortable. I'm going to prepare you a pipe.

I leaned back in one of the divans, not far from Louise, and I watched the young woman in the robe get to work. She deftly kneaded a ball of opium, placed it in the bowl, and lit it delicately.

Take a deep breath and continue to inhale, she said, bringing the pipe to my mouth, even if you think your lungs are going to burst.

I did as I was told. A silver blade slit my chest open, but instead of pain, I felt as if a curtain of light were descending from the sky. I lost all my strength.

Are you all right? my guide asked, caressing my hair. I nodded, wordlessly contemplating her goddess-like countenance, feeling as if both of us were slipping through a crack in space leading who knows where. Still leaning over me, she watched over my indescribable heaviness. Her words ricocheted, bursting in the air a thousand times, a crystal echo trailing them farther and farther away. Are you all right? she asked again, caressing my head and my face. I lifted my eyes, trying to retain her image, but it was escaping me. She crouched by my side. I felt the touch of her smooth, pearl-gray robe on my cheek. She had very white, thin, and delicately shaped legs. I tried to caress them before giving in to the drowsiness that was plunging me into unconsciousness. The robe opened imperceptibly. There was no trace of desire in my gesture, all my will toward pleasure was now in the pull of the opium, but I continued to watch the contours of her thighs, letting my eyes slip toward her crotch, when I realized that my guide was a man. He put the pipe to my mouth again and said, Breathe in, and I saw the spreading flame, like a cosmic explosion.

MARGUERITE

[Shortly before meeting Nadia.]

With Louise, in her Deauville studio, drinking:

We were at Corsair Beach, in a cave, Corsair's Cave. Well, the fact is that the beach was named after the grotto, which had once been used as a hideout by pirates. To get there you had to head off the main road and walk down a dirt road that bordered the vineyards. We went often when we were young. There were two ways to be there—so radically different it might as well have been two places, hundred of miles apart. One was with the family, on Sundays or holidays, the other when we skipped school and no adults were around to watch us.

She poured herself another scotch and set her eyes on an unfinished canvas. The large colorful swaths suggested a seascape.

I don't know why, but lately I've been thinking about Marguerite a lot, although I haven't seen her since she went off to college in Lille. I often wonder what became of her. That painting there is inspired by my memory of Marguerite. I'm working on it to get rid of this nostalgia. Maybe I'm reminiscing about her now because of what you told me about Sam Evans? Who knows? I hope nothing's happened to her, although—really—she ceased to exist for me when she left for Lille. I haven't heard from her since.

She looked back at me and said:

I had just turned thirteen. The boys wanted us to go inside the cave with them. They asked us to take off our underwear. They wanted to kiss us in the dark, touch us where they shouldn't—you know. Some girls agreed and pulled down their panties. As for me, I didn't even consent to step inside. But then there was the time Marguerite asked me. It was different. She asked me and I said yes, spontaneously, without even thinking about it, not even a bit afraid. She was a high school senior, three or four years older than me. The others had already gone into the cave and we were the only two left outside. Then she took my hand and said we should go in, and I let her take me.

THE DICE OF DEATH

[December 1988?]

Telegram from Paris. Louise pointed to a folded piece of thin blue paper on the glass table. Alston Hughes died, she said.

Alston Hughes? I repeated, incredulous, and things got a little blurry. Sylvie took my hand and pressed firmly.

Sit down. I know how it must feel. You want something to drink, Gal? she asked. And I said no.

The telegram is from Moreau. Well, I didn't expect anything like this so soon, but it isn't exactly a surprise, is it, Gal?

I told Louise she was right. In his last letter, Anzaldúa had told me that Alston was a mess. He pissed and shit on himself in bed, insulted everyone, said that he was going to win the Nobel Prize. He'd wake up with the DTs in the middle of the night. He only got out of bed to drink, and when he actually managed to make himself drunk, he would sing and scream until he was exhausted. Then he sat down to write. He wrote poems, letters, sections of books in which he mixed four different languages. (I have become an *alloglot*! he exulted in one letter, then explaining: "someone who writes in a language other than his mother tongue.") He ripped out pages from his diaries and glued them to the walls. He began to make a collage, a mural that took up his entire bedroom; he asked his friends from all over the world to send him photographs to add to the work in progress. He was saying his farewell to life. Sometimes, when he tried to write but couldn't, he would howl, like kids do when they don't get what they want right away. The amazing thing was that he was ever capable of writing anything at all, in such a state. He sent me a letter almost every week, and I wasn't the only one. His poems were another story—they got away from him more often than not, abruptly descending into nonsense and echolalia. Against all odds, however, there were times when he produced fragments of a strange and chilling beauty. It goes without saying that his private life was a shambles. He quarreled with Moreau, with Anzaldúa, with Gilgamesh, with everyone who had helped him financially. He bragged about it, boasted about biting the hand that fed him, said it with pride. He said he was going to donate a part of the prize money for his Nobel to the fight against AIDS.

He died the day before yesterday, Sylvie said. And that same day, an envelope mailed to you, care of my suite number, arrived at the Chelsea Hotel.

I don't know why he sent it to my address. She gave me a badly damaged envelope from a tray. I tore it open. Inside was an object that might have been intended to be a book, but more resembled a bundle of papers haphazardly sewn together. I looked for a letter, a note, but there was nothing else. Sylvie and I looked at the cover for a while, a lousy photocopy.

He sent us another one too, Sylvie said. Also without a note— just the book. According to Moreau, someone he knew at the Embassy of Panama in Paris agreed to publish a "limited edition," which he then mailed to a few friends, ten to fifteen copies at most.

At long last, he made up his mind to get into print, Louise laughed.

It's not his first book, I said. Anzaldúa showed me two others.

That's right, she confirmed.

His friend Gilgamesh published them under his own imprint, Invisible Editions. One is his correspondence with María

Zambrano, the philosopher who went into exile after the Civil War. The other one is a collection of poems titled *Mosaics*. I asked Gilgamesh to get copies for me and he found them in the Casa del Libro on the Gran Vía of Madrid. They were the last remaining copies of a tiny edition. Alzandúa bought them and mailed them to me.

Now I leafed through the book that Alston had sent before he died. The pages were unnumbered. There was no title or name on its paltry cover, which was a photocopy of a reproduction of the famous *Milk Drop Coronet* by Harold E. Edgerton—a photograph capturing a drop of milk at the moment of splashing into a body of more milk. Later, Moreau told me that Alston had taken it from D'Arcy Thompson's *On Growth and Form*, one of his favorite books. The image on the cover was so dark that it looked more like a coronet of blood.

The dark blood poisoning his heart, Louise said, trying to make me laugh.

I read Alston's book that very afternoon. It would be hard to describe it. A spiritual autobiography of sorts. As a memoir, it's very interesting—not just for those who knew him, but for anyone intrigued by the dynamics of literary creation. I wanted to rescue something from the mess and incorporate it into *Brooklyn*. And immediately I knew what to pick. An amazing story, especially given that Alston didn't write fiction. It's called "Salsipuedes." I'd numbered the odd pages in pencil as I read through, so I know that the story begins on page thirty-three. It's very short. Still, it took me an hour to copy it longhand. That night, I called Chus in Barcelona. He was very upset by Alston's death, and told me he was going to write something about him. After I hung up, I picked up Alston's opus and examined the cover in detail. It was so worn-out that it looked like a canvas coated with a layer of cracked gesso. When I had been examining it with Louise and Sylvie, I told them that it reminded me of a painting that needed to be restored. The splashing blood-milk was reminiscent of a crown of thorns. Behind it was a tall square, the night, finely edged, and above that was a bright distant point, the primeval eye of the moon.

It reminds me of something, but I don't know what, I told Louise.

It reminds you of Malevich's mystical squares.

She was right. It's fascinating to me how clearly she sees. White on white, an invisible surface over the nadir. I decided to use that same image as a cover for "Salsipuedes," the story I would put in *Brooklyn*. I would make a photocopy of the photocopy and write above it "The Dice of Death."

In the loneliness of my room, I opened Alston's book and began to read. As they say: I couldn't put it down. When I'd finished, I pictured him in his tiny apartment in Paris, writing to his friends at night, waiting for his death. It took me three days, but I was finally able to cry.

KADDISH & τπ

[*Below this enigmatic title there's a note in Gal's handwriting that says,* Story from *Atlantic Monthly*, translate and include here. Juxtapose with farce? Send both to Nadia. *In the* Brooklyn Notebook, *however, there's only a blank space. I'll do the same here.*]

Full text of the lecture given by Felipe Alfau before the Order of the Knights Incoherent. Transcribed by Lord Gin, permanent secretary and stenographer to the Brotherhood. The Periscope Bar & Grill, Lower Manhattan, April 1, 1964.

Ladies and gentlemen, members and guests, freeloaders and rate-paying attendees, enemies and friends:

We have gathered here today to celebrate, yes, that's the word, celebrate, the death of Mr. Tuttle, aka the Shadow, honorary if outlandish member of our distinguished Order. It is a proven fact that he lived underground, but we cannot know how and why he was brought to such straits. Neither do we know his place of birth, nor what he did for a living. He always wore the same outfit, his demeanor one of a weary elegance, but I am not going to describe his clothes. This is not a novel. Once a year, on March 16, he rented a room at the Chelsea Hotel. Today is April Fool's Day, a date on which our august society traditionally opens its doors so the public may attend our annual lecture. It is my turn to deliver the lecutre this year, and I have decided to dedicate it to the memory of our late friend, telling the story of the place in which he chose to mark his anti-birthdays and put an end to his life. My talk is also dedicated to the graduating class of the Miguel de Unamuno Program in Creative Writing, funded by our Order, and here with us today. After my lecture, they will receive their diplomas and so become fully anointed and accredited writers; may God have mercy on their future readers.

Before getting into today's topic, I would like to invoke the help of good old Don Miguel, by whom I have always been guided when it comes to methodology. I mean to say that it is not my intent to give a full and systematic dissertation on the peculiar building whose history I am about to recount. What I will do is make a few observations in my own manner, a process that, so far from being Teutonic, we might call Unamunian, which, conceptually speaking, is the exact opposite. I know this is a monster of a word, but I will coin it right here, protest though you might, much as we have been saddled with *Kafkaesque* or *Chekhovian*. Don Miguel more than deserves the same honor. In my future work, I shall employ the term *Unamunian* as a modifier vindicating the natural right to wipe one's ass with certain formalities that, masquerading as academic rigor, do nothing but set back the process of approaching the truth, which is never where we look for it. (And if I should fail to use it again in the course of this address, you may be assured that I will certainly have recourse to it in my future writings and allocutions.) As for this lecture, I don't have the least intention to pay heed to any narrative or chronological thread; if it should appear that I am doing so, I assure you that this will be mere coincidence. It is also my intention to do without any facts I happen to feel like omitting. That being said, let me start, it's about time.

The building we know as the Chelsea Hotel was opened in the year of our Lord 1884, at the height of the robber-baron era, ruled by such crooks as the Carnegies, the Morgans, the Astors, and the Vanderbilts, among others: a time of ostentation and corruption that would give rise to great dramatic episodes, such as when the mistress of the tycoon Jimmy Fisk blew her lover's brains out in the bedroom of a suite they were sharing . . . What, what's this here, Murphy, you moron. Fisk was actually shot by her lover's lover, although not in the hotel. But we'll leave it at that, we have to stay with the building.

The style of our building could be described as Victorian Gothic, a mixture of Queen Anne and free-style classicism. The apartments used to be (they no longer are) enormous, with very high ceilings and soundproof and fireproof walls. The interior stairwell, made of wrought-iron like the balconies, runs from the lobby to the roof terrace, and has a railing made of the finest mahogany. The roof terrace, made of red brick tiles, is an enormous, uneven space, scattered with steps, skylights, chimneys, studios, dormer windows, observatories, lounge chairs, parapets, gardens, and—though this might be hard to believe—an extensive grove of trees . . . *An extensive grove of trees,* what kind of assistant are you, Murphy? Okay, fine. I will take your word for this, but it makes it sound like a real forest up there.

Dear members of the audience, before continuing the water torture, I want to stress that for the most part I owe all this information to the efforts of my research assistant, who is in attendance today. Salute the audience, Murphy, don't be shy. Stand up so everyone can see you. A hand for Mr. Murphy Burrell. Thank you, friends, and thank you Murphy, please stop bowing like an epileptic, everybody's seen you now, you can sit down, that's enough.

We were talking about style. In the early days of the future Chelsea Hotel, the elegance of the furniture and accessories was on a par with the nobility of the materials used: marble for the floors; mahogany for the moldings, doors, and armoires. The enormous mirror frames were one of the trademarks of the place. The rooms had stained-glass windows. At one point, there were three large dining rooms, one of which became the property of some *Americaniards* who named it "El Quijote," which is still open today.

Its fame attracted all kinds of artistic types, in particular— for reasons that remain obscure—those who were mentally unbalanced. I'll go over a few, beginning with Sarah Bernhardt. The actress traveled everywhere with her own silk bedsheets and kept warm with a down comforter made to fit the padded coffin in which she always slept. Before you write this off as a simple caprice, let me inform you that La Bernhardt was not the first or the last tenant of the Chelsea to sleep in a coffin. Murphy has positively confirmed two other cases. Much can be inferred concerning the spirit and style of those individuals who over the years decided to stay at the Chelsea, including our good old Mr. Tuttle.

As for the fraternity of writers, to which I myself belong, the first prestigious entry in our guest book was Mr. William Dean Howells, who occupied a suite consisting of four rooms in 1888 . . . Er, Murphy, I can verify the year, but where did you get "four rooms" from? Are you sure? Oh, well. Let's move on. That same year, the author of the Yankee Quixote—in whose tales the swamps of the South stand for the plains of La Mancha, and the wide Mississippi is a mighty reincarnation of the elusive Guadiana—hung his hat there. I am referring, of course, as even the most dull-witted among you must have guessed, to Samuel Clemens, better known as Mark Twain. Sober or drunk—we won't go into that—the author of *The Adventures of Huckleberry Finn* was often to be seen at the bar.

Between 1907 and 1910, when the Chelsea was already a hotel, no less a figure than O. Henry lived in one of its rooms. Oh, the magnificent roundness of that initial, stripped and bared of any glitzy consonants, reduced to the perfection of a circle accompanied with the humility of a squire by an imperceptible ink stain, a thing devoid of dimensions, the most simple of the punctuation marks: the dot of the *i* fallen to the ground like a ball. A humble full stop, otherwise known as *period*. And since there is a period here, my fellow Incoherents, students, enemies, and friends, if you'll allow me to interject some remarks of a personal nature, I will digress for a moment to tell you that I had the honor of brushing up against the great O. Henry face to face. That's right. It happened at McSorley's, the Irish tavern in the East Village. He was carrying four mugs of beer, two in each hand, and I was carrying only two, one in my left hand and one in my right. Mine were pale, his dark. Mr. Henry, said I . . . Murphy, you're a bit sloppy, you know? I think you should be more careful when you're writing anything I might have to read aloud, in public. I can't read ahead to make sure I'm not about to make a fool of myself. Would I have really addressed the man by his pseudonym? Well, I can't remember. Makes it sound a little like fiction, really. And we oughtn't allow any. Anyway: Mr. Henry, said I brimming with admiration as he stood before me, but I was able to add nothing else to my plea. He gave me a funny look. There's no need to be so formal, he blurted out. Call me O, just like that, without the period, and turning around, he left me stranded with my admiration and my two beers. I'll never forget those eyes, round like his name, the dark points of his pupils fixed for a second on mine. I felt like the luckiest man in the city. The best writer in town (who cares what the highbrows might have thought) had deigned to address one of his humble admirers. My experience can only be classified as sublime, as much as my assistant, Murphy Burrell, may want to cast aspersions on it, reminding me that O. Henry often went on outrageous drinking binges during which he spent his time not composing immortal prose but trying to pinch the waitresses' asses.

But the Chelsea does not live on prose alone! In its hallways, there are the echoes of the footsteps of poets as fine as Hart Crane. If we had time, I would recite you his poem about the Brooklyn Bridge from beginning to end. Unfortunately, time's just what we don't have. But I will nonetheless if briefly talk about Edgar Lee Masters, the Poet of Death. The last time Mr. Tuttle set foot at one of our meetings, we the Knights Incoherent gave him a copy of *The Spoon River Anthology* by way of birthday present—a collection of poems as great as any ever written. Oh boy, Murphy. So you've become a critic now, into the bargain? Such strong opinions. I couldn't care less if Americans don't tend to rate *Spoon River* particularly high in terms of, what do you call it, "Great Writing"? Funny, I don't remember asking you for your opinion, smartass. The guardians of the canon can go chew their way through the *Cantos* for all I care. *The Spoon River Anthology* is a great book, end of story, in my humble opinion. A stroke of genius to write a volume consisting exclusively of epitaphs. And in each epitaph a story. Madmen, drunks, murderers, whores, everything is there, spoken from the grave.

Let's move on . . . where the hell did I put my notes? Do you have them, Burrell? You're sure? Oh no, you're right. Sorry. Here they are . . . let's see, who's up now? Vladimir Nabokov? But I wasn't going to tear into him till the end. Are you doing all this on purpose, Master Burrell? Well, your little ruse won't work. I don't care what the know-it-alls say. Nabokov's a hack and that's it. So let's set things in order here. What I wanted to do is tell you a juicy little anecdote, possibly apocryphal, about Sinclair Lewis. You're ready? In that case, I'll perform a little experiment. On a certain occasion, the good Don Sinclair was giving a lecture on writing to an audience of devoted fans. Let's see, how many of you here want to be writers? Raise your hands, please. No, no, not you, morons. That's what he said to his audience then—Sinclair Lewis did. Murphy, put your hand down, please. Everybody else has, in case you haven't noticed. You always have to make a scene. So yes, that's exactly right, just about everyone raised their hands, just like you did just now. On seeing that, Lewis struck the podium with his fist and exclaimed: Then why the hell aren't you home writing? I'm not quite sure why the hell I included that in my notes, but I didn't want it to go unsaid. Mind that, you lazy scribbler wannabes . . . And something else, too: the worst thing you can do is bore your reader.

Now I have to talk about the Knotts, Murphy? Why do you want me to do that? You should be giving this lecture, not me . . . Now why are you getting up and bowing to the audience again? You already got your round of applause, sit down, please. Okay, thanks. So, the Murphys . . . I mean, the Knotts built a library on the second floor. Did you double check this? What's this now? From an aesthetic point of view, they almost ruined the hotel.

They divided the suites to increase the profits, and if, to make room, something had to be broken, well, they broke it. They almost destroyed the hallways, lowering the ceilings, and . . . I better not go on . . . let's see, the years of the Great Depression . . . I think I'm going to skip ahead . . . the *Louisiana Story* . . . Wait . . . What does that have to do with the Chelsea? What? It was a collaboration between three prestigious Chelsea residents, you say? Who, may I ask? Robert Flaherty, Virgil Thomson, and Richard Leacock? Well, well. Who the hell cares, is my reply. Let's see now. Thomas Wolfe. Yes, this is good. Wolfe showed up at the Chelsea on a sunny morning in 1937. Someone had told him about the hotel and he came to take a look. It so happened that he ran into no other than Edgar Lee Masters . . . Ed recognized Tom, Tom recognized Ed. Ed asked what Tom was doing there. Tom replied that he was thinking of moving into the hotel. Don't say another word, you're staying, Edgar Lee said, and introduced him to the manager, who put him up in one of the most exclusive and lavish apartments in the place. Wolfe also had a nice suite, I mean it was dirty and cavernous but at least it had very high ceilings, which the gigantic Wolfe appreciated because he didn't have to bump his head on the doorframes. In the bathroom, upon a raised, canopied platform, there was a most impressive toilet bowl. What a nice detail. I get tears in my eyes thinking—I hope all of this is true, Murphy—that the manuscript of *Look Homeward, Angel* was written atop such a majestic throne. Once he'd finished a section of the novel, he would put it inside a wooden box next to his throne. Soon, a single box wasn't enough. He piled them up all over the bathroom, but soon he ran out of space and had to use the kitchen and then the living room until the whole place was full of boxes brimming with manuscript pages. When he died, the sheets of paper stuffed in the packing boxes numbered in the tens of thousands. One of the projects that was cut short by his early departure was a history of the hotel . . .

In 1939, the Knotts sold the Chelsea. None of these changes killed the spirit of the place. Its mysterious aura continued to attract new artists, younger blood, talented musicians, writers, poets, and painters, most of them drug addicts or drunks or both at once.

What are you saying, Burrell? Speak up, for God's sake, I can't hear you. Arthur Miller? No, I'm not going to say anything about Miller, I can't stand him. Who? Dylan Thomas? Everyone knows the story of the eighteen straight whiskies he drank before dying at St. Vincent's. What's wrong now? What's with the commotion? Why are you holding that gigantic alarm clock up in the air? You're a clown, Murphy Burrell. You can't just wear a wristwatch like everybody else? And now you're waving a red flag? Have you completely lost your mind? Ah, okay, I get it . . . My friends, we're out of time. As a matter of fact, I've gone over. Too bad, with all these notes left. William Burroughs . . . And so, that's it. All we have to do is observe a minute of silence for our friend Mr. Tuttle. Thank you for your attention. Please rise.

[There follows a large blank space that Lord Gin, the stenographer of the Society, intends to be the typographic equivalent of sixty seconds of silence, then the words *Requiescat in Pace. Amen.*]

THE AVENGING ANGEL

*[Original text from 1972.
Revised by Gal Ackerman
in February 1992.]*
Saturday at the Chamberpot with Marc Capaldi. Colm Talbot,
the ex cop, has just opened a bar right next to the Wilde Fire.

You know what he's calling it? Marc asks. The Green Snot.
Those Irish are genius when it comes to names. You probably
can't guess where the name comes from, I bet.

A squalid old man approaches and asks for a cigarette. Our
waitress comes out from behind the counter to steer him back
onto the street, but Marc stops her with a wave of his hand and,
pointing to the sky, barks:

The sea, the snotgreen sea, the scrotumtightening sea. *Epi
oinopa pontos*. Ah, Dedalus, the Greeks!

The old man blinks, not knowing what to say.

Marc lets out a guffaw and the old man laughs with him.

James Joyce, *Ulysses*, chapter one, Marc says and gives the
beggar an almost-full pack of L&M. The waitress tells him to go
away and stay gone.

The Green Snot is a shoebox wedged in between two other
foul places, the Mad Stork and the Wilde Fire. The Mad Stork has
jazz on Saturdays; the Wilde Fire is a shitty bar, where prostitutes
gather. On the corner is a gas station in front of an empty lot.
That's where it all happens after midnight. When we get there,
there's a patrol car at the gas station with its lights flashing. The
cops have their windows rolled down and are calmly chatting

with a couple of people. One of them waves at Marc. According to him, the cops take a cut from the pimps, the hustlers, and the bar owners. They hang out for a moment at the gas station before hightailing it out of there.

At the Green Snot, Marc goes directly to the back and starts chatting with a group of very elegantly dressed black men. A fat, tall man with red hair wipes the counter in front of me with a wet cloth.

I know you, he says. You're a friend of the Poet. Did you come with him?

I nod. I'm not sure how Marc gets everyone to call him that in these lousy joints.

The tall fat man offers a hand: Colm Talbot, he says. I'm sorry, I don't remember your name.

Gal Ackerman.

Pleasure to meet you. Is this your first time in the Green Snot?

I tell him it is.

First one on the house, then. What'll it be?

Marc disappears into the bathroom with one of the well-dressed black men. After a few moments, they come out together, laughing and wiping their noses

Have you got a light, *mi amor*? chimes a woman's voice behind me in a Spanish tinged with Caribbean inflections. When I turn around, I see a mulatta with green eyes who can't be older than eighteen. I search my pockets to no avail.

I'm sorry, I say. I thought I had a lighter with me.

And no fire here either? she says, cupping her hand on my genitals.

Careful, white boy, someone mutters in my ear. She's after your wallet not your cock.

It's Al Green, a friend of Marc's who plays the double bass at the Mad Stork. He bumps his shoulder into mine, placing a small bag of coke in my hand. No, thanks, I say. Al winks at the girl, offers her a light, and heads for the bathroom.

Will you buy me a drink? the girl asks.

I signal for Colm and she asks for a Budweiser. Her name is Esmeralda and she's from Spanish Harlem. She says they gave her that name because of her eyes.

Nothing to do with the name of this place? asks Marc, right before heading for the door to meet someone waiting for him at the parking lot. I wonder what he's up to or whether he'll come back. Years before, when we first met, I wrote this about him:

> Marc Capaldi, Italian American, publicity agent, forty-six years old, has published three collections of poems. We met at his apartment on the West Side. As we were leaving, he stuck one of his books in his pocket. It seems incomprehensible to me that he should carry his poetry with him when he goes to those desperate, lonely places where he likes to spend his nights, trying to mitigate the pain of living with a few crystals of coke and a few drops of semen. He's attracted to sinister guys—the more dangerous they look, the better; just like the dumps where he goes to look for them. Before leaving his apartment, we'd been talking about poetry. By the time we reached the fourth or fifth bar, he rounded on me, exclaiming:
>
> The rabble, blood and shit, the fucking asshole of the world, urban detritus, the loneliness and pain of humanity. Angels, but not those Rilke liked to yodel about   castrati who don't know what life is about.
>
> Which I found a bit adolescent, to tell the truth. On one hand, in his defense, he was very drunk at the time. On the other, though, I've had a chance to skim through his books, and his poetry is like that too—all blood and shit, reeking of desolation and rot. And yet, though of course I could be reading too much into it, I though I saw, from time to time, a

infinitesimal flame behind some of his work that allowed one to infer that there was least a sliver of hope in Marc.

Rilke's angels were *not* castrati, I said, but let's not argue about poetry now.

Why not? Because poetry's too good for the gutter?

No, not that.

It better not be that, because the shit we're wading through is the real world. That's why I don't give a damn about your poets. Not even Blake, much as he talks about hell. People like Burroughs or Bukowski, maybe. At least if they bother to talk to angels it's because they want to fuck them and then wipe their asses with feathers.

We'll talk about it some other time, Marc.

Why? *This* is where you'll find what you're looking for, not in Rilke or all those other sublime bastards you gorge yourself with.

We've barely just met, how do you know what I'm looking for?

Because you're looking for the same thing I am, you're just not doing it in the right place.

And where should I look?

I've told you. In the filth. You're knee-deep in it yourself, you just don't want to hear about it. But it's in blood, shit, and semen that you're going to find what you're looking for. Blood, shit, and semen, don't forget it, like when you get fucked in the ass, something you're too uptight to try because you think you're not a faggot. Oh, and a bit of coke. Asshole and nostril—they should take whatever comes, no protection, no second thoughts. And if it kills you—well, who cares? All the better. They'll burn you up, put you in an urn, and that's that. What are the so-called upright citizens of the world trying to prove? They want me to think I have to die just because I like to fuck? Well, fine. What counts is to be able to brush up against eternity, if only for a moment. Let them burn us. God couldn't care less what any of us do.

The owner of the bar pulled me aside and told me that I had thirty seconds to get Marc out of there, otherwise he would take care of it himself, and it could get nasty. He was clasping a gold medal pendant around his neck. We're Catholics around here and don't like this bullshit. And when he sobers up tell the son of a bitch never to show his snout around here again.

Marc was about to say something, but I put a hand over his mouth, and dragged him as best I could out to the street. I put him in a cab, and we got out of there.

The black man in the smart suit comes back from the empty lot by himself. I take a peek out the door but there's no sign of Marc. Esmeralda is leaning on the jukebox, smiling, when I head back for the bar. She raises her Bud and calls me over. She waits for the song to end, grabs my hand, and leads me out the front door. On Ninth Avenue, the shadows of the whores and transvestites are indistinguishable from those of the trees and streetlights. We pass blocks of buildings and more empty lots. A dirty moon floats in the sky. After a few blocks I realize that a scrawny guy wearing a ball cap with the Puerto Rican flag on it is following us. Esmeralda crouches over the curb and spits out a long, viscous string of saliva that clings to her lips, a worm of rotten light.

What have you been snorting? I ask her.

What the fuck are you talking about? she responds in her Caribbean singsong, still crouching. Her teeth reflect the light of the streetlight. I don't do that kind of thing.

What kind of thing?

She gets up nimbly.

I'm no whore, get it?

Now that her eyes are level with mine, I realize they're a bit crossed. The light changes to green. We look at it as if it's on the other bank of a river we have no way of crossing. The skeletal Puerto Rican watches us, leaning on a tree, always keeping exactly the same distance. Esmeralda begins walking against the red light. A car speeds by her, very close. I hear the trail of a yell, followed by a loud honk that vanishes into the night. I think she's completely forgotten about me, that she's heading off to some corner on Eleventh Avenue, but when she gets to the other side of the street she gestures for me to follow.

We walk a few blocks in silence. Every once in a while, her hand grazes mine. At the corner of 23rd Street, we stop again. In the distance I recognize the red sign of the Chelsea Hotel. I walk toward it and she follows me without saying anything. We pass by the restaurant named after Don Quixote and when we get to the striped awning of the hotel we stop.

Should we go in? I ask. A flash of fear flutters in her eyes.

You think they'll let us?

Don't worry, they know me, I say, taking her hand. The lamps, mirrors, marble floors, paintings, and sculptures, everything about the décor seems to intimidate her. From the ceiling, there hangs a papier-mâché figure painted green, a coyote about to leap. Esmeralda laughs and squeezes my hand. The front desk clerk recognizes me. I say good evening, but he doesn't respond. We go to the elevator. Esmeralda doesn't take her eyes off the lit floor buttons for a second. When the number 10 lights up, there's a metallic sound, and the door opens. I have no idea what I'm going to do after we step out. Up until this moment, I've pretended I was going to Sylvie's suite, but from here on that script doesn't work. I push open the swinging doors and glance at the long, dark hallway. To my left is a common restroom. It's always been there but this is the first time I really notice it. I open the door. Esmeralda goes in first. Once inside, I lean on the door until I hear it click shut. I look her in the eyes. She is vulnerable, defenseless. I wonder what she sees in me.

First the money, she says.

I stick my hand in my pocket. That morning, I had taken a hundred dollars from the box in the kitchen. I see twenties, tens, fives, and a few singles. I'm not sure how much it is. I give her the money without counting it. I'm surprised that she doesn't count it either. She opens her small red-sequin purse, puts the bundle of bills in, and takes out a pack of two condoms. The light from the ceiling has a greenish cast. On the porcelain enamel of the bathtub is a trail of rust that runs from the side where the faucet drip begins to the drain. How old are you? She's annoyed at the question. Nineteen, she says reluctantly and leans back against the wall tiles. Shifting her hips, she begins to take off her jeans, then her panties, until she's naked from the waist down. She opens her legs and waits. A light down covers her thighs. She throws one of the condoms into the sink, then rips open the other one with her teeth, and hands it to me. She helps me put it on as she cups my scrotum, just like she had done at the bar but now skin to skin. Her hand is warm and rough and she pulls it away suddenly. She's dry inside. I feel the hardness of her sex as I penetrate her. She grimaces and I stop. Go on, she says, but doesn't move. I don't know what she's seeing, where her mind is at. I forage for her breasts buried under several layers of clothes and she lets me caress them. She presses the palms of her hands against the tiles and pushes with her hips. A cavern of flesh. The rubbing of a blind animal against the ceiling of a grotto. A grunt, either hers or mine. The friction is painful, as if I were rubbing my eyes with fingers coated in sand. I feel the blood in my cock. I hope the condom breaks. This is how diseases find their way in. Esmeralda spitting on the curb. What had she snorted? Heroin? I knew she wasn't shooting up because there were no tracks in her arms. She probably smokes it. Who is this girl? What's her story? What's her mother like? Does she have any siblings? Who made love to her first? How old was she when it happened? The sound of trees falling, a forest felled by power saws, footsteps on a bed of dry leaves, the bloodshot eyes of a wild boar. Heavy breathing. Hers, mine? Animal panting. Is it me? I can't do this. I'm on a path carved through a granite quarry, breathing in marble and quicklime dust. Wait, I hear myself say, wait. I fish for the flask of vodka in my pocket. You want some? The animal out of its burrow, half flaccid, its cartilage throbbing like a fresh wound. This will help us both. You want some vodka? Esmeralda doesn't respond. What's in those deep green eyes? Emptiness. A vast vegetable silence without end. I think I see a path of light ahead of us again. Without saying anything, she reaches out her hand. Her skin is rough. I pick up a bitter smell. Mine, hers? She chugs and shivers. Go on, take another sip. She does as I say. Her eyes flare up. A trickle of alcohol oozes from the corners of her lips. Now it's my turn. We look at each other from the waist down, her eyes lifeless now. Mine want to erase all detail, so I drink what's left in one long swig. I feel as though I've climbed several steps at once. Above my eyes, her mons covered by a triangle of twisted hairs, a crack of living flesh, violently rosy, the skin bumpy. Now, clouds, I don't know where, a desert. She's finally wet. I slip in easily, pushing upward, burying my head in the depths of the night. Hot slime. She begins to move, hooking onto me, helping me move. She grabs my shirt, pushes toward me, digs her nails into my back, my ass, sinks her teeth in my neck, rubbing my balls. Our movements take on a mechanical rhythm. The girl is now a wild beast howling from down a well. She takes charge of my body, leading me, the muscles of her vagina pressing at the base of my penis, pulling me in and pushing me away without letting me out of her, dragging me in again. She doesn't say a word, waits until I collapse onto her breasts. As soon as I lose all strength, blood gone slack, she reverts to her initial passivity, her eyes vacant. She waits till I go soft, then expels me from her body. The greenish light from the ceiling blinds me. I see the second condom unopened in the sink. Esmeralda goes to the bidet and spits like she had done on the sidewalk. Her thighs are shiny with fluids. She straddles the bidet and washes. She asks me if I need to clean up and I tell her that I don't. The germs, those harbingers of death, are they already in me? I think for a second about Marc. Is he fucking some beggar? Where? In a public bathroom, like me? In a sewer, in the parking lot of the Green Snot, in his apartment? Is he reading his poems aloud to some illiterate homeless person, a truck driver, a toothless old man, a young hustler with a hard body who is set on stealing his wallet, and if he has to, cracking his head open?

Going out, the front desk clerk gives us an annoyed look. We've put one over on him. We pause for a moment in front of the display cabinet to the right of the front desk. It's full of books and other items relevant to the history of the hotel. On the glossy cover of a pulp fiction novel are some high-class whores with very white skin and their hair dyed platinum blonde. Esmeralda reads the title aloud: *Chelsea Girls*. What's it about? she asks me.

I don't know, haven't read it. Murder, I suppose, I tell her. Do you like to read?

Me?

It's almost dawn. The pimp is leaning against the window of El Quijote. Behind him is the knight errant's suit of armor. The visor of his helmet is up; one of his ironclad hands holds a spear and the other the menu of the day. I say good-bye to Esmeralda, wondering if she's just given me the gift of death, a death that someone else had already gifted her. Or maybe death will pardon me, pardon both of us, as it always pardons Marc. I feel like throwing up. Listen up, Ackerman, hold on, this is good, first-hand stuff you can use, turn into literary trash. Put together a good story, crude, raw, controlling, the material a quilt of writing, garbage-dump dreams. How about that? The crescent moon rests atop a cloud like an ashen scimitar. The desk clerk comes out to see what's going on. Four figures on the edge of dawn. What then, Marc, will you please tell me? Is this material for your poets or mine? Rilke's angels or Bukowski's? No, no. This shit is real, nothing to do with literature. That's why I want it in here, a part of *Brooklyn*, among so many other things, because it's the only way I'll cook up a meaning for it all—I think of Esmeralda's sex taking in my own, turning it into something significant, at least for a moment. I remember her green eyes, Esmeralda from Spanish Harlem, a girl addicted to crack or heroin, no doubt. A young woman from the projects who has to put up with sons of bitches like me. Note my choice of words. Sons of bitches. Language betrays me. My mouth is dry. Could it be that even though we belong to different worlds, when I was lost inside her, we got to share something, if only for a few seconds? Esmeralda! I yell out. She and her guardian turn around at the same time, the pimp and the whore. I take a few strides toward them. The Puerto Rican reaches into the pocket of his jacket, but she stops him. I'm too far away to look into her eyes, but if I could, I'd see that I've never existed for her, and I say nothing. I'll see you, she says and turns away. They walk together toward Eighth Avenue. When they get to the corner, they turn right, heading north, and disappear.

BRYANT PARK

[*May 1991*]

It's been almost five years. I had no way of knowing then, but I would never see Nadia again. June 1, 1986. She spent the night with me at the Oakland, but she was in a weird mood. The light woke us up and we left Brooklyn early, although her bus to Boston wouldn't leave for a good while. She was going there to say good-bye to her brother Sasha before taking a flight from Washington to Paris. She didn't know when she would be back. It could be some time. They had given her a scholarship to study at the Conservatoire National Supérieur, with Bédier. We took the subway. At the 23rd Street stop, she said she wanted to get off and walk up Fifth Avenue from the Flatiron Building to Grand Central Station. She was having trouble leaving me, perhaps because she was already certain, unlike me, that we would never see each other again. At Bryant Park, I told her that I wasn't going to walk her to Port Authority. She took my hand and nodded. A Slavic-looking old woman watched us from her little stall.

How about some tea? asked Nadia, and went up to the stall without waiting for me to reply. The woman didn't understand a word of English. Nadia tried Russian. That didn't work either. So she used her hands, and managed to order for us. The woman pointed to the tables in the park, suggesting that we sit in one of them. After a few minutes, she brought us two cracked china cups. The tea had a perfume-like, comforting aroma. When Nadia finished drinking hers, she examined the inside of her cup. I did the same. The inside of mine was stained with gray shadows and some leaves floated in the liquid remaining at the bottom of the cup. It looked like algae. The old woman approached us.

Do you think she knows how to read tea leaves? Nadia asked.

If she does, it wouldn't make a difference, since we don't speak the same language.

The woman smiled as if she had understood us, took the cups, and went away. We looked up. There was a light fluttering in the air, the rustle of slow white shapes raining upon us from above the tops of trees. The park was boxed in between skyscrapers, and a swath of swiftly moving clouds would occasionally drown it in near-complete darkness. The shadows of the trees trembled on the concrete paths and on the marble walls of the library. The white shapes were shreds of paper that someone had tossed out one of the buildings facing 42nd Street. Some landed on the grass, others on the surrounding tables or on the sidewalk below the park balustrade. A strip of paper, long and curly, landed on Nadia's lap. She picked it up carefully, smoothed it out, and read it to herself.

It's from a love letter, I think, she said, handing it to me.

The pieces of white paper continued to rain on us. When they had finished falling, Nadia stood up and began to pick them up. Piling them up on top of the table, she was able to put together two incomplete, rather wrinkled pages, loose pieces of a jigsaw puzzle. Reading in a low voice to herself syllable by syllable, she managed to reconstruct several passages. It's definitely a love letter, she confirmed, looking at me, and she read aloud from the fragments she had pieced together. She took a long envelope out of her bag, one of those with a plastic window for the address, and carefully slid the sheets inside.

Give me your notebook for a second, she said when she was finished, and buried the envelope in its pages. Then she closed it and looked up at the sky as if double checking there weren't any last shreds of paper about to arrive. You have to do something with this, Gal.

Something like what?

You have to find out about the rest of it, reconstruct the love story from this letter and write it. Why don't you include it in *Brooklyn*?

Fourteen
RETURN TO FENNERS POINT

"I once started out
To walk around the world
But ended up in Brooklyn."
LAWRENCE FERLINGHETTI
A Coney Island of the Mind

[*Brooklyn Heights, April 17, 2008*]
I've grown more and more obsessed with death, Ness. I know it sucks to talk about it, but the thing is that it's not easy to avoid when all your friends are dropping like flies, leaving you more alone than a car at night in the rain . . . Well, when you get to be my age, what can you expect? You know how old I am? That's right, eighty-six. I'm surprised you remember. I was born in 1922. My affairs are in order, both legal and otherwise—I don't mind telling you these things, you're family. Look at Raulito, 'member I was once so worried about him? He's making a fortune now. Everyone goes to him because they know he's honest to a fault. My daughters are both fine too. Camila left her husband and is now with a guy who works in a bank. They live in Tulsa. Wally was full of shit, so I get why she dumped him. My other daughter, Teresita, she's single, she's the brains. Teaches natural sciences at a college in Baltimore. You've never met my daughters, have you? Vincent you've met, that I remember. It's him I want to talk to

you about. I know I'm not going be to around much longer, so I've been worried about the bar. At one point, I thought I basically wouldn't have any options aside from hiring a management company or just selling the place. And that would have been the end of the Oakland. Luckily, though, there's been a new development. Vincent wants to run it. How about that? He got divorced too and is moving to Brooklyn. All's well that ends well. He sold his business in Rochester. A clean slate. He's going to be the one in charge of the Oakland when I'm gone, because the Oakland must go on, like life. My wife, Carolyn, is fit as a fiddle. She's fourteen years younger than me, so she has miles to go. The sad thing is that I lost Víctor, my assistant. Didn't you hear about that? He opened his own bar. And do you know what he called it? You got it, kiddo, exactly. The Oakland. So what can I say? My bar now has descendants. We're going to have to number them like kings in the old days and moguls now. Charles V, Ford III, Oakland II. But I miss Víctor like hell. Gal discovered him, I know you know that whole story backward and forward, I'm sorry, you know how we old farts repeat ourselves. Oh well, I have a new assistant, Danny, but he's just got no color, if you follow me, and I'm not just saying that because he's white. I'm saying it because he's useless, not to beat around the bush, although I like the guy and accept him as-is. That's how life goes, you get more tolerant, and if you don't, who the fuck cares anyhow. Like the saying goes, grin and bear it. And, you know, there's a Spanish proverb that comes in really handy here: No one goes to his own hanging willingly. So, yeah, the Oakland's gotten a bit rundown. Still the same regulars, a bunch of burnouts and has-beens, but look, if I took them all in when they were young, I'm hardly going to turn them away now that they've got one foot in the grave. They never had anywhere else to go—the Oakland's been the only home they've ever had. Take Niels, for example. He'll kick the bucket with his elbows on the bar—though I bet he'll bury all of us. My God, tell me one thing, Ness, when was the last time you stopped by . . . ? Fuck, really? In that case, we've got to get through a lot of background before we can tackle the important stuff. Let's see, who's still around from your time? Manolito *el Cubano* died of AIDS at Beth Israel. It was horrible. He wanted his mother to come and see him. One day, Nélida and I went to visit him in the hospital and it left our hair standing on end. He was howling, Mamá, mamá. It cut right through you. So I offered to pay for her plane ticket. I found out she lived in Tampa—and she's still there now. I got in touch with one of his sisters. She said their mother couldn't come. Alzheimer's. Didn't say a word about coming herself. I didn't push it at first, it wasn't my business, but at some point I just had to ask—I gave it to the sister point blank, and she said . . . well, she said she wasn't coming either, there was too much between them, bad ugly things that it was best not to stir up, so I left it at that. Manolito always said that he wanted to be buried in Cuba, though of course he meant when Fidel died, so . . . Anyway, we buried him at Woodside, in the original cemetery, yeah, that big one you can see from the BQE. And Ernie? He retired finally. And I say he retired because what else can I call it. He works as much as he ever did, which is to say not at all. He hasn't broken a fucking sweat once in his whole goddamned life. No, no, I tell a lie, actually, he probably works more now than he did before, because he offers you a drink without your having to ask for it, whereas, before, it was impossible to even get his attention. You asked him for a drink and he just looked at you like you'd taken a shit on his mother's tombstone or something. He's moved from one side of the bar to the other —that's basically what his retirement entails. Now he's just one more of the rabble of drunks. The only one who's exactly the same as ever is Nélida. I don't know how the fuck she does it, but she doesn't age. She gets younger every day, has more drive and energy. She reminds me of Celia Cruz. The truth is that I don't know anything about anyone not related to the bar. There are four or five old friends I still talk to. Though fewer and fewer as time goes by, I must say. It's different with you, because you're the one who calls all the time. Louise? The truth is, I never see her. Not that we saw each other a lot before. She was Gal's friend, really, so if he wasn't in the mix, we didn't see each other. I mean, I see her every year or year-and-a-half, if we're lucky. She's another one that never ages. She looks the same as twenty years ago. She's another one who calls pretty regularly, like you. I've always liked her, a good hardy woman, just like I like them. She broke up with Sylvie, you heard about that, right? What you probably don't know is that she went back to Europe. Sylvie, yeah, not Louise—no one could drag her out of New York. Who would have thought it after so many years? No, not Switzerland, she lives in Paris, thrilled, enjoying her fame—yeah, she won the art lottery too. I hope it doesn't eat her up. No, look, kid, come on, I'm not implying anything, don't get me wrong, I'm happy for her. Sure Louise is fine, she's the one who decided to end it anyway. It was me who called her last time. I was watching PBS, and all of a sudden something about the Spanish Republic came on, and I said: Fuck, of course. Today is April 14. I thought about Gal. When the show was over, I called her. It was a good thing, because she said she had been thinking about him all day too. We talked for hours. Don't forget to drink a toast to the Republic, she said in the end. To the Republic and for Gal. And I said what the fuck, and declared an all-night open bar in honor of Gal Ackerman. Half the patrons didn't even know who he was, but an open bar was just dandy with them. I didn't care about what they thought. All I wanted was for them toast him, and, of course, there were quite a few who did know him. I sat by myself at the Captain's Table and in between sips I remembered this and that. You have to take into account that Gal lived here for quite a few years. I also thought of you, 'cause you also spent quite a bit of time here writing that novel. How long did it take you? A couple of years, no? Holy shit! It was hard to get you to accept a salary, remember? Too bad you needed to leave after everything was done. Well, the important thing is that you finished the thing. And remember how at first you would come down with the boxes and we burned any papers you didn't need? When I told you we were like the priest and the barber, you cracked up. Admit it, you were surprised that I had read *Don Quixote* from beginning to end. It was the same with Gal, because I've never been much of a reader. It was my father's doing, Don José Otero, may he rest in peace. When he went blind, he made us read Cervantes to him aloud. My mother, my sisters, and I took turns reading him a few chapters at a time. The best part about that was to see how he laughed, it was a such a joy. In the end, I caught the bug too. Probably if it had been up to me, I'd never have done it, but on his deathbed my old man made me promise that I would read the whole thing myself, and of course I did. I still have the copy he gave me, and of course it keeps coming up. That's the thing about that book—all the things that happen in life are already in there somewhere.

What's gotten into this senile old man, you must be asking yourself, that first he calls me from across the pond—something he's never done before—and now he's gabbling on about books? I know, I know, it's all out of character for your old friend Frank. But that's right, I've called you to talk about books—just bear with me, I'm not going to tell you why yet. Let me do this at my own pace. Aside from *Don Quixote*, the only book that I care about is Gal's. Well, yours and Gal's, because it belongs to both of you, and hell, maybe it's mine too, though I didn't put in a single comma. And, actually, who knows how many people could claim a share, because in the end the book is about the Oakland and its people, right? So in a way it belongs to all of us. Well, that's why I'm calling you. The thing is, the other day, before hanging up, April 14th, I told Louise that if she ever wanted to go up to

Fenners Point again, all she had to do was ask, and I'd have a limo ready for her. I'd have Víctor take her and that'd be that. No, not Víctor, sorry, I mean Danny—see, I'm already losing it. She took a while to respond. She was quiet for such a long time that I had to ask if she was still there. And of course she was. Fuck, I thought, her voice is hoarser than ever—and it wasn't exactly delicate before. She sounded like a cement mixer. She coughed a few times, a bad cough, that woman is going to pay a heavy price for all her smoking. Finally she goes and tells me that no, she would prefer not to see Fenners Point again. I definitely didn't expect that. And I started to feel like maybe we'd all abandoned Gal after all—nonsense, I know, but as it was, the following day . . . I remember it was a Friday . . . I called Danny and told him: Danny, get ready, tomorrow we're going to Fenners Point. I mean, I told him that on Thursday, Friday was the day we went. He had no idea where Fenners Point was. Which makes sense, where would he have heard about that godforsaken place? So I explained it to him. Hadn't been there once, not a single time, I'm talking about me now. You see where I'm heading? No? We left early in the morning to avoid the weekend traffic. There wasn't a soul on the road. They've built a highway now—not even God uses the old route. Obsolescence, as Raulito, who's always been a bit pretentious, says. There's no life in the seaside towns either— they were fishing villages in the old days, but now everyone buys farmed fish and the stuff tastes like rubber. They built the fish farms crammed all together on the east side of the county, near the river, which is good, that way they don't ruin the shoreline. The thing is, the day we went, the sea was fucking gorgeous. The maple woods were beautiful. And you're not going to believe it, but the sign that says Danish Cemetery was still there. As we took the road through the woods, I thought about the funeral. There were so few of us there, remember? Almost no one. Just Louise, you, Víctor, and couple of other friends. I remember I had to bribe one of the town councilors so he would look the other way regarding the burial, because who the hell could get a permission for such a thing in less than two days? He sent me some workers and told me not to worry, that he would fix the papers in exchange for a nominal fee and everyone would be happy. Later, I thought that perhaps it hadn't been necessary, because, come to think of it, who the fuck remembered the Danish Cemetery? The consulate had done what they did after the shipwreck—which was big news, even the *New York Times* had a photo on the front page—but after that, nothing. The first ones who forgot about it were the Danes themselves. They put up the plaque, did their duty, and as soon as there was a change in diplomats, the new ones couldn't give a shit. Anyway, when I went with Danny, it was a cold gray day, raining a bit. The sea was choppy and the waves crashed against the reefs—it was petty harrowing up there. I'm not surprised they nicknamed the place the Devil's Pitchfork. But I'm getting ahead of myself again. There were some muddy stretches and it was hard getting up to the cemetery. Once there, everything was the same, or at least I didn't notice anything different. I like Fenners Point. It doesn't feel like a graveyard. It reminds me of that Japanese garden you took me to once in Queens, with all the white stone surrounded by grass. God knows the last time anyone set foot there. I went right up to Gal's grave. I took my hat off and stood there thinking, which is how I pay my respects to the dead. I don't know a fucking thing about praying, never been religious. Then, I noticed something strange. Someone else had been there after all. Danny was sitting on the stone wall and I called him over and told him about it. Do you remember, Ness, that I had a niche built into the gravestone, where we put the book? Well, I never went after that, although I arranged for everything. I called my friend the councilor again and he told me not to worry, a little more money and no problem, same old story. He had to send the workers back. You and Louise went, Víctor took you, remember?

After the work was done, I only saw it in pictures. I still have one somewhere. It was delicate work because the headstone was thin as it was. And that's where you put the book. So, well, that's why I'm calling. Someone took it, Ness, believe it or not. The novel is not fucking there. It took me a second to notice because they tried to cover up the mess they left, but the glass was broken and they couldn't close the latch. Who the hell could it have been? Someone who just found the place by accident? I have no idea. Or someone who wasn't in too much of a hurry, or who didn't like highways, a fisherman, a freak, an ecologist . . . ? Who knows? Maybe a driver saw the sign, and he got curious. That's all it would take to fuck the whole thing up. I don't have the slightest idea when it happened. It could have been weeks, months, even years earlier. There's no way of knowing, since none of us ever go there. Imagine how fucking pissed off I was. I started thinking about who could have been there. The last one to go was Louise, but that was years ago. It could be that whoever did it had nothing to do with Gal. We may never know, although that would be horrible. I mean, if it was someone who'd never heard of him, now he knows all his secrets. Well, that's why I was calling, *muchacho*, this is what I wanted to tell you. I'm sorry about the bad news. I'd like to do something about it, but I don't know what. You neither, huh? What could anyone do? With a case like this, there's not even a scent to follow. But, hey, how are you? Tell me something about yourself. When are you coming back to the States? Don't think about it too much, old Frankie is running out of steam.

May 6, 2008

Fucking hell, Ness, more than a year without talking and now we call each other every other day. But today's call comes with very good reason. Fasten your seatbelt. The motherfucking novel has been found. Pardon my French. I don't know what the fuck's happening to me, every day I curse more. Carolyn can't stand it. How? I got it in the mail, that's how. Believe it or not. Fuckin' A. I'm at the door of the Oakland, and I see Peter, the mailman, coming over. He hands me the mail as usual, and then he says to hold on and takes a package from his cart and hands it to me. A big package. I sign for it, go to the office, open it, and there's *Brooklyn*. What do you fucking think about that? No, no, it's in good condition given how long it was at the grave and then who knows where else. It's in pretty good shape, like it's never been out of its little niche. And it came with a note of apology. Yes, addressed to me. Well, there are two notes, in fact—the second one's for you. Shit, I don't know, I haven't read it. It's in a sealed envelope. Mine doesn't say anything specific. It's handwritten. The person who wrote it apologizes, says that as soon as he (or she) finished the book they began to inquire about the Oakland in case it was still around, since the bar plays such a big role in the novel. When they confirmed we were still kicking, they sent the book here by certified mail. To me, of course. Think how much they know about all of us, now. I feel . . . well, it gives me the creeps, when I think about it. No, man, it's unsigned. Isn't it enough that they returned it? What? Registered mail, yes. Oh you're right, I never even looked at the return address. Let me see. No, no, I have it right here in the office. Here it is. No name. Just PO Box 221, New York, New York 10021. There is also a note for you. No, goddamn it, I haven't read yours, I told you I wouldn't do that. What? Yes, that's the other reason I was calling, hold on, let me see. Now I've lost my fucking letter opener. No, I've got it. Ready? Okay, here I go.

Dear Mr. Chapman

I very much appreciate your prompt response. I wasn't sure if you and Frank Otero were still in touch after all these years. These last few months have been very strange and confusing for me, and it would be impossible to sum them up in just a few words, particularly by way of something as insubstantial as e-mail. But I had to tell you what a great relief it was to find you. I won't repeat what I said in my note. The important thing is that the book is back where it belongs. It's so odd to be writing to you like this, since I know so much about you and you don't even know my name. I apologize, but for the moment, I'd rather not be too explicit. For reasons too complicated to explain now, a number of Gal Ackerman's papers ended up in my hands, that's how I found out about the novel. I'll give you the details when we meet in person. There are things that it's better to say face to face. I realized that much right after I decided to return the novel. I have to admit, it was difficult, but you should know how good I felt afterward. Again, it's a long story, but I've come to understand that the best thing I can do is to rid myself of Ackerman's papers. It's not just that they have a direct connection to the book . . . For personal reasons, it's just painful for me to keep them. And since, on the other hand, I'm incapable of destroying them, I can't find a better solution than giving them to you, who are so familiar with Gal and his writings. Bear with me for now. I promise to explain everything when the right moment comes. As for our possible meeting, it's a blessing that you live in Madrid. I'm flying to Europe at the end of this month, specifically to Paris, right after the end of my semester. I'm studying architecture at Cooper Union. Once I take care of some personal business in Paris, getting to Madrid won't be much of a hassle. My apologies for keeping everything so hush-hush. I understand that from your perspective it must seem utterly bizarre and theatrical. This is very important to me, from a personal standpoint, and it would be impossible for me to furnish all the details by phone or, God forbid, by e-mail. I will need quite a few hours to explain everything adequately. Best wishes (and my apologies for the lack of a signature).

Saturday, May 10, 2008, 9:07 P.M.

Dear Mr. Chapman,

First of all, thank you so much for agreeing to correspond with me despite my insistence on remaining anonymous. I knew I could count on you. Really, thanks. I'm not playing games. If I told you who I am, I would have to rattle off the whole story, and for that, I insist, we must meet in person.

Oh, and about the return address—my roommate, Amanda Stevens, knows the whole story. After going through the novel and all the papers with me, she suggested that I rent a PO box especially for the occasion. Now that I've exchanged a few words with you, of course, I feel that I can trust you. Nevertheless, please allow me to take things at my own pace?

Sunday, May 11, 2008, 6:13 A.M.

I'm very sorry to hear about Frank Otero. I hope he recovers soon. Meeting in New York is another possibility, of course, but it won't be possible for me before the 21st. I'm very busy writing papers, and I can't afford any distractions till then. Look, it's only ten more days. You can make it.

Monday, May 12, 2008, 6:21 A.M.

No, it's not that either, don't worry about it. On the contrary, in a way it's a relief. Holding onto all these papers has been a source of terrible anxiety for me, and just speaking about them, even if it is by e-mail, is a relief. You ask how often I check my messages. In general, once a day, early in the morning. I love getting up before dawn, especially now that the sun rises so early (sometimes I go online more than once a day, but I never plan on it).

Your friend (if I may).

Tuesday, May 13, 2008, 7:55 A.M.

That's very sad, about Frank. It's the same for me as it is with Gal, with the rest of the characters in the novel, I feel guilty because I know so much more than I should. Please keep me informed about his condition. Do you plan to come to the States to see him? It's not clear from your message.

Tuesday, May 13, 2008, 9:31 A.M.

My friend,

I am writing you again before you have a chance to respond to my previous message, because something's come up that could affect our plans. My father was supposed to travel to London, but has now decided to stop over in Cádiz, Spain. A friend of his is curating an art exhibit there. This is rather sudden—I mean the change in my father's travel plans, not the exhibit.

Tuesday, May 13, 2008, 4:33 P.M.

After what I said before about checking my e-mail only once a day, here I am sending you three messages in a few hours. You're going to think I'm a flake. I'm writing in a rush, I'm not going to have time to breathe until I finish this damn paper that I don't seem to be able to get done. Yes, my father knows everything. You're the only one at a disadvantage for now. My father is an art expert. As for the exhibit, a friend of his—an Ensor specialist—is the one responsible for the change of plans. Ensor is one of my father's favorite painters. It's a small show, but exquisite, I hear. My father has to take care of something at the Tate Modern before going to the opening and he asked me to join him.

By the way, what you say about Cádiz is (really) striking! I had no idea. I'm joining my father in Madrid, where he has to spend a few days, so I could conceivably meet you there. But since I'm also going to Cádiz, where Ralph Bates's great-grandfather is buried—says you—I thought that we could meet there instead. Your call.

Wednesday, May 14, 2008, 12:44 P.M.
Dear Néstor,
I'm so glad to hear such good news about Frank! So where are we going to meet, finally? Madrid or New York? If you're still thinking about coming to see Frank, we can meet over here. My father will arrive in Madrid on the 28th. I'm going to take a few days off until I leave, probably on the 25th. Let me know what you think when you can.

Thursday, May 15, 2008, 7:11 A.M.
No, no, that's crazy. It would make no sense at all for me to meet Frank, nor am I interested in setting foot in the Oakland. I'm fond of Frank, sure, but for me he's just a character in the novel. Your relationship with him is a different story. You've met him in person, he's your friend, you've gone through a lot together. As for our own meeting, I have selfish reasons. For me, getting rid of those papers represents the possibility of bringing a very difficult

situation to its conclusion.

Thursday, May 15, 2008, 6:26 P.M.
It's a good thing for you to remind me that you'd rather look at things from a literary context. That's not how it works with me, but I guess that's irrelevant. As to the possibility of meeting in Cádiz, we can do that, if that's what you prefer.
Warm regards

Friday, May 16, 2008, 7:07 A.M.
Néstor! Please, don't insist. I thought we had an agreement. The reason I'm holding onto the papers has nothing to do with literature. You really can't wait a few days?

Friday, May 16, 2008, 7:50 A.M.
Okay, I give up. I'll send a list of Gal's papers, when I'm home in a few hours. It'll be pretty late, Madrid time, I fear.

Friday, May 16, 2008, 11:03 P.M.
You're in luck: I'm in a good mood because I finally finished the paper that was driving me crazy. Now I can concentrate on yet another assignment, my very last one. In the meantime, here goes: a bundle of seven letters, including the original in English that Abraham Lewis wrote Ben Ackerman; and yes, you'll be happy to know that I'm including the draft with the cryptic title "τπ," and "Kaddish," which is mentioned in the novel. "Kaddish" is the story that Gal published in the *Atlantic Monthly* (I have the original from the magazine as well as the Spanish translation.) As for "τπ," all I have is the Spanish version (which I haven't read). In the end, Gal Ackerman is dragging all of us toward his mother tongue. The rest of the stash is as follows:

—the beginning of a story called "Columbarium," accompanied by a clipping from the *New York Times* about the accumulation of urns filled with ashes of the patients from a madhouse in Oregon that nobody wants to claim;

—a story by Alston Hughes titled "Salsipuedes";

—"The Story of Ralph Bates, *aka El fantástico*";

—three poems by Gal's beloved Felipe Alfau, as well as an unsigned poem that seems to be Gal's (the last thing I bothered to read from all this);

—the "Chronicle of a Voyage to Patagonia," a document printed in cyclostyle (the first time I had ever heard that term, the librarian at Cooper Union explained to me what it means) signed by Henry Martínez, aka Lord Gin, the permanent secretary of the Order of the Incoherents;

—a *semblanza* (Spanish for "sketch," right? I love that word; it's what Gal calls the piece himself, at the top of the page) on Jimmy Castellano's gym;

And that's all as far as literary papers go—so what? The more relevant papers are strictly personal in nature. But I don't want to elaborate on that till we meet.

Saturday, May 17, 2008, 6:29 P.M.
Chapman, my friend, have mercy on me, I beg you. No, I haven't looked at the texts nor do I plan to.

Saturday, May 17, 2008, 9:08 P.M.
My dear friend, I'm sorry, but Amanda didn't show up until just moments ago, and I don't know much about computer stuff. Well then, I imagine that at this moment you are peacefully asleep. When you wake up tomorrow, you'll find

the story blinking at you from your screen. You'll have to thank Amanda, *eh voilà!*

KADDISH

Front page of the *New York Times*, Thursday, February 26, 1970:

MARK ROTHKO, ARTIST, A SUICIDE HERE AT 66

And then, under the byline:

> Mark Rothko, a pioneer of abstract expressionist painting who was widely regarded as one of the greatest artists of his generation, was found dead yesterday, his wrists slashed, in his studio at 157 East 69th Street. He was 66 years old. The Chief Medical Examiner's office listed the death as a suicide.

The obituary continues on page 39. Next to it, below a photographic reproduction of *The Black and the White*, a 1956 oil, is a short article titled "A Pure Abstractionist," which ends with these words:

> His passing reminds us that an entire era in the history of American culture is drawing to a close, and thus leaves us all—not only his faithful admirers but even those of us who still had serious questions about his ultimate achievement—a little older and a little emptier.

Painting is something primordial. A scream. It begins in the heels, trembles up the limbs, cuts across the heart, rises up through the heart, and comes out the eyes, bursting the skull open. Very few people understand my last paintings. I expected people to weep when they saw them, as it happens to me with when I hear Beethoven's last concertos. Black over gray, nuances representing nothingness, pigments buried under a slab of black light. The frames: caskets wherein the vanishing points of the canvas converge, waiting for a signal. Ad, Arshile, Willem, Robert, Jackson, so many others. Shreds of eternity, 60 by 60 inches, cruciform from an unknown region in Reinhardt's words, paintings pregnant with a mysticism that I didn't feel.

Upper East Side, one day earlier 19th precinct, 9:36 A.M. Thomas Mulligan and Patrick Lappin walk to a brownstone located a few blocks south of the police station. The removal of the body of a presumed suicide. The detectives enter a cavernous space with very high ceilings and a large skylight. A system of fabrics, strings, and pulleys works to control the light coming in. A century ago, the place was a riding school. There's still an interior gallery that looks out to a former courtyard in which equestrian exercises took place. Next to Rothko's is the studio of Arthur Lidov, a commercial painter (though it all depends on how you look at it—according to Lidov's opinion, Rothko's paintings are just expensive wallpaper). The two artists' studios are separated by a very thin partition. Lidov's work area is right next to Rothko's bathroom. The wall isn't thick enough to muffle the sounds of flushing or farting. Lidov has not yet been subjected to the sounds of Rothko fucking, however. Maybe the great artist is just too worn out for that. No, what he heard most often was classical music: Mozart, Schubert, and Beethoven, in that order. According to the deceased, the acoustics of the place were superb. The studio was only meant for painting, but on January 1st of last year, Rothko set up house there.

Before, as I was arranging the bottles of pigments in rows, I remembered helping my father to put away the poisons in his pharmacy. I can see you now fixing the flasks of Death, Jacob Rothkowitz. You were always so critical of me, you old tyrant. Still, when you died in Portland, Oregon, I had trouble imagining a life without you. You never took me seriously when I told you that I wanted to be a painter. I had to do it without help. But you were right about one thing: painting wasn't sufficient unto itself. No, it's not an end, but a journey. Mell, my love, my companion for twenty-three years, mother of my children, how did we come to such desolation? I liked drinking till my senses left me, in your company. It made me feel we were getting closer to the gods. I remember you too, Kate. You're gone away from home too. You live in Brooklyn now. Kate Lynn, my daughter; we never got along. You've already turned nineteen. And then that boy, whom I love with all my heart, Christopher, my son, I'm sorry. I'm going to abandon you, I'm going to leave you on your own. I was more than sixty when you were born, an unexpected gift, a shower of light, a luminous joy, but there was already too much mud in the water, flowing down the river. I have to leave you. I'm doing to you what old man Jacob did to us when he left Vitebsk. Rothkowitz the pharmacist left for Portland with his two oldest sons, leaving behind his wife and younger children, Sonia and me. By the time we finally joined him in Portland, it took him exactly seven months to die. Well, forgive me. You'll have to grow up without me. I wonder what you're dreaming now; am I part of your dream? I wonder what your life will be like. I only hope you'll find a way to rid yourself of my shadow.

After having dinner with Rita Reinhardt in a deli on Madison Avenue, Mark heads home. It's a very cold night. He secures all the entrances to the studio, locking doors he would normally not even close. There's an LP of Schubert's sonatas on the turntable. He goes into the bathroom and fondles the barbiturate bottles, opens and closes his shaving razor, perfect in its smooth pliability. The phone rings. He looks at the clock. Nine. It's his brother

Albert calling from California. The words come out of the receiver, expand in the spaciousness of the studio, and dissolve. He doesn't remember hanging up. He takes off his shoes, his pants, his shirt. He puts his glasses on the night table and lies down. He is wearing an undershirt, long underwear down to his ankles, and black socks pulled up to his knees.

The minute they discover my dead body, the dollars will start to dance around my legacy—oh, the incessant gush of capital. Do you remember, Willem, when we couldn't sell a thing? Now everybody wants their cut. The future is very clear to the dead, and I'm already gone. One day you'll have Alzheimer's, de Kooning, but they won't give a damn. Indifferent to your angelic transparency, the translucence of someone who's begun to let go of life, they will sit you down in front of a canvas, surrounded by brushes and paints. You won't know who they are, you won't know your own children, your wives. They gabble at you from the world of the living. Paint, you wretched old man, make more money, they'll tell you. You keep quiet, because you see what they can't. On the canvas you'll call forth bodies, women's bodies, eyes and teeth, grim smiles, the shapes and colors that so unsettled everyone once but which they've all learned to love because of the delirious amount of money they can make from it. They'll get nervous when the time comes to sign the canvas. Oh, it's all done very tastefully, very meticulously. They only come for the money, now. See what you get for bothering to stay alive so long? Me, I'm taking Nietzsche's advice: I'm getting out of the way before it's too late.

A cockroach peeks out from behind the glass ashtray, climbs up onto the edge, lowers its antennae, reading whatever's been written in those dunes of ash, and moves on toward the book near the lamp; it crosses between the first and last names of the author, William Gibson, and disappears behind the power cord. Rothko shuts off the light. A dim glow hovers in the studio. Hours later, the siren of a patrol car shakes him out of his stupor. He gets up, numb. He paces around the studio a few times. He sees the pack of Chesterfields but doesn't feel like smoking. He glances toward the kitchen and then goes in, turns the tap on, and continues to the bathroom. He sees his reflection in the mirror, a fat, old man, balding, his remaining hairs adhering to the skin on the sides of his skull, quivering like the legs of insects. Behind the thick glasses, swollen eyelids lower to narrow his myopic stare.

I can't stand my body. Yours is so young and beautiful, Rita. I don't understand why you let me touch it. After the aneurysm, I can hardly make love to you. I'm rotting away inside; I've already started to stink like old people, a nauseating smell that sticks to the sheets, the walls . . . just a whiff reaches out and stuns your pituitary gland as soon as you open the door. What do you know—it's the smell of death.

Thanks to the Sinequan, when the moment of truth arrives, he'll keep relatively calm. No pain, anyway. A brand new, shiny, double-edged barber's blade. He wraps one edge in Kleenex to get a better grip. With his right hand, he makes a test cut. A whitish line appears on his skin and is immediately filled with the redness of blood. He presses down hard on the blade, making a deep cut in the fold of his arm. Abundant blood, but he doesn't feel a thing. A single tick of the clock, and like a musketeer gamely tossing his foil from one hand to another, he passes the blade to his left hand and makes a second cut, making good use of his remaining and not insignificant strength. Two streams of blood fall simultaneously and symmetrically from the folds of his arms, filling the hollow of the sink. Before his sight begins to cloud, he lies on the floor face up and extends his arms.

I feel that I'm getting close to my mother. We're on an ocean liner, headed for the New World. When the boat rocks so violently that I

*think we're going to sink, she rests her hand on my head and sings.
I had no idea it would be like this, but who understands death? I'd
begun to miss her so much that I thought in death I would become a
black arrow shooting right back into the womb. She's waiting for me
somewhere, and when I plunge back into her belly and hear again
her heart beating through the strings of her veins, floating in that
interstellar space within her, I'll be able to look at the world through
her eyes, and I will see him, the pharmacist who abandoned us, my
mother's husband. Who will say Kaddish for him, for you, mother, for
me, for all of us? Yisborach, v'yistabach, v'yispa-ar, v'yisromam,
v'yisnaseh, v'ysadar, v'yis'halleh, v'yis'hallal sh'meh d'kudsha,
baruch hu. I liked listening to you, Rita, but I went numb when you
talked about your mother, your father, your little sister, all of them
dead in the camps. Sometimes you called for them in your sleep. And I
would watch you, your white skin in its milky light. I woke you up to
rescue you from your pain, and we made love. I heard echoes in your
panting and gasping—other times, other men. Your lips covered with
my foam, and the birds announcing the arrival of the morning in an
unseasonably cold late June.*

At 9:02, the painter's assistant, Oliver Steindecker, enters the
studio. A good kid, Oliver, if a bit shy. He uses his key to open the
first door and is surprised to find the second door locked. He can't
hear anything from inside. He calls out, but no one responds. He
hesitates before deciding to go in anyway. He sees the unmade
bed from across the room. When he reaches the space that serves
both as kitchen and bathroom, he discovers Mark Rothko's body.
He runs into Lidov's studio and talks to Frank Ventgen, Lidov's
assistant, his voice faltering. They make two phone calls, one to
the police and another for an ambulance. Not that the latter was
really necessary. An intern from nearby Lenox Hill Hospital
pronounces the old man dead. The first person to arrive at the
death scene is Theodoros Stamos, a painter friend of Rothko.

Stamos is trembling. His spine like an antenna picks up the waves of force emanating from the corpse. He asks Lidov for a camera. He knows the guy has some very sophisticated photographic equipment in his studio. And it's the right moment, before the police arrive. It would have been an unforgettable photograph. Think of it. An illustrious stiff for all seasons. But Lidov refuses. Anne Marie had arrived and she and Steindecker call Rothko's wife, Mell, and she takes a taxi to the studio. The detectives don't have much to do here. They're normal folk—that is, they have no part in the art world. They're Irish, probably, neighborhood kids who do their jobs as well as they can, and who learned what they needed to learn about life in the streets of Brooklyn. Here, they're superfluous—just like the ambulance. And, for them, the day's only begun. A reporter named Paul Wilkes had already been doing a ride-along with the two detectives for a *New York Times Magazine* piece, so he gets an inside line on the story— though he isn't actually there, that morning, by all accounts, for whatever reason, which is a real shame: a missed opportunity, in a literary-journalistic sense. When his article gets published on April 19, the writer will condense the weeks he spent with the two detectives into a single day, and when he gets to Rothko's suicide, he won't bother to make it clear that his account of the scene isn't first hand. Speaking of literature, Lappin likes to read, a detail that Wilkes finds interesting. In his piece, he will report that during those days the detective was reading *The Godfather*. A while ago he had read *House Made of Dawn* by N. Scott Momaday, which had won the Pulitzer, and *The Rise and Fall of the Third Reich*. Lappin glances at the scattered books all over the place. On the night table is a copy of *A Mass for the Dead* by William Gibson. The title catches his attention and he opens it. The book's structure is based on that of the Requiem Mass. Introit. Offertory. Rite of Darkness. A strange book, a meditation on death interspersed with personal memories and poems. He begins to read a poem but stops after a few lines. In the living room, there's a book, a biography of Arshile Gorky. He leafs through it, examining the color reproductions. He pays particular attention to a portrait of the artist as a young man, then continues to look through the book. He glimpses a sentence stating that the painter was Armenian. More pictures. Strange stuff. He decides that he doesn't like the book and closes it. Then, on top of a low table, he sees a novel titled *The Fixer* by Bernard Malamud. Guy sounds familiar. On a nearby shelf, a copy of a book by Joseph Roth. Name means nothing to him.

I read it in one sitting, as though it were a long poem. It filled me with a pungent mix of pleasure and grief. I identified with the bum who comes into a fortune, then drinks through it all in order to be in the presence of God as soon as possible—God, who appears to the drunk as a young prostitute, a little girl almost, Thérèse, a saint just like him. I cried when I finished it. The docks of the Seine, the bars and brothels of Paris. Miracles that don't need angels. Swells who need to give their money away so that others can benefit from it. It was the last thing you wrote, Joseph Roth. It was published the year of your death: 1939. You were spared the events to come. That was also the year the Spanish Republic was brought down. Which makes me think of those paintings by Bob Motherwell. Strange we never talked about it. I may have had nothing to do with it, but everyone I knew in those days lived through the events of the Spanish Civil War with the same anxiety, as though we already knew it was only a prelude to the horrors that awaited us. After I saw the series of paintings that Bob titled Elegy for the Spanish Republic, *a terrible sorrow got its hooks into me and I went home rattled . . . still hearing the screams buried in the canvases.*

Mark Rothko's body rests face up on the kitchen floor, arms outstretched, in a puddle of congealed blood six feet wide by seven and a quarter feet long. The tap in the sink is open, the water has been running for hours. Lappin takes a quick look around and sees that one of the sides of the double-edged razor blade is protected by a piece of Kleenex. *Suicides are amazingly careful not to cut their fingers as they slash their forearms*, Wilkes has one of the detectives say in his article, even though, as reported above, he wasn't actually there. Rothko left the tap running because he didn't want to leave a mess. He opened his veins in the kitchen sink after a little practice: some hesitant cuts on his forearms. *Hesitation marks.* Small incisions to test the sharpness of the blade. *An open-and-shut suicide*, Lappin says. Wilkes loves that bit. Everyone else who writes about the suicide will repeat it. *Rothko's wallet is intact and there is no sign of rifling in the studio, which contains scores of the artist's works, worth hundreds of thousands of dollars* (and in a few years will be worth millions). Once money enters the picture, Mulligan and Lappin, who till this moment hadn't had the slightest idea who Rothko was, exchange a look. Now they'll have to station a policeman at the door twenty-four hours a day, till things are squared away. For all the good this will do. It's not burglars they should be worried about, but criminals of the white-collar variety. The struggle for the artist's legacy, which is to say earnings, will end up being one of the great art-world scandals of the century. Corrupt critics, gallery owners, legal advisors, foundations . . . If tomorrow the art market determined that their mothers were all masterpieces, they'd sell them without hesitation. (And, speaking of hesitation, the autopsy determined that there was in fact only one hesitant cut in Rothko's arm.)

So this is how time comes to an end. I travel with my pockets full of silence, through huge holes that leave no room for color, precipices that leave no room for echoes, hallways that leave no room for words, spaces in which light is lost, and I feel like I am being dragged to the edge of dawn by the morning star. I always suspected that I'd end up swallowed by some blob of light. On the other side are empty ponds and wells full of snakes. That's where they throw the prisoners, their bones crack as they strike the rocks at the bottom. The snakes begin their work without delay, entering the orbs of the eyes, but they can't make it up the walls of the well—too slippery. They aren't fond of blood, they prefer milk. The whole thing only takes a few elastic seconds that extend like flaming fingers reaching for the absolute. Finally, I see into outer space. I didn't invent these shapes: they came to me and haunted me at night.

Case #1867. The artist's last name appears as Rothknow. Autopsy should really be a literary art, as necrology is. In England, they publish anthologies of obituaries—some of them are pretty damn good at that. The ones in the *New York Times* are all right, maybe not superb. In the city's public libraries they keep them in the reference section, big black clothbound books. A gloved hand rests on the thorax of the painter. The pathologist, Dr. Judith Lehotay, records marked acute senile emphysema, acute gastritis due to the ingestion of barbiturates, and irreversible cardiac dysfunction. He wouldn't have had much time to live anyhow. He must have known it, after the aneurysm. Two years, at the most? *One cut was two and a half inches long and half an inch deep on the artist's left forearm and the other two inches long and one inch deep on the right—deep enough to cut into and practically sever the brachial artery. Both cuts were made just below the crook of the arm*, reports, in turn, Rothko's biographer.

SELF-INFLICTED INCISED WOUNDS OF THE
ANTECUBITAL FOSSAE
WITH EXSANGUINATION
ACUTE BARBITURATE POISONING
SUICIDAL

You did a good job. Surely everyone will be convinced this was a suicide, will see that I left no room for doubt. Not an accident, not murder. With Jackson Pollock and David Smith, it was different. They were blind drunk when they got behind the wheel. They looked death in the face, all right, but behind glass, if you follow me—at a remove. There should be no doubt, as with Arshile Gorky. Rotten with cancer, alone in his house in Connecticut, deeply depressed, abandoned by his wife, he hanged himself from a rafter in a little shed. He was forty-four years old. He chalked his suicide note on the side of a crate. Me, I won't leave a single word. The living cling to the words you leave behind, looking for hidden meanings in them. Silence is much more accurate.

[February 26, the Frank E. Campbell Funeral Home. 2:30 P.M.]

Some decide to go to the funeral parlor on foot, their shoes stamping the asphalt, passing by puddles that reflect the winter light. Others arrive by limousine. Friends, family, predators. Among the artists: Willem de Kooning, a year younger, still attractive, his body slim and agile; Adolf Gottlieb, Robert Motherwell and his wife, Helen Frankenthaler; Philip Guston, who is beginning to explore new paths; Barnet Newman, a partner in thousands of conversations; Lee Krasner, the widow of Jackson Pollock, and an artist in her own right; the Menils, patrons who will erect a chapel for his most mysterious works; Elaine de Kooning, Willem's ex-wife. Malamud was there, and the one observation of his to come down to us—he was always prone to such peculiar fillips—was that the corpse was wearing glasses. Some of the mourners bring along objects to which the painter was particularly attached. His children don't want him to be buried without the musical accompaniment that, in life, filled his every hour. His oldest child Kate puts Rothko's favorite recording of *The Abduction from the Seraglio* into the coffin, while the young Christopher has brought along "The Trout Quintet."

Finally, Theodoros Stamos places a flower on Rothko's chest. Really a gala event, *très chic*, the performance of the season, as a reporter might say—my kingdom for a one-liner. Fur coats, perfectly tailored suits to pay respect to someone who didn't know how to dress, who would drive his friends crazy talking about this coat he was thinking of buying. He would call at the most unholy hours, hosanna! and begin talking about this damn coat. Ridiculous. All of them have good reasons for being here. Some people cry, others are in shock, lost in a circle of silence, and others still have come just because they smell money. Sorrow mingling with avarice. Stanley Kunitz, the poet, is the first to speak. The last ones are his older brothers, Albert and Moses Roth, who together sing the Kaddish: *Yisborach, v'yistabach, v'yispa-ar, v'yisromam, v'yisnaseh, v'ysadar, v'yis'halleh, v'yis'hallal sh'meh d'kudsha, baruch hu.* The black limousines return to their nests. Symmetries that reach beyond the grave: Mell will outlive her husband by only six months, exactly the same length of time that Jacob the pharmacist lasted after his youngest son arrived in Portland. Mell Rothko will be found dead one morning. It will be the young child, little Christopher, six years old, who will discover the body and have to run to tell his mother's lover.

Sunday, May 18, 2008; 1:25 P.M.

I understand what you say about the story he published in the *Atlantic Monthly*, Néstor, how could I not? But try to make an effort and put yourself in my place. I'm afraid we're just not on the same page—I don't mean inherently, as people, but it's like I told you: it's the end of the semester, and I have an insane amount of work to do. I have no time for anything but the papers I have to write. And I'm afraid I've hit a dead end in one of them. Nothing could be further from my mind right now than literary matters, and of which, I must confess, I know very little. Don't take it the wrong way. I'm not being selfish. I just don't have a choice. But I'm really happy to hear that Frank is feeling better and will be home again soon. So, anyway, I expect to be able to give you my full attention very soon. Wish me luck, Néstor!

PS. I almost forgot. No, I don't have the slightest idea what "τπ" is about. I know as much as you do, that Ackerman wanted the two pieces next to each other for some reason, at least that's what he himself hints in the novel. But because I feel that I'm beginning to know you, and for my own good—so that you leave me alone with my work, I mean!—I'm going to go ahead and send the story to you before you begin to bug me about it. I see you coming miles away, mister. You're transparent. I'd prefer to leave everything till when we can finally meet. So you have to promise not to insist for more things after you get your copy of "τπ." I'll ask Amanda to scan it, like "Kaddish," then forward it to you. After that, you can invent whatever stories about me you want. There's no way you'll be getting anything else after that.

Your friend—in spite of your stubbornness.

ττ

[A Farce]

At the table in the corner there was this grumpy-looking fucker whose freakish height didn't register with me till he took to his feet. He had thick curly sideburns running down to his chin, and a piratey sort of mustache, although his general demeanor made me think more of a werewolf. He must have been over six foot two. He was rather thin, his eyes a light blue, and his nose remarkably straight if somewhat thick. I went up to the bar, and as I sat on the stool, I heard someone make a hissing sound, and naturally turned around to see what the hell was going on. It was him. He raised his hand and grimaced at me. He had wide, yellow rabbit teeth that made him look rather ridiculous. He must have realized that I was looking at them, because he closed his mouth right away.

Psst, he called again. Here, my amigo! He was summoning me, arm still raised, and for some reason, I obeyed.

On top of his table, I saw a black leather briefcase with these two Greek characters embossed in gold:

ττ

Those gap-toothed incisors of his peeked out from under the lank bristles of his mustache.

I think I have one Hamilton left, I'm almost sure, he said,

speaking Spanish, to my surprise.

A Hamilton?

He stuck his hairy hand in his pocket, rummaging around until till he pulled out a bank note wrinkled into a ball. He flattened it into a rectangular shape. A ten-dollar bill.

Mr. Alexander Hamilton, he said, smoothing out the bilious face on the bank note. Now if you'll do me the favor of moving your ass in the general direction of the bar, I'll buy a round. Tequila sour for me.

He was clumsy, uncoordinated. When he stood up, he almost sent his chair flying. He left his briefcase on the table, apparently unconcerned that any of the other customers—by no means respectful of other folks' property, by the look of them—would take an interest in it. He was off to the pissoir.

So I came back with two tequila sours, planted them on the table, and waited. Two minutes later, the stranger came out of the toilet still pulling up his fly.

Mercibocu, he said and dipped his finger into a tequila sour and left it there. Code three, he said, taking out his finger and watching it as if it weren't his. He took a deep breath and added cryptically: I'm dedicated to mocking them. I make a point of slaughtering them up, raising my rhododendrums.

He took no notice of my confusion. Reclaiming his finger, he sucked the sour off it before asserting: They're after me, you know. They want to take my mug shot. He smiled. Some years ago, my editor alerted me that *Time* magazine had sent a photoharvester to Mexico City with the mission of erranding into me, so I made myself scarce. I vamoosed to Guanajuato, got on a meningitic bus that took fourhundredfiftysix rattling minutes to shake through the sierra. But the worst thing was when they started with the motherflocking awards.

This was all entirely impenetrable to me, but I asked:

Is that where you learned Spanish? I mean, in Mexico?

No, that's where I forgot it. The Spanish of Castilla I learned in Cascadilla.

Cascadilla?

Cascadilla Hall. It's the name of my old dorm at Cornell. He looked up and his teeth reflected the stream of light falling from the ceiling.

Prrost, he said, taking another sip of his cocktail. And where, pray, do you hail from? Where did you learn Spanish?

In Brooklyn, I said. What were you doing in Mexico?

I went to finish a novel. What's your favorite letter?

I've never given it any thought.

Mine's *V*. I have the Corvair outside. Let's go check out the other side of the night, he said, chugging down his tequila sour. Aw, shit.

He had a thing for light, I guess.

At the entrance to the bar he paused and positioned himself at the precise spot where two streams of light crossed each other, one yellow, the other blue. His striated figure floated indecisively in the liquid light.

There she is, he said, turning on his heels and stumbling toward a green Corvair with California plates.

He got behind the wheel, fastened his seatbelt, and reached over the sun visor on the passenger's side, where he kept a half-smoked joint that he referred to as a damselfly. He lit it with a purple lighter, and took a long, deep drag, shaking his legs as if he were about to piss his pants. He passed me the joint, still holding in his smoke, and it seemed a few forevers before he finally let out a cloud of bittersweet smoke that expanded until it filled up the inside of the car. It was my turn. A shiny silver scalpel sliced open my esophagus lengthwise, making way for the brightness that slipped in, slithered down, then came out again through my belly button.

$\tau\pi$ watched me gleefully.

Strong, huh? A drag is enough to gravebeyond you, he said as he put out the damselfly and shoved it back behind the sun visor.

I bet you've never tried nothing like this? He took a plastic bag from the glove compartment and opened it. Black ganja. The weed was the color of tar. Indians grow it at high altitudes. They beat the plantbushes with barges braided with silver threads so they can get the most retsin out of them. His voice sounded as though it were coming to me from a distant place. Where his eyes should have been I saw two live red embers. Brazilian fuckgrass, shilder than fuck.

His voice had become distorted. His words began to fuse into each other. The last thing I heard was:

Qu'est-Ce q [yilph kiameth] ue tea faye?

Then all sound became equally muted, unintelligible. It was like going through a tunnel. Coming out, all I could make out was this sentence:

Do you like jazz? Then: Thelonious Monk is playing today in the Village, he said, one voice dancing in a void. In a crypt. He hasn't played in years, you know. He ran down. Silence got him. He just stopped playing. Just like that. Rawturkey. Where he's at now has nothing to do with his gigs back in the fifties, when he played places like the Five Spot. And, shit, his sidemen. Bird. Coltrane. Anyway, Oedipa told me about today's gig. That's why I'm in New York.

At the club door, this gorilla bouncer has the gall to card ττ. The guy looks around forty but he needs to prove it, see. American literalness.

There's no birthdate here, the gorilla bouncer huffs.

ττ pulls out a handful of other IDs and fans them out. The bouncer goes through them till he comes across a driver's license, then grunts, satisfied:

Welcome, Mr. Lippincott.

Inside, at one of the front-row tables, there was a woman seated next to a skinny man who was wearing sunglasses and a baseball cap. They waved to us. τπ introduced them as Oedipa Maas and Don. We found seats and sat. Monk came on stage, wearing a leopard-skin hat. The room went church quiet.

Kneel down before the mystery, τπ told me. Monk over the keyboard. Another few forevers till he played the first note. The gremlins of entropy spare us even a single nervous cough. Don, in my ear: What he's listening to, we can't hear.

No doubt Monk's band knew the score. They weren't even scratching their noses. Everyone was waiting for the Man to give the high sign. Waiting for the great sphere to burn.

He's a genius, τπ said, a fuckingfagmotherlickingenius, that's what Thelonious Monks is. Extranversy. An extra transfaerial ecstasy.

When he gets like this, Oedipa said, when he goes into one of these, what? Linguistic trances. There's nothing you can do. She put one of her hands in τπ's pockets.

Driving, said Don, is out. Not like this.

I'm one ahead of you, Oedipa said, and she clinked in midair the keys she just liberated from our ward's pants.

Let's go to my place, she said. I have some mescaline.

Don said thanks all the same, he had to get to the Bronx. Oedipa got behind the wheel. τπ began to play the bongos in the back seat. I was about to ask him whether he was doing "A Night in Tunisia" when he passed out. So much for the rhythm section.

And where did you meet? Oedipa asked, once we were out in traffic.

In a bar a few hours ago. He brought me here.

So you don't know who he is.

Not a clue.

She named a name I'd heard around a few times, and asked if I'd heard of him.

I turned to look at the wreck snoring in the back seat.

I read one of his stories in a magazine about ten years ago. It stuck in my head. I think it even got into my dreams, once. There's this guy who winds up in a garbage dump, and a midget lives there, and she falls in love with him and won't let him go.

Name's Nerissa, I was told. Then: By the way, mine's not Oedipa, said Oedipa—It's Mel. Oedipa's another character of his. He loves playing games.

I was treated to what would wind up the only sane conversation that night. Mel told me what happened when our backseat bongoer's huge third novel won the National Book Award in fiction, a year and a half before. Apparently he shared it with *A Crown of Feathers* by Isaac Bashevis Singer.

Singer and this guy, I said. Now that's a schizoid pairing. Night and day.

That's right. Later it won I don't know what Medal from some Academy, not that he accepted the award. Then came the Pulitzer meltdown. The fiction jurors were pretty big names, that year: Elizabeth Hardwick, Benjamin DeMott, and Alfred Kazin, no less. Their decision was unanimous: give it to $\tau\pi$. But the bigwigs on the board were so frustrated or disgusted or who knows what, trying to read the book, that they declared no prize would be given that year at all. But the funniest thing was when it won the National Book Award. He wouldn't go to the ceremony. His publisher suggested they get the comedian Irwin Corey to pick up the prize. And he did, and he gave an acceptance speech too. You should have heard it. It was like a cross between *Finnegans Wake* and a Lord Buckley routine. Corey pretty much slaughtered the English language and left it there to die. One half of the audience laughed, the other half looked like it was doing the *Times* crossword puzzle . . .

Oedipa, $\tau\pi$ piped from the back seat, would you get me a beer and roll us gentlemen a joint?

You roll one, shithead, can't you see I'm driving.

Then τπ insisted we all sing "One-Eyed Riley," a song that appears in T.S. Eliot's *The Cocktail Party*. He happened to have the score on him, and so made us memorize it and then perform to his bongo accompaniment.

By the time he let us stop, we'd reached our destination on Riverside Drive. More music was leaking out of the entrance of the building in question.

Shit, I completely forgot about Amy's party. I think her thesis advisor is up there. I'm sorry, Tom.

Non ti preoccupare di niente. Arriviamo un momento, prendiamo la mescalina, un po da bere e partiamo.

There was a living room next, and in the middle of that room was a middle-aged man with a fair-to-middling goatee. I pegged him right away as a white tube-sock-and-jockey-shorts kind of guy, though I have to admit that this deduction was helped along by the fact that he didn't have anything else on. A guy with an overpowering French accent and hard-on bolted out from one of the bedrooms as we came in—seems he'd been fucking someone or something and at *le moment suprême* had had the misfortune of overhearing someone in the party pronounce this or that literary opinion—that Mickey Spillane was twice the writer Manly Wade Wellman ever was, perhaps (unless it was vice versa?). To let such a statement pass unchallenged was more than he could bear, so out he'd popped, and you'd better believe everyone got out of his way in a hurry.

Meantime, the man with the goatee was saying to someone ensconced on a futon:

Really, his novels are about the difficulties inherent in the act of reading. Well, isn't every novel? Of course, when I say "reading," I don't mean only the reading of little black letters on paper. Not at all! To me, reading is a figurative term alluding to the forms, all the ways and means by which individuals try to extract meaning from the world in which we live—and from themselves as well.

Leezen, you fucking whoredog, we're not in class, the guy with the French accent said. Don't you have enough fucking all the female students? If you want to bore the sheet out of everyone, go somewheres else. Look how poor Chandler is staring at you. He took acid. God only knows how much you're freaking him out! Fuck off.

Who's he? I asked Mel, referring to the guy in his underwear.

You don't know Genghis Cohen? He's the chair of the department of comparative literature in some prestigious university on the West Coast. He's a visiting professor at Columbia University this semester.

The man howled, let out a fart, and continued with his rant:

In the contemporary novel, the act of reading runs parallel to the act of decrypting a world problematized by a battery of dehumanizing codes . . .

Goddamn it. Shit on you, you fucking motherfucker, the Frenchman said. He wobbled closer and slapped Cohen in the face.

I warned you, the aggressor continued.

Professor Cohen, Professor Cohen, cried the young woman who now skittered out of the room she and the naked Frenchman had so recently occupied. She was wearing a nightgown through which light and therefore the sight of those gifts bestowed upon her by nature were able to move freely. Mel told me that the girl was working with Cohen on her thesis about entropy in contemporary fiction.

Why did you have to do that, Pierre? the girl whined. Poor old Genghis. There was no harm in what he was saying.

Let's go back to bed and finish what you left half done, Pierre replied.

Stately, obese, with a crafty double chin and lascivious lips, the egregious Harry Krug, aka the Philological Toad, opined from his place on the futon: You're entirely too late, young man. Obviously this fair lady is far more interested in what Professor Cohen and I have in hand here than whatever she might have had in hand in *there*. Ignore him, Genghis. In my opinion, it's imperative that we incorporate the aleatory irresolution of modern life, the chaotic forces governing the—eternally in flux—physical world, into our analyses. Only thus can we even begin to characterize reading as a means by which the individual might extract something approaching a linear narrative from their own experiences.

I see your point, but what if History, with a capital H is the greatest of fictions, Krug? History with its private army of authors. Perhaps even most random-seeming world-historical events only occur because *some* authorial figure (ah, but who, who, who, for Chrissakes?) has porvoked, I mean, provoked them? Isn't it true that his first novel deals with the notion of occult conspiracy as motivating force for all contemporary experience? A disturbing idea, because it undermines every rational understanding of History—be it micro or macro!—as a perceivable entity in which the random *randomly* attains the form of order.

Oh, said Mel. It's you. They're talking about your stuff. And she jabbed τπ, who shrugged.

Nobody knows what I look like. To me he explained: Actually, I'm the Invisible Man.

Who, then, is the mysterious woman for whom the book is named? Cohen asked.

A goddess, Krug replied. She is searched for through fragments of history—big H and little!—since the nature of conspiracy is that those who are not initiates may only ever be permitted to see little pieces of the grand design. Yes, she is an ideal, a woman whose first initial is the only thing we can ever really know about, the first letter of a name that on top of everything may be a fake.

Genghis Cohen looked over at Pierre, afraid perhaps to launch a new sally lest Pierre throw another punch at him, but the

Frenchman was busy with Chandler, who was drooling something about Wendell Willkie in the midst of his (increasingly) bad trip. When the two disappeared into an adjacent bedroom, Cohen felt it was safe enough to reply:

In that sense, our protagonist is a representation of the reader, who in turn performs the role of authorial stand-in, and since the creator is by nature unknowable, we can say, as some have regarding the Bible, that the *primum movens* is not a he, but rather a she—that it is more appropriate to speak of Goddess than of God.

Waitaminute, that's my theory, you thief. You can't steal it just like that. It's in print! Professor Krug protested.

Hush, hush . . . I was merely alluding to your worthy theoretical construction in passing. Consider it a tribute, if you will, Cohen intoned.

The Invisible Man came out of the kitchen then with two six-packs of beer, grabbed me by the arm, and led me out of the apartment. Oedipa! he yelled from the stairwell, let's get out of here. Mel came out of the apartment at a run.

Who is playing at the Inverarity tonight?

The Paranoids.

Perfect, somebody roll another joint.

From the street we could hear Genghis Cohen and Harry Krug continuing to spout off:

Genghis Cohen: A ghostly organization that functions underground . . . Its mission? To slow entropy down, diminish the level of disorder in the world. Enough with irrelevancies, redundancies, and confusions. Enough with disorganization, chaos and loss and waste! All of which, we must regreatfully [sic] admit, comes down to that most hideous and wasteful component of human life: language.

Harry Krug: The central image of the novel, the V-2, is at the point of convergence between two separate lines of thought.

You can see it as functioning in a similar way, narratively and structurally speaking, as the great white whale who still stands (swims?) proudly at the apex of our national literature . . . the V-2 is at once the Dynamo and the Virgin, but better, better yet, going back to the Melvillean symbolism, it is the White Whale and the Pequod at once.

The Wolfman: Oedipa, you've got the radio down too low. Turn it up! Man oh man, I already knew I was doing the right thing, but after tonight, I swear, no one's ever going to get a look at my mug ever again. I'm gonna outsalinger Salinger.

Turning toward me, he said: By the way, what on earth *is* your name?

[Appendix: Rejections]

I sent "ππ" to fourteen different publications, most of them quarterlies. Ten didn't even bother responding or making use of my excellently caligraphed SASEs. The other four sent rejections. Here's what the first three said:

Verbally inventive, but too crude and irreverent. [Eric Sorrentino, *The Nation*]

Abominable. I don't even know why I'm responding. [Cynthia Lump, *Story*]

No one is going to publish this, Ackerman. Why do you waste your talent like this? Send me something when you're sober, and let's talk. [Ron Abramovicz, *Atlantic Monthly*]

The last thing I got was a handwritten note on *New Yorker* letterhead, which said:

Our readers' reports on your piece were so unanimously virulent that they piqued my interest and I decided to read it. I am forced to agree that it's not publishable in a magazine such as ours. Which is not to say that I also believe that the *New Yorker* ought to always play things so safe—risk can be beneficial, but to print your piece would be a risk too far.

Nevertheless, I wish you luck, Mr. Ackerman, and hope this is not the last time I run across your name.

Cordially, William Maxwell.

And PS: Pardon the indiscretion, but did you really meet Pynchon?

Sunday, May 18, 2008, 6:00 A.M.

No, Néstor, I didn't read that one either. How many times do I have to tell you that I don't really go in for fiction? For me, *Brooklyn* isn't a novel. As for the other documents, I'd rather not talk about them for now. They're the only ones that really count for me. But don't let my relative lack of interest in literature worry you. I still plan to hand everything over.

Wednesday, May 21, 2008, 10:05 A.M.

Dear Néstor, Congratulate me! I'm a free woman. I've turned in all my papers and I'm going out in a minute to celebrate with my friends. I'll have a drink in your honor.

Friday, May 23, 2008, 9:56 A.M.

Néstor, I'm going away for a bit—Amanda's folks have a place in the country they let us use. Now that my mind is free of any academic obligations, I'm going to give our little dilemma lots of thought. You'll be glad to hear (won't you?) that after all your comments, I've gotten a bit curious about Gal's literary endeavors after all.

Friday, May 23, 2008, 8:30 P.M.

Dear Néstor, I'm writing from Williamsport, Pennsylvania, where Amanda's parents have a house on the shores of the Susquehanna River. Yes, that's "the country" to us. It's a beautiful place. How strange the power of fiction! I began to read Gal Ackerman's stories today, starting with the two I sent you a few days ago, and everything seems so different.

Anyway, we'll be seeing each other very soon. I'll write you again from New York, right before I fly. Greetings from your nameless lady (it is such a relief to know that aside from abundant patience you also have a sense of humor . . .).

Monday, May 26, 2008, 6:02 A.M.
Dear Néstor, This is to confirm that I leave tomorrow—American Airlines. I'll see you in Cádiz. I have your number and will call as soon as I'm down. Very much looking forward to meeting you in person.

Fifteen
CALL ME BROOKLYN

Cádiz, June 2008

I discovered the Oakland when my marriage was on the verge of collapsing. Days I threw myself at my work, going nonstop at the newspaper, and that was fine, but when I was done, in the evening, I had to scramble around looking for excuses not to go home. At one point, I even rented a room at Hotel 17 near Gramercy Park. One Friday night at the office, I'd been alone for over half an hour already, unable to make up my mind to leave even though I had nothing left to do. Nat, the security guard, tapped on the window with the butt of his flashlight and asked me if everything was all right. I said yes and realized how ridiculous I was acting. Out I went. On Lexington Avenue, I came across the subway entrance for *Uptown & the Bronx* and instinctively looked across the street for the corresponding entrance for *Downtown & Brooklyn*. When I got to the Borough Hall stop, I let my feet guide me to Frank Otero's place. It was as though they already knew the way. After that, I started going to the Oakland a few nights a week. What the appeal was, I couldn't tell you. On the one hand, it was like being in Spain, a distorted Spain to be sure, a kind of caricature; on the other hand, and for some reason this was comforting, going there gave me the curious feeling of being somewhat outside of reality.

I liked the owner, Frank Otero, from the moment I met him. I liked the way he looked at life. He was a carefree, generous guy, a people person, very open (not that he didn't have a dark side too). He loved striking up conversations with strangers. He had the knack—he could connect with certain kinds of people; particularly the kind the world called losers. If their lives had spat them out on the Oakland's doorstep, well, Frank was always quick to offer his protection. As for Gal Ackerman, we didn't hit it off immediately. It took time. For the first few months, I just watched him from afar. He was difficult to figure out. He could spend weeks coming down into the bar twice a day, in the morning and in the afternoon, just to write. He'd sit at a table in the back and became submerged in his world, indifferent to whatever was happening around him. And then, all of a sudden, he would disappear without telling anyone—and not even Frank knew where he'd got to. After some time (it could be days or weeks), he would show up again and start to write as if he'd only left off the afternoon before.

The bar had a few permanent residents, so to speak—it wasn't just Gal. Not all of them appear in *Brooklyn*, or if they do, are barely mentioned; among these, the one that I got to know best was Manuel *el Cubano*—he was gay, and alone; when Niels Claussen could no longer take care of himself, he became the former sailor's guardian angel.

The Luna Bowl folk were also trapped in the Oakland's gravity. Gal's best friend there was old Cletus Wilson, the doorman. Cletus had met Gal before Gal had discovered the Oakland, and he loved him like a son. Cletus had trained some of the greats, in his time, and he himself had once been quite a renowned professional boxer. In Frank's office, there was a picture of the young Cletus posing next to Rocky Marciano at the entrance of Madison Square Garden. If the Luna Bowl was the closest planet in orbit around the Oakland, the farthest was the Danish sailors. For me they were no more than faceless extras, but they were an essential element of Frankie's imagination.

The book doesn't say a single word about the tenants of the motel, as Frankie called the second floor of the Oakland, despite the fact that there was no doubt more than enough material up there for several novels. In the two years that I spent in Gal's studio, I got some glimpses of the mysterious inhabitants of that world, although I never exchanged a word with them. When we passed each other in the hallway, they didn't even look at me. The only person with whom I dealt during all the time I lived in Gal's studio was a woman named Linnea. She was very attractive, somewhere between thirty-five and forty; she looked like a femme fatale out of an old thriller. She came to the motel in the middle of winter, some eight months after me. Her hair was dyed platinum blonde and she was always wearing expensive furs and jewelry. Every time I ran into her, she would stop to have a chat with me. The first time we met, I was coming out of the studio and she asked for a light. I offered her one, and she told me she'd been a long-term resident once, in the old days, and asked me what had become of Gal. When I told her, she was quite upset. I told her too that I was putting together his writing, trying to finish the book that he had left half done, and she told me she'd always known that Gal was an artist. She went off without saying good-bye, as if she suddenly realized that it might be best not to be seen talking to a stranger in the hallway of a flophouse. The other times we ran into each other, she did exactly the same thing: she used the age-old excuse of needing a light, stopped a few minutes to chat, then suddenly broke the conversation and took off without saying good-bye. I never knew for sure whether she was a call girl or the mistress of some big shot. She came and went in a black limousine. No one aside from her and the driver—a tough guy with a Haitian accent—ever got in or out of the thing. One afternoon, I was surprised to see a bunch of suitcases in front of her room. The Haitian appeared and, seeing me loitering by her property, gave me a nasty look. I remember it was snowing. From my window, I could see the limousine double-parked outside. Out of one of the half-lowered, tinted windows, I could see Linnea's cigarette holder and its squiggle of smoke. After a few moments, the driver put the luggage in the trunk, climbed behind the wheel, and took Gal's friend away forever. And that's it for interactions with Frank's tenants. Weeks passed between brief stairwell or hallway encounters. I always knew when a room had been vacated: Nélida would leave its key in the lock.

What Frank called the motel comprised six rooms of different sizes, all of them unnumbered save mine, which is to say Gal's. Some were deluxe, as far as this went, while others were real dumps. After Linnea left, I got in the habit of going inside the various vacant rooms and looking around. I'm not sure why. I would go up to the windows overlooking Atlantic Avenue and stand for a long time watching the traffic and the lights of the port. And then some morning, that room's key would disappear from its door, and that's how I would know the room had been rented again. It wasn't at all unusual for people to disappear from the motel after having spent a few months there—and without my ever setting eyes on them.

Frank was very careful about making sure that the world of the motel and the world of the Oakland never met. They were parallel universes: no communication allowed. With one obvious exception, the tenants of the second floor didn't go into the bar, and vice versa—it would have never occurred to any Oakland patron to peek upstairs. Each establishment even had a separate entrance, although, oddly enough, there was a revolving door behind the dance floor that led to the adjacent building. Frank always kept it unlocked, which I found odd in itself, but people rarely used it, Gal notwithstanding. Frank had reserved one of the rooms upstairs for Gal's use in perpetuity. It started out as Raúl's. He spent years there. When he went to live in Teaneck,

Frank offered it to Gal, and when I started working on the novel, he offered it to me. On the door, in bronze, was the number 305, which Gal had put up himself. I never figured out what it meant, but I have my suspicions—for one thing, the number of the room at the Chelsea where Mr. Tuttle committed suicide was also 305. Frank pretty much acted as though the motel didn't exist. He never talked about it and there was nothing in or outside of the building to betray its existence—neither a sign on the street nor a reception desk. The names of the tenants weren't kept in any registry book. They could spend their lives there, but they stayed invisible. Certainly there were some fishy things going on up there. A few glimpses have stayed with me: a Bentley that pulled up in the middle of the night and spent a few hours parked out front, vanishing by morning; groups of people who came and went as if in fear for their lives. One moonless night, I saw Frank distribute cash to several guys who had climbed down from a canopied truck—Víctor was watching his back. And then, once, I ran into a group of girls wearing strange masks in the lobby.

If in fact there were illegal goings-on at the motel, I never found out what kind. I don't believe Frank was directly involved. My impression is that he rented the rooms without asking too many questions. Otero allowed Gal into that world because he knew Gal was the soul of discretion. When I arrived, he saw no reason to treat me any differently. As for the Oakland, it too was somehow occult; not hidden, but then not exactly open to just anyone. You had to discover it. You could wander in at random, of course, and people did from time to time; but, in the end, it was up to Frank to select the regular clientele. And he had a weakness for the weird, people with shady pasts breathing down their necks. More than a few of them actually depended on Frank for subsistence; a select few even received a weekly allowance. In exchange for his aid, those under his aegis were required to do certain chores. Nélida and Ernie were in charge of assigning these duties, and they did it with great equanimity. A number of customers ran tabs, and when the time came to settle them, it could be that Frank only made them pay part of their debt, asking them to do some job for him. In any case, Frank's selection criteria weren't always clear. It came down to this: if he thought that you didn't fit in, you weren't admitted—and there were no appeals possible.

Once inside, though, you had to abide by Frank's unwritten laws. He ran the Oakland according to a scrupulously enforced code of conduct. You could see why they put up with it, though. Frank's beneficence didn't end with people's material needs. Many of the regulars at the Oakland were, to use Gal Ackerman's expression, people who had been defeated by life, individuals who had lost their way. Here, they felt safe. The Oakland gathered them in one by one: Manuel *el Cubano*, Niels Claussen, even Gal. It almost happened to me too, but I was able to get away in time. Not Gal. He was so tired of wandering around that, when he chanced into the Oakland one day, he was trapped at once: a lifer. He didn't notice it himself, at first. It was a creeping sort of paralysis. At first, of course, he could leave at will, travel far away, get on with his life—and it didn't seem odd to him that he always came back to the Oakland whenever inertia finally caught up with him. By the time I came into his story, the fight had almost completely gone out of him. Those sudden disappearances of his were the last thrashings of a fish on a hook. It was as though, on that distant afternoon when he had first arrived at the Oakland, someone had drawn an invisible circle around him. A very wide, loose circle in those days, but with the passing of the years it tightened around him until he could hardly take a step.

His name was Bruno Gouvy and he was a diplomat. She met him in Paris in September of 1985, at an art exhibit sponsored by the Belgian embassy where Bruno was a First Secretary. She had a scholarship to study with Bédier in the conservatory. A very brief courtship. They married in December in a more or less secret civil ceremony. I was born in late 1987. When I was sixteen or seventeen years old, Nadia confessed to me that she had never fallen in love like that before. She meant that she'd never been in a relationship so peaceful as that one. Her love life had always been quite turbulent.

It unnerved me to hear my mother talking about such intimate things so candidly. Listening to her tell me about all the other men she'd been involved with made me horribly anxious. My parents were the pillars that sustained my world. I looked at her both fascinated and frightened, trying to imagine what her previous life had been like. What I'd thought was solid ground was in fact an abyss. I didn't want this new version of my mother. I wanted the one I'd always known. I knew my mother adored Bruno—that had always been the case, and it would never change. She felt safe with him—he made her calm. By his side, she discovered that being in love was compatible with feeling at peace. Before meeting Bruno she never suspected that such a thing was possible.

Years later, when she was very ill, she told me that she had only been capable of giving birth because of the stability that my father had given her. Before she met him, she'd been pregnant many times, but around the fourth month, each time, she would inevitably miscarry. The terrible thing was that there was no physiological cause for it. She was convinced that it was her fault—that there was a will toward self-destruction inside her that made new life anathema to her body. That's what she told herself, anyway. The last time it had happened to her, the doctor was unequivocal: no more. Even one more miscarriage was too risky. She would have to resign herself to being childless. That was before she met my father, while she still lived in the United States. A few months after they were married, she got it into her head that with Bruno she would be able to overcome her jinx. She told me she'd never been so sure about anything before. So she waited to become pregnant, which didn't take long—she didn't have any trouble with conception, the problem always came afterward. She found a good gynecologist. She filled him in on her history and warned him that she was intent on bringing this pregnancy to term. After examining her, the doctor told her that her miscarriages had done a lot of damage, although from a physiological point of view, she was still capable of bearing children. He gave no credence to her theory that it was she who had provoked her own miscarriages, and suggested that perhaps she should see a psychologist. My mother replied that this was no longer necessary, that things had changed. The gynecologist finally assented, assuring her that he would do whatever he could. Nadia waited until the middle of the third month before she announced to Bruno she was pregnant. He'd suspected that something was up, but now that he knew for certain, he told her that he shared her certainty that everything would turn out fine. The pregnancy reached the fourth month, then the fifth. She had never gotten that far. Recalling this, she later told me that her body sent her little messages at night—little reassurances that everything was going according to plan. The sixth, seventh, and eighth months came. In due time, she went into labor and gave birth without any complications whatever.

I know I'm breaking the rules here—generally, you don't tell these stories because nothing happens in them. But the unbelievable thing about my mother's pregnancy was precisely the lack of anything notable. The extraordinary thing about it was that there was nothing out of the ordinary. And that was also the story of Nadia's life after I was born: a remarkable absence of anything remarkable. As she herself told me, motherhood changed her character, although in my opinion the change had begun earlier—when she met Bruno. All in all, it was a change for the good, although there were certain things that were lost in the process. Various edges of her personality were smoothed over, and she lost that rage that had always been a part of her and that was inseparable from her creativity.

It was a complicated phenomenon that I didn't fully understand until much later, when I no longer had her around to talk with. What happened to her was most evident in her relationship with music. Music continued to be the center of her life, of course—as it had always been since she was a child. She'd gone to Paris in the first place because of her musical talent. Her studies with Bédier were the culmination of many years of effort. But there was a difference, now. She had no ambition. Love, yes—she would never stop loving music. But the ambition that till then had been the engine of everything she did had disappeared. Nadia Orlov, the prodigy of whom her professors expected so much, lost interest in competing, struggling, excelling. Being better than others ceased to be a motivation for her. She continued to live up to the rigid standards that Bédier imposed on her until her scholarship ended, but in her heart she had abandoned the idea of becoming a concert violinist. Her involvement with music was, from then on, purely spiritual, shall we say. Internal. The world and its pomps and vanities had nothing to do with it.

In that, she was exactly like my father. You could say his profession was in his blood. Bruno Gouvy was the son and grandson of diplomats. But, in his blood or not, it wasn't his calling. It's not that he didn't like what he did, but the truth was that he had mainly resigned himself to follow in the family tradition because he saw it as a way to keep himself concealed. For him, being a diplomat was the perfect cover— elegance, good manners, and unfailing discretion are barriers behind which almost anything could be hidden. Diplomacy allowed Bruno to keep his true self hidden, protected. And it was only when he found himself far from all protocol, behind closed doors, in private, that he allowed himself the luxury of being who he really was—which is to say, something of an aesthete. There was something sacred about all this, for him. Few things, if any, were more important to him than privacy. I realized all of this little by little, but now that the time has come for me to go out into the world and deal with all its traps and snares on my own, it all seems quite clear.

As for me, I was coddled to ridiculous extremes. I might as well have been raised in a sterilized capsule, completely outside of the reality surrounding it. It was the three of us, and that's all. All my parents needed was their daughter and each other; beyond that, perhaps, a very limited circle of friends. And inside that fortress (and this point is crucial if you want to understand what their marriage was like), the only thing that had any value was art. They lived in an artificial world whose only religion was beauty. Papa brought his passion for painting into their partnership, Mama hers for music. Between those two planets swarmed the various constellations of the other arts. But if it didn't have anything to do with beauty, it didn't even register.

Of course, if I had wanted to tell an exciting story, Nadia's before her marriage more than fits the bill. She was born, grew up, and went to school in Laryat, Siberia, in a makeshift town whose residents were all scientists. If she wound up an adherent of the religion of beauty, she began in a world where rationality and knowledge were seen as the center of life. The school in that non-town was run by educators whose pedagogical philosophy necessitated giving their children an encyclopedic education: music, languages, physics, mathematics, astronomy, history, literature (broadly speaking, I mean), philosophy, and the social sciences. Nadia left when she was still quite young. Early on, in the States, it became evident that she had an extraordinary talent for the violin. Before she was twelve, she was accepted to the Boston Conservatory. The admissions committee was astonished when they heard her play during her audition—and bear in mind that these were people for whom child prodigies were as common as rocks. Years later, when she auditioned for Juilliard after graduating from Smith College, they gave her a similar reception. She easily surpassed the expectations of her professors throughout her career. When she graduated, she was awarded not only her degree but—as you know—a scholarship to study in Paris. I'm reiterating all this, Chapman, because the end of the story links up with the beginning. The idea, as far as she was concerned, was to construct the perfect conditions for her becoming a concert violinist, but after she met Bruno, and I was born, all that got put aside. A new leaf. Now that I can look at it with some perspective, it all strikes me as somewhat sinister. Nadia Gouvy, formerly Rossof, although I know nothing of that period of her life . . . disappeared, making way for a very different person: Nadia Gouvy.

My father and I never talked about personal things, and we still don't. He just can't do it. A very refined man, with an exquisite sensibility, no doubt capable of truly profound feelings—but putting them into words is beside the point. Bruno Gouvy's great passion could never have been anything other than painting: a static, visual, contemplative medium. Me, I've inherited my parents' inclinations in equal parts. For me painting and music are perfect partners. If I decided to study architecture, it's because I think that, as a discipline, it's halfway between my parents' interests—it is the perfect point of equilibrium between my parents' two worlds.

Don't get me wrong—it wasn't all tranquil contemplation. Perhaps Bruno was so guarded because he knew that his passion for painting bordered on madness, sometimes. It was nothing at all to him to travel thousands of miles simply to stand in front of a particular painting. I remember when I was, I don't know, around ten years old, he asked Nadia and me to accompany him on one of those trips. He had been assigned some duty at the Vatican. Once his mission was completed, he told us that instead of returning to London we were going to continue on to Palermo, and the following morning, he chartered a plane! All because he wanted us to see Antonello da Messina's L'Annunciata.

We got to the museum too late, after they'd closed for the day. Still, the curator of the palazzo was waiting for us. Bruno had made an appointment with him through the embassy. They were opening back up again just for us. With the curator leading, we went directly to the room where L'Annunciata hangs. I was too young to really take it in, then, but in retrospect, Bruno was right. It was absolutely worthwhile traveling to Sicily for no other reason than to see Antonello da Messina's tableau. We spent the night in a hotel in the middle of town, and the following morning, we went to see the painting one more time to say good–bye, as if we were taking leave of a loved one. After that, we headed back to Rome. That's Bruno Gouvy for you, Néstor.

So, my father has a peculiar pet theory. According to him, there's one masterpiece out there in the world for each of us, one great work that holds the key to our character, one work of art that in some mysterious way (he doesn't care to elaborate) corresponds to what we are, stands as a précis of our soul, who we are, how we feel, the way we look at life, and so forth. During that trip, as she stood in front of Da Messina's tableau, Nadia came to feel that L'Annunciata *was the painting assigned to her, according to the terms established by my father. She kept her feelings to herself until we were in London, where she asked him if the reason he had wanted us to accompany him all the way to Palermo was that he knew that when she saw it, she would recognize herself in the painting. He answered—I think in earnest—that she had it all wrong; the reason he'd asked us to go with him to Palermo was that being in Rome had for some reason made him itch to see the original of a work that had fascinated him for a long time. Even though he only knew it through reproductions, he was sure it would be magnificent, and he had wanted to share the experience with those he loved most in life.*

Bruno's favorite painting? Of course I don't mind telling you, it's no secret. Vermeer's View of Delft. *My father keeps a catalogue containing the particulars of the locations all of the canvases of the Dutch master, which are scattered all over the world, and which also provides substantial information about the works that have been lost. He's made a pilgrimage to every single place where the known Vermeers are kept—all of them, without exception. He's managed to get even the most intractable owners of the most inaccessible paintings to open their doors for him. Even the royal house of England granted him permission to study the Vermeers in their possession. When my father comes to see me in New York, the first thing we do is go to the Frick Collection on Fifth Avenue. There are several Vermeers there that aren't allowed to leave the museum under any circumstances. When Bruno tells me about his trips to the Frick, it's like hearing someone talk about visiting friends under house arrest. He hasn't let up—he's always traveling, always heading off on some adventure to meet up with a new painting he's dying to know in person, or else to revisit the ones that he misses most: Kandinsky, Fragonard . . . well, it's an endless list, and it takes in pretty much all of human history . . . His last trip, as you know, was to the Ensor exhibit. I try, whenever possible, to go with him on his pilgrimages, like we used to do with my mother before she died. I hope he never gives it up.*

 Don't take this the wrong way, but I've never seen anyone make quite the same face as you did, earlier, when I told you my name. I wish you could have seen it yourself. Some people are kind of surprised when they first hear it, although heaven knows you have more reasons than most. Do you see, now, why I didn't want to tell you? I wasn't trying to be melodramatic or anything. It's just that since everything is interrelated, giving you an isolated fact like that was entirely out of the question. You would have needed context, and before we knew it, things would have snowballed. That's also the reason I was reluctant to give you any of Gal's papers ahead of time. And, for your information, my name is by no means as rare as you seem to think it is. Not that it's very common even today, but, you know, it's gotten to be kind of fashionable in recent years. When I was a kid, sure, it got its share of comments, but not lately. Unusual or not, Brooklyn is my name. It's a mysterious, musical word, to me anyway: full of hidden meanings, like all place names. I remember one day, at school, when I was nine or ten years old—we were still living in London at the time—one of the girls in my class came up with the idea that we should all pick "true" names for ourselves—ones that really corresponded to our personalities, since the ones we bore had been chosen by our parents, not us. Well, you probably did the same thing when you were a kid. No? Anyway, my friends started trying on new names as if they were buying dresses. When my turn came, I said that I loved my name.

 That was another reason why I didn't want to tell you everything by e-mail. I'm not really over it—losing my mother. I was devastated.

Maybe I'll never be over it, really. She died in the middle of the summer. Bruno had already been transferred to Tokyo, so that's where she left us. Thankfully, it was a relatively quick death. My uncle Sasha, who had always been very close to her, stayed with Nadia till the end. Some of Bruno's family from Belgium also came. She was cremated, you know, and once it was all over, Bruno and I couldn't quite get back to reality. Hallucinatory solitude, I'd call it. We lived more alienated than ever from the outside world. I don't remember the rest of the summer very well. Each of us tried to comfort the other as best we could. Mostly, Bruno spent all his time looking after me, neglecting himself—that's just the way he is. Who knows how many weeks had passed before he was able to pull himself together and go back to work. At the end of the summer, we had to separate. He had no intention of letting me abandon my studies. As much as it hurt, I had to return to Cooper Union. We were so far away, it was impossible for us to see each other more than once a semester. Bruno had an absolute horror of long phone conversations, but this was our only comfort during these days. He called me two or three times a week. During a conversation in mid-October, he announced apropos of nothing that when we next saw one another, he would tell me something or other about my mother. I got very nervous. It wasn't like Bruno to be mysterious—I guess I'm not a chip off the old block, in that respect. Anyway, he wouldn't worry me like that if it weren't something very important. He picked up on my anxiety and told me there was nothing to get all upset about. He didn't say anything else and I didn't insist. Knowing how difficult it is for him to speak about personal stuff, I didn't have the heart to push him.

When your mother disappeared, Gal sought refuge in his writing as never before. It became his obsession—or, perhaps, better said: more of an obsession than ever. What he wanted was to write a book so that *she* would read it. Gal Ackerman had a fragmentary mind-set. He thought, spoke, lived in discrete segments. He wrote constantly, but was incapable of instilling any sort of unity into his work or life. Our pact—so to speak—was something I only became aware of gradually. Looking back, after he died, I saw how Gal had been showing me, very subtly, what he wanted his book to be like—what sort of message he wanted your mother to read, someday. I was in Taos working on a story. One night, when I got back to my hotel, there was a message waiting: call the Oakland immediately. When Frank told me the news, I thought: that's it. I had to follow through. I had to honor our pact. Frank Otero played a crucial role throughout the process, as you know. If it hadn't been for him, Gal's book would never have seen the light of day. Frank loved Gal Ackerman, and he wanted to see his friend's last wish granted. If the novel remained unfinished, what had Gal's life been for, in the end? Gal never shut up about the thing, Frank told me, and Frank had watched Gal write it year after year at the bar, seated at his table, the Captain's Table. Moreover, and this is important, Frank had witnessed firsthand the end of Gal's so-called love story with Nadia. He got to know her a bit, as well. Your mother spent more than a few nights at the motel. She even lived there for a while, if not too long. And, before he died, Gal gave me the key to his studio. See, he'd planned it all in advance. And, without his even knowing about Gal's scheme, Frank decided in all innocence to offer me the room soon thereafter. So you'll see how much responsibility I'd inherited: I'd become not only the bridge between Gal and your mother, but also between Gal Ackerman and Frank Otero. How could I refuse? I dug in. I practically moved into Gal's room—because that's where the material was, for one thing. And it's just an ideal place to write. I never really understood why Gal insisted on going down to the Oakland to work instead of staying put. At first, I would spend just a few hours a day on the book, late in the afternoon. It wasn't long, though, before I began to see the true dimensions of the project—all the material I would have to revise, sort, reconstruct, or destroy. A few hours a day weren't going to be enough. If I wanted to finish the novel, I had to really make a commitment, and that's what I did. I would get up at four-thirty in the morning so that I could work for a couple of hours before going to the newspaper, and then when I left the office I went right back to the motel to keep on working, as if my time actually earning money had just been a regrettable parenthesis. Weekend or weekday, holiday, blackout, drought, or storm, I kept on working. And that's not to mention all the research and legwork I had to do—talking with people who'd known Gal, hoping to fill in the gaps in all the stories he'd left for me to piece through. Yes, "all the stories," because Nadia's is just one among many—he might have been writing his novel *for* her, but he would be damned before giving her the pleasure of its being all *about* her into the bargain. But, look, I was still in the early stages of the process—I didn't know what I was dealing with, yet. It was a staggering amount of work, so much so that I really did begin to worry I'd lose my mind before being able to set down the final period. After a while, I began to see everything else in life as a distraction—just a bunch of obstacles trying to prevent me from bringing the project to an end. The biggest hindrance continued to be my full-time job, naturally. I had begun writing pieces for *Travel Magazine* shortly before Gal's death, but when work on the novel began in earnest, I didn't feel as though I could keep interrupting *Brooklyn* to jet off to the other end of the country to write a piece. I explained to Dylan Taylor that my contributions to the magazine would have to take a back seat, and he didn't hold it against me; but even without having to leave New York, it became less and less possible for me to steal time from the book project. I couldn't spend my day working at the *New York Post* and then just plunge right back into the world of Gal's novel. It was then that Frank offered to be my sponsor—that was the word he used. I laughed it off at first, but he was serious. He said he'd pay me a salary until I finished, and he wouldn't back off. How long would it take for me to finish *Brooklyn*? What are you making a month at the *Post*? I refused, but I might as well have been trying to convince the sun to stay down. No matter what excuse I made, he responded the same way: ours was a perfect arrangement. The best I could do was convince Frank to only give me half of what he'd offered. I may add an extra allowance here and there he replied, not fully understanding my motives, and shook my hand as if we had just signed a contract.

My bosses were understanding, as far as it went. They told me not to worry, that although they couldn't promise me anything, they would more than likely have a job for me when I returned. And who says New York is so cutthroat? After that, I guess you could say that I stopped living for a couple of years—that I spent two years in someone else's skin, a prisoner of a world Gal had created, reading letters, diaries, notebooks, story drafts, choosing which papers to keep, which to burn. During the second year, I hardly left the studio. I was living in a fiction, albeit an "autobiographical" one, as they say. It was the only way to finish the book, I thought—someone else's book, that is. Now I can't help but feel it's a little bit mine as well. The last thing I worked on was a bunch of disparate odds and ends that dated from various points in Gal's life. He had been conscientiously correcting them during the months before his death. His intention was to place them at the end of his manuscript. The novel has an open ending, as you know—a section describing Gal and Nadia's last meeting at Bryant Park, two avenues away from Port Authority where everything had begun. They would never see each other again. Nadia had to catch a bus to Boston at the 42nd Street terminal, but Gal had decided not to accompany her all the way . . . Anyway, I had to write around the clock if I wanted to get the novel to Fenners Point on the second anniversary of his death. I almost didn't make it. On April 10, 1992, I typed in the last word. The last weeks were a maddening frenzy. *Brooklyn* was an imperfect creature, as all books are—some more than others, of course—but now it existed, it had taken form, it had a life. I said to myself: that's it, mission accomplished. I went to the Danish cemetery and put the book in Frank's niche . . .

The worst was yet to come, however. I was done, but I didn't *feel* done. It was the beginning of a very serious crisis. I'm not talking about the post-partum emptiness you always stumble into at the end of a long and intense project, although of course that was part of it. No, what was bothering me was that even after having carried out my part of our pact, the shadow of the author continued to haunt me. I was still waking up every morning in the world of Gal's book. I'd fallen into a trap—a trap that included not just the novel, but the Oakland, Brooklyn, the States. I had to get away, put some distance between us, do other things, live my own life. There's something dangerous about the Oakland. It doesn't want to let go, once it's gotten its hooks into you.

Frank insisted I could stay in the motel as long as I wanted. But that was just what I didn't want. I was afraid that what had happened to Gal and others before him would happen to me. Niels Claussen was a good example. One of the things that I learned, writing the novel—and I learned quite a few things, I'll have you know—was how difficult it is to get past the sense that what you read on a page has some basis in fact. The story of Niels wasn't in the book just because it had inspired Gal to start collecting material for his *Death Notebook* . . . No, it was a sort of parable. Tragedy comes for all of us, sooner or later. Tragedy is all around us, all the time. But that's not the important thing. No, the really bone-chilling thing about Claussen's story wasn't what had happened to him—it was that he was incapable of reinventing himself afterward. He just gave up. See, the Oakland didn't finish him off *physically*; it did something worse. It turned him into a zombie when he was all of twenty-six years old. Gal was just as much of a goner, if you think about it. He couldn't function away from the site of his defeat. So, no, there was no way I would stay in the motel. I had to go off on my own. I'd taken a long detour, but now I was back on the main road I didn't bother to call Tom Archer. If I had, no doubt he would have offered me some kind of gig. But, no, I had to be strong and sever all ties, just go, go, go—find a life somewhere else, keep moving forward. I had just turned thirty-four. Old enough to give up forever, if I wasn't careful. I didn't know what to do, only that I had to do something—perhaps return to Spain. Anything but stay put.

Things couldn't go back to the way they had been before. Finishing Gal's book shook the foundations of my personality. Forced me to review my entire life. So much that I thought had been stable had been blown to bits. But that was fine. I decided to reinvent myself, a very American conceit that—ironically—I now utilized precisely to sever my ties with that country forever. I renounced my future as a journalist, into which I (and so many others) had put so much stock. I said good-bye to Brooklyn, to New York, to the States, the friends I had made there, the landscapes that I had come to love, the beauty of American literature. I said good-bye to the things that had made me what I was. I said good-bye to Frank, to Gal, to Nadia, to Nélida, to Niels Claussen, to Victor Báez, to Abe Lewis, to Umberto Pietri, to Teresa Quintana, to Felipe Alfau, to Jesús Colón, to Mister Tuttle, to all the characters who had paraded in front of me and were now ensnared forever in the pages of a novel I had managed to complete for a dead friend. I needed to do it—to be myself again. And with all the clarity of a ray of light seeping through a crack in a sealed basement window, I saw that I wasn't leaving empty-handed. No: I had, after all, become a writer.

At the beginning of November, around the time of my birthday, Bruno had to go to Paris; he invited me to spend a week with him in the city of my birth. We would go on long walks, see as much art as we could, attend concerts, and eat out. On my birthday, we would go to Dominique, Nadia's favorite restaurant. It's in Montparnasse, a real storied sort of place—it was founded back in the twenties by a White Russian exile. Knowing I might be a little disconcerted at the venue, Bruno told me that it was difficult for him too, but we had to make an effort, because that's what Nadia would have wanted. I acquiesced; he had me dead to rights. When the time came, though, I couldn't handle it. Right before going into the restaurant, everything went blurry, and my knees got weak. Bruno held me by my shoulders, trying to comfort me as well as keep me upright. He repeated what he had told me over the phone from Tokyo, that wherever Nadia might be, she would be happy that we were celebrating my birthday at one of her old stamping grounds. Seeing him so self-assured, I managed to recover, and in we went. The maitre d' recognized us right away, even after so long, and led us obligingly to "our" table. The tradition with the three of us had been to give presents only during dessert. When we had it in front of us, Bruno brought up that phone conversation—when he'd made those ominous hints about some big secret concerning my mother. He put a metal box on the table. I asked him if it was my gift, and he said that it was. Before he told me where he got it, he implored me not to open it until I was alone in my room at our hotel.

He had come across the box one morning after having mustered the fortitude and composure required to go through the papers that Nadia kept in her bureau. The box was the first thing he'd seen when he rolled up the top of her writing desk. He took off the lid in the same state of anxiety as when he had gone through her chest of drawers, or the armoires where she kept her wardrobe and jewelry, or when he had inspected the knickknacks she kept in her numerous music boxes. The first thing he saw were some old papers, on top of which were an old silver necklace and earrings. He pushed aside the jewelry and cast a quick glance at the papers. Somewhere in the pile was a clothbound diary. He hesitated before opening it. A few fragments picked out from the text at random were enough for him to know what it was about. He put the lid on the box again as though he'd seen a dozing cobra inside—those were his words. The passages he had read brought other things to mind. Things my mother had told him in passing, but that were begging to be assembled into a whole that my father nonetheless determined he had no right to know about. But I was her daughter, and that was different. The loss of my mother was still very fresh in my mind, he knew. This would probably bring me closer to her. It would help me to get to know her better. Besides, I was like Nadia in so many ways. He grabbed my hands firmly, urging me to finish my dessert, because we had to leave for the opera very soon.

I opened the box later that night. The necklace and the earrings were very beautiful, the silver engraved with Aztec figures. I looked at them, knowing somehow that these were gifts another man had given my mother. The diary is news to you, I know, but the papers you already know about. I'm sure you understand now why I resisted sending you the full inventory by e-mail—don't you?—although in the end, I gave in, I know. As I've already told you, my interest in the papers varied piece to piece, depending on the subject matter. What we've ended up calling the "literary" papers, I only glanced at, and they failed to capture my interest—sorry. And the letters, yes of course, I read them all in one go, but what I kept going back to was the diary. It was a medium-sized journal, black, like the ones you say Gal used to write in. It was no longer than a hundred pages and was about half filled. It wasn't easy to read, but not because of the handwriting, which was so familiar to me, but because of the language my mother used—solipsistic, I guess: cryptic, the syntax disjointed, the language of someone talking to herself. She mixed hermetic references with descriptions of events so lacking in detail that at times it was impossible to know what on earth she was talking about. It was like reading poetry in a language you barely understand. But yet I did get something out of it. I mean, one thing was very clear. The majority of the entries referred to the relationship that my mother'd had with Gal Ackerman. She didn't mention any

lovers, specifically, although I knew that Gal hadn't been the only one.
(I don't count my father—his name does appear in a couple of entries
too.) Reading Nadia's diary was like a journey to some remote and
secret place. It was clear that the journal, along with the stack of papers
and the objects that accompanied them, all meant a lot to my mother.
She'd found a way, through her annotations, to keep alive the feelings
she'd had in those days, good or bad—her writing had nailed them
into place forever. Trapped in those pages, the love that my mother had
felt for that strange man remained alive, although in real life she had
moved on long ago. The entries were brief and sparse, covering a span
of several years. At first, there was a sort of continuity between them,
then the entries became more sporadic, and then dropped off entirely.
The last entry floated alone on a recto page, as though it had gotten lost.
The handwriting there was a little more legible than usual for her, as
if she had written it very slowly. She writes about a letter in which
someone had succinctly communicated to her that Gal Ackerman was
dead—had died, in fact, two years before. When I first read it, I didn't
pay attention to the date or the name of the sender or the name of the
place in which this Gal person was buried. I only registered the fact
of the death. I went through the rest of the diary, but there were no
further entries. I cried for a long time, until I was left feeling utterly
devoid of energy. I hadn't even realized they were coming, those tears.
It was a cloudburst, and I was surprised at myself.

I turned off the light, exhausted. Though it had slipped from my
hands long before, the diary's words went on parading in front of
me, out of order, stirring up a new onslaught of images. I had read
everything in one sitting, condensing into a few hours what had taken
my mother years to live and write. It was too much to come to terms
with—or not with any coherence. Some details of the story were very
clear, while others, likely, hadn't even registered. I don't remember
how long it took me to fall asleep; I didn't notice it happen, and my
dreams were about waiting to sleep; it felt interminable, as though I'd
never get back to the sunlit world. I saw Nadia in the room with me,

reading aloud from the diary as she caressed my head, which I had laid on her lap. Since I thought I hadn't fallen asleep yet, I almost believed she was really there.

Had I done the right thing by reading everything straight through? Should I have exercised restraint, like my father, and so have avoided looking into the void? But of course, he'd been the one to hand it over. He must have wanted this. Wanted me to get to know my mother better. Wanted me to go into the secret place from which he was—necessarily—barred. Perhaps even to report back on what I'd found there. But what about the effect on me? On her memory? Fresh from my semi-dream, I caught myself imagining her watching me from someplace unimaginable . . . what would she think of me now? The question kept coming: The diary was exclusively centered on Gal Ackerman. Why not other men too, except for in passing? They had existed—I was certain of that much. She had even married another one after leaving Gal, that musician whose name she had taken for a few years . . . not even a hint of that guy in there. The diary had been reserved for one man only. Why such devotion to a man who seemed—to me, anyway—like nothing more than a stain that had tainted so much of her old life?

I'm young, I know, but even so—I've been hurt plenty in what must seem to you a very short time. Maybe a man like you would find it all pretty ridiculous if I made a clean breast of all my amorous catastrophes. But Nadia was different. Her wounds were very deep— the real thing, if you like. That's what I discovered reading the diary. Bruno and I didn't talk about this at all, of course, although during breakfast he could see perfectly well how affected I had been by reading the diary. I took the whole package back with me to New York, but kept the box shut tight. I was almost scared to disturb it again. I remembered what Bruno had told me, that the moment he realized what was inside the box, he put the lid back as if he had seen a dozing cobra inside. Later, early in December, I think, Nadia made another appearance in my dreams: She was barefoot and wearing a tunic, and her hair was up in a bun. She looked very young, younger than when she gave birth to me. She wore the earrings and silver necklace that she had put away inside the box. She wouldn't talk to me. I wasn't even sure that she could see me. She was standing up, leaning on a marble column like a Greek goddess. She was carrying the box. I tried to approach her but I couldn't. I called on her, sometimes by her name, Nadia, Nadia. Other times, in a much quieter voice, I just said Mama. She didn't respond. At some point, she glanced toward me, perfectly composed, beautiful, but she remained silent. I asked her if it was okay that I had read her papers. She put the box on the floor. The lid lifted off on its own and a horrible bird popped out to fly off and perch on some brambles that were there, and had always been there, you know, the way things are in dreams. My mother turned around and walked away, ignoring my calls. I woke up sweating and disoriented. I know, it sounds like a movie—the echo of my cries seemed to hang in the air around me. I went looking for the box as soon as I came to my senses. I'm not sure why. Maybe I just wanted to be sure it was still there, and that it wasn't concealing any avian stowaways. I certainly had no intention of reading anything. If I wanted anything concrete, it was just to touch the pages, to run my finger across the words that my mother had written, to caress the necklace and the earrings she had been wearing in the dream. Sure, I leafed through the pages, but I did my best not to understand whatever phrases my eyes couldn't help but light upon. When I reached the last page she'd used, I stopped, winded, as though I'd been climbing a mountain and had finally reached the inhospitable peak. It took a while for the words I had in front of me to register:

May 6, 1994

Poste restante—the last letter sent to Gal was returned—unopened—inside the envelope a note from Frank Otero—Gal died almost two years ago—buried at a place called Fenners Point, near Deauville

I put away the diary and shut off the light, although I knew that I wouldn't be able to get back to sleep. Right next to the bedroom window there's a neon sign that flickers on and off all night long. I leave the window shade up on purpose, usually, because instead of bothering me the incessant blinking makes me sleepy. The room is completely dark one second (or as dark as any room ever is in New York City) and in the next bathed in a halo of red and blue. In May of 1994, when my mother had written the last entry in her diary, I was six years old. I thought about all the blank pages that followed it. It was as if with the death of that man a very heavy door had been slammed shut, cutting off Nadia's contact with her past. It's funny how the imagination works. The name Fenners Point bounced around in my head. I'd never heard of the place, just as I had never heard of Deauville. It sounded made-up.

I tried to picture the cemetery, but the blinking of the neon sign finally worked its magic, and I dozed off. For a moment, on the threshold of a new dream, the neon signs outside seemed to spell the place names that Nadia had recorded in her diary. Fenners Point. Deauville. The following morning, I looked them up on a road map I have in my room. I couldn't find them. I had to use one of those enormous atlases that sit on lecterns, in the Cooper Union library. I felt a bit silly, being so curious about the resting place for the mortal remains of a man I couldn't help but wish had never been a part of my mother's life. It wasn't long before I'd gotten it into my head that I had to go to that cemetery. I needed to see the grave of my mother's lover. I told Amanda, my roommate, all about it. She asked me what I expected to find there. Nothing, really, I told her—it was just scratching an itch, so to speak. I told her that I was set on going, one way or the other, and asked her to come with me. We went in her car. The rest you know.

As for the novel, reading it changed things for me. It was no longer my mother's history alone. Gal's book is where so many stories cross paths—and a lot of them have nothing to do with Nadia, as you said.

For one thing, it's also about the man who actually did the work of finishing the book—you, Néstor Oliver-Chapman. You know, the papers that I found in the box my father gave don't always agree with the finished texts in the novel, in terms of how the stories go, the details that get presented. Gal Ackerman wasn't the most consistent writer— or person, for that matter. It's not that he lied to you, but he did use you. He left a particular version of things in place so that you would finish the book as he wanted it finished, never mind the truth of the matter. Well, it is fiction, after all. For instance, Gal knew about me and never told you. Nadia wrote a long letter to him to tell him she'd borne a child, a girl, and Gal replied. It's one of the letters that she kept. Read it, it's excruciatingly sad. Another thing is that Gal and Nadia did see each other again after that time at Bryant Park. Gal wanted his novel to end with the story of the torn love letter falling from the sky, so he let you believe that that was that. I'm not saying he invented the love-letter thing—my mother refers to it in her diary as well. But, then, she also records—in some detail, actually—their real last meeting, which was very painful. Literature is one thing, life another, as perhaps you need reminding now and again. So, yes, they shouldn't have done it, but the truth is that they met again. Their last meeting, which Gal forced on my mother, was—naturally—a little traumatic. And I could keep going. There are other things, other remarks in the diary that would have changed the book you wrote, sometimes drastically. I wouldn't say that they disprove Gal's version of events—I guess you could say that they complement it. Anyway, Gal made my mother the keeper of certain texts. Clearly, he considered them vital. They're here, they're in the box. As far as I'm concerned, though, it all belongs in the novel, and so, rightfully, it all belongs to you. As for me, I just want to forget about it.

I'm glad that I went to Fenners Point, silly though it was. When I saw the title of the book through the glass, my heart leapt. Amanda and I forced open the latch, took out the novel, and started to look through it together. It wasn't long before we stumbled upon the name

Nadia Orlov. Amanda soon stepped aside, seeing I intended to read every word; though, of course, I couldn't finish the book there and then. We went back to the city immediately, hardly exchanging another word on the drive. As soon as we got home, I locked myself in my room. It felt like one of those dreams or not-dreams I'd been having since Nadia died. When I finished the book, I realized the magnitude of my transgression. Aside from all the things related to my mother, which I perhaps did have the right to know, I'd also meddled my way into the lives of a bunch of strangers. I was trespassing. After a few months, I knew what I had to do: return the novel to Frank Otero, if he was still alive, if the Oakland was still there after so many years. And if I found Otero, maybe I could get to you through him. And if I found you, I could at last get rid of my mother's papers without having to destroy them.

EPILOGUE

"And over there where dreams are invented
There were not any
For us."
ANNA AKHMATOVA

Fenners Point, September 2010
Everything had been going so well, but then she interrupted herself to suggest I talk about me for a bit.

I stared at her. About me? I asked. I have nothing to say about me.

Please, she insisted.

The malicious glare in her eyes unnerved me.

My story is irrelevant. I . . . I . . . had nothing to do with all that. Circumstances dragged me into a world I didn't belong in . . .

I stopped making excuses. Her big green eyes went on drilling into mine. What was it about that those damn eyes? She was giving me vertigo.

In a very sweet voice, she said:

It's exactly the opposite now from when we were talking by e-mail. Now it's you who knows everything about me while I know practically nothing about you.

What is there to know?

I'd like to know more about Néstor the man. What you were like before and after *Brooklyn*. We're never going to see each other again, so why not? I insist.

The tone of her voice, the way she pronounced her words, the particular angle of her smile, the gestures she made while listening to me, how she brought her index finger to her lips whenever she began talking again after a pause—in short, all her body language during our long conversation seemed to add up to an imperative that I give in, seemed to add up to a sort of seal of approval. And then that stare. The stare above all.

Before and after *Brooklyn*? I repeated.

She nodded, pushing some hair away from her face.

If you want to know the truth, Gal, I think she could have done whatever she wanted with me. After a while, I realized that I was telling her things that I'd never told anyone, not even you or Frank. Did you know that my mother, Christina, was from Seattle, and my father, Albert, was Catalan? Or that I was born in Trieste? Well, those are the things Brooklyn wanted me to tell her about, so I started at the beginning, though I did it in broad strokes, in a rush, because the only thing I wanted just then was to finish as quickly as possible. I told her about my parents' bohemian lifestyle, their countless trips all over Europe, of my erratic education, the years I spent studying at Summerhill with that amazing nutcase Neil, and later at the University of Madrid, about how Lynd, my mother's friend, helped me with my master's in journalism at Columbia. I told her about my beginnings as a freelance journalist, writing for the *Village Voice*, then my work for the *New York Post* and *Travel*. When I reached that part of the story, I told her that I liked to be invisible, and asked her to let me be, that all that had been left far behind. She thanked me, and I knew our meeting had come to an end.

Too bad we never found the grave of Ralph Bates's great-grandfather, she said, smiling. It would have been a nice way to say good-bye to all this.

I tried, but it was a dead end, I said. Maybe I'll try again before

I leave. Who knows? It's definitely here, that's for sure.

There was a long silence. I lifted my eyes to the blue sky of Cádiz. The midday sun battered the graves, the whitewashed walls with their niches, the mausoleums. When my eyes came to rest on Brooklyn again, she stood up and said:

I really appreciate your taking charge of my mother's papers. Pushing the hair from her face, she shook my hand and added:

It's been . . . very strange, Néstor, but I'm glad I met you.

Brooklyn, I said.

She waited for me to go on, but when she realized I wasn't going to, she turned and walked away.

You know how people say, sometimes, "I wasn't myself at the time"? Well, I wasn't. I had become you. It was a dream, or a hallucination, or perhaps I was finally losing my mind for good and all. Yes, I must have gone completely mad, because none of it made any sense, or maybe it made too much sense. As Brooklyn said, it was like a movie—but I felt that I was a spectator now, not an actor; as though I was watching myself up on the screen in one of those old movies that feel like they have to toss in a dream sequence designed by Dalí, or something, in order to wrap up their plots. I took very precise notes on my conversation with Brooklyn as soon as my faze passed. I wanted to be able to read it to you now. It wasn't that difficult. I remembered each and every word with painful clarity. Although I no longer had Brooklyn in front of me, her body, her face, especially her eyes, were still very much present. I felt as though I were under siege—everywhere there were signs and symbols pulling me into the past, and then into my own very uncertain future. It took a while, but I was finally able to make some sense of the feelings pressing in on me.

I stared at the box of papers Brooklyn had left with me, and said her name aloud twice: Brooklyn, Brooklyn. I felt a pain in my side, as though I'd been stabbed. I felt that and I felt thirsty, a terrible thirst. And I came to understand what was happening to me. I probably don't need to tell you. You probably guessed ages ago. It was the most elementary and primal feeling that exists, the most basic—the same thing that set our novel into motion in the first place. I recognized the feeling, or to be more exact, I remembered it. But it couldn't be. It couldn't be happening to me. It was as if time had shrunk. It was . . . as if I had fallen in love with Nadia. And after I thought that, after the idea took shape, after the words aligned themselves in my head, I was relieved. I hadn't fallen in love with Nadia because the woman I'd had in front of me wasn't her.

As all those thoughts whirled in my head, my eyes remained fixed on her receding figure. Brooklyn Gouvy was walking between two rows of graves, moving farther and farther away from me. The sunlight sparkled on the graves, the flowers, the metal of the epitaph plaques. A very hot morning. Wisps of sultry air rose from the ground in little clouds, as though the earth were a giant, asthmatic animal expiring in the dust. The haze softened the edges of things as clouds of mist continued to rise from the asphalt, translucent little clouds that trembled and danced. I kept my eyes on Brooklyn Gouvy, feeling that odd pain in my side, until she made it to the gate and disappeared without having turned once.

We will never see each other again, she'd said.

Absurdly, I dashed after her. My footsteps echoed and cracked down the alley, widely spaced, mixing with the other indistinct midday sounds. As I ran, the silhouettes of the cypresses danced in my peripheral vision like drunken sorceresses. A horde of unconnected scenes were piling up in my imagination. I felt as if I were being dragged from myself, as if I would have to die in the dust in a moment or two. But I made it to the gate. She had turned left. I looked in that direction and saw a silver-gray Mercedes with diplomatic plates, and next to it, two figures.

Brooklyn was resting her head on the shoulder of a tall, elegantly dressed, aristocratic-looking gentleman. The man ran his hand through her hair and gave her little taps on the back as she sobbed. Neither Bruno Gouvy nor her daughter realized that they were being watched. The image remained frozen in time for a while. There was a whitewashed wall, a row of cypresses, a stone path that led to the door of a chapel. The Mercedes was parked very near the curb. Bruno Gouvy took his daughter by the shoulders then, raised her chin, pushing it up delicately with his index finger so she would look him in the eyes, and gave her a handkerchief so she could dry her tears. Then he walked her to the passenger door of the car and opened it for her. Gouvy's movements were gentle, delicate. He closed the door and then went around and got behind the wheel. The engine came on with a slight whirr and the tires bit into the gravel. I made myself visible. With uncertain steps, I moved to the middle of the street. The car stopped a short distance away and both of them looked back at me. Through the windshield I could see their faces clearly—his fine-featured, with a bronze complexion, hair the same color as the Mercedes. And Brooklyn, the living image of her mother. I stepped to one side and the car continued on its way very slowly. Bruno Gouvy raised his hand and smiled with his eyes, without moving a muscle in his face. As they passed by, I put my hand on the window, the fingers spread in a fan, and Brooklyn did the same, she put her small, delicate hand on the glass, though her fingers were pressed together, not apart. It could have been a good bye caress, had it not been for the hot glass between the palm of her hand and mine. Then she pulled away and waved. The car moved past the gravel path, turned right to get on the main road, and disappeared.

I stood motionless in the middle of the road, not sure what to do, as I replayed everything in my mind, rewinding and then sitting through the surreal dream sequence once more. It was as if night had suddenly fallen, as if a total eclipse had descended on the Bay of Cádiz. I remembered one such eclipse, the only one I had ever experienced, when I was a child at Summerhill. Mrs. Dawson had warned us it was coming, around noon. When the time grew near, instead of going to the main pavilion to witness the event with the others, as we had been instructed to do, I hid in the nearby woods. Sitting on a rock, I watched as something that was not quite night descended upon us, a nameless darkness that covered everything like a big black sheet, until little by little, things returned to normal. It was the same, now, at the cemetery. What before had been clear images became shadows. Shadows, I thought, or maybe it was a voice inside me giving dictation. Shadows, the voice said, only shadows, shadows without end. Everyone who was once a part of that world was gone forever—a whole universe had been erased. The beings that once inhabited it, full of life, were now little more than smoke. I could hear again the chorus of pealing bells near Hotel 17, where I rented a room when my marriage was disintegrating. Those dreadful hotel rooms occupied by old homeless couples who smoked marijuana and watched cartoons on TV all night long. Back then, first thing in the morning, as I woke, the peal of the bells of a nearby church made me think for a moment that I was still in Europe, still a child. In the calm of the cemetery, I heard the wind whistle down on me from afar, a wind that as it passed wanted to erase everything still remaining. And, at that moment, I, who thought I'd been dreaming of the shadows cast by everything that bore the name of Brooklyn, realized that there were no shadows, only brilliant lights that bleached the world. Everything was white, ash-white in the heat—the walls, the box holding the papers Brooklyn had given me, and which she claimed contained what's missing from this book. But I knew I wasn't going to read any of it. Because *Brooklyn* already had a life, the one you wanted to give it. It was the book you wrote for Nadia, and it was done, and nothing and no one could ever change that.

EDUARDO LAGO was born in Spain in 1954, and has been a resident of New York City since 1987. The author of numerous interviews with American writers, including Philip Roth, John Updike, Norman Mailer, David Foster Wallace, and Don DeLillo, he has translated fiction by Henry James, William Dean Howells, Junot Díaz, and John Barth into Spanish, among other authors. *Call Me Brooklyn*, his first novel, was declared the best book of 2006 by the daily *El mundo*, and won the Nadal Award, Spain's oldest literary prize, as well as the City of Barcelona Award, the National Critics' Award and the Lara Foundation Critic's Award, all in 2007. Between 2006 and 2011, Lago served as Executive Director of the Cervantes Institute in New York. He teaches at Sarah Lawrence College, where he has been a tenured member of the faculty since 1994.

As well as a translator, ERNESTO MESTRE-REED is the author of three novels, *The Lazarus Rumba*, *The Second Death of Única Aveyano*, and the forthcoming *Sacrificio*. He is Assistant Professor of Fiction at Brooklyn College.

SELECTED DALKEY ARCHIVE TITLES

MICHAL AJVAZ, *The Golden Age.*
The Other City.
PIERRE ALBERT-BIROT, *Grabinoulor.*
YUZ ALESHKOVSKY, *Kangaroo.*
FELIPE ALFAU, *Chromos.*
Locos.
IVAN ÂNGELO, *The Celebration.*
The Tower of Glass.
ANTÓNIO LOBO ANTUNES, *Knowledge of Hell.*
The Splendor of Portugal.
ALAIN ARIAS-MISSON, *Theatre of Incest.*
JOHN ASHBERY AND JAMES SCHUYLER,
A Nest of Ninnies.
ROBERT ASHLEY, *Perfect Lives.*
GABRIELA AVIGUR-ROTEM, *Heatwave
and Crazy Birds.*
DJUNA BARNES, *Ladies Almanack.*
Ryder.
JOHN BARTH, *LETTERS.*
Sabbatical.
DONALD BARTHELME, *The King.*
Paradise.
SVETISLAV BASARA, *Chinese Letter.*
MIQUEL BAUÇÀ, *The Siege in the Room.*
RENÉ BELLETTO, *Dying.*
MAREK BIEŃCZYK, *Transparency.*
ANDREI BITOV, *Pushkin House.*
ANDREJ BLATNIK, *You Do Understand.*
LOUIS PAUL BOON, *Chapel Road.*
My Little War.
Summer in Termuren.
ROGER BOYLAN, *Killoyle.*
IGNÁCIO DE LOYOLA BRANDÃO,
Anonymous Celebrity.
Zero.
BONNIE BREMSER, *Troia: Mexican Memoirs.*
CHRISTINE BROOKE-ROSE, *Amalgamemnon.*
BRIGID BROPHY, *In Transit.*
GERALD L. BRUNS, *Modern Poetry and
the Idea of Language.*
GABRIELLE BURTON, *Heartbreak Hotel.*
MICHEL BUTOR, *Degrees.*
Mobile.
G. CABRERA INFANTE, *Infante's Inferno.*
Three Trapped Tigers.
JULIETA CAMPOS,
The Fear of Losing Eurydice.
ANNE CARSON, *Eros the Bittersweet.*
ORLY CASTEL-BLOOM, *Dolly City.*
LOUIS-FERDINAND CÉLINE, *Castle to Castle.*
Conversations with Professor Y.
London Bridge.
Normance.
North.
Rigadoon.
MARIE CHAIX, *The Laurels of Lake Constance.*
HUGO CHARTERIS, *The Tide Is Right.*
ERIC CHEVILLARD, *Demolishing Nisard.*
MARC CHOLODENKO, *Mordechai Schamz.*
JOSHUA COHEN, *Witz.*
EMILY HOLMES COLEMAN, *The Shutter
of Snow.*
ROBERT COOVER, *A Night at the Movies.*
STANLEY CRAWFORD, *Log of the S.S. The
Mrs Unguentine.*
Some Instructions to My Wife.
RENÉ CREVEL, *Putting My Foot in It.*
RALPH CUSACK, *Cadenza.*
NICHOLAS DELBANCO, *The Count of Concord.*
Sherbrookes.
NIGEL DENNIS, *Cards of Identity.*

PETER DIMOCK, *A Short Rhetoric for
Leaving the Family.*
ARIEL DORFMAN, *Konfidenz.*
COLEMAN DOWELL,
Island People.
Too Much Flesh and Jabez.
ARKADII DRAGOMOSHCHENKO, *Dust.*
RIKKI DUCORNET, *The Complete
Butcher's Tales.*
The Fountains of Neptune.
The Jade Cabinet.
Phosphor in Dreamland.
WILLIAM EASTLAKE, *The Bamboo Bed.*
Castle Keep.
Lyric of the Circle Heart.
JEAN ECHENOZ, *Chopin's Move.*
STANLEY ELKIN, *A Bad Man.*
*Criers and Kibitzers, Kibitzers
and Criers.*
The Dick Gibson Show.
The Franchiser.
The Living End.
Mrs. Ted Bliss.
FRANÇOIS EMMANUEL, *Invitation to a
Voyage.*
SALVADOR ESPRIU, *Ariadne in the
Grotesque Labyrinth.*
LESLIE A. FIEDLER, *Love and Death in
the American Novel.*
JUAN FILLOY, *Op Oloop.*
ANDY FITCH, *Pop Poetics.*
GUSTAVE FLAUBERT, *Bouvard and Pécuchet.*
KASS FLEISHER, *Talking out of School.*
FORD MADOX FORD,
The March of Literature.
JON FOSSE, *Aliss at the Fire.*
Melancholy.
MAX FRISCH, *I'm Not Stiller.*
Man in the Holocene.
CARLOS FUENTES, *Christopher Unborn.*
Distant Relations.
Terra Nostra.
Where the Air Is Clear.
TAKEHIKO FUKUNAGA, *Flowers of Grass.*
WILLIAM GADDIS, *J R.*
The Recognitions.
JANICE GALLOWAY, *Foreign Parts.*
The Trick Is to Keep Breathing.
WILLIAM H. GASS, *Cartesian Sonata
and Other Novellas.*
Finding a Form.
A Temple of Texts.
The Tunnel.
Willie Masters' Lonesome Wife.
GÉRARD GAVARRY, *Hoppla! 1 2 3.*
ETIENNE GILSON,
The Arts of the Beautiful.
Forms and Substances in the Arts.
C. S. GISCOMBE, *Giscome Road.*
Here.
DOUGLAS GLOVER, *Bad News of the Heart.*
WITOLD GOMBROWICZ,
A Kind of Testament.
PAULO EMÍLIO SALES GOMES, *P's Three
Women.*
GEORGI GOSPODINOV, *Natural Novel.*
JUAN GOYTISOLO, *Count Julian.*
Juan the Landless.
Makbara.
Marks of Identity.

HENRY GREEN, *Back.*
Blindness.
Concluding.
Doting.
Nothing.
JACK GREEN, *Fire the Bastards!*
JIŘÍ GRUŠA, *The Questionnaire.*
MELA HARTWIG, *Am I a Redundant Human Being?*
JOHN HAWKES, *The Passion Artist.*
Whistlejacket.
ELIZABETH HEIGHWAY, ED., *Contemporary Georgian Fiction.*
ALEKSANDAR HEMON, ED., *Best European Fiction.*
AIDAN HIGGINS, *Balcony of Europe.*
Blind Man's Bluff
Bornholm Night-Ferry.
Flotsam and Jetsam.
Langrishe, Go Down.
Scenes from a Receding Past.
KEIZO HINO, *Isle of Dreams.*
KAZUSHI HOSAKA, *Plainsong.*
ALDOUS HUXLEY, *Antic Hay.*
Crome Yellow.
Point Counter Point.
Those Barren Leaves.
Time Must Have a Stop.
NAOYUKI II, *The Shadow of a Blue Cat.*
GERT JONKE, *The Distant Sound.*
Geometric Regional Novel.
Homage to Czerny.
The System of Vienna.
JACQUES JOUET, *Mountain R.*
Savage.
Upstaged.
MIEKO KANAI, *The Word Book.*
YORAM KANIUK, *Life on Sandpaper.*
HUGH KENNER, *Flaubert.*
Joyce and Beckett: The Stoic Comedians.
Joyce's Voices.
DANILO KIŠ, *The Attic.*
Garden, Ashes.
The Lute and the Scars
Psalm 44.
A Tomb for Boris Davidovich.
ANITA KONKKA, *A Fool's Paradise.*
GEORGE KONRÁD, *The City Builder.*
TADEUSZ KONWICKI, *A Minor Apocalypse.*
The Polish Complex.
MENIS KOUMANDAREAS, *Koula.*
ELAINE KRAF, *The Princess of 72nd Street.*
JIM KRUSOE, *Iceland.*
AYŞE KULIN, *Farewell: A Mansion in Occupied Istanbul.*
EMILIO LASCANO TEGUI, *On Elegance While Sleeping.*
ERIC LAURRENT, *Do Not Touch.*
VIOLETTE LEDUC, *La Bâtarde.*
EDOUARD LEVÉ, *Autoportrait.*
Suicide.
MÁRIO LEVI, *Istanbul Was a Fairy Tale.*
DEBORAH LEVY, *Billy and Girl.*
JOSÉ LEZAMA LIMA, *Paradiso.*
ROSA LIKSOM, *Dark Paradise.*
OSMAN LINS, *Avalovara.*
The Queen of the Prisons of Greece.
ALF MAC LOCHLAINN,
The Corpus in the Library.
Out of Focus.
RON LOEWINSOHN, *Magnetic Field(s).*
MINA LOY, *Stories and Essays of Mina Loy.*

D. KEITH MANO, *Take Five.*
MICHELINE AHARONIAN MARCOM,
The Mirror in the Well.
BEN MARCUS,
The Age of Wire and String.
WALLACE MARKFIELD,
Teitlebaum's Window.
To an Early Grave.
DAVID MARKSON, *Reader's Block.*
Wittgenstein's Mistress.
CAROLE MASO, *AVA.*
LADISLAV MATEJKA AND KRYSTYNA POMORSKA, EDS.,
Readings in Russian Poetics: Formalist and Structuralist Views.
HARRY MATHEWS, *Cigarettes.*
The Conversions.
The Human Country: New and Collected Stories.
The Journalist.
My Life in CIA.
Singular Pleasures.
The Sinking of the Odradek Stadium.
Tlooth.
JOSEPH MCELROY,
Night Soul and Other Stories.
ABDELWAHAB MEDDEB, *Talismano.*
GERHARD MEIER, *Isle of the Dead.*
HERMAN MELVILLE, *The Confidence-Man.*
AMANDA MICHALOPOULOU, *I'd Like.*
STEVEN MILLHAUSER, *The Barnum Museum.*
In the Penny Arcade.
RALPH J. MILLS, JR., *Essays on Poetry.*
MOMUS, *The Book of Jokes.*
CHRISTINE MONTALBETTI, *The Origin of Man.*
Western.
OLIVE MOORE, *Spleen.*
NICHOLAS MOSLEY, *Accident.*
Assassins.
Catastrophe Practice.
Experience and Religion.
A Garden of Trees.
Hopeful Monsters.
Imago Bird.
Impossible Object.
Inventing God.
Judith.
Look at the Dark.
Natalie Natalia.
Serpent.
Time at War.
WARREN MOTTE,
Fables of the Novel: French Fiction since 1990.
Fiction Now: The French Novel in the 21st Century.
Oulipo: A Primer of Potential Literature.
GERALD MURNANE, *Barley Patch.*
Inland.
YVES NAVARRE, *Our Share of Time.*
Sweet Tooth.
DOROTHY NELSON, *In Night's City.*
Tar and Feathers.
ESHKOL NEVO, *Homesick.*
WILFRIDO D. NOLLEDO, *But for the Lovers.*
FLANN O'BRIEN, *At Swim-Two-Birds.*
The Best of Myles.
The Dalkey Archive.
The Hard Life.
The Poor Mouth.

The Third Policeman.
CLAUDE OLLIER, *The Mise-en-Scène.*
Wert and the Life Without End.
GIOVANNI ORELLI, *Walaschek's Dream.*
PATRIK OUŘEDNÍK, *Europeana.*
The Opportune Moment, 1855.
BORIS PAHOR, *Necropolis.*
FERNANDO DEL PASO, *News from the Empire.*
Palinuro of Mexico.
ROBERT PINGET, *The Inquisitory.*
Mahu or The Material.
Trio.
MANUEL PUIG, *Betrayed by Rita Hayworth.*
The Buenos Aires Affair.
Heartbreak Tango.
RAYMOND QUENEAU, *The Last Days.*
Odile.
Pierrot Mon Ami.
Saint Glinglin.
ANN QUIN, *Berg.*
Passages.
Three.
Tripticks.
ISHMAEL REED, *The Free-Lance Pallbearers.*
The Last Days of Louisiana Red.
Ishmael Reed: The Plays.
Juice!
Reckless Eyeballing.
The Terrible Threes.
The Terrible Twos.
Yellow Back Radio Broke-Down.
JASIA REICHARDT, *15 Journeys Warsaw to London.*
NOËLLE REVAZ, *With the Animals.*
JOÃO UBALDO RIBEIRO, *House of the Fortunate Buddhas.*
JEAN RICARDOU, *Place Names.*
RAINER MARIA RILKE, *The Notebooks of Malte Laurids Brigge.*
JULIÁN RÍOS, *The House of Ulysses.*
Larva: A Midsummer Night's Babel.
Poundemonium.
Procession of Shadows.
AUGUSTO ROA BASTOS, *I the Supreme.*
DANIËL ROBBERECHTS, *Arriving in Avignon.*
JEAN ROLIN, *The Explosion of the Radiator Hose.*
OLIVIER ROLIN, *Hotel Crystal.*
ALIX CLEO ROUBAUD, *Alix's Journal.*
JACQUES ROUBAUD, *The Form of a City Changes Faster, Alas, Than the Human Heart.*
The Great Fire of London.
Hortense in Exile.
Hortense Is Abducted.
The Loop.
Mathematics:
The Plurality of Worlds of Lewis.
The Princess Hoppy.
Some Thing Black.
RAYMOND ROUSSEL, *Impressions of Africa.*
VEDRANA RUDAN, *Night.*
STIG SÆTERBAKKEN, *Siamese.*
Self Control.
LYDIE SALVAYRE, *The Company of Ghosts.*
The Lecture.
The Power of Flies.
LUIS RAFAEL SÁNCHEZ, *Macho Camacho's Beat.*
SEVERO SARDUY, *Cobra & Maitreya.*

NATHALIE SARRAUTE,
Do You Hear Them?
Martereau.
The Planetarium.
ARNO SCHMIDT, *Collected Novellas.*
Collected Stories.
Nobodaddy's Children.
Two Novels.
ASAF SCHURR, *Motti.*
GAIL SCOTT, *My Paris.*
DAMION SEARLS, *What We Were Doing and Where We Were Going.*
JUNE AKERS SEESE,
Is This What Other Women Feel Too?
What Waiting Really Means.
BERNARD SHARE, *Inish.*
Transit.
VIKTOR SHKLOVSKY, *Bowstring.*
Knight's Move.
A Sentimental Journey:
Memoirs 1917–1922.
Energy of Delusion: A Book on Plot.
Literature and Cinematography.
Theory of Prose.
Third Factory.
Zoo, or Letters Not about Love.
PIERRE SINIAC, *The Collaborators.*
KJERSTI A. SKOMSVOLD, *The Faster I Walk, the Smaller I Am.*
JOSEF ŠKVORECKÝ, *The Engineer of Human Souls.*
GILBERT SORRENTINO,
Aberration of Starlight.
Blue Pastoral.
Crystal Vision.
Imaginative Qualities of Actual Things.
Mulligan Stew.
Pack of Lies.
Red the Fiend.
The Sky Changes.
Something Said.
Splendide-Hôtel.
Steelwork.
Under the Shadow.
W. M. SPACKMAN, *The Complete Fiction.*
ANDRZEJ STASIUK, *Dukla.*
Fado.
GERTRUDE STEIN, *The Making of Americans.*
A Novel of Thank You.
LARS SVENDSEN, *A Philosophy of Evil.*
PIOTR SZEWC, *Annihilation.*
GONÇALO M. TAVARES, *Jerusalem.*
Joseph Walser's Machine.
Learning to Pray in the Age of Technique.
LUCIAN DAN TEODOROVICI,
Our Circus Presents . . .
NIKANOR TERATOLOGEN, *Assisted Living.*
STEFAN THEMERSON, *Hobson's Island.*
The Mystery of the Sardine.
Tom Harris.
TAEKO TOMIOKA, *Building Waves.*
JOHN TOOMEY, *Sleepwalker.*
JEAN-PHILIPPE TOUSSAINT, *The Bathroom.*
Camera.
Monsieur.
Reticence.
Running Away.
Self-Portrait Abroad.
Television.
The Truth about Marie.

DUMITRU TSEPENEAG, *Hotel Europa.*
   The Necessary Marriage.
   Pigeon Post.
   Vain Art of the Fugue.
ESTHER TUSQUETS, *Stranded.*
DUBRAVKA UGRESIC, *Lend Me Your Character.*
   Thank You for Not Reading.
TOR ULVEN, *Replacement.*
MATI UNT, *Brecht at Night.*
   Diary of a Blood Donor.
   Things in the Night.
ÁLVARO URIBE AND OLIVIA SEARS, EDS.,
   Best of Contemporary Mexican Fiction.
ELOY URROZ, *Friction.*
   The Obstacles.
LUISA VALENZUELA, *Dark Desires and*
   the Others.
   He Who Searches.
PAUL VERHAEGHEN, *Omega Minor.*
AGLAJA VETERANYI, *Why the Child Is*
   Cooking in the Polenta.
BORIS VIAN, *Heartsnatcher.*
LLORENÇ VILLALONGA, *The Dolls' Room.*
TOOMAS VINT, *An Unending Landscape.*
ORNELA VORPSI, *The Country Where No*
   One Ever Dies.
AUSTRYN WAINHOUSE, *Hedyphagetica.*
CURTIS WHITE, *America's Magic Mountain.*
   The Idea of Home.
   Memories of My Father Watching TV.
   Requiem.

DIANE WILLIAMS, *Excitability:*
   Selected Stories.
   Romancer Erector.
DOUGLAS WOOLF, *Wall to Wall.*
   Ya! & John-Juan.
JAY WRIGHT, *Polynomials and Pollen.*
   The Presentable Art of Reading
   Absence.
PHILIP WYLIE, *Generation of Vipers.*
MARGUERITE YOUNG, *Angel in the Forest.*
   Miss MacIntosh, My Darling.
REYOUNG, *Unbabbling.*
VLADO ŽABOT, *The Succubus.*
ZORAN ŽIVKOVIĆ, *Hidden Camera.*
LOUIS ZUKOFSKY, *Collected Fiction.*
VITOMIL ZUPAN, *Minuet for Guitar.*
SCOTT ZWIREN, *God Head.*